EMPEROR'S MERCY

For the last hour, as ammunition had run low, they had resorted to simply giving up their spare rounds and allowing the huntsman to snipe away at the encircling foe. They guessed that Silverstein had fired at least two hundred rounds in that time. Many of them had been kill shots.

They waited a while. The enemy fired no more shots as if testing, no, taunting them into firing back. But they had nothing left and it would not be long before the Archenemy realised that.

'How long do you think it will be before they roll up a tank to flatten this whole thing?' asked Goa, a foundry worker in his late sixties. Sunstroke had affected him the worst and he spoke with his eyes closed, his head lolling.

'Death by artillery would be lucky. They won't give us that luxury,' Silverstein replied matter-of-factly.

As if on cue, they heard the gate at the base of the tower being breached with some sort of a piston ram. Voices began shouting harsh words in the dark tongue.

'Here they come,' shrugged Silverstein.

More Warhammer 40,000 from the Black Library

EISENHORN

Dan Abnett

(Contains *Xenos, Malleus* and *Hereticus*)

RAVENOR: THE OMNIBUS

Dan Abnett

(Contains *Ravenor, Ravenor Returned* and *Ravenor Rogue*)

THE IMPERIAL GUARD OMNIBUS: VOLUME ONE

Mitchel Scanlon, Steve Lyons and Steve Parker

(Contains books 1-3 in the series: *Fifteen Hours, Death World* and *Rebel Winter*)

A WARHAMMER 40,000 NOVEL

EMPEROR'S MERCY

Henry Zou

To my folks and Biffle. For letting me run wild.

A BLACK LIBRARY PUBLICATION

First published in Great Britain in 2009 by
BL Publishing,
Games Workshop Ltd.,
Willow Road, Nottingham,
NG7 2WS, UK.

10 9 8 7 6 5 4 3 2 1

Cover illustration by Raymond Swanland.

A CIP record for this book is available from the British Library.

UK ISBN: 978 1 84416 734 0
US ISBN: 978 1 84416 735 7

See the Black Library on the Internet at
www.blacklibrary.com

Find out more about Games Workshop
and the world of Warhammer 40,000 at
www.games-workshop.com

Printed and bound in the UK.

IT IS THE 41st millennium. For more than a hundred centuries the Emperor has sat immobile on the Golden Throne of Earth. He is the master of mankind by the will of the gods, and master of a million worlds by the might of his inexhaustible armies. He is a rotting carcass writhing invisibly with power from the Dark Age of Technology. He is the Carrion Lord of the Imperium for whom a thousand souls are sacrificed every day, so that he may never truly die.

YET EVEN IN his deathless state, the Emperor continues his eternal vigilance. Mighty battlefleets cross the daemon-infested miasma of the warp, the only route between distant stars, their way lit by the Astronomican, the psychic manifestation of the Emperor's will. Vast armies give battle in His name on uncounted worlds. Greatest amongst his soldiers are the Adeptus Astartes, the Space Marines, bio-engineered super-warriors. Their comrades in arms are legion: the Imperial Guard and countless planetary defence forces, the ever-vigilant Inquisition and the tech-priests of the Adeptus Mechanicus to name only a few. But for all their multitudes, they are barely enough to hold off the ever-present threat from aliens, heretics, mutants – and worse.

TO BE A man in such times is to be one amongst untold billions. It is to live in the cruellest and most bloody regime imaginable. These are the tales of those times. Forget the power of technology and science, for so much has been forgotten, never to be re-learned. Forget the promise of progress and understanding, for in the grim dark future there is only war. There is no peace amongst the stars, only an eternity of carnage and slaughter, and the laughter of thirsting gods.

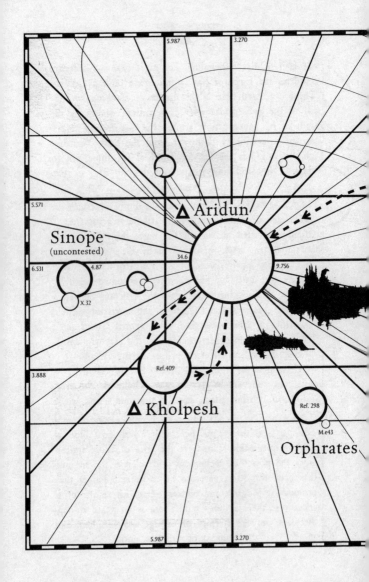

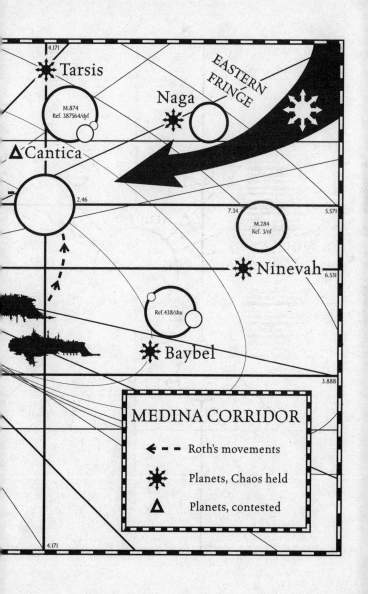

PROLOGUE

THE FIRST PROJECTILE thundered into the tenement bazaar. It hit with a percussive blast that could be heard in the terracotta valleys far beyond.

Carving a plume of debris, the vessel ploughed into a picket of tea stalls and spice carts, its fifty-tonne bulk skipping with momentum. Finally it penetrated one of the tenements that flanked the commercial district, demolishing the entire bottom tier.

Jolted by the seismic collision, human congestion in the narrow market lanes sounded a shrill chorus of panic. Streets began to flood with hurried, confused foot traffic, like a sprawling river system. The stacked buildings and overhanging roofs gave them no room to flee or see the commotion. Dust clouds of ochre yellow, the powdered stone of ancient buildings, formed a solid wall around the crash site.

Vinimus Dahlo had been toiling at his tea cart when it happened. He had been nursing urns of sweet black tea over an iron griddle with expert hands, and had not seen the collision at all. Rather he had felt it, a sonic tremor that shot up his spine and rocked the base of his skull. When Dahlo looked up, the locals perched or squatting on the stools around him were all pointing in one direction and exclaiming in shrill agitation.

They were pointing down the narrow avenue. Down past the canvas awnings and the rafts of grain sacks, silk fillets of various hues, porcelain and dried fruits. Down to where the mezzanine avenue had been ruptured by some colossal cartridge from the skies.

Dahlo left his tea cart unattended, an uncharacteristic act for a man of his sensibilities. Suddenly seized by fear, he pushed and prodded his way into the crowd, craning to catch a glimpse of the destruction. Traders, labourers and flocks of women in shawls faltered in their work, gravitating towards the crash site.

When the rolling blossom of dust began to wilt, it revealed a long iron pod nestled within the rubble. It resembled some beached ocean submersible, its metal hide flaking with rust and oxidised scorching.

No one knew what to make of it. Naga was a frontier world of the Medina Corridor, and the only aeronautical vessels that frequented these ports were the Imperial ships that claimed their tithes of textiles, ceramics and spices. Perhaps because of this, when the belly of the vessel popped free with a hydraulic hiss, the throng only edged closer.

Dahlo, however, began to back-pedal against the tide. He was not one to be swept up by an inquisitive herd. Something, whether it was the hot prickling in the nape of his neck or the coiling sensation his stomach, warned him that all was not right.

An armoured figure clawed out of the hatch, like the birth of some ghastly newborn. Its head emerged first, humanoid in shape yet wholly bound with bars of some ferrous alloy. It then dragged its armoured torso over the lip of the hatch, a cuirass of chainmail and iron petals. Simultaneously, turret hatches began to peel away on both sides of the beached vessel. Armoured silhouettes began to surface. That was when the killing started.

It began with a solitary shot that echoed in the awkward stillness of the bazaar. A las-round crumpled a young girl. She slumped lifelessly against the press of bodies behind her as panic began to ripple outwards like capillary waves. Screams of outrage and confusion interspersed with the whickering snaps of rifles broke the calm that had existed mere seconds before.

High above the tenement bazaar, more vessels pierced the clouds. Against the ochre sky a dozen vessels turned into hundreds, the hundreds turned into thousands.

LESS THAN TWO kilometres from the bazaar, high up on the garrison walls, the 22nd Naga Air Defence Squadron stood sentry. Even at extreme optical zoom with their sentry scopes, they could not see the killing in the markets. But the soldiers could see the pulsating lights of pink and purple las throbbing in the distance, and it made their palms sweaty and their jaws tense. Around them, like autumnal shedding, craft similar to the speck which had plummeted into the commercial district, were falling in thick sleets.

The monstrous rigs of their quad-linked autocannons nosed out over the haphazard tiers of terraces and tenements. Like most military hardware on Naga, it was obsolete and had been harboured behind an abandoned chariot shed almost as an afterthought. The weapons themselves were Onager-pattern anti-aircraft platforms. A primitive yet reliable indigenous design, each 50mm barrel was pneumatically driven. The combined rate of fire was typically six thousand rounds per minute of low-altitude air deterrence. Mounted on the flat-tiled roofs and minarets of most Nagaan cities, it was a workhorse of the Naga Militia Combine squadrons against both ground and air targets.

Major Meas Chanta of the 22nd Naga Air Defence Squadron wanted nothing more than to unleash those six thousand rounds as he watched strange foreign objects fall from the sky. Standing on the disc platform high above the cityscape, the major squinted through his magnoculars as the distant specks plummeted with an eerie grace.

'What orders from the division HQ?' asked Chanta.

'Stand by until further direction, sir,' replied his vox operator. It had been the same answer for the past forty minutes, and in truth Chanta had not expected anything different. A curtain of vessels were dropping down, bruising the amber cloud bars an ominous black, but still they waited.

The squadron company were arrayed in an overlapping fire pattern, batteries of Onager anti-air platforms anchored on the highest points across the city. They were one hundred and twenty men in all, clad in quilted gambesons of khaki twill – the uniform of the Naga Combine. The padded flak coats had high collar guards that shielded the lower face from the biting perennial dust storms. These part-time citizen soldiers had been summoned to their ready stations less than forty minutes ago, when the first vessels had entered the atmosphere. But the mobilisation had faltered there, milling into the disordered confusion of a hesitant defence strategy.

Chanta chewed on his lower lip, a habit of anxiety that he had not indulged in since childhood. This time he drew blood. He was a ledger clerk by trade, and his commission had been passed down from his father on account of his high education and public standing. But Chanta was not a soldier; his hands were uncallused and inked from years of wielding the quill. This was no place for him. Around Chanta, the 22nd squadron were braced in tense silence, some looking up vacantly at the sky, others looking to him for direction.

He had none to give them. Naga was a tiny rimward world in the Lusitan Sub on the Eastern Fringe, and military prowess was not a defining feature. The military seniors were in disarray and unable to provide decisive leadership to the soldiers that manned Naga's increasingly obsolete military arsenal.

For most of his men it was the first time the klaxons had summoned them to their stations for anything other than a drill. They were looking to him and he had nothing to give them. Still the vessels continued to fall.

'Tell me again in exact words why we are to hold fire,' Chanta asked his vox operator. He had asked him before, but he needed to hear it again.

'Sir, long-range signal instruments have failed to identify the incoming objects. Although they appear to be landers, preliminary defensive measures cannot commence until proper identification can be ascertained, sir,' came the reply.

Chanta wasn't really listening any more. To describe Naga's signal instruments as archaic would be a generous assessment. The corroded array of listening stations strung up across the dune spires of the western Naga continents would be hard-pressed to pick up a ship's presence let alone its source signature.

He looked up into the sky as if searching for some divine guidance. Whether he found it or not, the galaxy of landers swarming across his field of vision made him resolute.

'Corporal, commence vox orders to fire,' Major Chanta ordered.

'Sir?' asked the squadron vox operator, his features creased with confusion.

'Commence firing orders. Please, corporal, do hurry,' Chanta said as he cinched the padded khaki of his collar guard tight across his lower face. He did not want his men to see his bloodied lower lip, already clouding his ivory uniform a vivid pink. Major Chanta had never been so wracked with fear in his entire life. If he was wrong there would be hell to pay, but if he was right, then it would not matter either way.

IN THE SUBTERRANEAN depths, the repository trembled. Tunnels and vaults, networked beneath the continents like coiled intestinal tracts, were not spared the cataclysm, despite their deep insulation. Grit shook from the rafters as multiple impacts from the surface continued the rhythmic pounding. The aftershocks travelled through the catacomb libraries and were felt even in the archives. The script silos too were trembling violently. It seemed that Naga would collapse from the inside out.

Elhem Meteadas, senior archivist, was beginning to fear the worst. A buttress of books three hundred metres high began to shiver precariously, rocking on wooden supports so old they were ashen. A volume of *The Movement of Stars*, a nine-hundred-year-old almanac, was dislodged from its shelving seventy metres up the northern vault face. It came whistling past Meteadas and exploded on the tiling next to him in a fluttering swirl of parchment.

'Meteadas! Meteadas! What is happening?' shrieked Scholar Amado.

'I–' he began. But the senior archivist did not know how to finish the answer. Meteadas was well into his one fifties and had been a keeper of the texts for almost all of those years. Some would consider him a polymath, a man with encyclopaedic depth of knowledge. If anyone on Naga understood the catastrophe that was occurring on the surface above, he would likely be one of them. Yet Meteadas did not want to incite panic.

'Earthquake of course,' he lied.

'That cannot be! This section of the repository does not lie under any planar fractures or subduction zones,' yelled the scholar as he gripped the sleeves of Meteadas's linen shift.

'Are you familiar with the works of Aloysius Spur?'

'No…'

'Excellent. Then you have absolutely nothing to worry about,' Meteadas quipped as he shrugged off Amado.

'But Meteadas, some of the others say it is fighting! Are they fighting? Why would there be fighting?'

Elhem Meteadas sighed deeply. Perhaps the others already knew, or perhaps they had already read the same texts he had. The labyrinthine libraries tightly woven beneath the surface of Naga served as the central repository of the Medina Worlds. Although they archived everything from the war poetry of pre-Heresy to subsector trade outputs of last month, it was a possibility. The writings of Aloysius Spur may have been a lesser-known work, but all archivists were at heart hoarders of obscure knowledge.

'Why would anyone bother fighting for the Medina Worlds but for the Old Kings of Medina?' Meteadas admitted solemnly.

At this Amado threw back his head and laughed. 'The Old Kings of Medina are one of the great mythical tales.'

'Then for what reason, Amado? You are a learned man, a polymath. Have you learned nothing? Naga is a minuscule planet of a frontier sector. It has neither strategic relevance nor resources of note.'

It was the elder's turn to seize the younger man's cotton chemise. 'Aloysius Spur warned us about the Old Kings of Medina. He foretold that they would bring war from the stars. Why do you laugh about it?'

'Because, Elhem, they are a child's stories! Relics from the Age of Apostasy, buried and lost on one of the

Medina Worlds? There is not even a plausible account of what or where they may be! Pure fabrication!'

'Aloysius Spur did not fabricate; he observed the laws of inevitability. If the Old Kings were lost in the Medina Worlds, it is inevitable that someone will try to claim them, now or in a hundred thousand years' time.'

'Who was Aloysius Spur? A prophet?'

'No. A military tactician. A lord general during the Age of Apostasy.'

'Ah,' nodded Amado, suddenly taken aback.

Meteadas released the man from his fervent clutch. His postulating was interrupted as more archivists spilled into the northern vaults from the myriad catacomb entrances. Some were shouting, some were crying, others still were petrified with glassy-eyed shock.

'They are here! Naga is at war!' Through the confusion, that much was clear.

Before Meteadas could discern any more, a rumbling tremor from the surface punctuated the cacophony. Three buttresses of texts collapsed, two on the northern vault face and one adjoining the western silos, as the tortured wooden supports could hold no longer. The hundred-metre stacks swayed preposterously before they liquefied into a rolling tidal press. The avalanche of prose, poetry and epic history came down and decimated the repository chamber.

Mercifully, Elhem Meteadas blacked out. He did not have to hear the dying screams of his colleagues or the deathly quiet that followed.

IN THE SLAMMING, teetering crush of people, Vinimus Dahlo had lost his abacus. His tea cart had been upturned too, but that could be repaired. The abacus was precious to him. It had been carved out of a fragrant red wood and bought for him by his wife. His wife, who had scraped together two years' worth of her own savings in a dented tin hidden in his daughter's bassinet.

He foraged on his hands and knees, covered in a sienna dust kicked up by the stampede. Bodies surged around him, trampling down the picket stalls, pushing and falling. A merchant balancing decorative bird cages on a carry-pole trod on Dahlo's heel. Close by, a potter wailed piteously as her raft of earthenware was stomped into fragments. And through all of this, the steady snap of gunfire remained a constant.

Dahlo's scouring led him against the human current until he finally glimpsed a wink of carved wood in the chalky ground ahead. Staying low and shielding his head with his forearms, Dahlo drove himself against the crowd. He stumbled through the remains of someone's rouge stall; the little pots of colours – red for the lips, purple for the eyes, cream for the cheeks – were all crushed underfoot. At one point the swell of the stampede was so great that he was lifted bodily off his feet and dragged backwards for several metres.

Forcing a wedge into the stampede, Dahlo spied his abacus on the ground. The varnish had scuffed but it was otherwise intact. He lunged for it, seizing the prize against his chest. Then, as he turned to run, a rough hand seized the beaded collar of his jacket and snapped him flat onto his back.

He landed hard on his spine. Dazed, it took Dahlo's vision several seconds to swim into focus. What he saw next almost froze his heart with sheer terror. Standing over Dahlo was one of the armoured killers.

Its frame was tall and raw, swathed in weighty layers of chainmail, scrap and gunmetal plating. It was a monster, wild and savage. Across its chest were slung multiple bandoleers of ammunition and grenades.

But it was the head that terrified Dahlo the most. Its head was bandaged in iron. Strips of metal enclosed it

from skull to jaw, with a slight gap for the mouth and
narrow slits for vision. Up close, Dahlo could see the pus
that wept between the gaps of each iron slat.

Slowly and deliberately, the Ironclad killer raised a
gauntleted fist. A thirty-centimetre spike was welded to
the backplate, and the Ironclad traced a slow arc with it.
Dahlo was certain that behind the metal bindings, it was
smiling at him.

'Shoot me instead, please,' Dahlo gasped and immediately wished he hadn't. He had always fancied that his
last words would be profound and measured.

TRACER FIRE HAMMERED into the stratosphere, scuds of
flak darkening the sky like ashy condensation. Despite
the florid resistance, the vessels continued their bombardment. Dozens were snared by screens of shrapnel,
disintegrating in their burning, tumbling descent.
Dozens more continued to scream through the orange
twilight and land in great mushrooming clouds on the
surface below.

Major Chanta crouched behind the mantlet of an
Onager. He traversed the iron-sights, hosing up quadru-
ple streams of firepower. His primary gunner had been
shot. They had been receiving enemy fire from positions
on the ground for some time now. The invaders had
advanced into Central Naga, overrunning the Militia
Combine ground units. The vox-links were dead. Much
of the city was burning.

As far as Major Chanta could tell, he was the highest-
ranking officer in the region by default. His air defence
squadron had done all they could, but it would not have
been enough, even if they had acted earlier. The seething
aerial deployment was absolutely overwhelming. The
PDF training manuals had never prepared him for anything like it. Against the horizon of the cityscape, enemy
formations were amassing.

It was so loud, so brutal. The clatter of guns had reduced his hearing to a constant ringing. Across his field of vision the searing flashes burned afterimages into his retinas. It was little wonder then, that Major Chanta never saw the flanking force that swept across the rooftops and engaged his heavy guns in hand-to-hand. He didn't even notice the Onager platforms being picked off, one after another. To his immediate left, thirty metres away, an Onager of Delta Squadron was overwhelmed by Archenemy soldiers, the gunners and loaders being thrown off the platform onto the rooftops below.

'Corporal, vox to all units and report back the ammunition levels. Are they depleted?' Major Chanta ordered as he continued firing.

There was no answer from his vox operator.

'Corporal. Affirmative?' he repeated. Still there was no answer.

The hairs on his neck prickled with chills. Major Chanta slowly turned to look behind him. What he saw was singularly the most terror-inducing thing he had ever experienced.

Corporal Anan was dead. His corpse was being cradled by one of the Archenemy. The Ironclad rocked back on its haunches, humming tunelessly. He was playing: tracing geometric patterns on the ground with the corporal's blood.

'What do you think you are doing?' bellowed Major Chanta with a bravery he did not truly feel.

The Ironclad looked at Chanta. His metal-bound skull was featureless and betrayed no emotion. The Archenemy raider tilted his head, almost quizzically, and rose to his feet. From the bandoleers festooning his chest, this one unsheathed a hooked machete.

The major leapt off the Onager's bucket seat and seized the closest weapon. It was a discipline rod. A fifty-centimetre truncheon of polished hardwood, issued to all officers of the Naga Combine. It was not really a weapon but he hoped it would suffice.

Breathing hard, Chanta lashed out with the rod. The Ironclad parried with his machete and stepped inside Chanta's guard. The enemy revealed an embedded razor running the length of his forearm. Pressing hard with the machete, the Ironclad ran his bladed forearm across Chanta's abdomen.

The paper-thin blade scissored into the twill gambeson, eliciting a bloom of blood against the ivory fabric. Chanta gurgled. He took a step back and his knees buckled underneath him. It was all over. The Archenemy soldier pounced and straddled him, hacking down with the machete again and again.

IT COULD HAVE been the rubberised crump of combat boots that woke him. Or it might have been the harsh voices shouting orders in a clipped military tempo. Either way, Elhem Meteadas slowly regained his consciousness to the sounds of intruders in the repository.

He could not move. His spine was bent in such a way that, with every laboured breath, his shoulder blades spiked his lungs with agony. Books, thousands of them, had buried him. The *Horticulture of the Western Naga Archipelago* nudged into his kidney. He knew it was that book because the elaborate copper curling on the tome's edges was unnecessarily pointy. A good archivist remembered such things.

Around him voices barked back and forth in a language he did not understand. It was a human tongue, but nothing he had ever encountered in his studies. Meteadas could only assume, through tone and inflection, that it was the tongue of Chaos.

The thought that Chaos was ransacking his duty region of the labyrinths plagued his mind with impending dread. He did not fear for himself – his old arthritic bones were well past their prime and he had come to accept his fate with a mellow reluctance. Instead, his rational mind began to fear for Medina.

War, at least on an absolute scale, had not scarred the star cluster for four thousand years. Yet the earth-shaking ferocity of this assault bespoke of more than a cursory raid. This was war.

Meteadas knew wars were not fought on miniature rimward worlds such as Naga without pretence. No, wars were ghastly affairs only waged when the prize exceeded the costs. The Medina Corridor was not a strategic route in the subsector. It did not collate in Meteadas's rational mind.

Within seconds, Meteadas's brilliant intellect had reached a conclusion. Whatever the machinations behind the conquest of Naga, it would only be a means to an end. That notion pumped more dread through his veins than anything else.

He knew what he had to do. Deny the enemy their prize, whatever that may be. *'Scorch the land and leave no seed or fruit in passing,'* was a quote from one of Meteadas's favourite military philosophers. He had no choice.

With laboured gasps of pain, Elhem Meteadas wormed a hand through the debris of the book avalanche until his fingers brushed his belt. Immobilised as he was, it took Meteadas's fingers some time to hook onto the shuttered lamp at his waist. Easing it free, Meteadas slid open the hinge plate and sparked the gas condenser. A tiny flame fluttered into being.

At first nothing happened. But then, the naked flame began to catch on the sheaves of brittle manuscript that pressed down upon it. After the combustion, it did not take long at all for the lapping flames to erupt into a whirling pyre, sixty metres high.

Old Elhem Meteadas, senior archivist, died without much pain. He had burnt ten thousand years of Imperial history and literature, some irreplaceable and lost forever. But in doing so, he had struck a body-blow against the invasion. Naga would die, but perhaps Medina could live to write the histories again.

CHAPTER ONE

THE DISPATCH TO Inquisitor Obodiah Roth was urgent, couriered directly from the Ordo Hereticus. It had reached him, by way of clockwork pigeon, in a waxed envelope sealed with the highest order of authority, the scarlet seal.

The letter had been a cordial invitation to convene with a Conclave of Medina, for a matter of 'no small calamity'. It was the Inquisition's way of informing him that he had no choice in the matter. In Roth's experience, the more understated the situation, the more apocalyptic it would likely be. The very fact that the message had been sourced from the Medina Corridor, three weeks of non-warp travel by frigate, attested to its importance.

As it was, the request could not have arrived at a more inopportune moment. For months, Roth had been embroiled in a treasonous scandal concerning the oligarchy and the governing administration of the Bastion Stars. For the most part, it had been dry, paper-sheaving work, endless hours of cross-referencing tax ledgers and metric data. Now his investigation was on the cusp of fruition. He had narrowed down the conspirators to a clandestine circle of elites within the Bastion militocracy.

But now Roth would not be participating in the raid. The message arrived, as most messages do, in the most inconvenient of times, as Roth was cleaning his weapons, surrounded by gruff, growling Interior Guard troops who were eager to exact retribution on the political conspirators. The guardsmen had laughed, consoling the inquisitor with claps on the back and heavy handshakes, but it did not change the fact that Roth would not bear witness to the fruits of his labour. No amount of cursing and ranting would change that. Regardless, it didn't stop Roth from cursing or ranting.

By the time Roth embarked on his three-week journey from the Bastion Stars to the Medina Corridor, the invasion of Medina had been seething for five months. By that stage the war had, in the words of Inquisitor Roth, reached an apocalyptic scale indeed.

Archenemy forces had swept through the system, dismantling the unprepared Imperial resistance. They were the Ironclad, corsairs of the Eastern Fringe that had plagued Medina shipping lanes with sporadic small-scale attacks for the past six centuries. But now they fought with cohesion and in unfathomable numbers under the command of a Khorsabad Maw. Conservative reconnaissance estimates placed enemy numbers at seven million.

The regiments of the Cantican Colonial, the primary Imperial Guard formation of the Medina Worlds, numbered no more than nine hundred thousand, including auxiliary support units and non-combat corps. By the first month the CantiCol had suffered a successive series of staggering defeats in the frontier planets. Their noses bloodied, the High Command had recoiled, the entire front on the verge of collapse.

Far more troubling was the constant stream of intelligence that the Ironclad were only a vanguard force. Khorsabad Maw's seven million Ironclad were the spear-tip of a Chaos armada en route from beyond the Fringe.

For this reason, Imperial reinforcements amassed in the neighbouring systems of the Shoal Clusters and the Bastion Stars. Medina had little strategic value for the subsector. Despite a combined population of sixteen billion, the Medina Corridor was, for all intents and purposes, a sacrificial lamb.

AMIDST THE ELLIPTICAL crescent of the Medina Corridor, the Imperial 9th Route Fleet moored at high anchor.

They were five dozen ships submerged by pink sparks of starlight, floating like a trillion motes of dust. The barbed, knife-like frigates and ponderous spears of Imperial cruisers clustered in protective formations. As fleets went, this was by no means a large one. Against the depths of space, the flotilla seemed almost vulnerable, so absolutely eclipsed by the smoky infinity of galactic nebulae.

The *Carthage*, the nucleus of the 9th Route Fleet, was a grand cruiser over nine kilometres in length. It was an old ship, even by Imperial standards. From its gilded arrowhead prow to the fluted reactor banks of its warp drives, the cruiser displayed a decaying elegance of ages past.

Since the Chaos offensive on Medina, the *Carthage* had been the military nerve centre of the dogged Imperial resistance. On board the cubic kilometre expanse of the *Carthage's* docking hangar, Lord Marshal Varuda Khmer waited. He did not like to be kept waiting, especially aboard his own ship. It irked him that a man of his rank should have to swelter in the oppressive heat of the docking bays alongside the common ratings.

Underneath the vertical lancet arches of the hangar, fork-loading servitors with chirping sirens ferried supplies from cargo carriers. Labour crews toiled and sweated at repair bays and fuelling stations. Throughout the organised pandemonium of blaring alarms, shouted directions and choking heat, the recycled oxygen of the pressure vents added a burden of drudgery that chafed the lord marshal no end. The fuming anger rising out of Khmer was tangible like a shimmering curtain of heat, and crewmen and servitors alike gave him a wide berth.

The stratocraft he had been waiting for had touched down on the cradle clamps almost six minutes ago. But still no one had emerged. Khmer checked his chron, a timepiece affixed by a gold chain to his breast pocket, for the sixth time.

'If he doesn't haul himself out of there by the time I count to ten, I'll shoot him when he does,' growled the lord marshal. His bodyguards around him, tall and powerful provost marshals, chuckled meaninglessly. Some did so out of fear.

Lord Marshal Khmer was not a physically imposing man. He was on the short side of average, with a lean build for a man in his sixties. Yet he carried his authority like a mantle about his shoulders. Despite his size he had an alarming presence. It was everything about him, down to the smallest detail. His movements were surgical, every gesture swift and intense. Khmer was so intense that when he clasped his hands behind his back, he clasped them together so hard the leather gloves emitted a low creaking groan.

It seemed too much energy and vehemence had been concentrated into such a small vessel, so much that it sparked and hummed like an overcharged powercell.

Finally, the gangway of the stratocraft detached from its fuselage with a hiss of steam-driven hydraulics. Lord Marshal Khmer stiffened. His two score bodyguards, flexing muscles beneath their rubberised sheath armour, rose like guard dogs.

Inquisitor Obodiah Roth sauntered out of the hatchway. He appeared unhurried. He was a young man, young for an inquisitor. His face was handsomely equine. Even though he had just transited into a war zone, he eschewed the vestments of combat. Instead he was stripped to the waist in white jodhpurs and leather ankle boots, his torso taut and wiry. His knees were still strapped with thick leather kneepads, his hands still bound in sparring mitts.

Khmer hated him immediately.

'Lord Marshal! I was just indulging in some fist-fencing. I hope I did not keep you waiting,' Roth said as he brushed past the forest of bodyguards.

The lord marshal, bristling in ceremonial finery, complete with gold frogging, war honours and embroidered velvet, eyed the down-dressed inquisitor with a look of abject revulsion. Khmer had expected more. Obodiah Roth had been requested by the Inquisition's Medina Conclave to aid the war effort. Previously, the lord marshal had serious doubts as to the relevance of Inquisitorial actions during the war effort. This new arrival just cemented his suspicions.

'You did. Is this going to set a precedent in relations between the Imperial High Command and the Inquisition?' Khmer retorted.

'Have it as you take it, sir.'

By this stage, Roth was less than an arm's length away from the lord marshal. At two metres tall, the Inquisitor reared well above the shorter Khmer. The phalanx of provost marshals squared up and edged in. Their tower-length ballistic shields and shock mauls were held low but ready.

'You needn't have brought me a welcome party, lord marshal.' Roth nodded at the provosts. The bodyguards were a subtle insult and one that the inquisitor could not let slip.

'Just as you've brought yours.' Khmer gestured at the man who had followed Roth down the ramp.

Bastiel Silverstein gestured back with a nonchalant wave. He was man on the spry side of forty. Whippet-thin and dressed in a waistcoat of finely tailored pirahnagator hide, he cut a sternly patrician figure. A scoped autogun was nestled in the crook of his left arm, a self-loading rifle painted in a camouflage of stylised foliage.

He stalked across the decking, looking unimpressed at the slab-shouldered provosts.

An Inquisitorial agent, thought Khmer. Probably another one of the many specialised pawns employed by the Conclave. As far as he was concerned, they weren't soldiers and therefore weren't to be trusted. He'd already had enough of the Inquisitorial circus troupe on board the *Carthage* to suffer any more.

'I'm here to make one thing clear, inquisitor. I did not want you here. Nor did I want other members of your Conclave,' the lord marshal stated.

'Oh, very clear,' Roth replied, unfazed.

Khmer continued. 'Yet Warmaster Sonnen ordered the collaboration of the Medina Conclave with my general staff. In turn the Conclave has requested you. Keep out of way, and our cooperation will be smooth, clear?'

Obodiah Roth wiped the perspiration from his wireframe shoulders with a square of linen. He appeared uninterested. Finally, he looked the Lord Marshal of the Medina Corridor square in the eyes and winked.

'Can you fetch me a fresh towel?'

Lord Marshal Khmer stiffened. Unseen to anyone else, he gripped the timepiece in his hand hard, spider-webbing the glass lens. Both men, soldier and inquisitor, were guilty of a monumental temper, and things might have played differently had Forde Gurion not appeared at that moment.

'Obodiah! Welcome, welcome,' called Inquisitor Forde Gurion as he strode towards them, his augmetic legs clapping out an irregular rhythm.

'Master Gurion,' said Roth, bowing deeply to his elder.

The lord marshal cleared his throat. 'Gurion. I was here to welcome our esteemed guest. We have come to a mutual agreement,' he said with a reptilian smile at Roth. 'I expect to see the Conclave at our command briefing this evening at sixth siren. Do not be late.' And with that, Lord Marshal Khmer turned briskly with the practiced ease of a parade officer and marched away, flanked by his provosts.

'I can see the partnership is blossoming,' quipped Roth once the Imperial commander had disappeared into the roiling press of the docking bays.

Gurion shrugged wearily. 'Diplomacy is not one of the lord marshal's strong points but his efficiency is beyond reprove. We need officers of his mettle if we're to see out this campaign.'

'That bad?'

Gurion looked solemn. 'Come, Obodiah. There is much you need to know.'

THE STATEROOM ASSIGNED to Gurion might once have been lavish. A large apartment in the officers' quarters, sections of the room had not been refurbished since the *Carthage's* maiden voyage six thousand years ago. Inside, the light was a smoky orange from lanterns. The walls were draped with elaborate floral velvet, which were once vivid primary colours but had now faded to creams and tans. Towering wardrobes, recliners and chairs had twisted columns, broken pediments and heavy carvings. A harpsichord dominated the centre of the room, its wood hand-painted with thousands of nesting birds and stylised botany.

Inquisitor Roth paced over to the harpsichord where a map of the Medina theatre had been spread-eagled across its decorative lid. It was a cartographic antique,

centuries old, depicting the three core worlds of Medina
– Cantica, Kholpesh and Aridun – alongside their various
ous satellite planets. Gurion's handwritten notes and
annotations marked the vellum surface.

'We are losing the war,' Gurion said from across the room.
He placed a wafer plate onto the phonograph. Francesci's
Symphony of the Eldest Season crackled out of the flared trumpet
pet cone. It was the same concerto that Gurion had played
from their APC when they had incited the loyalist Counter-
Revolution on Scarbarus eight years ago. Roth had only
been freshly ordained then and Gurion had led the joint
ordos operation. The strident compositions of Solomon
Francesci reminded him of past loyalties.

'Losing, or lost?' Roth asked.

'The rimward world of Naga was conquered five
months ago. Since then, Chaos forces have pushed their
advance onto the satellite and core planets of Medina.'

Gurion joined Roth by the strategy map. Under the
smoky light of reading candles, Roth noticed for the first
time how much his ordos senior had aged. Gurion
looked drawn and grey. To Roth, the man had always
been the scarred veteran of almost two centuries of service
vice to the rosette. His spine had been broken and
reinforced during the Fall of the Fifth Republic in the
Corsican Subsector. Below the hips, his legs had been
lost during the Orpheus Insurgency and replaced by augmetics of fluted copper skin and fibrous muscles of
wiring. Yet he looked older than Roth remembered.

'Naga is conquered. Ninvevah, Baybel and Tarsis. All
satellite planets taken by Chaos,' said Gurion as he indicated each planet on the map. 'Imperial forces have
retreated to a war of attrition on the core worlds of Medina – Cantica, Aridun and Kholpesh.'

'How is the campaign faring on the core worlds then?'

'Judging by manpower, supplies and enemy disposition, Imperial forces cannot hold the core worlds for
more than three months.'

Roth's expression darkened considerably. 'Seems like we are wasting our effort here. Why doesn't the military retreat and consolidate in the Bastion Stars?'

'So the High Command keeps telling me, but no. I am clearly of the opinion that if the enemy sought to claim the Bastion Stars, they would have circumvented the Medina Worlds entirely. This cluster of planets has no strategic relevance to the subsector.'

'Then I don't follow you,' Roth admitted.

'The Archenemy is fighting for a reason. It wants Medina for a reason. That's why the Conclave was formed. Circumstance, logic and intelligence indicate that the Archenemy is seeking to claim the Old Kings of Medina. Come now, Roth, I don't need to explain this to you.'

At this, Roth nodded slowly, raising an eyebrow. '"The Old Kings of Medina. Here be the relics of the Emperor's cause. Wielded for the dominion of worlds and lost in the aperture of civilisation",' Roth recited, an old verse from Medina's historical annals.

'Yes, Obodiah. Our objective here is to gather and collaborate on a network of intelligence which will hopefully unveil the nature and exact location of these relics, and present them to the Imperial High Command,' said Gurion.

Roth was not convinced. It seemed like they were clutching at straws.

The sliding screen of Gurion's stateroom rolled back. A young woman entered, taking slow and measured steps across the carpet. She was suited in an egg-yellow bodyglove, an Inquisitorial rosette worn as a choker on her throat.

'Ah, she arrives on time. This is Inquisitor Felyce Celeminé,' said Gurion, introducing the newcomer with a welcoming sweep of his arm.

Roth bowed deeply and offered his hand.

'Inquisitor Roth, it's a pleasure. Lord Gurion has had nothing but praise for you,' she said, folding Roth's hand in both of hers.

Roth studied the newcomer with a gentleman's appraising eye. She was not tall, nor was she beautiful in the conventional sense. Rather, Inquisitor Celeminé was delicate, almost girl-like in stature. Her copper-blonde hair was cropped stylishly short and a lip ring tugged at the centre of her pout. She was, Roth decided, handsome in a demure and eccentric kind of way that verged on the bookish.

'Oh he has? I think he's been too liberal with his liquor then,' Roth dismissed lightly.

'Not at all. And a body's got a right to be curious.'

'Maybe you should keep that body in check, and remember to let go of my hand,' smiled Roth.

Celeminé started and slid her hands away, chewing her lower lip in slight embarrassment.

Gurion cleared his throat. 'Inquisitor Celeminé is newly ranked. I am confident in her abilities, but I hesitate to send her to Cantica and investigate alone. I want someone with experience with her, as we can't afford to take chances. She will be your second.'

'Settle down, sir. I haven't agreed to this yet,' said Roth.

Gurion, looking crestfallen, didn't say a word as he crossed over to the harpsichord. He studied the map closely. Under the yielding light, his face looked weary and battered. It was a face of flat planes and corners, brows polished by fists and forceful blows. Slowly, it dawned on Roth that Lord Gurion was scarred and sharpened through two centuries of service to the Emperor. And yet, Roth had never seen his colleague so filled with such barely suppressed fear.

'There will be a war council tonight. You will be there. After you know what I know, I trust you will do the right thing. I wouldn't have brought you here if I didn't,' said Gurion with conviction.

CHAPTER TWO

THE COUNCIL OF Conclusions was the plenary organ of the entire Medina Campaign.

Present were the senior commanders of the Imperial Guard and Navy, representative officers of neighbouring regions and, of course, the inquisitors. Even the titanic form of a Space Marine was present, an envoy of the Stone Gauntlets Chapter as denoted by the markings on his shoulder plate. The Astartes settled in his dusk-red armour like a dormant fortress.

Far removed from the opulence and grandeur of a congressional council, this was a regular assembly of briefing and intelligence dissemination. The representatives of the Governate and other political bodies were not invited. It was no place for bureaucrats.

For this reason, the Council of Conclusions assembled in the war vault of the *Carthage*. It was a tactical chamber constructed specifically to house the most powerful military and political chieftains of the subsector.

The war vault was a domed chamber, armoured within the hammerhead prow of the cruiser. The walls and ceiling were of ribbed ceramite, sparse and spartan when compared to the haughty elegance of the *Carthage's* design. The seating galleries were steel benches, forming U-shaped tiers around a hololithic projector. The chamber was unlit except for the ethereal glow of the projector. It was raw and reflected the blunt, unrelenting attitude of military leadership. Truly, this was the nerve centre of the entire war effort.

Inquisitor Roth had suited up in his Spathaen fighting-plate. He decided it would be prudent, considering the occasion. The chrome trauma-plates afforded him a degree of buoyancy against the disapproving glares of blade-faced military seniors.

The Council began with a detailed briefing of the war situation: production output, fuel, ammunition, food, a comprehensive analysis of casualties. The officers debated with each other in a terse, clipped military fashion, their words coming in tight bursts like gunfire. Roth was content to listen. From what he could gather, the situation was very bad indeed. It seemed the general consensus amongst the Council was that Medina was, for all intents and purposes, defeated. The remaining Imperial forces should be re-routed to shore up defences in the strategically vital Bastion Stars.

At one point, a Naval admiral stood up and brandished a scorched wad of papers for all to see.

'This is the war journal of a captain of infantry, salvaged from the trenches of Ninvevah. It contains intelligence of Archenemy tactics prudent to our discussion.'

The officer opened the papers, tracing the words with his finger until he found the entry he was looking for.

'"Day sixty-two. The Archenemy, perhaps by design, parade the captured civilians of Ninvevah before our positions daily. They execute them within sight of our trenches, arranging the bodies in ranks. By my count, the entire city is dead and arrayed before us. Among those who are not killed, stout, healthy young men are marched in slave columns towards an unknown fate. This is appalling, I very much want to go home."'

As the admiral finished reading, there came a murmur of unease from the gallery. Even Roth, who had travelled widely, had never experienced war on such a scale.

'The captain and his 161st were overwhelmed shortly thereafter. This journal was retrieved as the remaining Cantican forces withdrew from Ninvevah following a surge of Archenemy aggression,' the admiral announced flatly before returning to his seat.

Then it was Forde Gurion's turn to speak. The inquisitor rose slowly, looking imperious in a long cape of carbon-ceramic polyfibres. The loom-woven armour glowed brass under the light of the hololith.

'Gentlemen, as you are well aware, our respective ordo have drawn together a Conclave in order to reveal and deny the objectives of the Archenemy in this subsector. Today, our Conclave is complete with our final member – Inquisitor Obodiah Roth.'

For a brief second, several dozen unfriendly eyes focused on Roth. Their distaste was palpable.

Gurion continued smoothly. 'Further, our Conclavial Task Groups on Kholpesh and Aridun have been toiling ceaselessly these past months in analysing intelligence regarding the Old Kings of Medina.'

A voice called from the assembled officers. 'And are you any closer to finding out what these mythical pieces are? Or where we can start digging them up with shovels and spades?'

Gurion shook his head politely. 'As of yet, we know not their exact nature or location. We have, however, obtained new findings from collated data over the past several months. According to the sources, the origins of the Old Kings began no less than twelve thousand years ago, and no more than twenty. Across the span of the Pre-Imperial galaxies, many lost outposts of man were bequeathed with visitation from what the sources described as "Early Sentients". The visitors brought with them their worship of the stars and constellations, as well as mathematics, astronomy and technology. In return, man adopted their worship of astronomical bodies.'

A Naval staff officer raised his hand. 'What sources are these?' he asked flatly, clearly unimpressed.

'Old scriptures, folk literature, but most importantly intelligence briefings gathered during the initial War of Reclamation, when Imperial fleets first moved to reclaim the Medina Worlds. The fleet acknowledged that when the Early Sentients left the Medina Worlds for whatever reason, they left for their subjects a parting gift. It was a monument of worship. The gift was known by many names – the Old Kings, the Star Ancient, the Guardian of Medina. According to the intelligence gathered by the Naval Expeditionary Fleet, this monument would strike down the enemies of Medina, at a time of dire need.'

'These gifts certainly didn't help the Pre-Reclamation Medinians from fighting the Imperial Crusade. This is Imperial territory now, is it not? Didn't we smash these barbarians thousands of years ago?' another officer retorted.

Under the barrage of scepticism, Gurion kept his composure. 'We can only ascertain, from archived scripture, that the Old Kings rest on one of the three core worlds. Historical experts postulate that the Old Kings were worshipped by Pre-Imperial Medinian culture, and to this effect it is believed that when the stars and the magnetic properties of the star system are in alignment, the Old Kings can be woken from their dormant state and be reborn as the "Star Kings".'

There was a ripple of derisive laughter. Gurion, however, remained unfazed.

'I have also come into possession of orbital reconnaissance photos detailing the mass excavations which have taken place across the surface of conquered worlds.'

He cued the grainy high-altitude reconnaissance pict. Roth squinted at the black and white hololith of excavation quarries that, judging by the comparative size of nearby terrain features, were a kilometre deep.

Gurion reviewed a slideshow of various picts. 'It is our belief that the slaves collected post-invasion, are utilised in an immense mining effort on these worlds. This leads us to believe the Archenemy are actively searching.'

He zoomed out to show a high orbital shot of the several subjugated worlds. The Archenemy had been so voracious in their digging that they had gouged into the equator lines of the planets, like a series of zagging claw marks. Most of the excavation quarries seemed to navigate the entire circumference of a planet.

After a moment of contemplative silence, the lord marshal himself stood up. The scar tissue on his face was alive, twitching and livid as he spoke.

'This is Chaos; they act without pattern or logic. We cannot hope to understand them, and certainly we cannot base our own campaign strategy around their madness. You mean to ask us to clutch at straws? To formulate a war plan because of some historical narrative?'

The marshal's rebuttal was met with a raft of applause. Roth noticed that even the giant in power armour – the Space Marine – shifted his massive weight and leaned in, his broad features eager to hear Gurion's response.

Roth would have brandished his Inquisitorial rosette then and there to remind Varuda of his authority. In truth, his fingers twitched to do so. But Gurion's response reminded Roth how young and unlearned he was in comparison. There was no substitute for two centuries of experience or the cold, steady head of a veteran.

With his composure unswayed, Gurion turned his wrists out in placation.

'Gentlemen, please. I only ask to re-establish my case again. We know the Medina Corridor is of little strategic merit in the context of subsector conflict. We know the Archenemy are utilising slaves in mass excavations. We know all this.' Gurion paused, panning his eyes across the gallery, waiting for a challenge.

'Regardless of the Old Kings, the question remains why the Chaos vanguard would choose to attack Medina. At the very least, Imperial forces must defend core worlds until we can define Archenemy objectives and neutralise them. That is all we ask.'

Varuda opened his mouth to speak but was cut off by the resonant collision of metal on metal. It sounded like a forge anvil, slowly and rhythmically hammering together.

The gallery all turned to see the Space Marine clapping gently. The ceramite gauntlets that sheathed his massive paws reverberated through the chamber. Nodding his shaven head in approval, the Space Marine even dipped his head in respect to Gurion.

The lord inquisitor bowed once and retreated back to his seat next to Roth. As another officer took the stage to make his report on fuel supply, Roth whispered to Gurion, 'Do you think you've swayed them?'

Gurion snorted. 'Definitely not. But I've made my point. Besides, if all else fails I'll force this down their throats.' He dangled his rosette from a chain on his wrist.

Roth arched his eyebrows with equal parts surprise and revelation. He should have known. It was a fundamental principle taught to all ordos candidates – move in soft, then bring their whole damn world crashing down around their ears, if you have to. His mentors had coined the term 'being a smiling pirahnagator'.

Roth's reaction summoned a chuckle of amusement from Gurion. 'Oh my Roth, you have a lot to learn regarding Inquisitorial diplomacy.'

INQUISITOR ROTH RACKED the slide against the receiver of his stripped-down plasma pistol, checking for slick lubrication.

The parts of his MKIII Sunfury were laid out neatly at the foot of Gurion's bed. Barrel, cocking cam, trigger assembly, bolt assembly. The weapon was a monster, a gas-operated cyclical pistol, carapaced in plates of insulating brass.

Despite its firepower, the pistol was subtle and that was what Roth admired the most. It was a gentleman's Parabellum with the bark of a military-grade cannon. He holstered it in a shoulder rig and continued with his equipment check.

He limbered up, checking the smoothness of his Spathaen fighting-plate. The fluid interlocking plates of chromatic silver were fitted in such a way as to allow complete fluidity of movement. Everything from the shoulder domes to the sleek shin greaves were designed to slip and turn the ballistic properties of an attack.

Satisfied with its condition, Roth then donned a knee-length tabard of tiny tessellating obsidian scales. As he moved, the tiny panes of psi-reactive glass clinked like the scales of a sea serpent.

Finally he checked the feedback of his power fist. His right hand hummed with a low magnetic drone. The weapon was a Tang War-pattern power fist, a slim-fitting silver gauntlet. Lighter and smaller than the standard designs issued amongst Imperial officers, this elegantly slender power fist had been seized from the armoury of a narco-baron on Sans Gaviria during Roth's tenure as an interrogator. An artist, a gentleman and a connoisseur, the narco-baron had been like

Roth in many ways. He had had a fine taste for arte-facts of both utility and style.

Bastiel Silverstein was likewise making his own prepa-rations. He had upended his luggage next to Gurion's well-stocked sideboard, chasing shots of oak-aged bram-sch as he sorted through his array of hunting equipment. For Silverstein, it was a matter of selecting the proper tools for the job.

Repeating crossbows, hunting autos, long-las, needle pistols and even a harpoon-throwing rig were piled up around him. From his carry cases, the huntsman selected a bullpup autogun, slender and spidery in frame. He played the weapon in his hands, feeling out its balance and its weight. Shaking his head, Silverstein placed it back in its case and took out a scoped autorifle. This one was much longer, its stock painted in dashes of greens and greys. Silverstein tested the trigger with a click, tog-gled the safety and racked the bolt. He fired again with an audible click. Satisfied, Silverstein slammed back a shot of bramsch and placed the weapon aside.

Ever conscious of style, the huntsman was still dressed in his tailored coat of green leather, with jackboots pol-ished to gloss-backed sheen. Over this, he grudgingly struggled into a flak vest, a basic piece of Guard kit that Silverstein had hand-painted a woodland camouflage onto. The huntsman did not trust the tools of his trade to anyone else.

Strapping on a utility belt, the huntsman began to stuff items into the various pouches – composite-polymer cord, auspex, tranquillisers, bolos and a large serrated skinning knife. Looking pleased with his preparations, he stood up and bounced on the balls of his feet, listening for loose straps or rattling pouches. He was as quiet as a hunting cat.

Wordlessly, the inquisitor and his hunter continued to adjust buckles and load magazines, latching and unlatching various large and ominous luggage cases. Neither of them looked up as Gurion, Celeminé and a CantiCol officer entered the stateroom.

'Are you planning on starting on a war?' asked Gurion.

'No. Joining one,' replied Roth without looking up. He was working out a knot in the release latch of his harness with his teeth.

Gurion nodded sagely. 'You will head the Task Group to Cantica then?'

'If that's where I'm needed.'

'I knew you would.'

As he spoke, Roth glimpsed the newcomer in his peripheral vision – the young staff officer who had accompanied Gurion into the room. Although he wore the rank-sash of a captain, he was too young. The brown felt of his jacket was loose on him, and his white kepi hat sat oddly on his head.

'Who is the young scrapper?' Roth said, nodding towards the captain.

'I am Captain Leyos Pradal, sir,' announced the boy, his eyes staring straight ahead in severe military discipline.

Gurion smiled apologetically at Roth. 'Captain Pradal will be your adjutant. He is a fine marksman and has seen combat experience.'

'What experience?' Silverstein snapped from across the room.

'Oh... I... uhm, limited skirmishes with rogue bandits on Cantica,' Pradal said.

'What kind of bandits?' Silverstein pressed.

'Hinterland raiders,' said Pradal.

'You mean Cantican bandits who shared one autorifle between five men,' Roth called to Silverstein.

Pradal puffed his chest and piped up again. 'I also score 95 out of 100 on our graded shooting classes,' the young captain said.

'Hitting a target at a shooting range is one thing. The game is different when you have explosives going off overhead and the enemy is rushing you with a large axe,' Silverstein explained as he slipped rounds into a curved magazine.

'I see what you are saying,' Captain Pradal said. 'I am not here to boost your combat capability, but to liaise on your behalf with Cantican command staff. I can look after myself.'

Roth sighed. Gurion did not look pleased either. The last thing Roth needed was an inexperienced field officer on his task group. But if it would help smooth over some of the friction with High Command, then perhaps he could accommodate. Roth nodded curtly at Captain Pradal, then returned to his preparations.

Gurion picked his way around the clutter of spilled baggage and settled down in his armchair. 'Before you do go, I should tell you that there is already another Con-clave Task Group on Cantica headed by Marcus Delahunt. They have been there since almost the beginning.'

Roth spared Gurion a look as he counted out fusion canisters for his pistol. 'I know Marcus. So why are our services still required? Or perhaps I am missing something?'

'We believe they are dead.'

'Ah,' said Roth, his expression unchanged.

'High Command has not established any comms with Cantica for the past twenty-seven days. Likewise, the Conclave hasn't been able to make astropathic contact with Inquisitor Delahunt for that same time.'

'Convenient.'

'Roth, please listen to me. If you still choose to go ahead onto Cantica, we need you to find Delahunt and to extract intelligence about the state of Cantica.'

'This keeps getting better, sir,' smiled Roth.

'I will contact you during the Cantican dawn on the fifth day, by astropath. Have Celeminé prepare herself for conveyance. In the event I am not able to reach you, I will repeat the conveyance once every second day, for a week. After that…'

'You can assume we're dead,' Roth finished for him.

'Be serious, Obodiah,' Gurion said, assuming his paternal tone. 'We cannot afford any chances here. You will be carving your path into the lion's den. Are you certain you are prepared to do this?'

Roth unholstered his Sunfury and loaded a fusion canister into the pistol grip. With habitual ease he expelled a tiny spur of gas from the venting assembly, toggling the weapon to *dormant-safe*.

'Well, Master Gurion, of course I'll go. Dressed as I am now, it would be terribly embarrassing of me not to.'

CHAPTER THREE

BYRSA PRIME HAD fallen. Sibboeth had fallen. Iberia had fallen. The city-states of Cantica were collapsing and Central Buraghand would be no different.

Although Cantica was the defensive buttress of the Medina Corridor, its military had collapsed under the invasion. Within the subsector, Cantica was strategically insignificant, yet within Medina the planet was a lone sentry. The archeo-world, its ancient geography appearing as an orb of yellowed parchment from orbit, had been assaulted with the full force of the Archenemy invasion, a heavy blitzing attack that had allowed the Cantican Colonial Regiments no time to formulate a cohesive defence. The CantiCol, a formation of light infantry spread thin over the entire star system, had not been enough to even temporarily slow the Archenemy momentum.

The invasion had begun with a surgical, probing attack. It had started four months previously with an aerial deployment of Archenemy Harrier-class raiders that perforated the Imperial Naval pickets.

Corsairs of Khorsabad Maw – the Ironclad, raiders well versed in the art of amphibious warfare – stormed the beachheads of the Cantican Gulf. An enemy force, primarily infantry numbering some one hundred and fifty thousand.

In the eleventh week of invasion, Lord General Dray Gravina wrote in his journal, 'The Archenemy, having resolved to make an amphibious landing, have amassed their forces in a stalemate along our coastal defences. It is our intention to deny the Archenemy access to inland routes. This shall be achieved by concentrating our resources in the sea-forts of the eastern and northern Gulf. It is a favourable opportunity to allow the enemy to disperse themselves like waves against our curtain defences.'

In that event, it was precisely what the Archenemy pre-empted. The Cantican Guardsmen were stretched thin across the coast against a diversionary assault. In the sixteenth week, the Ironclad began aerial deployment into the undefended Cantican heartland. Legions of mechanised and motorised infantry and fighting vehicles were inserted, almost directly into population centres. Significant urban sprawl covered the majority of Cantican continents, yet these low-lying clay forts and sprawling terracotta cities were prime targets for high-altitude deployment.

What followed would be remembered as the Atrocities. Estimates made at a later date indicated that the total number of civilians and prisoners of war massacred during the first two weeks of the Archenemy occupation was well over four million.

An Imperial missionary by the name of Villeneuve made pict-recordings and first-hand spool reels of the Atrocities. He died but his recordings were later retrieved by Imperial intelligence. The infamous Villeneuve recordings revealed mass live burials, and slave columns marched into the wastelands, presumably for excavation. Lord General Gravina was publicly executed. The Archenemy unceremoniously dragged his body, in full military regalia, through the streets of the government district.

The journal entries and letters of dead civilians uncovered from the ashes were the worst. Within the scorched pages of a diary, one man wrote, 'I fear I have gone mad with the obscenity of these circumstances. Yesterday the occupiers discovered the language scholam where the local children have been hiding. They were loaded onto trucks and driven to the outskirts of the city. I do not know where those children may be. They were screaming "save our lives" as they passed my house.'

The conquest of Cantica, the largest core world of the Medina Corridor, heralded the beginning of the end for the Imperial war effort.

ROTH COULD SEE the plumes of smoke that rolled off the shattered spine of Buraghand from the high altitude of his stratocraft. The panoramic wilderness of bomb-flattened debris and impact craters made him realise he was in the land of the enemy now.

The stratocraft swept in on an arcing descent. It hurtled low, hugging the ocean surface of the Cantican Gulf to reduce its radar signature. The servitor pilot skimmed so close, its turbine burners hollowed out a tail of steam and boiling water in its wake. On the horizon Roth could see Buraghand, the central city-state of Cantica, rise like a thousand-tiered pyramid.

Snarling hard on thunderous thrusters, the stratocraft skimmed along the western coastal ridge of Buraghand. The craft was a modified Naval sixty-tonner, its armaments stripped to carry exhaust dampeners, counter-stealth radars and extended fuel capacity. Had it been spotted from the ground, the craft would have appeared as a dart, its needle-like cockpit perched on massive quad-engines. Toothless, sharp, its profile had a minimal radar cross-section and its dampeners reduced its infrared footprint, rendering it almost invisible to Archenemy surveillance.

It traced the seawall, a towering curtain of mosaic that fortified the seaboard for fifty kilometres. They trailed it for forty, until the servitor pilot found a breach within its defences. The stratocraft shot in through the opening, flying no more than twenty metres above sea level.

They were going so fast, Roth was overcome with inertia. The visual blur was too fast for his eyes. He barely caught glimpses of the Cantican city, structures of terracotta and heavy copper shaped in ascending tiers.

The city was defined by its masonry. Shaped without plumb lines or spirit levels, the masons seemingly improvised as they built. The buildings were teetering affairs, with blunt edges, curvaceous parapets and lean-ing walls that lent the city a dizzying effect. Between the structures, webs of open-air staircases connected the multiple city strata from the minarets of the upper tiers to the fossilised ruins many kilometres below the ground.

Still maintaining a recklessly low skim, the stratocraft entered the stack ruins of lower Buraghand. An archaeo-logical wasteland spilled down the slopes from the city-state's apex in a rambling scree. Broken-toothed ruins chopped past them, so precariously close they whispered past their wingtips with subsonic sighs. Finally, the stratocraft banked hard, rolling almost belly up before it decelerated underneath a mess of exposed wooden frame supported by crumbling pillars. Roth could not tell what the building had once been, perhaps a shrine judging by the copper dome that dominated the ceiling. Regardless, the rusted ceiling would shield the craft from enemy radar sweeps.

The stratocraft's monstrously snorting thrusters settled into a soft purr as the servitor-pilot powered off. He deactivated the stratocraft into hibernation. Slowly and wordlessly, the members of Roth's task group emerged from the lander, weapons ready.

Inquisitor Roth stalked out of the craft first, hunched low, the chrome of his Spathaen fighting-plate friction-less and silent. With a running crouch, he sprinted for cover behind a revetment of rubble. Drawing the plasma pistol from his chest rig, Roth took up a firing position and scanned his surroundings. Turning to the stratocraft, the inquisitor signalled the all-clear.

Captain Pradal and Silverstein appeared next. With practiced precision they sprinted down the ramp, boots crunching on the carpet of crushed stone as they went to ground, taking up firing positions on Roth's uncovered flanks. Celeminé was the last to emerge, clad in her egg-yellow bodyglove that seemed at odds with the desolate environment.

'Get on your guts!' Roth hissed from his position. Celeminé settled into an awkward crouch, suddenly aware that the wilderness of disintegrating masonry could hide any number of unseen gunmen.

'Silverstein, I need you to fix me a position,' the inquisitor said as he squinted into the ragged flames on the horizon. To Roth, Upper Buraghand was just a silhouette of ragged spine-like buildings, but to a huntsman with bio-scopic lenses it was a different matter.

The xenos game-hunter reared up, the yellow lenses of his pupil augmentations narrowed to targeting reticules as they homed in on distant targets. A tabulation of data began to scroll down the periphery of his vision, analysing the distance, climate and movement signatures.

**+++ Buraghand, Upper city state –
Cantica: 7255 metres distant.
Visibility Spectrums: Noon Visible
Heat/Wind: High/High
Movement Signatures: 41% +++**

'Sire, I'm picking up a lot of movement, probably enemy patrols. If we stick to a north-east route, we should avoid the majority of it,' said Silverstein.

Roth nodded and turned to the others. 'Delahunt's last known position was a garrison fort in Upper Buraghand, roughly seven kilometres due north. That's our destination. This is enemy territory now, so stay sharp and keep moving. Good?'

The others primed their weapons and nodded. As one, they rose and picked their way through the ruins towards the burning metropolis. Far away, the echo of sporadic gunfire and the screams that followed were carried on gusts of wind and wisps of blackened ash.

THEY EDGED INTO the desolate, shell-scarred remnants of a fortress compound. Within the terracotta walls, the marshalling ground was pockmarked with shrapnel and shot. An artillery shell had found its mark in the central keep, caving the command tower inwards like a collapsed ribcage. Blood and death had seeped into the porous earth and a pall of gun smoke still hung heavily in the air.

Silverstein was running point, his bioptic pupils dilating and contracting as they tracked for targets. His autorifle was braced loosely against his shoulder, the camouflaged weapon blending hazily with his long coat of reptilian hide. Crouched and running as he was, Silverstein resembled a hunting hound seeking his quarry.

Fifteen paces behind, Roth and Celeminé followed. Roth looked long and lean in his fighting-plate and obsidian scale, his most favoured regalia of war. He ran with long loping strides, the fighting-plate seeming to facilitate, rather than hinder, his grace of movement.

Beside Roth, Celeminé gripped a bulky two-shot flame pistol in both hands. Extra fuel canisters were secured to her chest webbing, along with her med-kit and other utilities.

Bringing up the rear was Captain Pradal, lasrifle held at the hip, spike bayonet socketed in its lug. The weapon was CantiCol-pattern, distinctly longer yet thinner than standard, with a stock and grip of low-grade comb wood. His uniform was Cantican standard issue – a brown cavalry jacket and widely cut grey breeches, tapered around the calves by canvas binding. Upon his swarthy head was the distinctive regimental kepi cap with its circular flat top and forager's bill.

The captain turned around and panned his rifle at the empty marshalling square every few paces. He held a wad of tabac in his lower lip. His eyes were wide and wired as he chewed slowly.

Inquisitor Roth had researched the Cantican Colonials prior to entering the star system. It would have been rude of him not to. Although a little-known regiment, the CantiCol were the Medina Corridor's primary troop formation. According to census, four hundred thousand Guardsmen were garrisoned thinly across the Medina system alongside indigenous PDF elements. But like the planets they defended, their heritage was swathed in antiquity. The regiments had been raised six thousand years ago from the Cantican loyalists of the Reclamation Wars. They had been the few warring dust tribes to aid the Imperium during the Reclamation and were thus the only regiment granted the right to defend the entire region. Unified under Imperial colonisation, these soldiers had only seen intermittent actions against frontier raiders and minor xenos incursion on the Eastern Fringes. Nothing in their long and lengthy history had prepared them for an absolute war against the millions-strong legions of Chaos.

OF DELAHUNT, THERE was no sign. The main barracks block of the inner bailey was empty. The team crept into the blockhouse, silent except for the grinding of broken glass beneath their boots. There was no movement there, nor had there been any signs of life anywhere in the compound.

Inside the barracks, slashes of dried blood stained the walls and congealed in the corners and crevices of the tiled flooring. Spent casings and power cells littered the area. Ranks of bunk beds had been toppled over, some had evidently been used for defensive cover, their metal frames twisted and scorched. The fighting had been heavy here. In one corner of the housing unit, nestled behind an improvised barricade of granary sacks, a heavy stubber had fired its last rounds. The barrel was heat-warped from continuous firing and a bed of brass casings covered the area around it. Evidently, the Guardsman here had put up a dogged resistance.

Roth looked out the broken window into the outer courtyard. He saw the bodies of the entire garrison company, a hundred and twenty men in all, strung up across the battlements. As a member of the ordos, Roth had seen brutality before but he was thankful that he had not yet become inured to it. The massacre was painful to see and he knew it wounded Captain Pradal even more. Those were his men up there, swinging in the humid breeze. Even though the captain had not known them personally, they were his brothers in arms nonetheless. It saddened Roth immensely.

'Live target! South-east corner of the compound,' Silverstein called. Immediately, the four of them dropped to their stomachs.

Roth hit the tiles with a clatter. His cheek pressed against the semi-dried blood. Some of it was still viscous and felt like oil on his skin. Cursing softly under his breath, he leopard-crawled towards Silverstein, who had been watching from the window.

'How many?'

'Three movement signatures, at least. Maybe more. Want me to look again?' Silverstein asked.

'No, I will,' said Roth. The plasma pistol in his gauntlet began to vibrate as he thumbed it off safety. He hazarded a peek through the sepia-stained shards of the glass window.

Sure enough, the huntsman had been correct. Roth spotted a ghost of movement, darting between two squat storage sheds no more than fifty metres away. Then another flicker of movement, this time closer still, heading for their barracks block. Roth had seen enough; he ducked back down and gestured to the others.

'Enemy. They've got us cornered. We can either make a break from the barracks across the open marshalling grounds. Or we wait.'

'I say wait, at least until we know how many of them there are. They'll flush us out and cut us down otherwise,' replied Captain Pradal fearfully. The others nodded in agreement.

'Fine. Celeminé, Pradal, cover that window. Silverstein, with me.' Roth said as he scrambled behind an upturned bed frame. He made a quick assessment of the entry points to the barracks. Besides the main door, and a central window on the courtyard-facing side of the housing unit, there were no other entrances.

The four of them settled into a tense silence, eyes darting, jaw muscles clenching. Roth kept his eyes fixed to the main entrance. It was a thin metal door, so warped and perforated by small-arms fire it tilted on its hinges, unable to close. It hung there, slightly ajar, as Roth

waited for the slightest creak of movement. To his left,
Silverstein had stabilised his rifle on top of a storage
trunk. He had settled into a pattern of rhythmic breathing, slowing his pulse and easing out his muscles. He
aimed down the scope of the weapon and briefly closed
his eyes before opening them again to check for realign-
ment. Roth wished he too had the same hunter's poise.

'Do you hear that?' Celeminé whispered. Her voice
suddenly seemed so loud, Roth flinched inwardly.

Sure enough they could hear the scuffling crunch of
boots on a dirt floor. They were barely audible at first,
but increased in pitch and rhythm rapidly. Something
was starting to sprint towards the barracks block. Several
somethings.

Then the door began to swing outwards. Roth's index
finger slipped into his pistol's trigger guard. He raised
the weapon with both hands. A figure appeared in the
doorway, a dark silhouette framed by the harsh sunlight
that flooded into the room and haloed around it. Roth
aimed for the centre of mass, his synapses firing the
impulse for his hand to squeeze the trigger.

'Hold fire! Hold fire!' Silverstein screamed. At the
same instant, the huntsman had instinctively made his
shot. He shifted the weight of his rifle at the last
moment, bucking the aim upwards and unleashing his
round into the ceiling. The noise was deafening.

Roth faltered, paralysed with confusion. His brass-
plated plasma pistol wavered in the air. He paused...
drew a breath. Slowly his vision adjusted to the influx of
light, and the figure in the doorway swam into focus. It
was a Cantican soldier.

The Guardsman stared back at him, frozen in the
doorway. At that moment, Roth imagined their expres-
sions of shock would have mirrored each other. The
soldier was no more than seventeen or eighteen standard; dirty and dishevelled as he was, he was not old

enough to have nursed a growth of beard. His brown felt jacket was missing a sleeve and his grey breeches had no leg wraps, so they flapped voluminously. Roth noted the sash around his abdomen denoted him as a corporal.

'I'm a friendly,' the young Guardsman finally stuttered. He lowered his CantiCol lasrifle. Several other men appeared behind him, tired and ragged and all dressed in Cantican uniforms. Another soldier slowly nudged the surprised corporal out of the way. He was a much older man, with a thick handlebar moustache. The rank sash stretched taut across his abdomen denoted him as a sergeant major. He looked at Roth, unsure what to make of the situation until he spotted the Inquisitorial rosette embossed on Roth's left shoulder guard. The sergeant expelled a soft gasp of hope.

'Praise the Emperor. You are inquisitors,' he muttered under his breath.

Roth holstered his pistol back in its shoulder rig and rose up to his full height. He was an impressive head and shoulders taller than all the Canticans. Several of the Guardsmen retreated a step or two.

'I am Inquisitor Obodiah Roth of the Ordo Hereticus. This is my field team,' he said. As he spoke, Roth noticed in the periphery of his vision that Silverstein and Pradal had not relaxed their weapons. It was a necessary precaution considering the circumstances.

'I am Sergeant Tal Asingrai. Formerly of the Cantican 6/6th Infantry.'

It was Captain Pradal who spoke next, rising from his position by the window. 'Sergeant. Are you deserters?' he asked with his lasrifle gripped in both hands.

The sergeant's jaw hardened visibly. 'No, sir. We still fight.'

'Cantica fights? Cantica has fallen,' Captain Pradal stated flatly.

'Cantica has fallen, yes. But some of us still fight. Resistance cells have formed in the under-ruins. We don't do much, but we do what we can,' the sergeant replied.

The reaction in Captain Pradal was overwhelming. He dropped his rifle, letting it droop on its sling, and squeezed the old soldier in a heavy bear hug. Roth could only guess how it must feel for the captain to realise his home was not dead, that its people still lingered. Perhaps they had a fighting chance yet.

The Cantican Colonials surged into the room, exchanging names and handshakes; it was unusual for an officer to act with open candour with enlisted men, but this was an unusual situation. Roth allowed the atmosphere of jubilation to wane before he spoke.

'Gentlemen, this is the first glimmer of positive news I have heard for weeks. The Archenemy, have they subjugated the surface?'

Sergeant Asingrai stole a furtive glance out into the courtyard where the garrison company had been butchered, and over the walls into the enemy-held city beyond. 'It's not safe here. Follow us to the under-ruins. We can talk there.'

CHAPTER FOUR

WHEN MEN HAD colonised the Medina Worlds so very long ago, they had raised cities from the arid plains. These were ancient structures of clay, mortared with the crushed sea shells of long-extinct ocean-dwellers. Over the centuries, these cities were eroded by the seething dust storms and relentless suns until new cities were raised over the skeletons of the old. This natural cycle of construction had continued over the course of millennia, strata upon strata of ossified structures, growing as vertically as it did laterally, forming a mantle of architectural under-ruins, a labyrinth of archaeology that went five kilometres deep.

It was here, driven four kilometres underneath Upper Buraghand, that Inquisitor Roth came upon the isolated pockets of Imperial resistance. Down through an arterial maze they descended, groping their way through structures so old that natural rock growth and man-made construction had fused into one organic cavern. Crops of fungal growth grew wilder and more monstrous the deeper down they went.

Roth lit his way by the dull blue glow of his activated Tang War-pattern power fist. At one stage, Roth tripped and pushed his power fist through an ashlar wall. He found himself peering into a house that had not been visited by a human presence in at least seven thousand years. The structure was empty but for the petty ornaments of everyday living that lay undisturbed under swathes of dust and white mould – ceramic urns and plates, a crumbling copper-framed cot that had verdigrised to deep turquoise. The thing that seized Roth's attention, however, was an aquila shrine mounted on the far wall. A stylised double-headed eagle of black ore, housed within a shrine box of porous, flaking wood.

Roth was seized by a desire to brush the cobwebs from the shrine but thought better of it. If something had remained such a way for millennia, it was not up to him to disturb it.

After two hours of black, dusty, claustrophobic descent, Roth assumed they had reached their destination. He saw a stratum of ancient structures that had collapsed, forming a natural valley two hundred and fifty metres in length. The shoulders of the ravine were clustered with buildings so old and ossified they had fused with the planet's geology into a honeycombed warren. Overhead, rock pillars supported another stratum of ruins like the buttressed ceiling of a cathedral. As they entered the underground valley, Roth smelt rather than saw the signs of a camp first. He smelt boiling broth, chemical fires and the stale warmth of humans.

'This is it,' Sergeant Asingrai said as he gestured at the rock cubbies that rose up around them.

Judging by the number of drumfires and the refugees that huddled around them, Roth estimated there were over a thousand people seeking shelter in that small underground enclave. Men, women and children shuddered in the subterranean cold, swathed in blankets and rags, their faces hollowed by starvation. A small-bore autocannon, bronzed and ageing, was manned by a Cantican Guardsman and an armed volunteer. Sandbagged within a nest overlooking the mouth of the valley, it provided the enclave's only defensive hard point.

Roth rubbed his face wearily with his hands. The situation was woeful. He had hoped for something more, perhaps an underground command bunker, or at the very least some semblance of effective resistance. As far as he was concerned, his mission to gather intelligence on the Cantican warfront was over before it had begun. Cantica was utterly defeated.

'Sergeant. I don't want to waste any more time. I need answers about the nature of the defeat on Cantica. I need you to tell me what you know,' Roth said.

'You look disappointed, inquisitor. But we haven't been defeated, not like that,' Sergeant Asingrai replied. 'There will be a time for questions once you speak to our senior. I know he would like very much to talk to you.'

He led them through the settlement, and as Roth walked amongst the people he began to see what the sergeant meant. Despite the almost sub-zero temperature and lack of nourishment, women in beaded shawls danced and clapped on tambourines. Tired-looking men warmed their hands over drumfires while sharing the ashy stubs of tabac sticks. Although their clothes were shredded and greased with dirt, the people still carried themselves with an air of quiet dignity. As they walked, a boy of no more than fourteen ran alongside Roth. His cheeks were hollow and his hair was matted but a stern fury smouldered in the boy's eyes. Although he wore no shoes, he cradled a lasrifle in his arms.

'Cantica lives!' the boy shouted, hoisting the rifle above his head.

'Indeed it does,' Roth smiled. He was beginning to understand.

They finally came upon a man ladling broth to refugees. He was an elegantly dishevelled fellow, especially so with his leonine mane of hair and sternly ferocious eyebrows of black. A neatly trimmed beard edged the determination in his jaw line and when he met Roth's gaze, his eyes were a flinty grey. The man reminded Roth of the sort of rough face an Imperial propagandist might model for a conscription poster.

'This is our elected senior, Shah Gueshiva.'

Roth had expected a military man, but Gueshiva was a civilian. A civilian who nonetheless wore a leather jerkin slung with ammunition belts and slung a drum-fed autogun across his chest with accustomed ease. Upon seeing the newcomers in his camp, Gueshiva carefully passed his pail and ladle to a nearby woman. He approached Roth slowly, his face furrowed with incredulity. It was as if Gueshiva did not believe the inquisitors to be real. He first scrutinised Roth up and down before turning his attentions to Celeminé, studying them both from odd angles. He shook his head and ran a hand through his snarling mane.

'Master Gueshiva, I am of flesh and blood and so are my colleagues. You have my word on it,' Roth said, proffering a hand in greeting.

'Doctor. Doctor Gueshiva. I was a physician before this, but please, just Gueshiva will do,' he said as he gripped Roth's forearm. 'It is good to know the Imperium has not forsaken us,' he said, more to himself than Roth.

Roth bowed. 'I am Inquisitor Roth of the Ordo Hereticus. This is my colleague, Inquisitor Felyce Celeminé.' In turn, Celeminé also bowed low, smiling her bow-shaped smile.

'This is momentous indeed. Please, I have so many questions and need so many answers. Will you and your companions join me for tea?'

'Lead the way,' said Roth. His only concern was that Gueshiva did not have unrealistic expectations. Expectations that two inquisitors, a huntsman and a good captain could not hope to meet.

DOCTOR SHAH GUESHIVA'S tent was nothing more than a tarpaulin erected over a rock shelf on the valley gradient. Hooded sodium lamps powered by a ballast generator kept the perpetual night at bay.

Roth slid cross-legged onto a sandbag. His team did likewise, settling down onto sandbags arranged around a plank of wood set across an ammunition crate. A taut sheet of canvas had been erected overhead, strung with beards of hemp and medicinal sundries. As was the custom, Gueshiva began to set out food for his guests – hardtack boiled with water into a creamy sludge, a ration tube of salted grease and tinned fish.

They were desperate rations and Roth hesitated, unwilling to erode their evidently dwindling supplies of food. Although he was hungry Roth nonetheless considered declining the meal, until he saw Gueshiva smiling broadly at him.

The man made shovelling motions with his hands towards his mouth. 'Eat, eat!' Gueshiva bade enthusiastically. He himself did not eat and looked like he had not done so for several days.

Roth reluctantly added a smear of salt grease to his cup of tack porridge. He exchanged a concerned glance with Celeminé, who clearly shared his sentiments. She sipped softly on her battered tin mug. Nobody touched the prized tin of fish. The team ate what was in their bowls appreciatively but did not reach for seconds. Roth swallowed the last of his cereal and nodded his thanks. When they had finished the Cantican custom of breaking bread, Gueshiva cleared his throat.

'Will the Imperial Guard save us?' Gueshiva started.

'Forgive me, Doctor Gueshiva, but at this stage the Imperial High Command are at a loss regarding Cantica. We do not even know the situation. All contact between this world and the 9th Route Fleet ceased twenty-seven days ago. I must answer your question with a question and ask you – what has happened here?' Roth replied in measured tones.

'Look around you, inquisitor. This is Cantica now. The enemy took it from us and drove the survivors into hiding. Vox systems are dead. Communications are non-existent. For all we know, we could be the last and only survivors.'

Roth paused, digesting the information. 'The defeat has been so sudden, so total. How did the enemy overwhelm us? Was it...' Roth hesitated, trying to find the right words, 'was it... the Old Kings of Medina?'

At this, Shah Gueshiva leaned forwards almost as if he did not hear the inquisitor properly. 'You mean the mythical relics of the Old Kings?' He chuckled. 'If that is what you mean, then no.' He leaned back and shook his head softly.

'The Archenemy had been fighting hard but our soldiers fought harder. Morale was good and we did what we could for the war effort. Knitting blankets, pickling foods, rationing. We thought we would pull through.' Gueshiva paused, a lump in his throat making it hard for him to continue.

'But a month ago hundreds of thousands more came from the skies, deploying column after column of armour and mechanised infantry. The depleted garrisons didn't last out for more than two days.'

'Then they have not found the Old Kings yet,' Roth muttered under his breath.

'Pardon my candour, but the Archenemy will break apart the Medina Worlds just to find them,' said Gueshiva.

Roth was taken aback. He was surprised at the good doctor's uncanny insight. He looked to Celeminé but she too was too astonished to ask anything.

'Don't be surprised, inquisitor. I'm not a fool. Why else would war of such a scale be brought to rimward Medina, if not for some grander pretence?' Gueshiva smiled humourlessly.

'Which brings me to my next question – Inquisitor Marcus Delahunt was an ordos operative dispatched to Cantica six months ago, in order to investigate the Old Kings of Medina. His last known location was a distress beacon from the above-ground entrance to the garrison fort where Sergeant Asingrai found us. Is he perhaps within your camp?'

'I'm sorry, inquisitor, but no. Thousands of above-ground portholes, tunnels and hatchways lead into the under-ruins. If he is still alive he is not here.'

Roth let everything he had been told seep and settle. The situation was grave, but the revelation that Cantica had been subjugated by conventional warfare was reassuring in an ironic way. He and his Task Group would have time to establish a temporary base of operations within the enclave until they could ascertain Delahunt's fate. There would still be much to do.

'Do you hear that?' Celeminé asked, leaping up from her seat. Her sudden enthusiasm intruded on the contemplative mood.

At first Roth thought Celeminé, a kappa-level psyker, had felt something he did not. But slowly he realised he heard it too – the distant barking of dogs. Roth turned to Gueshiva but the doctor had already risen from his sandbag, racking back the cocking handle of his autogun. The gesture did little to assuage Roth's sudden concern.

'Were you followed?' Gueshiva asked.

Before Roth could answer, the physician had dashed out of the tent. The barking was louder now. Louder and closer.

'With me,' Roth said to his team. The rattle of loading ammunition and hollow clacks of primed weapons was his reply. Without looking back, Roth pushed aside the tent flap and emerged into the subterranean valley.

Outside, panic was total. Fires were doused and tents were flattened. Refugees scrambled into the rock warrens, snatching up their children and carrying the old. Roth spotted a dozen armed volunteers sprinting in the opposite direction towards the steep entrance of the valley. Roth followed, heading for the autocannon nest at the lip of the defile.

He heard someone shout an order to cut the lights. Immediately, the enormous floodlights that lit the settlement were powered down. Roth dived onto the ground beside the gun nest just as darkness dropped around him like a black curtain. He landed hard on his stomach.

Just as abruptly as the commotion had begun, the settlement became quiet. It took Roth's eyes a moment to adjust to the darkness but the fluorescent glow of subterranean flora allowed Roth to make out murky shapes. He found himself lying prone next to Gueshiva, the man distinctively outlined by his wild hair and beard. On his left was Silverstein, his bioptic vision unaffected by the absence of light as he aimed down his scope. Together they formed a static firing line that stretched for perhaps fifty metres if not more, covering the notch entrance and western flank of the valley depression.

Roth squinted into the depths and traced out vaguely humanoid shapes cresting a hog-backed mound of rubble to their front. The figures stood atop the mound and peered directly down at him, well within shooting distance. Roth swore that they were staring at each other. They were so close Roth could hear them snarling at each other in a slurred guttural tongue heavy with awkward consonants.

Gueshiva leaned in close and whispered. 'Archenemy murder squads. They've been sweeping the under-ruins for signs of Imperial resistance. Don't move a frakking muscle.'

Roth held his breath and pressed himself further against the gritty sediment of the underground. Several of the figures had moved away from the squad on the ridge and were stalking cautiously down the scree.

'Sire, I count fifteen men. Five approaching,' Silverstein whispered.

'The dogs. What about the dogs?'

'Just untrained maulers, not scent hounds. I've targeted seven of them, one hundred and twenty-two metres away up on the ridge, and I don't think they've got a scent. No wind currents or circulation down here.'

'Stay put and wait out then,' Roth hissed back.

The approaching figures were climbing over a tumble of masonry and blunted pillars. They were so close now, Roth could make out the razor-edged lines of their armoured silhouettes, metallic petals and corollas sweeping from their shoulders and arms. Three of them aimed lasguns as the other two probed at the boulders and rock slabs with long metal pikes and roving torch beams.

Roth closed his eyes and clenched his fists. Perspiration beaded his upper lip. The white beams of light oscillated wildly and several times flickered dangerously close to their hidden positions. Finally, after an agonising eighty-five seconds, by Roth's count, the intruders turned to go. They prodded their way back up onto the ridge, growling in their language. Whether they were cursing or reporting to their squad leaders, Roth could not discern. After a few more glances in the direction of the collapsed ravine and the hidden settlement, they disappeared over the ridge.

Roth let out a prolonged breath. Without consciously doing so, Roth had held his breath almost the entire time. They waited for a few seconds, straining to see into the darkness before climbing off their fronts.

'Routine patrol,' Gueshiva observed.

Everyone else had risen to a crouch, yet Silverstein stayed prone. Roth shook his friend by the shoulder. 'Bastiel, are you good?'

The huntsman looked up at Roth, stunned, blinking his bioptics. 'They had no faces,' he said.

'Bastiel?'

'I saw them. They had no faces,' Silverstein repeated as he rose. For the first time in almost ten years of service, Silverstein was visibly shaken. For a xenos game-hunter, who pursued bone kraken and carnodon unperturbed, the visage of the Archenemy had truly unnerved him.

CHAPTER FIVE

HE WAS TRAPPED and he was done.

When Inquisitor Marcus Delahunt awoke, those were the first thoughts that came to him. He tried to sit up, but pain lanced up from his broken femur. Rolling over onto his side he vomited onto the cold, wet flagstones.

Delahunt tried to remember where he was. Panning around, he could see he was in a darkened hall of some sort. The floor was lined with polished wood and cylindrical leather bags hung in rows like gutted carcasses. A fresco along the far wall painted in crude pigment depicted stylised athletes, naked, punching and kicking. A training facility, thought Delahunt.

Yet he had no idea how he had got there. His last conscious thoughts were of being hounded by murder squads through the streets of Buraghand. Vaguely he remembered colliding with a heretic raider mounted on some sort of motorised bike. That was how he had broken his leg, of that he was sure.

Delahunt eased himself up on his quivering arms and spotted a water basin, just out of reach. It was an earthenware oblong, undoubtedly placed there for the athletes to sup. But the athletes were dead now. Delahunt flash-backed to their barracks cots, red with blood as he had made his way to the training hall. That memory had stayed vivid above all else.

With slow agony, Delahunt reached out a hand and dragged himself towards the basin. But the splintered ends of his bones grinding against each other almost blacked him out with pain. He collapsed in a heap on the floor, his throat too dry to vomit.

Utterly defeated, the inquisitor lay down for a while, not even blinking. He considered killing himself with the autopistol at his hip. It was a thought he nursed for some time. Finally, he came to a resolution. Lifting his left hand, he pressed his signet ring to his lips and began to speak. The ring, although bronze and unadorned, bore the authority of his Inquisitorial seal. As he spoke, his words were crystallised into data and conducted along microscopic veins of quartz within the signet. The current of information flowed through the circuit and was encrypted, transforming sound waves into codified symbols.

In his state, it was a trying task. Despite lapsing in and out of consciousness, slowly and with great deliberation, Delahunt began to record everything he could remember since he had set foot on Cantica.

IT WAS MORNING as far as Roth could tell. It had only been his second day in the under-ruins and already he had lost all sense of day and night, dark or light. The only reason he knew it was morning, was that he was fatigued. His eyelids felt caustic with lack of sleep and his head was throbbing.

He and Celeminé had been awake all night attempting to establish psychic communion in order to find

Delahunt, with little success. Not only had the psychic strain been totally draining, it had been dangerous too. They had taken turns to disembody themselves, soaring their psychic entities high above the minarets of Buraghand. The threat of being ambushed by other psychic entities, especially on a world subjugated by the Archenemy was all too imminent. While one of them was disembodied, the other had kept constant vigil ready to intervene, psychically if need be. Yet as their night wore on, their efforts had floundered as exhaustion set in. Roth had ingested three tablets of melatonin, but even that did not kept his mind fresh.

Celeminé was asleep now, laid out on the freezing stone floor. She was still clad in her yellow bodyglove and boots, her hair tussled and falling into her face. Celeminé's raw psychic potential could be eta-level but she was still young, and at best she currently skimmed a very potent kappa-level. As a consequence, she had borne the brunt of their efforts. By the third attempt, Celeminé was so spent, her speech was barely coherent.

They had taken up residence in a sheltered cove, a flat-topped house of Cantican design that had collapsed into the ravine aeons ago. It had accumulated so much chalk and calcium deposits that it resembled a rocky shell of natural flowstone. Considering their circumstances, the ruins at least provided the tranquillity and shelter necessary for psychic meditation. Gueshiva had also been a gracious host, giving them a plastek groundsheet and a coal stove to keep the temperature affable.

Roth pulled the groundsheet over Celeminé's sleeping form. Sleeping as soundly as she was, Roth did not want to wake her. He took up a perch in the tiny rock hut, sitting cross-legged on the millennia-old flagstones. He swallowed another two melatonin and mentally steeled himself for another communion. This time he would do it alone.

Roth let his mind drift like a dinghy unmoored from its pier. He floated up as an invisible mote of light, looking down on himself and Celeminé. He was already tired, and the ebb and flow of spirit winds threatened to carry him away into the abyss. It took all of Roth's focus to buoy himself against the current. Hardening his mind's eye into a knot, he began to ascend.

It was slow at first, wafting up through the honeycombed strata of the under-ruins. Roth tasted the lingering ghost-prints of each ossified strata. He moved through the earliest stages of Cantican history, passing a domed palace of the dynastic Imperial governors. He empathised with the guilt of a governor-general who had suppressed a rebellion of horse nomads. The governor-general had ordered their steeds and menfolk executed by live burial six thousand six hundred years ago. The guilt lingered as a sour aftertaste.

He soared up through a layer of single-storey houses stacked from mud brick and covered in mosaics of red, brown and turquoise stones. Although the seismic pressure had crushed the structures into flattened rubble, Roth could smell the vigour of hearth and home. The oily scent of cooking was so strong; he was tempted to stay a while. But up and up he went, gathering in velocity.

Soon the under-ruins flashed past in an overwhelming surge of sensation until he erupted onto the surface. Roth braced himself. Immediately, the turmoil of a city at war threatened to flay open his mind. A tidal wave of brutality and sheer paralysing terror impacted hard against his mental defences. Had it not been for the many hours of tutelage Roth had received under the ordo's finest psychic-duellists, he would have died. Roth recoiled, spiralling inwards into a helix shell as he concentrated internally. Four kilometres below the surface, Roth's physical body tremored momentarily and his left lung fibrillated.

He could feel the terror of families hiding in cellars and basements, the suffocating hopelessness of many who were just waiting to die. Worst of all, he could feel the addictive rush of Ironclad murder squads on a rampage. He could see their black auras, hideous and nauseatingly evil. They haunted the city like a plague of laughing ghosts.

He knew he could not last long. Roth flew low and fast, skimming the haphazard stacks of the tenement quarters. He cut across ornate structures of terracotta and heavy copper and reached the major Buraghand canal. He cast his mind snare wide, hoping to catch any tentative sign of Delahunt – a thought, an ornament, a cry for help, anything.

He searched as best he could. Compared to Celeminé, Roth was not a powerful psyker by any means, but what he lacked in raw potency, he made up for with a singular will to focus. Like the body, the mind could be vigorously trained. Meditation, psychic sparring and even the simple puzzle book could all be tools for psychic prowess, as much as weights, callisthenics and nutrition could build the body. Roth regularly honed himself, and was considered omicron-level by his peers.

Combing the city block by block was a torturous effort. Delahunt was nowhere to be found. Instead Roth glided over the central plaza of Buraghand, a flat hectare of unbroken ground paved with a billion sea shells to resemble the stars and planets of the Medina Corridor. Once the central basilica and forum of Buraghand, it was now a mustering field for Ironclad slavers to herd their Cantican captors for the excavation quarries. The misery and hopelessness of those people, beaten and prodded into the plaza, was so poisonous that capillaries in Roth's physical form began to bleed, threads of blood lacing down his eyes and nose.

It was all too much, and momentarily Roth almost lost control and lapsed into a coma. He strained hard to anchor himself, a single flower against a gale. One more sweep, Roth decided. Narrowing his search area down to the region surrounding the garrison-fort where Delahunt had last transmitted his distress beacon, Roth flew in a concentric circle.

Many thousand of metres below, Inquisitor Roth's body became wracked with seizure. Blood poured from his face. It poured from his nose, his eyes, his ears and from every pore in his cheeks. The atmosphere of holocaust was consuming him.

Unable to maintain his psychic form any longer, Roth decided to return. He recoiled from the conical metal caps and bronze roofs of Upper Buraghand. But as he did so he snagged a glimpse of a sign, the sparkling wink of an Inquisitorial seal being activated. Roth halted, holding his ethereal breath. He searched for it again and sure enough, it was tangible. Down amongst a vast amphitheatre in the commercial district of Upper Buraghand, Roth could almost reach out and touch it. It had to be Delahunt.

Throwing caution aside, Roth shot in like a bird of prey. Assuming the form of a psychic spear, he lanced into the amphitheatre and aimed for the training barracks attached to the western wing of the complex.

Streaming through the stone columns, the psychic manifestation rocketed into the sparring hall. There, crumpled against a wall, lay Inquisitor Delahunt. He was unconscious and his despair was palpable, but he was alive.

Roth roused Delahunt with a brisk mental probe.

+Marcus Delahunt.+

'That is I,' wheezed the inquisitor. He squinted up towards Roth like a man staring into the sun. Delahunt was not a psyker and he could see nothing. Despite bleeding and spasming, Roth drew into his mental reserves and summoned a visage that Delahunt would recognise. It was of a much younger Roth, from their youth as orphans of the Schola Progenium. The image was painted into Delahunt's eye, a spry lanky Obodiah Roth in his mid-teens, lost within the folds of a scholam robe several sizes too large.

+Marcus. It's me, Obodiah.+

'You old bastard. How long has it been, sixteen, seventeen years?' chuckled Delahunt through a mouthful of broken teeth.

+Too long, Marcus. I knew you'd be here, you always were too tough to die, the warp would only spit you back out.+

'If only. I don't know how much longer I have. This whole city is crawling with Archenemy. I can hear them banging on my door.'

+I know, Marcus, I've seen it. Tell me quickly, where exactly are you?+

Delahunt shrugged. 'I think I'm in the Gallery of Eight Limbs. It's an old training facility and tournament pit for maul-fighting. Buraghand commercial quarters. I think I crawled here somehow.'

+Hold on until sunset, old friend. We'll be coming to fetch you.+

'Wait, Roth,' Marcus started.

+Marcus? Quickly. I'm slipping.+

Roth had already stopped breathing for over a minute. Hypoxia was setting in and carbon dioxide began to poison his blood.

'Roth. If I don't make it, I've recorded everything I know in my signet,' said Delahunt.

+Did you find the Old Kings?+

Delahunt shook his head. 'I don't even know what the Old Kings are. I'll explain when you get here, unless the Archenemy get to me first.'

+We'll find you first, Marcus. We will.+

And with that Roth had nothing left. He broke his psychic link, too fast and too abruptly for his weakened state. Asphyxiated and seizuring, he collapsed onto the ruined flagstones.

WHEN BASTIEL SILVERSTEIN found Inquisitor Roth, he was folded backwards over a kneeling position. Arching his spine with his stomach pushed outward, his face was smeared with a film of blood.

He looked like he had died. At least that was what Silverstein thought until a cursory scan with his bioptics revealed a pulse. The huntsman rushed forwards and handled him by the underarms, easing Roth's weight into an upright position.

'Sire, what happened here?' asked the huntsman.

Roth blinked blearily, his words slurring into each other. 'I'm fine, just psychic communion.'

Silverstein propped the inquisitor up against the wall and handed him a steaming tin cup. 'I came in to bring you some tea.'

'Thank you.' Roth wrapped his hands around the warmed metal appreciatively and took a moment to gather his breath. He sipped the tea slowly. It was only a watery Guard-issue infusion, but the earthy bitterness did much to mend his spirit.

By this stage, their conversation had awoken Celeminé. She shrugged off the groundsheet and began to instinctively smooth down her hair. When she spotted Roth, her eyes widened.

Roth raised a hand to halt the questions before they left her mouth. 'Relax. I'm well, but that's not important right now.'

'Roth–' she began.

'Hush. Delahunt is alive and I know where he is. Fetch Gueshiva for me and gather what aid he can spare. We move out at nightfall.'

CHAPTER SIX

Esaul usually didn't mind roof sentry. It was a chance to shoot down any stray flesh-slaves who were lax enough to wander the streets after dark. From his position on the highest tenement roof, he felt like a god. But tonight was a cold night and he was impatient to join his unit. Since the invasion he had almost collected enough ears and teeth to decorate the sling of his newly looted lasrifle, and he was hungry for more.

The prayer towers struck twelve and began to mark the hour. Speakers nestled in the minarets and temple alcoves had once crackled with the flat-toned warble of holy Imperial prayer. Chaos had changed that. Now, on the hour, they broadcasted the incantations of Khorsabad Maw in a guttural Low Gothic. It was a ghastly sound, with its wailing inflection and sinister drone of voices all muted by a static crackle.

Such electronic incantations reverberating through a silent city were a great demoraliser to the dissidents and resistance cells. The trembling acoustics were conducted so well by the conical copper roofs of the city that the echo lingered for many minutes after. Esaul revelled in it. He drew a stick of obscura from one of the many loot pouches harnessed across his breastplate and lit it. Taking a moment to savour the ghoul's gospel, he inhaled deeply on the opiate.

Smoke wafted from his mouth slit and coiled from the gaps of his iron headpiece. The hot desert days and dry freezing nights had irritated the raw facial skin underneath. With a bayonet, Esaul nonchalantly scrapped and prodded into the gaps between the slats to satiate the itch.

Suddenly there was a ripple in the shadows on the streets below. His boredom and discomfort were quickly forgotten and Esaul leaned over the ledge of the roof. Drawing another lungful of obscura, he squinted through the vaporous smoke at the darkness below. Again he saw it: someone detached from the shadowy walls and broke into a sprint. For a brief moment Esaul wondered if it was the hallucinogenic obscura playing phantoms with his vision. But no, sure enough the second was followed by a third figure.

Esaul flicked aside the obscura and nestled down behind the scope of his lasrifle. The gun had been set on a tripod mount and placed over a ledge overlooking the main boulevard. By the way they scurried, they must be live-plunder. He wriggled into a comfortable firing position and tapped his metal cheek against the stock of his weapon. Tracking through the scope, he hunted the jogging figures down the length of pavement. The target reticules wavered onto the back of a running live-plunder. He made ready to ring a shot out into the night and make known his presence. He was a god again and they were his play-things.

The sudden impact to the back of his head jolted Esaul out of his delusion so hard he almost lost his rifle over the edge. Surprised and off-guard, the Ironclad rolled onto his back and placed his forearms over his head, taking the next blow on his rusty vambraces from sheer muscle memory. His assailant pressed the initiative, straddling the prone Ironclad and striking again.

Up close under the pale moonlight, Esaul could see his attacker clearly. It was a man, dressed in civilian clothing but equipped with the military paraphernalia that marked him as a resistance fighter. He had killed enough of them to recognise one in the dark by now.

'Eshulk!' barked the Ironclad. He came alive in the surging panic of close combat and unhinged a flick razor folded beneath his left wrist. It was just one of the many blades he had in his possession. Bridging up on his neck, Esaul rolled his attacker off his chest and reversed their positions. Without pause, he gripped the throat with his free hand and brought up his flick razor.

An unseen knife cut his throat first. Rough hands seized Esaul from behind and a forearm cranked the Ironclad's head back as the bayonet plunged in.

HIGH UP ON the roof ledge, the guerrilla hand-signed the all-clear. The sentry had been silenced.

Roth signalled back and his Task Group fanned out to secure the main street. It was an arterial lane that ribboned up towards the commercial district, narrow, tight and winding. Roth and Silverstein sunk into a crouch behind the remnants of a little blue fruit cart, hand-painted and gilded. As the pair covered the street ahead, Celeminé and Captain Pradal ghosted past them on the opposite side, hugging the terraced workshops that flanked the thoroughfare. They passed the terrace of a tailor, a barber, a clocksmith, all empty and abandoned. On the overhanging eaves above, birdcages clustered like lanterns, once filled with songbirds. The birds were dead and drying now.

Behind the Task Group came the resistance fighters, running low with their weapons tracking the rooftops. Gueshiva had been gracious enough to volunteer a fifteen-man escort of his guerrillas. They were resilient men who knew the city well. Even though most of them had been civilians who had once plied their trade in this very district, the recent months of war had scarred and sharpened them into fighters.

One of the volunteers, a youth who had lost his hand to a grenade, padded softly next to Roth. The inquisitor knew his name was Tansel, a boy who had once been an apprentice rug weaver. He could not weave rugs any more, even if Cantica were to be liberated. Now ammo pouches had been sewn onto a vest far too big for his coat-hanger shoulders, and he gripped a stub-pistol in his remaining hand.

'Beyond this lane, we come to an open bazaar and past that is the Buraghand Amphitheatre,' whispered the boy.

Roth nodded and waved the resistance fighters on, past them to cover the next section of the street. Celeminé and the good captain then leapfrogged the next secured area. The Task Group maintained this cautious advance for some time before reaching a junction in the lane.

The volunteers prowled ahead, half of them nuzzled down with their weapons to give suppressing fire as the other half-dozen disappeared around the winding bend. They waited for some time before re-emerging. Roth could not discern what was happening but the volunteers appeared to be arguing in hushed voices amongst themselves.

'Can you see what they're doing?' Roth asked Silverstein.

The huntsman shrugged. 'We'll see soon,' he said, nodding in the direction of Tansel who was crouched over and running back towards them.

The boy waved the stump of his arm and shook his head. 'It's blocked off, we can't get through.'

'What do you mean it's blocked off?' said Roth.

'Barricaded. The Archenemy have barricaded the avenue into the plaza. Tires, rubble and razor wire about twenty metres high. I think we're going to have to double back the way we came and find another entry point.'

Roth swore colourfully under his breath. Then repeated himself for good measure.

'It's not too far, inquisitor. My old weaver merchant had a workshop five hundred metres back. There was a rear door that would take you straight onto an adjacent alley. We can reach the amphitheatre that way,' Tansel assured them.

'That's quite all right. You lead the way then,' Roth replied.

The Task Group began the agonisingly slow advance back the way they had come. They had not gone far when their tactical caution was validated by the low rumble of engines. The string of guerrillas began to hiss sharp, urgent words down the line.

At first Roth did not recognise the bass tremor that shuddered through the stillness of night.

'Enemy patrol, break track,' whispered one of the volunteers. The warning rippled down the column.

There was nowhere to hide in the cramped confines of the lane. Roth spied headlamps and searchlights thundering in. Spears of white light pierced the darkness. The silky darkness of the night was suddenly penetrated by a brilliant flush of incandescent white. They were caught.

Roth turned to a nearby window with a lattice-work screen of ageing wood. He shouldered his way into it and came crashing through the other side, rolling onto his knees in a fog of dust. Silverstein came spearing through the window after him. The terrace was a humble bookshop. The shelves had been overturned and most of the texts had their pages torn out and carpeted the floor. A bank of narrow arched windows faced out onto the street. The two of them ripped the latticed shutters off their hinges and rested their weapons on the sills.

The outriders appeared first, raiders astride motorised bikes that shrieked like chainsaws. Two light trucks followed behind, patrol vehicles painted in off-white enamel streaked with rust and grease. On the flatbeds, two Ironclad murder squads and braces of attack dogs rocked on the shrieking suspensions.

Most of the resistance group had been caught out in the open. They exchanged stray shots as both sides sought cover or went to ground. The patrol trucks pulled up just short of the group and their troops dismounted. The attack dogs came off first, slab-chested mastiffs bounding and snarling. The Ironclad clambered off after them.

Roth opened fire with his plasma pistol. The mini-nova of energy pulverised an Ironclad as he was dismounting, liquefying his breastplate into molten metal and fusing him to the truck chassis. From an alcove opposite Roth, Celeminé and Pradal exchanged small-arms fire as they bobbed and ducked behind cover.

Someone shot out the searchlight on the leading patrol vehicle and visibility winked out instantly. The sudden loss of light turned everything black. Roth could see nothing except for the flickering exchange of las-bolts and sporadic muzzle flashes. Vaguely, he could hear the slavering growl of dogs as they tore into something wet and fleshy.

'We're as good as dead unless I draw them away,' said Silverstein. He had moved next to Roth, his vision unfazed by the night.

Before Roth could disagree, Silverstein clasped his forearm. 'I'll see you back here before dawn. Open your vox-link for contact.' And just like that the huntsman vaulted over the windowsill into the street.

He paused briefly, picking off two outriders with two clean shots. The soft-point rounds poleaxed the riders off their bikes. Barely breaking stride, he cut across the narrow lane to where the resistance fighters had been pinned down by fire underneath a tympanum arch. Several more well-aimed soft-point rounds in the direction of the enemy patrol gave them the respite they needed. Silverstein and a handful of Canticans broke from cover and sprinted directly towards the murder squads. The remaining guerrillas sprinted back towards Roth and signalled for him to follow.

It was the decoy that Roth needed. Wasting no time, the inquisitor leapt back onto the street. He didn't really know what happened next. He could barely see the back of the man in front of him. Somehow, in the confusion, Celeminé's hand found his and he held on hard to make sure he didn't lose her in their flight. They crashed through plywood boards, hurtled up flights of stairs, stumbling blindly. At one point, Roth put his foot down through something that gave way with a snap, almost turning his ankle. He hoped the men in front knew where they were going.

After another headlong lurch up a rickety flight of steps they spilled out of a trapdoor onto a roof landing. The resistance fighters began to climb across the rooftops but Roth pounced onto the limestone ledge to peer down the street below. The murder squads were still directly below him. Further up, he saw what could only be Silverstein and his volunteers, the muzzles of their guns barking in the night. Even further away, more headlamps were converging on their position. With pained reluctance, Roth turned his back on Silverstein and began scaling the rooftops.

Cutting across a snag-toothed row of terraces, they finally shimmied down a drainage pipe onto a stack

alley. The pedestrian lane was no more than ninety centimetres wide and tapered up into a mess of irregular
stairs. A sodium vapour lamp strung up on wire lit the
way. The place stank of bile and urine.

'Quickly now, up this way,' said Tansel.

The remnants of the Task Group drew out into a staggered column and followed the boy. Close by, far too
close, could be heard the angry rev of engines.

THE CARTHAGE'S CONGRESSIONAL chamber was a vaulted
hall, the ceiling crowned by a canopy of tapestry and
banners. Heavy leather benches were arranged in a geometric octagon, ringing the central dais. The walls
themselves were the most remarkable triumph of Imperial grandeur – glazed tiles, mathematically arranged,
rendered the historic battles of pre-Unification in shades
of brilliant blue. There were three hundred thousand
tiles all told, no two the same, a task that had taken the
prodigious painter Jorge Seville the better part of half a
century to complete.

Here, Lord Marshal Khmer addressed an assembly of
the most powerful men in the star system. Present were
nineteen generals, stately and resplendent, twelve divisional commanders, two score Naval officers of the
highest order, chosen regimental officers and a representative of the Officio Assassinorum. In all, they were men
with enough power to destroy galaxies.

Staff cadets mingled in the congressional benches,
serving light refreshments. Despite the pomp and dignity
of the war council, luxuries were eschewed for basic
rations. The officers ate what their men ate, they did not
expect anything less of themselves. Staff bore silver trays
piled with hardtack, and salvers of the finest sterling containing nothing but raw onions and tinned fish. Even the
crystal decanters held barley wine of the standard half-
pint ration. These were dire times indeed.

Lord Marshal Khmer waited until the drinks were dispensed and the officers were settled before speaking. The address was pronounced in measured tones, the fluid acoustics carrying his voice around the chamber. 'Brothers-in-arms, I have ordered a military council today to reassess the grand strategy pertaining to the execution of the Medina Campaign. For too long, military command has been indecisive, inadequate and hamstrung by external elements.'

There was a polite raft of applause from the military council. Some of the commanders stomped their boots on the ground in approval. The lord marshal raised his hands for silence and continued, 'Our men have fought bravely and beyond reprove. But we cannot deny the fact that our strategy of attrition will lose us this war. Our one clear objective is to halt the Chaos advance. To achieve such an objective, a tactical retreat is our only option at this point. It is in my informed opinion that it is the Bastion Stars we must hold. To this end, I declare we withdraw and consolidate with gathering Imperial reinforcements in the inner subsector.'

The declaration caused no small degree of consternation amongst the delegates. Khmer had expected this. Among those seated, many were loyal to him, but many could be considered rogue dissidents, intent on complying with the Inquisitorial edict to defend Medina.

To this end, Lord Marshal Khmer had already arranged for a plan. He had made certain to order the presence of several outspoken rogue officers, men not loyal to him. It would be a chance for Khmer to make examples of them.

As if on cue, a gaunt, shaven-headed officer scarred from scalp to chin stood up from his bench. The rank sash around his waist denoted him as a brigadier of the 29th Cantican Light Horse. The cavalry officer cleared his throat elegantly. 'Sir, if I may say, we are restrained by the

edict of the Inquisition. We must, according to the Conclave, hold the Medina Worlds with all available
resources until they can discover what objectives the
Archenemy have in securing Medina. Is it not a fundamental objective of war making to deny your enemies
their objectives so as to satisfy your own?'

'No you may not *say*, brigadier! I will not have my soldiers suffer defeat, for some mythical old wives' tale. The
Medina Conclave does nothing but hamstring our efforts
to secure the subsector. Sit down, brigadier, before you
embarrass us all,' scoffed Khmer.

'Sir, with respect. The edict of the Inquisition is clear.
Hold the Medina Corridor. As much as it pains me to
say, they are the highest Imperial authority here,' replied
the scarred officer.

The fool was playing straight into his hand, Khmer
thought to himself.

'I am the highest Imperial authority here! These men
are my men, this ship is my ship. I will deal with Gurion
and his travelling troupe, is that clear?'

'Sir,' said the brigadier through clenched teeth. He
folded his cap to his chest and sat back down.

It seemed the air in the chamber had cooled several
degrees. The military seniors growled amongst themselves. Some glowered, seeming to agree with brigadier.

'My fellow soldiers. Understand that I do not wish to
abandon our home, our planets. But it is not a choice
any more. Civilians do not have to make the choices we
make. It is our duty to protect the Imperium and to do
so we cannot give our lives needlessly here. We must
reinforce the defences in the Bastion Stars for the major
Archenemy advance.'

Khmer waited for the dissenters, knowing full well he
was about to lure them out. Indeed, the brigadier stood
back up. 'This is our home, sir. What you are telling us to
do is to allow Chaos to destroy our homes, and defy the

edict of the Inquisition, the work of the God-Emperor. I find it abhorrent and I will not have any part in it.'

It was exactly what Lord Marshal Khmer had hoped for. Now came the denouement. The chamber hushed. Lord Marshal Varuda Khmer said nothing for ten long seconds. He even counted them precisely himself. Finally, his hands reached into his pistol holster and he drew his laspistol and shot the brigadier through the sternum.

The cavalry officer's face lit up in shock. He was dead before he slumped back into his seat, his eyes and mouth still wide. No one said a word. These were the senior architects of war; there was little they had not seen but even this shocked them.

The lord marshal finally broke the silence. 'Remember. I am the highest Imperial authority here.'

He delicately drew a silk cloth from his breast pocket. Calmly, he wiped down his pistol before holstering it. The gallery was still silent as Khmer strode to the front gallery and held out his hand to the Officio of the Assassinorum.

Gloved in a cameleoline bodyglove that shifted with every spectrum of grey and black, the man appeared like a deathly spectre. The Assassin clasped Khmer's hand in allegiance. Again, it was another brilliantly orchestrated affair that sent a clear message to the Imperial High Command.

'Brothers-in-arms. For the sake of this campaign, I declare myself the highest regional authority in the name of the God-Emperor. If anyone sees otherwise, please speak now.'

As Khmer expected, nobody did.

CHAPTER SEVEN

IT WAS ONLY three hours past the middle of night but dawn was approaching. Already the triple suns were bruising the horizon from dark blue to amber, shortening the shadows and airing out the dark. It would not be long before the sticky pall of the day's heat turned the cool of night into condensation.

By Roth's calculations, that meant they had thirty minutes to reach their objective and return to the under-ruins. Forty at the most. Fortunately, the Gallery of Eight Limbs already rose into view. It was a natural amphitheatre, a crescent-shaped stadium built into a precipitous curve of red, white and orange rocks. The stepped seating overlooked an oval arena covered in a mixture of sand and salt. That had been where the maul-fighters in their prime had fought for the entertainment of thousands. It was also where they had been rounded up and executed during the initial Atrocities.

The team swept around the perimeter of the stadium into the gymnasia of training barracks attached to the wings of the Gallery. These were spartan quarters, a grid-work complex of palaestra and fighter-stables where the athletes trained and slept.

Tansel and Captain Pradal led the way, followed by Roth and the rest of the team in a herringbone formation. They entered through the central yard of the palaestra, essentially a rectangular court framed by colonnades. The columns ran along all sides of the court, creating porticoes that led into spacious training halls.

They cleared each hall with methodical precision. The team moved quickly, silhouettes flickering through the colonnades as they prowled through rooms dedicated to steam baths, striking bags and weights. Beautiful friezes were chiselled into the stone walls, depicting the athletes and their patron saints. The Ironclad had evidently already raided here, desecrating the artwork with vulgar graffiti, almost juvenile had it not been daubed in blood.

Roth recognised the striking figures as practitioners of Medinian maul-fighting. As an avid theorist of the unarmed arts, Roth's interest had been piqued at a young age by the gentlemanly pursuit of fist-fencing at the progenium.

As a pugilist, Roth respected the brutal art of Medinian maul-fighting. The combat sport of maul-fighting prohibited the use of hands or feet. Fighters instead sought to strike with forearms, elbows, knees and headbutts. Most bouts were short, scrappy affairs usually concluding in a knock-out. It was a shame his first encounter with the sport was under such trying circumstances.

The rest barracks were the worst to see. The fighters had slept on straw mats, their living spaces cluttered with the personal effects – books, blankets, clocks, prayer ornaments and even the detritus of dead relationships.

Yet as the team filed past the mats, they saw the gore and shrapnel that feathered the area. Flashes of blood dripped from framed photo-picts and curtains. The barely recognisable remains of humans festered on the floor, the stench cloying the sinus passages and lingering forever behind the palate. Roth's rudimentary grasp of forensics revealed the story – the maul-fighters had tried to hide in their barracks and the Archenemy had filled the hall with grenades. The destruction was gleefully excessive and not much had remained intact.

'See that, inquisitor?' Pradal said, pointing to the ground.

Roth looked down, seeing nothing at first. But sure enough, he followed Pradal's pointing finger until he saw a fresh trail of blood, brighter than the browning crust around it. Amidst the drying carnage, fresh, perfectly circular dots of blood left a speckled trail across the gallery into a side portico. It was barely perceptible.

'Delahunt?' asked Celeminé, crouching down to inspect the sanguine trail. Her voice came muffled through the kerchief she held against her face.

'A rather astute observation, madame. One can only hope,' Roth observed. The pattern of blood-fall indicated light wounding, perhaps sub-dermal incision or puncture. It might not have been life-threatening but, in any event, Delahunt needed aid. Urgency got the better of him and Roth sprinted the last several metres through the tetrastyle columns.

He rounded the entrance and saw Inquisitor Delahunt, flayed open on the clay tiles.

Roth halted, his breath caught in his lungs. Someone had got to Delahunt first. From the way the inquisitor had been laid out, someone had left him there to be found. It had to be a trap. Someone was playing their game and staying one step ahead. Eyes wide in sudden realisation, Roth spotted ghosts in the periphery of his vision, shapes and silhouettes moving on his flank. Roth opened his mouth to shout but the word *ambush* never reached his team.

The concussive stutter of auto-weapons engulfed his warning. Roth went to ground as the resistance fighter closest to him was poleaxed off his feet. High-velocity rounds shrieked overhead. A single slug impacted into his shoulder pauldron, piercing the fighting-plate and mushrooming within the armour. Spinning shrapnel bounced around, lacerating his shoulder. Hollow points for tissue rending, was the only thought that ran through Roth's mind. Cursing, spitting and scrambling on his hands and knees, Roth dived behind a salt basin. He hazarded a look at the ambushers, detaching themselves from the columned shadows.

Expecting to see soldiers of the Archenemy, Roth instead recognised something else entirely – the most feared mercenary formation of the subsector if not the entire Ultima Segmentum: the Orphratean Purebred. Eugenically bred humans with their long lean frames poured into snakeskin bodygloves, there could be no coincidence in them being here. In the gloom they moved like diamond-backed spectres, shifting through shades of brown, mauve and crimson. A harness of chest webbing carried the tools of their trade, ammunition, pistols, wire cord, field dressings and other military kit. Torch beams underslung on their weapons dozed through the lightless room in blinding circles.

Each mercenary shouldered an EN-Scar autogun. The matt-black carbines cut the air with snapping barks of fire. They fired single well-aimed shots in overlapping arcs of fire as they manoeuvred into position.

In one corner of the training pit, behind a stack of wooden mannequins, a heavy stubber had been set up on a tripod. The Purebred gunner raked enfilade fire in a diagonal cone, pinning Roth's team in the open. Lambent threads criss-crossed the air creating a solid lattice of tracer.

Panic was not something inquisitors were accustomed to. Acting as the hands of the God-Emperor, the Inquisition were seldom placed in compromising situations so utterly out of their control, influence and preparation. But compromising was an understatement right now. Celeminé huddled behind a stone sparring post, bullets gnashing into the stone and biting off the wooden arms and legs. Shot slammed into mural carvings behind Roth, showering him in chips of rock and a fine powdery talc dust. Two of the six resistance fighters had been shot dead. Pradal was nowhere in sight.

But more than the shock and ferocity of the ambush, the one thing that really rattled Roth was the simple fact that these were not Archenemy. Genetically superior men of the warrior caste in Orphrates, the Orphratean Purebred had seen limited action since the beginning of the Medina Campaign. Utilised by Imperial forces to augment special operations capacity that the Cantican Colonials so severely lacked, these mercenaries had been and still were, as far as Roth was aware, under the employ of Imperial High Command. But now they were freelancers contracted to kill Inquisitorial agents. Whatever their motives, they were damn good at it.

So fierce was the suppressing fire that Celeminé could not gather her mental faculties to generate a concerted psychic counter-attack. She hesitated, strangely undecided. Popping a buttoned pouch on her chest webbing, she slid a grenade into her hands. The device was stencilled 'fragmentation' in a yellow munitorum script. Celeminé wrenched out the pin and rolled the grenade out like a croquet ball before bobbing back behind cover and pressing both hands to her ears.

+Duck for cover!+

She jettisoned the urgency directly into the mesocortical pathways of her comrades.

Henry Zou

Roth, emptying his Sunfury into the pillars directly to his fore, barely managed to swing back behind the stone basin before the grenade erupted. The detonation was felt with a physical rumble. Roth felt like someone had slapped his back, hard. The enemy fire abated for several seconds.

It was all the time Celeminé needed. She immediately threw up an illusory wall at her enemy, hazing the darkness into a formless, nauseating depth of vertigo. It was her favourite trick, and in the low visibility of night it was enough to throw off aim and destabilise equilibrium. Even sheltering outside the radius of her focus, Roth was seized by rolling inertia.

It was only then that Celeminé vaulted from behind the sparring post. She announced her presence with a hand-flamer. The jet of liquid fire roared into the shadows, flushing the Purebred from their cover. She killed five before the flames lost pressure and licked back into the muzzle. Her second squeeze of the trigger sent the Purebred scuttling for cover. An incandescent spear lit the hall in dazzling shades of amber.

+Holy Throne, woman. You never told me you were so dangerous!+ Roth telepathed.

+If I had, would you have believed me?+ She ended the thought-speech with a brush of girlish laughter.

No, Roth admitted to himself. In fact, he still found it hard to believe. Under the exaggerated shadows and extreme lighting, Celeminé in her yellow bodyglove and harness of heavy-duty military gear looked like a scholam-child playing soldier.

But there she was, a virgin inquisitor, alone and slight of build, scattering at least forty killers of the Orphratean Purebred before her path of war.

'Fall back and disengage!' shouted Captain Pradal. He had reappeared, firing his lasgun on full auto. Seizing the initiative, the remaining resistance fighters followed him out the portico they had entered from, firing as they went. The last two to leave took a knee by the portico, laying down suppressing fire for Celeminé and Roth.

+Time to go,+ she called.

Inquisitor Roth unfurled from his crouch and made ready to sprint for the exit, but halted in mid-step. +No! Wait, not just yet!+

He pivoted on the balls of his feet and dashed towards Delahunt's body. Psychically, he could feel Celeminé urging him to leave. The Orphrateans were recovering, shouting fire drill and target coordinates in precise military inflections. Their shots were building in tempo and accuracy.

Roth was not far from Delahunt. He could see his old comrade, supine against the wall, his neck cranked in an absurd backwards angle, his arms prostrate like a martyr. In the background, he could hear Celeminé's flamer, snorting and choking out its last coughs of fire. It would not be long before the three dozen Orphrateans caught the both of them in the open. Ludicrously, Roth wondered what six hundred rounds of sustained fire would do to his body.

That was when the Orphratean speared out from behind a pillar and collided with Roth. They went tumbling over and hit the ground hard. Barely recovering, Roth was pinned by the Purebred's raw-boned frame. Up close, Roth could understand how the planet of Orphrates had made an economy out of killing. The man was bred for combat. His father and his father before him, interbred with the warrior caste. In that way, the genetic purity maintained a dynasty of long, lean and ruthless killers.

The man astride Roth betrayed no emotion on his equine features. He simply reached up to a cord on his shoulder strap and extended a fine thread of razor wire. In one well-practiced motion, the Purebred looped the garrotte around Roth's neck. Gripping hard on the mercenary's wrist to prevent him from tightening the noose, Roth raised his Tang-War power fist.

It hummed to life with a corona of static.

The razor wire slitted down onto Roth's epidermis, slicing so clean it didn't draw blood. Before his carotid arteries could be severed, Roth shovel-hooked his power fist into the Purebred's floating ribs. Power fists, Roth knew, were primarily developed as anti-armour devices. From experience, a power fist could rend the flank armour of a battle-tank, scooping out great handfuls of molten steel. Against human flesh, the results did not bear thinking about. Roth was literally covered in Orphratean Purebred within a matter of seconds.

He heaved the eviscerated body off him and dived the last few metres to Delahunt. The dead inquisitor's eyes were still open and glazed, almost accusatory. They had not found him, as promised.

'I'm sorry,' mouthed Roth. He reached down towards Delahunt, deactivating his power fist as he did so. The signet ring gleamed at him. Roth plucked at Delahunt's hand and the ring, slick with blood, popped into his palm.

As he did so, Celeminé's flamer depleted its fuel canister with an oxygenated burp. +I'm out!+ she cried.

Roth pivoted hard on his heels and powered towards the portico. In the corner of his vision, bristling phalanxes of EN-Scar autocarbines steadied their aim. Three rounds almost scalped his head. He shouldered into Celeminé, hooking an arm around her waist, and just kept going. A round slammed into the segmented trauma plates of his abdomen. The ballistic apron tensed on impact, absorbing the kinetic force. Although the deep tissue bruising would be severe, the round did not penetrate.

Less than ten sprinting strides away from the portico, Roth saw a shot find its mark on one of the resistance fighters covering the exit. The young man, a former administrative clerk of the Governor's palace, spun completely around. His face hit the wall behind him, his neck spurting out arterial crimson in a three metre stream. Roth ran through the portico and kept going.

He emerged in the rest-barracks. The survivors, Captain Pradal and young Tansel, sprang up from their firing positions as soon as they saw him emerge.

'This way, we can cut through the gymnasia,' beckoned Tansel.

Roth acknowledged with a frantic motion for them to keep going. Behind him, he could hear the last surviving resistance fighter following close behind, turning to snap off several last defiant shots into the chamber of ambush. No doubt, the mercenaries would give chase. The Orphrateans lived by their reputation. Roth just kept running, focusing on Tansel's darting form before him.

'You can put me down now,' Celeminé said. Roth had forgotten that Celeminé had been thrown across his shoulders, her head bouncing on his back. He quickly lowered her back down.

'My apologies, madame. I didn't mean–'

Celeminé put a delicate finger to his lip. 'Not the time for your verbosity.'

'But I–'

'Shush. You talk so much all the time.'

The resistance fighter bringing up the rear waved his arms frantically, motioning for them to keep moving. They headed from the gymnasia down an arched tunnel.

When they emerged from the complex, the night had receded and day had come. Roth found himself in the arena proper. The suns were already out in full, low and swollen embers that crested the skyline. Gasping for breath and dazed in defeat, the Task Group slogged across the stadium and back out into a conquered Burag-hand.

CHAPTER EIGHT

BASTIEL SILVERSTEIN SLOTTED the last round into the chamber. The thought crossed his mind to save the last shot for himself. But he was too stubborn. With an almost weary resignation, Silverstein raised his weapon and fired his last shot.

The bullet hissed down from the minaret fifty metres above street level, cutting diagonally over the jostle of tenement roofs. It traced towards the blockade of Ironclad that had sectioned off the city block and found its mark on an Archenemy raider hunched down behind the flank of his patrol vehicle. The round entered his forehead. With an explosive spray it exited out the back of his skull, his iron headpiece opening up like a flower in bloom.

Silverstein ducked back under the balcony of the prayer tower. The expected volley of return fire clattered overhead in fierce reprisal. Placing down his empty autorifle, he sat his back against the smooth red clay of the balcony and sighed.

'Anyone have any rounds left?' he asked.

The six resistance fighters around him shook their heads. They had emptied their canvas pouches and webbing. They were tired and spent. It was early morning, but the Medina suns were already searing the city with intense shimmering heat. Dehydration and latent heat exhaustion were beginning to set in.

The siege itself had already taken the better part of five hours since the group had splintered away to run decoy. It had been a tight run and they had lost three on the way. At one point, it seemed like there were dogs and patrols waiting them for them around every bend. They had fled into the highest prayer tower in commercial Buraghand and there they had held the Archenemy at bay. To their dismay, the accuracy of their fire had driven the Archenemy into a protracted siege, cordoning off the block and gathering nearby patrol units.

For the last hour, as ammunition had run low, they had resorted to simply giving up their spare rounds and allowing the huntsman to snipe away at the encircling foe. They guessed that Silverstein had fired at least two hundred rounds in that time. Many of them had been kill shots.

They waited a while. The enemy fired no more shots as if testing, no, taunting them into firing back. But they had nothing left and it would not be long before the Archenemy realised that.

'How long do you think it will be before they roll up a tank to flatten this whole thing?' asked Goa, a foundry worker in his late sixties. Sunstroke had affected him the worst and he spoke with his eyes closed, his head lolling.

'Death by artillery would be lucky. They won't give us that luxury,' Silverstein replied matter-of-factly.

As if on cue, they heard the gate at the base of the tower being breached with some sort of a piston ram. Voices began shouting harsh words in the dark tongue.

'Here they come,' shrugged Silverstein. The six others began to fumble for their spike bayonets but Silverstein sat without a sound, hands on knees.

The huntsman was feeling strangely morose and eerily complacent. He wished he could feel the same motivating fear that the others felt, but he couldn't. The sounds of the Archenemy ascending the spiral staircase of the shaft should have elicited some panic if not terror, but he didn't feel either. Perhaps his three decades of Inquisitorial service had deadened his nerves. Perhaps his adolescent years as a 'beater', driving out large carnivores for his senior huntsmen on his home world of Veskipine, had hardened him. Boys tended to mature fast when they spent their youth flushing tusked lupines from their dens with little more than a switch cane. Most things just didn't affect him. Instead he popped the ivory button of his top coat pocket and drew a rolled stick of tabac. He ran it under his nose, wishing he had time to smoke one more.

The Ironclad thundered up the upper gallery landing. They surged out from the stairwell, baying and snorting for blood. For the first time, Silverstein saw them in the daylight. They were wild, bestial men roughly shod in a disarray of hauberks, breastplates, jack plate, brigandine or splint. Some brandished machine pistols, others lasguns. Silverstein even spotted a flak-musket somewhere.

They crashed onto the balcony. Silverstein closed his eyes, unwilling to examine them so close with his bioptics. He didn't want the last thing he saw to be a statistical analysis of the Archenemy.

'Tung etai!'

The killing blow did not come. A voice had barked them to a halt. Silverstein had coordinated enough times with the Imperial Guard to recognise an officer's authority when he heard it. Slowly, the huntsman opened his eyes.

The Archenemy stood at bay within arm's reach. They towered around him like a curtain of iron. Silverstein was not sure why, but his bioptics flickered and washed with static. His augmetics had never failed before, almost as if the circuitry could not bear to siphon such insidious visual imagery into his brain.

Staring into the eyes of Chaos, the six Canticans dropped their rifles and sank to their knees. Without the adrenaline of battle to fortify them, their nervous systems just gave out. It was just all too much.

'Kehmor avul, Kehmor eshek avul,' ordered the Chaos officer in a strangely lilting, free-flowing dark tongue. The minor warlord was a monstrous creature. Tall and sinuous, he was clad in a cuirass of nailed splint that tapered down into an armoured apron, giving him the frame of a rearing viper. Unlike his subordinates, the metal banding of the skull-piece that enclosed his head was patterned. It formed a symmetrical braid that ran down the centre of his head, some sort of rank, Silverstein surmised, that placed him as leader of this raiding party.

The underlord leaned in to examine them, tilting his head curiously. Without warning he lunged forwards and gripped Goa's throat. The elderly resistance fighter didn't react, even as he was dragged up to his feet. With one swift overhand motion the Ironclad hurled the man over the balcony.

Silverstein stood up. He did not want to die sitting down. The commander turned on him. He snagged the huntsman up by the lapels of his leather coat and forced Silverstein's torso over the balcony railing. Silverstein looked down at the fifty-metre drop. On the pavement below, Goa was laid open in a halo of blood.

But the Ironclad did not throw him. Instead, he paused, running his thumb along the collar of Silverstein's coat. The Inquisitorial service badge, a delicate little pin of silver, winked under the sunlight.

'You are a watchdog of the dead Emperor?' the Iron-clad leader slithered in Low Gothic.

Silverstein clenched his jaw and said nothing.

'Orday anghiari inquiszt', the underlord said to his men. Judging by the crestfallen reactions, Silverstein surmised that they had just been denied the privilege of summary execution.

'I am Naik Ishkibal. Naik is my rank. Ishkibal is my blood name. You may not call me by either. To do so is sacrilege and I will have to kill you. I tell you this because I do not want to kill you yet. Understand?' His voice had a metallic resonance that carried the threat well.

'Stick your fist up your own rear,' spat Silverstein.

'Good. Good. You learn quickly, watchdog. Let's see how long we can keep you around for. I think my war-lords may want to have a word with you.'

'I'm not an inquisitor. I'm a game hunter,' replied Silverstein.

'All the same. You wear the pin, you have the answers,' chuckled the underlord. He turned to his subordinates and rattled off a series of orders in the dark tongue.

The Ironclad seized up the resistance fighters, laying in with punches and kicks as they did so. With heavy hands they began to bind hands and feet with wire cord.

'Amel buriash!' snapped the underlord. 'I need them in one piece for interrogation. I will eat the face of anyone who bleeds them without my permission.'

IT WAS THE third night they had spent in hiding. Roth was laced in blood, some of it his own, most of it not. Brick dust, grit and grime coated his armour in chalky enamel the colour of filthy teeth. Exhaustion had exceeded his physical limits, his tendons felt disconnected and his muscles throbbed.

Of his whereabouts, Roth was also vague. He guessed that he was hiding in the ventilation shaft of some semi-demolished tenement in Upper Buraghand. He couldn't even be sure of that, as they had dared not stay in any one location for too long. The roving murder squads were thorough in their patrols. Once, on the second day, they had nearly been caught. Desperately hungry, they had ventured into a semi-demolished granary processing plant in search of provisions. Instead they walked straight into an Ironclad patrol. They had barely escaped. Roth had canine bite-marks on his greaves to prove it.

Yet his suffering was purely physical. Roth's mind was still reeling from the system shock of his past seventy-two hours. Within that time he had lost Bastiel Silverstein, his unit of Cantican guerrillas had been decimated and now he was hiding in the crawl-space of a tenement basement, hoping he would not be discovered and shot. To add venom to his laments, he could not fathom who would hire the Orphratean Purebred to orchestrate such a premeditated ambush. He had been down every cognitive path, trying to piece together an answer, but nothing logical or even remotely rational could be gleaned. The only plausible explanation was betrayal. Betrayal from within his own cadre. In Roth's current state, that didn't bear thinking about.

Through the pandemonium of his thoughts, the only clear decision was that he could not flee Cantica aboard his lander. Although Celeminé had been adamant about withdrawal, Roth had refused to leave the planet, thoroughly defeated and no closer to the truth than when he started. Roth was stubborn when he wanted to be, and the Task Group was under his command. They had stayed, if only to salvage some semblance of a mission objective.

'I've brought you some soup to share,' said Celeminé. She was crawling along the tunnel towards him, one hand running along the overhead drainage pipes for balance. In her other hand she proffered a steaming cup canteen. 'It's only dehyd but it's cold tonight.'

Roth nodded his thanks and cradled the cup. He sipped it and rested his head back. The warm metal felt so good in his frost-numbed hands. The soup, despite being Guard ration, was not bad either. Thick and salty, it just reminded him of a rich cattle consommé. But only just.

Celeminé settled next to Roth, wedging her boots against the opposite wall as she rested her back against the cramped confines. Perhaps it was his fatigue, but under the phosphorescent glow of gas burners she looked especially beautiful. The chemical lighting made the profile of her face positively porcelain. Even the ring in the centre of her lip, something Roth had never been fond of, gave her mouth a particularly innocent pout. Roth didn't even realise he was staring.

'We can't stay like this, you know,' Celeminé urged.

'Twelve more hours. If Silverstein hasn't voxed us by then…' Roth trailed off.

'Roth. We can't stay here. I'm sick of running and hiding. We have no food, we're low on water. We transit back to the *Carthage* and allow the Conclave to decrypt Delahunt's signet. It's reasonable and it makes sense.'

'In any other time or place, I would be inclined to agree with you, madame. But with so much at stake, we cannot leave Cantica until we are certain that the Old Kings will not fall into Archenemy hands. We haven't done enough here.'

Roth was not sure how much of his reply was false bravado and how much of it was simply his stubborn streak. But he just could not allow it. His mentor, the late Inquisitor Liszt Vandevern, had disparaged Roth as being too impetuous and far too possessed by emotion. Initially, Roth's lack of the rhythmic rationality so common amongst inquisitors almost cost him his sponsorship to full inquisitor. But throughout the years, Roth's gut instinct had stood him in good stead. Now his instincts told him he could not flee back to the Conclave with his tail between his legs, on account of two demoralising gunfights. Infiltrating a Chaos-held world, Roth had expected to be shot at. Indeed, it was part of his Inquisitorial duty to be shot at. Or maybe he just wasn't thinking straight.

'Roth, this is idiocy. I'm sorry but it is and I won't tell it any other way. At the very least, we have to move because we can't stay here,' Celeminé protested.

Roth noticed that when she was upset, she could not look Roth in the eyes. Instead she looked away and bit the tips of her fingers.

'I promised Silverstein I would wait for his vox in the tenement district. I can't move out of vox range.'

'Roth. Please. You said it yourself, we haven't done enough here. As much as it pains me to say it, this can't be about Silverstein. The Conclave has ordered us to establish whether the relics exist on Cantica.'

At her words, Roth expelled a ragged breath. She was right, and Roth knew it. They could leave now, or push on with the original mission. Roth could not leave, so that left him with only one option. 'We'll go,' he relented.

'I'm glad you've said that, because Captain Pradal has a wonderful plan!'

Roth laughed for the first time in four days. 'Please, do tell.'

'Have you heard artillery in the past few days?'

'No,' Roth admitted.

'Well I have. And so has the good captain. Which meant the Archenemy were still fighting. Evidently this would suggest Imperial forces are still active in the region. Captain Pradal risked raising vox contact on an Imperial frequency. He's very clever with comms and I don't think the Archenemy were able to tag on our location for long enough to get a fix. Unless we want them to.'

'And?'

'And he made contact. There is a battalion of Cantican Guardsmen, fighting hard about twenty kilometres north-west of Buraghand city.'

'So we proceed on foot for twenty kilometres through enemy territory?'

'No. Here's where the plan gets good.'

THE MURDER SQUAD thundered down the empty street, predatory machines roaring from brute engines of diesel. Two trucks painted off-white, escorted by two fighting patrol vehicles growling with throaty exhaust. The FPVs were squat, hog-nosed four-wheelers with an open passenger side chassis. A side-mounted heavy stubber panned out from the exposed opening, the gunner hunched down behind a mantlet. Since the Atrocities, the distinctive shuddering scream of an FPV engine was the most feared sound of the night. Resistance fighters and refugees were right in coining them 'preds and prowlers'.

Ripping down the war-torn streets of tenement quarter nine, the vehicles rolled to a juddering halt outside a tenement stack. The whole frontal façade of the building had sagged away from its structural frame like wet paper, exposing girders and twisted struts.

Someone had been broadcasting a distress signal on an Imperial frequency. A frequency that had been compromised since the Ironclad had overrun CantiCol forces. The signal had been pin-pointed to that very building.

The murder squads dismounted from their vehicles, checking weapons and cinching ammo belts the moment their boots hit the ground. The full complement of two squads, twenty killers in total, sprinted up the short stoop of steps towards the front entrance. Ironically, even though the wall around it had been demolished, the door in its door frame stood intact and alone. The squad leader – a Naik – bashed off the lock with his mace-gauntlet and the others formed a tactical column after him, weapons raised.

Inside, shafts of moonlight lanced in between the puncture wounds of masonry. A third of the tenement had fallen away like a cross-section cut. On the seventh storey, a child's bassinet balanced off a jagged edge of flooring, one wrought iron leg suspended over empty space.

The Naik homed in on the signal with auspex in hand. The signal was vibrant and clear, no more than a fifty metre radius away. Soon, he expected another dissident cell would learn the error of sustained broadcasts in an enemy zone. The Naik trained a heavy-calibre machine pistol into the geometric shadows ahead.

The murder squad sloshed down a communal corridor. Somewhere, a drainage pipe had ruptured, filling the bottom level with ankle-deep water, a soupy mixture of ash and sewerage. Most of the tenement doors had been torn off their hinges, the insides thoroughly ransacked. Furniture spilled out into the hallway, soggy, brittle wood crunching underfoot.

The auspex's chirping reached a shrill crescendo. Ahead, a locked utility door barred the way into the tenement's boiler basement. The vox beacon was broadcasting from within there, of that they were certain.

A piston ram, thirty kilograms of solid metal, was brought up from the rear of the line. The murder squads made final weapons checks. They were hungry for the kill, so much so that agitated clicking sounds came from behind their face bindings. An Ironclad swung the battering ram back with both hands and drove it into the door. The wood gave way like crunching bone.

The murder squad stormed the boiler room. The Naik entered first, swinging his pistol back and forth for a target. But the second he stepped into the room he noticed two things.

One, the room was empty except for a single military vox set. It was planted underneath a pool of moonlight, chattering away on the highest vox channel setting. Two, the door had been rigged up to a rudimentary pulley trap. A thread of wire fastened to the door had been hooked up to an overhead cinch, which in turn pulled taut on a brace of grenades. The stoved-in door, which now lay a good ten metres away, had snapped the pin loose with an audible clink.

By the time the Naik noticed, it was already far too late. He didn't bother to call out a warning, he just turned on his heels and tried to push his way back out through the door. He was nowhere near fast enough.

The grenades exploded with the sound of clapping concrete. Sixty thousand anti-personnel ball bearings shredded the boiler room. In an instant the plastered walls eroded into a perforated sponge. Of the Archenemy who had stormed the room, most were caught in a solid curtain of expanding shrapnel. The after-shock blew out every window of the tenement block that had not already been broken, and the windows of tenements several streets way.

THE SHATTERING WINDOWS gave them the signal to move. Roth rushed from his hiding place in a drainage ditch adjacent to the tenement's communal courtyard. The remains of his team followed close behind.

Scurrying low, hugging the walls of the building, they spotted the vehicles of the murder squad parked outside the front of the tenement. Roth ran towards an armoured truck, convinced he would be downed by an unseen shot before he reached it. No shots came and he hurled himself into the open door of the vehicle. Once inside, he turned and pulled Celeminé into the cab after him. In the rear-view mirror, he saw Captain Pradal and the two resistance fighters clamber onto the flat-bed.

The belly of the truck stank of machine grease and ammonia. He was glad it was too dark to see in detail. Reaching down underneath the heat-warped dashboard he fumbled for the keys. They were still warm in the ignition. He cranked it and nursed the truck to life like a winter-waked bear. Two spears of white light stabbed from the headlamps, pale and incandescent.

The truck began to roll, heavy and sluggish at first. Roth edged the vehicle forward, pressuring the accelerator. In the side mirror, Roth spotted an Ironclad stumble from the tenement entrance, dazed, wounded and brandishing his lasgun wildly. Captain Pradal put him down with a well-aimed shot. He then shot out the over-sized wheels of two stationary FPV Prowlers in quick succession.

'Go sir, now now now!' Pradal shouted. He slapped the back of the cab frantically.

Finally roused from its gear-seizing sleep the truck found its rhythm and surged away, trailing a cone of exhaust. The cracked speedometer clocked a high seventy, leaving the tenement quarters far behind.

LORD MARSHAL KHMER was brooding in the depths of his armchair when an adjutant announced the arrival of the Orphratean emissary.

The silk screen panels of his stateroom door slid smoothly open on intricate cog rollers. Aspet Fure walked into the chamber, bowing respectfully at the threshold of the entrance. Like the others of his clan, Fure had the bronze skin and pale olive-green eyes that marked him as Purebred, a product of human eugenics. The bodyglove of snakeskin sepia did little to hide the hard muscular lines of his limbs. He was evidently a fighting man, and even though he had shed his wargear out of etiquette, a Lugos Hi-Power autopistol was holstered at his hip.

Khmer was not impressed. He did not even bother to rise out of his chair. To him, they were little more than uncultured freelancers. Indeed, the lineage of the company could be traced back to the barbarian soldiers of the Ophratean sub-arctic, during the lost times of pre-Unification. These were the very same savages who had worshipped sky pythons and raised pillars from the painted jawbones of their enemies only ten thousand years ago. Now the entire economy of Orphrates relied on the capital inflows of its famed mercenaries.

'Salutations, lord marshal. You seem morose, so I will keep this brief and civil,' began the Aspet.

The lord marshal raised an eyebrow. Obviously the barbarians had chosen an emissary who could string together sentences without growling between words, he mused.

'I'm listening,' said Khmer.

'An attack was orchestrated for the priority targets on Buraghand, Cantica, eighty hours ago. Your informant from within the target group was able to contact my company with ample intelligence. Unfortunately, the attack met with limited success. The priority target still lives–'

'Shut your mouth!' roared the lord marshal. He had sprung up from his chair, veins of anger popping livid against his neck. He stomped over to a dresser of chocolate satinwood. It was a masterpiece carved by the late Toussaint Pilon in the early Revivalist style. The furniture was inlaid with a veneer of pearl; the iridescent patterns resembled cherubs at play when viewed from a distance. Khmer put his boot straight through the lower cabinet.

'Do you know what this means? Your incompetence, the incompetence of your men may cost me everything! Do you know what we are dealing with here? We are dealing with the damned Inquisition. There was no room for error!'

'Which reminds me, lord marshal. You did not inform us prior to contract that the initial bait-target was a sworn member of the Inquisition. Such a high-risk killing brokers an eight hundred per cent increase on the initial amount.'

Khmer almost drooled with fury. 'I hired you idiots expecting full competency. Now you expect me to deal with this garbage?'

The Orphratean shrugged. 'We don't ask questions. We fought, we bled and we expect full payment. That's the way it works, lord marshal.'

'Not this time. You think I needed you to tell me of your failures? I already knew. I've known for some time that your men fouled up.'

The Orphratean was slightly taken aback. For once, confusion creased his noble features. 'Then why the facade? Why did you request a brief if you knew the answer?'

A cold slivered sneer crept up the corners of Khmer's mouth. 'Because I wanted you here when I told you the news of my own. I wanted you here so I could savour your reaction.'

The Orphratean took a step back. His fingertips rested lightly on his holstered pistol. Behind him the screen door rolled open and a full squad of provosts greeted him with a wall of shotguns and shock mauls.

The lord marshal cleared his throat theatrically for all to hear. 'I want to tell you, Aspet Fure, that twelve hours ago CantiCol garrison forces stationed on Orphrates raided your company holdings. They have broken your network, and what little remains of your enterprise have scattered into hiding. Your crimes, which include collusion with the Archenemy and murder of an Inquisitorial authority, have given me the right to terminate dealings with the Purebred across the subsector and process punishment accordingly.'

The Orphratean mercenary shook his head in mute disbelief.

'I'm sorry it had to be this way. But silence is a heavy price worth paying,' said Khmer as he turned his back on the Purebred.

CHAPTER NINE

THE LAST BATTALION of the 26th Colonial Artillery had been fighting for the past thirty-one days. Since the Atrocities, twelve hundred men of the 26th had fought for the cave temples twenty kilometres west of Buraghand city.

They had held, even as the meat-grinding advance of Ironclad mechanised columns had crushed ninety per cent of CantiCol forces. Every day the Archenemy had assaulted that pale, coarse-grained intrusion of igneous tusk over three hundred metres in height. Every day the warren of caves within the batholith had repelled them with guns and artillery.

Strategically, the low-lying scrubland provided limited enemy cover. Erosion had weathered the surrounding ruins and trace fossils into sculptural rock. Bulbous succulents and taproot knotted in the gaps of man-made geoforms. Ever since the Guard had been stationed at the cave temples they had coined it the 'Barbican'. The three thousand Archenemy dead that littered the dry prairie attested to that.

Spitting up great plumes of smoke, sixty-pounders had bombarded the Archenemy positions, harassing them and taunting them into suicidal charges. The great guns vibrated the caverns with their recoil, lobbing shells beyond the Erbus canal five kilometres out.

Although sustained enemy assaults had inflicted five hundred and ninety-two casualties, the battalion kept fighting. The 26th fought on almost in spite of the fact that they had nothing left to defend. Before the conquest, they had been tasked with defending the only motorway that connected Buraghand to the western outlands, but that didn't matter any more.

It was during the early hours of the thirty-first day that Inquisitor Obodiah Roth and his retinue sought refuge within the Barbican. Their captured truck had been left beyond the perimeter defences of the cave temples. By virtue of superstition the vehicle had been set ablaze beyond the razor wire.

Lurching up the escarpment, the inquisitor and his men looked bloodied, ragged and delirious with fatigue. They stumbled towards the nearest cave bunker, an outlying sentry post that could fit no more than three or four men.

It was camouflaged with prairie grass and fortified by a breastwork of mud and basket-woven sticks. From the cave, Troopers Prasad and Buakaw rushed out to meet them. At the sight of the Guardsmen, in the brown jackets and rank sashes of the CantiCol, the inquisitor fumbled out his rosette. Exhaustion tarred the words in his mouth. Instead he cast the rosette onto the ash before him, as he collapsed onto one knee.

ROTH DID NOT know how long he had been sleeping for. He could not even remember falling asleep. When he awoke, the high-noon suns filled his vision, flaring from the cave mouth in a prickling wash of white light.

He found himself in a small cave, asleep over a bed of packing crates. The cuirass of his Spathaen fighting-plate had been shed like a metal husk on the ground. He was still armoured from the hip down, but on top he had been stripped down to a loose cotton shirt that was stiff with sweat mineral. Somehow he still holstered his plasma pistol in its shoulder rig.

Squinting against the light, Roth eased himself up. He winced as his stiff limbs stung with lactic build-up. A cursory inspection yielded bruised ribs, minor lacerations and stress fractures in his lower legs. Given his circumstances, Roth considered himself extremely fortunate.

He took stock of his surroundings, realising he was in a hand-carved cave with a smoothed floor and low ceiling. Dimly, he remembered he was in some sort of cave temple complex, a place of pilgrimage before the war. Small shrines and votive offerings to the God-Emperor cluttered one side of the grotto – crude clay aquilas, painted candles, beads, scriptures on parchment strips feathering the walls.

Shuffling over to the cave mouth he peered down at the Barbican, which sprawled out beneath him. It was a shelved cliffside of grey and ivory stone, smeared with banks of thorn-bush, reed and toothy stumps of cactus. The slope was broken by almost vertical cliffs in some places – rocky, bare, precipitous and irregular. At its plateau, batteries of field artillery bristled like a roc's nest, heavy Earthshaker barrels saluting the horizon.

'Sleep well, inquisitor?' asked Captain Pradal. Roth turned to see the man emerge from a stooped tunnel at the rear of the cave. The officer had shaved and scrubbed most of the bloodied filth from his face. His head was bandaged and so was his left wrist.

'Like a beaten-up child,' said Roth, rubbing his face with his hands. Flakes of dried blood and filth dislodged into his palms.

'Welcome, inquisitor. It's about time we had some conscious activity out of you.' A second man had appeared beside Pradal. His rank sash denoted him as colonel, but he was young for a man of such rank. Thick-necked, square-jawed and shaven-headed, the officer looked more like gang muscle than a colonel of the artillery. When he spoke his voice was sandy and coarse, whether from chain-smoking tabac or gun-smoke inhalation, Roth could not tell. Both suited his rough-edged demeanour.

'My thanks, colonel–'

'Colonel Gamburyan, battalion commander of the 26th,' he said.

They briefly shook hands. The colonel's grip was hard and callused, from years of gripping awkward shells and pulling artillery pieces. It made Roth ashamed of his own well-manicured hands.

'Captain Pradal here has given me a full briefing of your situation. I wouldn't have a frag's clue how we can help, but if there's anything you need, I can try my hardest to accommodate,' rasped the colonel as he drew a stick of tabac from behind his ear and lit it in one deft, well-practiced movement.

In truth Roth could have done with some sustenance, or even some water and a rag to scour the solid filth that caked his body, but he had his priorities.

'I need a cipher machine, a cryptographer. Military-grade will do, you must have one somewhere.'

The colonel savoured a mouthful of smoke and nodded. 'I thought you would. The other inquisitor, Sella-meanie I think her name is. She said you might need one. I've got it set up in the main command bunker.'

'Excellent. You are quite on the ball, colonel,' said Roth as he struggled to his feet.

'Have to be. We're alive aren't we?' He shrugged with a grin, tabac stick clenched between his teeth. 'Anything else I can do for you?'

Roth sighed wearily. 'Yes, colonel. May I be so frank as to ask for a smoke?'

WHEN ROTH HAD requested a military-grade cryptographer, he had forgotten that military-grade often stood for obsolete, un-serviced and possibly broken.

The cipher machine was a heavy-duty cogitator set up in the sand-bagged belly of the Barbican. Its porcelain casing was furred with dust, the spindles and keystrokes cracked and faded. Several hundred rusty cables spooled out from underneath its skirting like the tentacles of an undersea leviathan. Roth had never in all his years of service seen a cogitator like it.

With neither patience nor an inclination for technology, Roth left most of the work to Celeminé. She was a natural, tapping on the loom pedals as she adjusted the bristle of cogs and dials. The machine purred, and a flower of ivory set above the mantle of the machine began to gyrate, signalling the decoder's activation. Roth tried to busy himself with the cables, trying to look useful.

'The sooner you stop fussing over my shoulder, the sooner we can begin the decoding,' admonished Celeminé.

Roth mumbled an apology and sat himself down on a bench improvised from plywood and ammunition trunks, content to watch. Celeminé plugged Delahunt's signet into the cipher's central feed, winking data pulses into the machine's logic engines. Her other hand began to spool paper out from the mouth of a porcelain cherub's face set into the machine's side casing.

'Is it done?' asked Roth, craning for a look from his seat.

'No. This signet is magenta-level encryption and this decoder is garbage-level *de*cryption. Its logic engines

have to penetrate the data's enigma coding and polyal-
phabetic substitution. You can figure out the rest.'

Roth stared at her blankly. Celeminé stood, one hand
on her hip, her suede boots tapping in reprove. She had
changed out of her bodyglove and procured a cotton
shirt and some baggy CantiCol breeches. The trousers fit
her so loosely that she had to double them over and
cinch them tight around her tiny waist with a silk scarf.
Likewise, the shirt was so voluminous that she knotted
the hem up above her midriff. Roth thought she looked
like some sort of hive dancer. She rolled her eyes at him.

'It means this might take a while.'

'That's quite all right. We can wait,' said Roth.

As if to prove him wrong, the cave bunker suddenly
shook with a low tremor. Grit loosened from the rafters
in a dusty downpour. Roth felt the percussive heave in
the depths of his diaphragm.

'Are we under attack?' Celeminé said. Her playful
demeanour vanished in an instant. Her chest webbing,
sloughed off and hung on the rafters overhead, was
snatched down.

'I don't think that's incoming artillery,' answered Roth.
The cavern shook again, jarring the sand-bagged walls.

'What is it then?'

'Outgoing, of course. The Guard are firing on targets.'
His reply was punctuated by a rhythmic trio of blasts, the
decibels echoed by the acoustic warren of the cave temples.

Soon enough, Cantican officers began clattering into
the command bunker. The bank of vox arrays that
encompassed an entire wall of the cave began to hiss and
chatter with multiple open stations. The sound of distant
gunfire and commands, washed with static began to
grate out of the speakers.

Roth snagged a passing captain by the sleeve as he ran
by. 'What's the situation?' Roth asked.

The captain looked at Roth like he had been just asked a rhetorical question. 'Uh… well we're fighting, of course. Again. Ironclad infantry offensive, crossing the Erbus canal and making another break across no-man's-land.'

'Does this happen often?'

'Every damn day,' came the reply.

CAPTAIN PRADAL SIGHTED the Archenemy first. He had volunteered for sentry in one of the forward observation caves overlooking the northern approach when he saw them – Archenemy foot scouts silently scouring up the steep scree slope no more than two hundred metres away.

Through his magnoculars, he saw them skulking low against the tumbled wedges of igneous rock, slowly rustling through the crops of mountainous flora. They made good use of the sparse cover, crawling on the loose gravel and hugging the dry, stunted vegetation. At first he counted no more than ten, but then he saw twenty, fifty, perhaps more. A full company advancing in open file.

Pradal turned to the two Guardsmen in the gunpit alongside, handing one of them his magnoculars as he reached for the vox radio. There was no need. The Archenemy fired first. A flak rocket, most likely from a shoulder launcher, screamed overhead, trailing a ragged spine of smoke. It spiralled wildly before exploding forty metres uphill in a scatter of rock fragments.

And just like that, the Archenemy announced their presence. With a bestial roar that swelled in volume, the Ironclad surged to their feet and charged. All told, Pradal counted four, maybe five, full infantry companies, most emerging from cover. They thundered up the slope in a staggered line, closing the two hundred metre distance fast. But beyond the infantry screen, kicking up a curtain of dust, mechanised columns rolled across the Erbus canal in support. It was the fighting vehicles that terrified Pradal most of all.

All at once, the three perimeter positions, two cave bunkers and a concrete pillbox opened fire. Captain Pradal had bellied down behind the gunpit's lone heavy bolter. The forty kilogram gun bucked like an industrial drill, even when Pradal threw his weight behind it. Fat nosed bolt shells slammed out of the barrel.

'Command one! This is forward observation eight. Enemy infantry advance at north bank!' barked Private Chamdri into the vox-set. He was hunkered down next to Pradal, one hand over his kepi hat as he screamed into the mouthpiece.

By now the Archenemy had reached the first line of defence, a cordon of razor wire three coils deep. Pradal hammered rocket-propelled bolt shells into them at a range of fifty metres, throwing up a mist of blood and fragmented metal wherever he raked the gun. The enemy answered with spikes of las-fire.

Pradal's vision began to tunnel. He smelt the methane stink of fyceline as his weapon ejected steaming-hot cartridges. A las-round punched through an empty ammo pallet by his side. Smouldering splinters of wood drizzled the air, prickly warm against his cheek.

'Come on you fraggers. This is my house!' Pradal shouted. He clenched the spoon trigger hard, the long burping bursts of fire muting his words into angry grimacing.

Through the cross hairs, Pradal shot an Ironclad pawing through a clutch of brush-tail reed. The shell's mass-reactive payload ruptured its target, throwing up a fan of blood and dry brown grass. His next shot went wide, hitting an arrow-headed slab of scree. It didn't matter. The rocket-propelled round exploded into a boulder, sending fist-sized fragments of rock shearing through the air. It killed more Ironclad than a direct hit.

On and on he fired as Private Chamdri fed a looping belt
of ammunition into the chamber. Throwing out an automatic stream, Pradal was ignoring the standard Guard
doctrine of tightly controlled bursts. There were too
many enemies for that.

Further up the incline, other cave temples fired
within their interlocking arcs, throwing up a solid curtain of fire. Bolters, autocannons and heavy stubbers,
their elemental roars combining into decibels so deafening it reduced Pradal's hearing to a soft tinnitus
ring.

'–fun without me–' came a voice, muffled as if spoken
through water. Pradal only caught broken snatches of it.
Turning to his side, he saw Inquisitor Roth emerge from
the connective tunnel at the rear of the gunpit and slide
next to him.

'Not yet, sir! You've only missed the prologue,' Pradal
yelled back. At least that's what he thought he said. He
couldn't hear a damn thing.

Nonetheless he was correct. The infantry advance had
only been a screen. Ensnared in razor wire and pulverised by heavy weapons at close range, the Ironclad
infantry assault had withered. Now half a kilometre off,
the mechanised assault was only just closing in. Growling, fuming, howling – no less than fifty fighting patrol
vehicles, gun-trucks and Chimeras supported by a full
lance of KL5 Scavenger-pattern light tanks. The eight-
wheeled tanks gleaming white and up-armoured,
looming like ghosts.

'–light tanks are going to ruin our day–' mouthed
Roth. The Guardsmen cramped in the gunpit echoed the
inquisitor's sentiments with colourful language. In a
way, Pradal was glad the weapons had dulled his hearing.

'Can you crack them?' Roth screamed, practically
directly into Pradal's ear.

Pradal shifted the heavy bolter and lined up one of the fast-approaching KL5s under the iron sights. He unleashed a long sustained blast that sent shockwaves rippling up to his shoulders. The heavy rounds *spanged* off the tank's frontal hull, erupting in a chain of small explosions. Underneath the coiling smoke and punctured plating, the tank was not affected.

Despite their sustained fire the mechanised assault rumbled on. Now only three hundred metres away, the columns began to fan out into a cavalry line. Tracers flashed into them, the shriek of solid slugs impacting on metal. A handful of FPVs and gun trucks caught fire as fuel tanks combusted, shedding peels of flaming wreckage as they spun out of control.

Enemy fire intensified, chopping into the Guard positions. The Archenemy were upon them now. Ironclad infantry dismounted from their motorised convoy, struggling up the hill against the teeth of Imperial fire. To Pradal's right, a light tank rolled in line with the forward pill-box. Its turret slowly traversed, lining up the fortification with a chain-fed autocannon.

'We have to move!' shouted Roth. He grabbed Pradal by the collar and dragged him away. Pradal didn't see what happened next. He didn't need to. The KL5 fired and he felt rather than heard the cataclysm, as sixty kilotonnes of kinetic energy split open thirty-centimetre thick rockcrete.

HALF A KILOMETRE up, a whickering salvo of enemy fire belted the highest defensive line. Defensive breastworks of interlacing logs, sticks and clay mortar bore the ruptured scarring of heavy-calibre rounds.

Celeminé threw herself flat as a javelin of las-fire fizzed into her cave bunker. It dissolved a neat hole into the pilgrim's shrine at the rear of the cave. Jugs, candles and blessing dolls clattered off the rock shelf.

'Anti-armour weapons, over there, give it to me!' Celeminé shouted at the two troopers sharing her gun-pit. In the panic of war, she lost all semblance of grammatical eloquence.

'Are you sure? The enemy are too far out of range, inquisitor, it would be a waste,' Trooper Jagdesh shouted back.

'Yes, yes! Just hand it over,' Celeminé beckoned as Jagdesh belly-crawled over with a shoulder-launched missile. He was right of course; at five hundred metres, the frag missile would likely propel away in a wild spiral at two hundred. She had a different idea.

'Load me,' she said, chewing on her lip in contemplation. Jagdesh held the launcher tube upright as Trooper Gansükh fixed the shaped-charge warhead. As they handed her the weapon they gave her a look that implied she was totally mad.

Shouldering the rocket, Celeminé peered over the breastworks. She saw tinder sparks flashing from camouflaged gun-holes, weapons nests and fortified cave-temples. She saw Ironclad dismount from their transports to storm the defences like tiny silver beetles below.

Celeminé adjusted the cross-hairs for angle and distance. She armed the fire control lever and took aim. A solid slug cracked past her shoulder but she was too deep in psytrance to notice. Resting the launcher over the edge of the breastwork, she aligned the sights on a KL5 light tank, two hundred metres and closing.

'Watch for the back-blast!' she warned.

The weapon clapped with a hollow bang. A cone of pressurised exhaust jetted into the rear of the cave, the thermal gas destroying what remained of the pilgrim's trinkets. The warhead itself trailed a coiled serpent of smoke in its wake, stabiliser fins snapping. For over two hundred metres it stayed on trajectory, until the rocket lost momentum and crazed off target.

Celeminé concentrated hard and reached out with her mind, snagging the warhead and forcing it back on path. She could feel the whirr of the gyro motor, jumping against her control as if she were cradling the rocket in her hands. It flew up in a catapulting loop before spearing back down on the KL5. Celeminé hooked it down onto the turret and the missile did what it was designed for. Its copper rocket sheath punched through the enemy plating and high explosives rocked the tank from inside out. The turret flew off. Wheels collapsed. A side hatch popped open and flaming figures staggered out of the tank, before collapsing on the rocks. They writhed like tortured beetles before lying still.

'That's one,' breathed Celeminé. As if in reply, a salvo of impact slugs chopped overhead. The inquisitor and her soldiers ducked into an exit tunnel, just as a volley of autocannon rounds hammered into the cave-bunker they had held scant seconds ago. The cave collapsed behind them with a seismic bellow and a mournful shudder.

IN THE CENTRAL command bunker, deep within the heart of the Barbican, the command post pounded with activity. Signals officers hunched at vox-bays, screaming into headsets, each louder than the next. Battalion commanders surged back and forth, relaying orders and communiqués, scraping knees against supply crates and yelling over each other's shoulders. Overhead, explosions throbbed through the thick stone. The single sodium lamp swung on its cord, casting wild claustrophobic shadows.

Roth and Pradal dashed into the command post through one of its many connective tunnels. Between them they dragged Private Chamdri, who was crying with fear, his hands held up above him like he was already surrendering.

'Colonel Gamburyan!' Roth bellowed. He juiced his words with psychic amplification, so he could be heard above the pandemonium.

From a circle of officers huddled around a map table, Gamburyan looked up. The colonel had shed his cavalry blazer and his braces hung from his breeches. Crescents of sweat soaked the chest and arms of his undershirt. The officer excused himself from his peers.

'Inquisitor. How do you do?'

'I've just had an autocannon almost rearrange my gentlemanly graces. But I'm otherwise in perfect health, thank you. What's the situation?'

'The situation is under control. Nothing we haven't seen before,' replied the colonel as he dragged on a tabac stick.

'Sir, the perimeter bunkers are being overrun,' Pradal interjected.

'As is expected, captain. Defensive nests on the north and west banks are scrapping with a mounted infantry offensive. I've already ordered artillery to flatten the perimeter as our forces withdraw deeper into the Barbican. Trust me, we've seen much worse than this.'

As if to reiterate the colonel's assurance, the low bass rumble of artillery thrummed like muzzled thunder. Deep within the cave complex, it sounded like an avalanche rolling down the escarpment.

THE FIGHTING CONTINUED well past sundown, ebbing and flowing in intensity. Three more times that day, the Ironclad mounted a concerted offensive of mixed-order advance – mechanised columns scattered with infantry platoons. They met tenacious resistance, scythed down in ranks by the furious torrent of Imperial fire. More than once, the Ironclad overran the first-line defences, breaching the bunkers with grenades and flamer. At one stage, a squad of Ironclad had even penetrated up into the tunnel network, massacring an artillery crew before they were put down.

The Canticans had manned their posts in short shifts, fingers tense, eyes glazed and shaking with adrenaline. They had fired a total of over sixty thousand shells, missiles, las-charges and solid slugs. By evening the enemy had receded, slinking away into the dusk-bruised horizon.

Sustained assaults on the north and western banks had inflicted sizeable casualties. Major Aghajan, the battalion's deputy commander, had been one of those killed. He and five other senior officers had been on routine inspection during a break in the assault when a single enemy mortar had claimed them all. It was an irreplaceable loss to the battalion. In all, forty-one men of the 26th were killed in that day's fighting. Many more were wounded.

CHAPTER TEN

FOR NOW THE field was quiet. The following morning had passed without further enemy movement, or even gas or shell attack. Yet the weariness of battle was still fresh in Roth's mind, while his ears were ringing with the hum of post-battle. At night the ringing had become so persistent that Roth had not slept, and now he welcomed the quiet. The fighting at the Barbican was by far the most confrontational and desperate siege he could have imagined.

He stood on the flat mesa plateau of the Barbican, watching the sweeping expanse of knotted rock that fell away like a stretched grey blanket. So high up, the wind fluttered against Roth's plating, a stirring buffet that numbed the tips of his ears and nose. It carried with it a fine ashy dust from the tomb flats between Buraghand and the western coast, coarse and cold. Before the war, the ascent of the cave temples had been known as the Pilgrim's Stairway.

It was not that any more. The bodies of the Archenemy littered the slopes like beached carcasses, tangled in

127

razor wire and scattered between stones. Dark, scorched rings and jag-toothed craters scarred the earth. The scene was still and grey, trailing curls of smoke like every battlefield Roth had ever surveyed. But in its own way Cantica was also different. There was no hope here; the fighting was done, like the curtains had already fallen. The atmosphere was quiet, contemplative and deeply morose.

This was where he was going to die.

Roth picked up a wedge of flint and threw it towards the horizon where the Archenemy amassed. Out there, four hundred thousand soldiers of the Ruinous Powers prowled the landscape, burning and butchering. His work here was done. He would give the Conclave what he found and he would be allowed to die here, at least with some dignity and defiance.

He heard footsteps clapping up the tunnel steps that led onto the plateau. Roth presumed it was Celeminé, returning with the readouts from the cipher machine. But it wasn't just her.

The hatch door, camouflaged with a nest of thornbush, slid aside. Colonel Gamburyan climbed from the hatch, dragging on tabac as always. Celeminé emerged after him, clutching a sheaf of wafers.

'Marvellous view from here,' said Roth, turning back to stare into the distance.

'Always good to see the results of a hard scrap,' Colonel Gamburyan nodded as they moved to join Roth at the edge of the precipice.

'How many did we lose today, colonel?'

'We lost Corporal Alatas in the infirmary just five minutes ago. He lost a leg from a tank round and bled out, poor bastard. That makes forty-one today.'

'Oh,' said Roth, his shoulders visibly sagging.

Gamburyan proffered a little envelope of waxed paper. 'Would you like a stick of tabac? You look terrible.'

Roth laughed at the soldier's blunt observation as he drew a stick. Roth had not seen a mirror in so long. He dreaded what he would look like, if he ever saw one again.

'Where do you keep finding these anyway?' sighed Roth.

At first, the big man almost looked sheepish. 'Votive offerings. You'd be surprised how many pilgrims had left tabac for the pleasure of the God-Emperor.'

The inquisitor snorted. 'The Emperor provides.'

A rustle of paper behind him reminded Roth of Celeminé's presence. His mind had grown absent of late. It was not at all like him. He turned to her and bowed deeply.

'How rude of me. I'm sorry, madame, was there something you wished to speak to me about?' Roth asked.

She nodded, oddly straight-faced. Celeminé handed Roth the sheaf of papers. 'I have the decrypted text from Delahunt's research log.'

Roth took the papers and flicked through them absent-mindedly, not really reading anything. 'What does he say?' Roth asked, looking up from behind the wafers.

'Delahunt seems to have thought the Old Kings cannot be on Cantica.'

Roth shrugged. 'I thought as much.'

'You did?' Celeminé asked.

'If they were, do you not think the Archenemy would have found them by now? Cantica has been their playground for well over a month.'

'I did find something of importance in his research,' said Celeminé. She rifled through the pages until she found it and held it up for Roth to see.

'Here. He writes that, "It is with some degree of certainty, judging by historical evidence and geological composition, that relics from the War of Reclamation do not reside on Cantica. Rather, the myth of the Old Kings became a pillar of institutional identity, so embedded within the historical collective and creational narrative of the planet, that it has become difficult to separate myth from reality."'

'What does that mean?' Colonel Gamburyan asked.

'It means our work here is done. The Old Kings must reside on one of the other core worlds, colonel, one of the core worlds under the jurisdiction of another Conclavial member.'

'So where do we go from here?' Celeminé interjected.

Roth thought for a while. It was not that he needed to work out what he needed to do. No, he had given that much thought already. It was how he was going to propose it to Celeminé.

'We stay here, madame. The colonel could do with our help, I am sure.'

'We… stay?' Celeminé repeated. She found it hard to roll the words off her tongue. Even Colonel Gamburyan was surprised. He let the stub of his tabac slip out of his fingers to be carried away by the wind, spinning and tumbling.

'Yes. Of course. We are inquisitors. We fight the enemies of mankind until we die. That is our role. We accepted that the moment we became what we are. What good would fleeing do?' said Roth. He couldn't look into Celeminé's eyes. Instead he kept his gaze level with the horizon.

Celeminé stopped talking. By the expression on her face, she was not prepared for his answer at all.

'Inquisitor. You do not have to do this,' the colonel began.

'But we must. What other choice do we have? We cannot reach the stratocraft. Not surrounded as we are. Better to die here fighting than to be shot like dogs running.'

'This is about Silverstein isn't it?' Celeminé snapped.

Roth didn't say anything.

Celeminé shook her head softly. 'Let me convene with Gurion.'

'If you must. But I do not think the choice is ours anyway. Out there, the four hundred thousand killers disagree with your prognosis.' Roth gestured into the distance.

'I–I see your logic. But I will ask Lord Gurion as I relay him our findings,' Celeminé replied in unconvinced, yet soft deference.

'As you wish,' said Roth finally. He took a drag of his tabac and turned away without another word.

AT ONE HOUR past midnight, when the night was at its coolest and quietest, the Ironclad attacked again. A line of infantry waded out from the shadows of the prairie, flanked by fast-moving FPVs in a sweeping pincer. The forward observation bunkers, barely repaired from the previous day's fighting, engaged the Archenemy at a range of no more than fifty metres. Above, the artillery banks on the crest of the Barbican did not fire, their muzzles threatening but silent. Ammunition was low as it was, and far too precious to squander on anything short of enemy armour.

By all accounts of the Guard at his side, Inquisitor Roth fought furiously. He led a thirty-man platoon on a counter-attack, bayonets fixed. They hooked around wide to pinch the flanks of the Ironclad pincer, disrupting their advance with enfilade fire. The Canticans under Roth's command fought like men with nothing to lose. It should have been suicide, unarmoured Guardsmen on open terrain exchanging shots with Ironclad fighting patrol vehicles. They hammered away with shoulder-mounted rockets, and when those ran dry, they charged. It was rough, dirty fighting. Hand-to-hand, face-to-face.

Men of the 26th witnessed Inquisitor Roth drive his power fist through the engine block of an FPV. The inquisitor tore the light-skinned vehicle right down the middle and gunned down the occupants in the cab. Visibility was poor and the men fought blind, gouging and flailing at heavy black shapes.

Despite their small numbers, the counter-attack blunted the momentum of the Ironclad push, halting them just short of the razor wire. At eight minutes into the assault the Ironclad withdrew, chased back into the shadows by drizzles of las-fire.

CELEMINÉ SETTLED INTO a cross-legged lotus posture, drawing deep, relaxing breaths. It was severely difficult to concentrate with the constant fighting outside her cave bunker. Since her arrival, the fighting had almost been constant. There was nothing she could do about that.

She had tried her best to find the most suitable cavern for her needs. After a little searching, she had come upon a shelved pocket deep in the heart of the Barbican. A gaudy papier-mâché saint slathered in garish pastels had once dominated the chamber, draped with garlands of grain and prayer beads. Since the Atrocities, the saint shared her shrine with ammunition pallets and stacked drums of fuel. Cantica had once been beautiful, and wistfully, Celeminé wished she could have visited it before the Medina War. If only.

Slowly, Celeminé drew herself into a meditative state. The distant drumming of gunfire faded. She was trancing. The temperature in the cave plummeted. Candles arranged in geometric patterns flickered out all at once. Celeminé's breath, steady and rhythmic, plumed frostily.

A gentle calm pervaded throughout the chamber. The saint, kneeling with hands in benediction, watched over Celeminé with glassy eyes. Condensation formed on the saint's cheeks, curling the paper skin and melting the pigmentation from her face. As Celeminé's consciousness drifted from her body, the last thing she saw was the gaudy saint crying in prayer.

FROM THE PORT side of the *Carthage*, the satellite suns of Medina glimmered through the glare-shutters of the tall, arching viewing bays. Judging by the alignment of the suns, it would be hazing dawn on Cantica.

In his stateroom, Forde Gurion's chron, synced to Cantican time, struck three in the morning. He sat in a deeply cushioned high-back. Because of his hoofed augmetics, Gurion seldom needed to sit, but he often did out of courtesy and to make his guests at ease. It was very important to make the man, sitting in the chair across from him, very much at ease indeed.

'Would you like a drink?' Gurion said, gesturing at the thimble of ambrose in his hand. He did not need to gesture, however: the man was blind.

'No, my thanks. Liquor distorts mental clarity,' said the man with the sunken, hollow eyes. The embroidered robes, spilling over the armrests in a radiant sheen of emerald, marked him as an adept of the Astra Telepathica.

'Oh but of course. I ask you every time, don't I?'

'The last two times we have tried this. Yes.'

'Let us hope we are more fortunate this time,' said Gurion, webs of worry crinkling the corners of his eyes.

'If the Emperor wills it,' replied the astropath in his monotone voice.

With this, the astropath sidled down deeper into his robes, sinking back into the chair. His head tilted forwards and for a long time he was very still. It almost looked as if the psyker had nodded off to sleep. Then, despite the wrought-iron heating grille set into the stateroom fireplace, it grew colder by a dozen degrees. The air took on a scent of residual ozone.

Gurion felt uncomfortable, but not because of the chill. It was the astropath. In over a century of service to the Inquisition, Gurion had dealt with astropaths many times, but it never made it easier. It was the way they writhed and squirmed in their trance, their faces twisting and leering in pantomime agony. Or perhaps, it was the fact that their minds were swimming through the warp. Gurion had always believed that the only barrier between the warp ghosts and him were the astropath's eyelids. That if the man were to suddenly arch up his stomach, with his mouth partially open, then his eyelids would snap open and all the warp would come streaming through.

Gurion slammed down the thimble and shook his head vigorously to clear it. The tart spice and earthy terroir of the Mospel River vintage anchored his senses. Just in case, he placed a small nickel-plated autopistol in his lap and waited while watching his chron.

'Gurion…' the astropath murmured after a long period of silence.

Gurion started inwardly. When the man spoke, it was not with the monotone he had grown accustomed to. Instead, it was the soft, canting lilt of Felyce Celeminé. It never failed to disturb him. Someone had once explained to Gurion that through the psychic connection, the mediator became one with the messenger, mimicking emotions, voice patterns and even body language. That did not make it any less disconcerting to an old non-psyker.

'Gurion…' called Celeminé's voice.

The old inquisitor leaned forwards, the servomotors in his hip whirring. 'Yes. Yes, Felyce, I am here, it's Forde Gurion.'

'Gurion. I don't know if it's safe to commune. It's very loud here. Very violent and colourful. I need you to listen to what we know,' mouthed the astropath.

'Of course. Tell me, dear,' nodded Gurion. He picked up a data-slate from an adjacent stand and made ready to scribe with a gilded stylus.

'Where do I start?'

'From the beginning, please, dear.'

Word after word, Celeminé began to recount their findings. She told him of Delahunt's fate, his research, and the fall of Cantica. Most importantly, she told him that the Old Kings were not on the conquered planet. That it must be, by reason of deduction, hidden on one of the other two core worlds. By the time the astropath finished talking, Gurion realised his augmetic left hand had clenched so hard it had gouged small crescent moons into the leather armrest of his chair.

'And what of you two? Are you well? Is Obodiah well?'

'Roth is… I am well. But Inquisitor Roth wishes to stay and die on Cantica. He says we have nowhere to run, so we should die fighting… I–' began the astropath.

Gurion shook his head. 'No no no. That will not do. The Conclave still needs you.'

'I thought as much,' said the astropath. Gurion was not sure, but it seemed the man actually breathed a sigh of relief.

'No. Celeminé, listen carefully. Inquisitor Vandus Barq on Aridun has uncovered something crucial to our work here. We can't risk transmitting the information by vox or telepathy so I need Roth and the Overwatch Task Group to travel to Aridun. It matters not how you get there, just depart with all possible haste. Vandus Barq is in the Temple of the Tooth, on the Antillo continent. That is all I can tell you and I fear I may have already said too much. Can you rendezvous with him?'

'We can try,' said the astropath, shrugging his shoulders up high like Celeminé would.

'That's all I expect, Celeminé. Try to arrive within two weeks' time. Vandus will wait for you.'

'Yes, Lord Gurion. I have to go now,' said the astropath, octaves wavering between a female and male voice.

'Take care of yourselves,' Gurion pleaded. He gripped the astropath's hand earnestly, then immediately felt foolish for doing so.

ROTH HAD BEEN waiting for news from Celeminé for some time. Anxious with anticipation, he had attempted to occupy his mind with other activities. At the behest of Colonel Gamburyan, Roth and the battalion commander elected to conduct a general assessment of the forward defences.

He followed Gamburyan from bunker to bunker, conversing with soldiers at their posts, praising them for a job well done and sharing tabac. It was the standard officer's inspection. But it also served to give them a realistic assessment of their situation. The Guardsmen were tired, their nerves frayed from ceaseless fighting. Some took it well, becoming inured to the threat of constant enemy attack; others less so, their hands trembling, their faces offering only blank stares. Supplies, especially clean water, were running low and dysentery was becoming endemic. If the Archenemy didn't kill them, starvation and infections would.

At designated cave bunker two-two, a mid-line gunpit housing a heavy stubber draped with camouflage netting, they came upon a dying man. His name was Corporal Nabhan, and he was feverish with gangrene. Wrapped in a blanket and clutching his lasrifle, the Guardsman had volunteered to hold bunker two-two on his own until he died. Dehydration and infection had leeched the corporal into a pale wisp of a man. Colonel Gamburyan knelt by the Guardsman and administered him several tablets of dopamine. There was little else Roth could do.

As Gamburyan nursed capfuls of water from a canteen for Corporal Nabhan, Roth heard a knock on the support frame of the cave tunnel. Celeminé entered the cave, ducking low to avoid bumping her head on the support beams.

'Lord Gurion's astropath contacted me,' she said, biting her lip.

'Very good. What does the Conclave say?' Roth asked. For a man who seldom flinched when being shot at, Roth was suddenly nervous.

'Well, in light of our recent findings, Gurion orders us to make for Aridun and–'

'Absolutely out of the question,' Roth interrupted.

His answer evidently jarred Celeminé. Her eyes took on that particular tint of rose before tears, a sad ruby kohl that made her seem suddenly vulnerable. Roth felt a spike of guilt.

'Apologies for my lack of courtesy, madame. I simply mean that it is not possible for us to leave. We have been hunted ever since landfall. Better we make a stand here.'

Celeminé's eyes hardened. 'In truth, Roth, I don't want to die here. There is still much to do.'

'I understand how you feel, but we have little choice. We've finished what we needed to.'

'Roth, I'm sorry but I really don't think you do. I'm too young. I have more to accomplish.'

But Roth did understand. He remembered his virgin deployment to Sirene Primal in 866.M41. Caught between a secessionist insurgency and an alpha-level xenos threat, that first assignment had almost killed him. The fatalistic part of him always believed he should have died on Primal, and that every moment since was an extension granted by the God-Emperor. An inquisitor could not function to his fullest capacity if he was preoccupied with self-preservation. That was what he had always believed, anyway.

Roth walked close to Celeminé and touched the tips of her hair. He was not sure why he did it. It was an awkward gesture but it had a calming effect. 'Be as it may, Celeminé, we can't leave. Look around you. We are under siege. We are surrounded and nowhere close to our transport. Our work here is done. There is nothing left to do.'

'There is one thing, inquisitors,' said Colonel Gamburyan crisply. He stood at the cave mouth, trying to light the frayed end of a tabac stub. Taking his time, he walked towards Roth with his rolling officer's gait and paused contemplatively before continuing.

'The 26th can conduct a ground assault from the Barbican. All of us, every last one. You and your Task Group can make your escape under the cover of our offensive,' announced the colonel in slow, measured tones.

Roth considered himself a scholar with a rogue's wit, seldom at a loss for words. But he quite simply did not know how to react. Colonel Gamburyan continued to speak before Roth could muster any protest.

'Let's be realistic for a moment, inquisitor. We are running dry of food, water and most critically ammunition. Every day I lose more good men. How long can this go on for? Two weeks? A month? It wouldn't matter. What you could do for the subsector would far outstrip anything my battalion could potentially achieve here.'

'I cannot have your men die for me,' muttered Roth weakly.

'We're already dead, Roth. No one will remember us here, unless you go. Let us have one last moment under the stars. A strident last charge, wouldn't that be grand?' laughed the colonel.

Roth paused, hesitant to answer. They were right of course; they were both right, damn them. An inquisitor should not live in fear of death, or he could not serve the Emperor, Inquisitorial doctrine had taught him that. But his mentor, old Inquisitor Liszt, had also taught him no service could be done for the Imperium if he died a stupid death. Roth's reflection was interrupted by a weak voice from the gun-post of the bunker.

'Sir... if there is a last charge can I please go with my unit?' rasped Corporal Nabhan, his eyes staring at the dripstone on the cave ceiling.

'Son. If there is a last charge, I would not be the one to deny you,' answered Colonel Gamburyan. At this, he levelled his gaze on Roth and smiled broadly.

THE LAST CHARGE was scheduled for 06:00 hours on the thirty-sixth day.

At 05:00, the five hundred and twenty-five men of the 26th Colonial Artillery began last equipment checks. At the foot of the Barbican, a sombre line of soldiers locked their bayonet spikes and adjusted their canvas webbing in silence. They loaded up their equipment satchels with musette pouches, grenades and exactly two spare cells each.

By 05:30, Colonel Gamburyan made last inspections. In close order rank, his five hundred men stood to attention in the brown blazers and tall white kepi hats he had grown so accustomed to in his twenty years of service. They stood in the open prairie, waiting for the enemy to see them, taunting them with their presence. The colonel thought of his wife, the wife he had not seen since the Atrocities and who would never again tease him for his scowl, or pick the loose threads from his uniform. He thought of her because it steeled his resolve.

At 06:00, it was Gamburyan who sounded the charge. Strung out in an open line, the battalion broke into a steady cant that rolled momentum into a roaring charge. Bugles sounded, officers blew on tin whistles. Guardsmen screamed themselves hoarse as the regimental standard was borne aloft. The wind caught their colours, the sabre and stallion of the CantiCol regiment, embroidered with the chain-link wreath of the 26th Artillery snapped high on a brisk easterly.

It was during all this that Inquisitor Roth, Celeminé and an understandably reluctant Captain Pradal made their escape. They threaded west, hugging the Erbus canal towards the coastal headlands. During their flight, they went to ground many times in order to avoid the Ironclad elements moving in the opposite direction, storming towards the cave temples. By the time the battle was over, Roth and his group were clear of the red zone. Regional Archenemy commanders were so preoccupied with the last stand of the 26th that a lone stratocraft powering up on the western shores did not warrant their attention.

Roth never saw the last stand on that hot, brittle plain of undulating grass husk and dog-tooth stone. In the thick of the fighting, the battalion formed a large defensive square, two soldiers deep. For the first time the Ironclad engaged the Imperial Guard point-blank. The Archenemy were seized by a predatory glee, eager to pounce upon the Guardsmen who had held them at bay for so long. They were eager to claim heads and ears. Even the crew of light and heavy armour clambered from their vehicles with blades and weapons of blunt trauma. Every Ironclad warlord and underlord within a twenty-kilometre radius mustered his forces for the attack. No less than eight thousand Ironclad foot-soldiers and as many armoured and light-skinned fighting vehicles converged on the Barbican plains.

Despite the shock of the Ironclad charge, the Cantican Colonials seemed like a bulwark that could not be moved. They stood firmly, shoulder to shoulder, forming a bristling phalanx of lasguns, heavy weapons, cannon and rocket. They laid down a furious killing zone two hundred metres out, hewing down the churning press of Ironclad.

Despite sustaining las-rounds to the leg and upper torso, Colonel Gamburyan continued to rally the battalion. At the battle's apex, when the CantiCol phalanx was punctured, ragged and beginning to fracture, Gamburyan attempted to hold a breach in the line alone. The colonel died behind the post of a smoking heavy bolter. He was shot a total of thirteen times, but it was a ricochet slug entering beneath his chin that finally claimed him.

In all, the Guardsmen withstood the assault for eighteen minutes even though the Archenemy several times broke into the interior of the Cantican square. Many years later, this scene would be rendered in oil pastel by the revered muralist Niccolo Battista. Awash with vivid colours on the ceiling of the Saint Solomon Cathedral on Holy Terra, it gave the men of the 26th CantiCol a voice in history.

CHAPTER ELEVEN

THE HOLDING CELL was a cold, rusted, disorientating affair.

Silverstein no longer knew how long he had been captured for. He spent his days wrist-chained to the grate alongside the Cantican five. Their cage was no larger than a Munitorum shipping crate, and hung like a pendulum from the ceiling of a docking berth. By the nature of its design, there was no room to sit or crouch and the constant shifting of his companions to ease their joints caused the cage to swing nauseatingly. His captors sporadically dealt them scraps of sustenance, at odd hours and without any semblance of pattern.

All that Silverstein knew was that he was aboard some kind of frigate in transit. It was a bloated Archenemy troop carrier en route to somewhere. The Elteber had promised Silverstein that they were being taken to 'dine' with Khorsabad. Who or where Khorsabad was, Silverstein did not know. Regardless, the huntsman had vowed to escape at the first opportunity. He and his fellow captives discussed the escape endlessly. It was the only thing that kept them sane.

Sometime into their journey, whether it was days or weeks, an Ironclad slaver lowered the suspended holding cell by means of a clanking lever. The slaver was swathed in chainmail and a frilled mantle of feathery scrap iron. Slinging a two-handed mace casually across his shoulders, he entered their cage and chose Varim, a clocksmith with steady hands who was a keen shot with the las. Without warning the Ironclad lashed the studded maul into Varim's head. It was one swift brutal strike that lathered everyone in a mist of blood.

Then, just like that, the Ironclad latched the cage and left. There had been no reason, no provocation, no warning. Creaking on cabled chains they were hoisted back up, along with the bleeding corpse of Varim. Throughout the ordeal, no one made a sound. Silverstein, pressed against the body, could not look away. His bioptics watched the heat signature slowly fade, and the pulse signs taper flat to nothing.

ARIDUN, THE SMALLEST of the Medina Worlds, was at once both ancient and new. Six thousand years ago, the planet had suffered mass extinction. The atmosphere was eroded and its alignment to its satellite suns had bleached the planet, evaporating the great ocean basins and baking the soil with a shimmering curtain of heat. This change birthed new flora and fauna, evolving to flourish under the primordial environment. It was a new dawn only six thousand years old.

Across the ash plains were the remnants of prehistory, the crushed bones and fossil dust painted in hues of faded sepia. Where oceans once lay, vast tracts of evaporite deposit sprawled into salt flats.

On the southern belt of the horizon, a dry savannah of dunes formed the core of Imperial settlement. At least there, the seasons were temperate enough to sustain thousand kilometre reefs of cycads, ferns and ginkgoes.

The structures of settlement here predated Imperial colony. Known as the Fortress Chain, the cities formed a line of strongholds, strung out across the southern savannah. They were twenty-three city-states in all, Percassa, Argentum, ancient Barcid, dead Angkhora and nineteen others, each twenty kilometres apart in a line of squat stone chess pieces. A rampart wall four hundred kilometres long connected the walled cities in a defensive grid. The wall itself, an earthen rampart of lime and sandstone, was simply known as the Fortress Chain. Bombasts and mortars peered from embrasures that stretched across the horizon like a stone rind. It was the only bastion of civilisation and, indeed, fertile life on Aridun.

Sparsely populated and lightly garrisoned, it was odd that Aridun was the least ravaged by war. Thus far and for reasons unknown, the Archenemy incursion had been probing and sporadic. The deployment of the Ironclad was limited; CantiCol reconnaissance estimated seventy thousand enemies at most, judging by drop-ship disposition. Even then, most had been driven away from the inhabited southern belt by the chain's aerial defences, into the Cage Isles and scorching wastelands many kilometres out.

It was on the temperate belt in the ninth chain-fortress of Argentum that Roth and the Overwatch Task Group found the Temple of the Tooth.

ROTH STRAIGHTENED THE sapphire folds of his brocaded silk robe, a fine piece of attire he often wore at rest. It had been less than a week since they had arrived on Aridun, but it was remarkable how a bath, a shave and few days of sleep had made the conflict on Cantica seem decades past. Roth stepped out into the elevated temple rooftop, his toes warmed by the soft, loamy clay tiles. Over the low parapet of the temple walls the roof offered an expansive view of the southern savannah belt. For the past two mornings, the temple priests had suggested Roth seek meditative solace on the temple walls, to recuperate himself. It was sage advice, as the landscape seemed to banish doubtful thoughts and the sharp worrying stones of his mind. Out there, bars of floral green wreathed the outskirts of the Fortress Chain. Narrow canoes meandered from the swamplands and up the city viaducts, wending towards the market districts. Further out, herds of sauropods, grey reptiles long of neck and thick of limb, grazed on the sprawling vegetation. Silverstein would have loved to hunt here, Roth thought.

The temple itself, as befitted its namesake, resembled the cusp of a human molar. An edifice constructed entirely of mud, it was a circular monument crowned by a ring of minarets some forty metres in height. Every year, before the mild rainy season, new mud would be smeared over the old walls. The city's plasterer guilds were the only masons deemed worthy of this task.

Work started only on an auspicious day, determined by star-gazing, religious debate and when the mud in the canal channels was of the right consistency. The foundations would be blessed amid holy prayers, a mixture of Imperial verse and local incantation. Each phase of reconstruction was marked by ritual.

Once a monastic retreat, the Temple of the Tooth was now a convalescence run by the priesthood of Saint Solias. It was a genteel facility, the gymnasium and courtyards filled with the murmuring, resting infirm. Inquisitor Barq could not have selected a more suitable location for their rendezvous. After the ordeals of the past month, it was the least he could do in order to function in his official capacities. Roth had spent only two days at the convalescence, most of it in deep sleep.

Nourished by the restoring meal of potted rice simmered in poultry broth, his vigour was already renewing and his wounds healing.

'Are you feeling better? You look morose.'

Roth turned and saw Celeminé emerge from a brass door at the conical base of a minaret. Much like Roth, she had shed her battlefield attire days ago and had not donned it since. She now wore a chemise of alabaster, her throat chased with white lace. Freshened, rested and reposed, Roth thought she looked absolutely radiant.

He bowed deeply. 'Celeminé. I am fine, thank you.'

She glided in close and pretended to pick a loose thread from his collar. 'Don't lie, Roth. You're certainly not very good at it. What's on your mind?'

Roth sighed. Although he had first thought Celeminé too young and too green to be an inquisitor, he now knew better. She was sharp, perhaps much sharper than he. More than that, despite her demeanour she was a hellcat in a firefight. Gurion had selected his colleague well.

'It's the ambush,' he began. 'The enemy, they were not the Archenemy. But more than that, they knew where we were going to be.'

'You suspect an infiltrator,' she said flatly.

'I suspect,' Roth said, choosing his words carefully, 'that someone very high up in Imperial Command wants us dead. By all accounts, the Orphratean Purebred have been deployed in surgical strike roles by the Imperium since the onset of the Medina Campaign.'

Celeminé crinkled her nose and bit her lip-ring thoughtfully. It was a gesture Roth had grown strangely accustomed to.

'You suspect Captain Pradal is the leak?'

'He would be the most likely suspect, yes.'

Celeminé thought about this. 'Or perhaps me? There *is* me, you know.'

Roth chuckled. He realised Celeminé was standing very close. So close that he could smell her cosmetic fragrance, hints of citrus and fresh milk.

'If it were you who wanted me dead. Why don't you kill me now? You could have shot me any time you wanted.'

She crinkled her nose again. 'Or perhaps Silverstein? I mean no offence, Roth, but the puzzle fits. I'm sorry.'

The suggestion startled Roth. It had not occurred to him that Silverstein, old Bastiel, his primary agent, could have been the one to betray his whereabouts to the mercenaries. He had departed before the ambush, perhaps not on circumstances of his own choosing, but he had departed nonetheless.

'There is a distinct possibility, yes. But–'

'But?'

'It would be immoral of me to regard a lost friend in such light without the Emperor's own verification. I'd be a lesser man for it.'

Celeminé nodded. 'I'd think less of you too. Don't make me do that.'

Roth looked away. In the distance he spied a flock of winged reptiles, circling lazily on the solar currents. When he turned back he had recomposed himself.

'Was there something you wanted to see me about?'

She smiled. 'Yes. Inquisitor Barq has been waiting to see you since you arrived here. He said you both have much catching up to do in the gymnasium.'

'The gymnasium?'

'Of course,' she said, taking him by the hand, 'He's been waiting for some time.'

TUGGING HIM BY his hand, she led Roth down the spiralling stairwells and helix corridors of the temple.

They finally entered a cloistered court adjoining the main structure. Although the temple was four thousand years old at last census, the cloister was a recent addition of the plasterers' guild. Balance beams, vaults and pommel horses sprouted from the packed dirt flooring while still rings and high bars swung from the ceiling like wooden fruit. They all served as excellent instruments of recuperation, but this early in the morning the courtyard was largely empty.

Empty but for Inquisitor Vandus Barq, limbering up at the centre of court. Although it had been decades since the progenium, Roth recognised him immediately – a young man with a wrestler's build. His bull-neck and hulking shoulders tapered into a narrow waist wrapped in a lifting belt. The wrestler's leotard he wore exposed forearms ridged in sinew and inked with tattoos. If Roth didn't know him better, he might have mistaken him for gang muscle.

Barq looked up from his stretching as Celeminé drew Roth into the court.

'Obodiah! My Throne – you've become ugly,' smiled Barq as he clinched Roth in a crushing hug.

'I haven't had the same luxuries you have had for the past months, no,' acknowledged Roth, still clasping forearms with his old friend.

'By all accounts, no you have not. Gurion has thoroughly briefed me on your misfortunes.'

Roth shrugged, almost dismissively. He looked around at the gymnasium and realised he could not remember the last time he had indulged in his daily routine of fist-fencing and callisthenics.

'What is the situation here? On Aridun, I mean,' asked Roth.

Barq flexed his wrists and rolled his jaw to warm it up. 'I'll tell you all about it while we spar.'

In a way it was their ritual. It was almost but not quite a rivalry that had developed ever since they were twig-limbed progena at the academy. In his day, Roth had been the champion tetherweight fist-fencer for his age group. He was slim but he was whippet-quick. Roth's multiple knockouts over anchorweight fencers several years his senior were still the stuff of legend within the progenium dormitories.

On the other hand, Barq was a scrapper. He was well versed in the linear system of military self-defence developed for the Cadian regiments and its surrounding subsectors. His rough brawling style was complemented by progeniate-level wrestling. Chokeholds, leg-locks, armbars and neck cranks composed the core of his unarmed arsenal.

'It's been years, Vandus. Either you've got better or you've too much confidence,' remarked Roth. He adopted a low fist-fencing stance, wide-legged, springing on his toes like a dancer. The lead fist was held straight forwards, poised like a swordsman in en garde. Across the dirt floor, his opponent Barq coiled up into a wrestler's half-crouch, hands held up in front of his face.

'Still practising that wimpy punch-fencing nonsense, I see.'

'It is a gentlemanly pursuit,' chided Roth. 'Now, are you just going to taunt me or will you tell me how Aridun fares?'

Barq stepped in cautiously. 'Aridun is at war. But with the slaughter across the region, Aridun is low-scale in comparison. The Archenemy have deployed mass aerial landings but the numbers aren't anywhere near as overwhelming as on the other core worlds.'

'How about the Ironclad motorised elements? They ran roughshod through Guard infantry back on Cantica.' Roth punctuated his question by pirouetting off his back foot and snapping his fist into a double jab.

The blows stung Vandus on the nose, catching him off guard. Growling like a wounded bull, Vandus circled off to the right. 'Archenemy forces have been mainly infantry. Vigilant aerial defence have limited their drop zones to the wilderness at least some three hundred kilometres out from the Southern Savannah.'

Seizing upon his pre-emptive blows, Roth glided forwards and uncurled his right hand in a straight cross. The blow connected with a satisfying snap against Barq's upper jaw. In reply Barq lunged out with a looping overhand punch, throwing all his weight behind it.

Roth took a pendulum-step backwards. With forearms raised like pillars, Roth trapped Barq's punch. It was a technique known as 'sticking hands'. Besides its array of fist strikes, fist-fencing also contained a thorough syllabus of fifty-one hand blocks and trapping techniques. Roth believed he had mastered forty of them by the last count. Pulling Barq off balance with his trapping block, Roth disengaged and pedalled away.

'What of the Medina Campaign? Does the defence hold across the system?' Roth asked between sharp intakes of breath.

'Worse than we'd feared. Of the half-dozen satellite worlds, only Sinope remains free and even then, recent weeks have seen some heavy fighting there. Kholpesh has mired to a war of attrition that we do not have the numbers to win.'

Barq shot in for a wrestler's takedown, dropping to his knees with his arms outstretched. Roth had been waiting for his tackle – Vandus ate several more sharp punches. Tap-tap on the jaw and nose.

'Which leaves me to ask. Why is my task group here? Gurion said I was needed,' said Roth, his breath becoming more laboured. To give himself space, his feet glided in radially symmetrical spirals, confounding his opponent.

'Because I requested you.'

'I'm flattered, old friend,' said Roth as he scored a jab right between Barq's eyes.

Livid red welts were beginning to appear on the cheek-bones and bridge of Vandus's nose. He shook his head to clear it and continued to speak as if unscathed.

'I've been here six months and I've unearthed a lot. I have a contact, a xeno-archaeologist who tracked down an item of interest being held for auction by a relic collector on Kholpesh.'

'You think you've found the Old Kings?'

Barq shrugged. 'Most likely not, but the relic dates back to the War of Reclamation and we may have a lead. Inquisitor Joaquim's agents have contacted me and seem to think it's important enough. I trust them, so it's the most solid lead we have thus far.'

Barq took a big penetrating step and tried the tackle again. This time Roth pivoted on the balls of his feet and whipped a flurry of punches at Barq's head. Six punches in under a second. Despite Barq's thickly corded neck, the wrestler was visibly rocked. He bulled forwards, striking with a series of knees, elbows and looping punches. The two fighters traded, exchanging a barrage of haemorrhaging strikes.

'Kholpesh – why not have Inquisitor Joaquim pursue it? He heads the Conclave Task Group on Kholpesh, does he not?' panted Roth as he circled away.

Barq closed the distance between them with a sweeping low kick. He lashed explosively in a wide arc with his shin but missed as Roth quick-stepped. Suddenly vulnerable, Barq shelled up his torso as Roth snapped his lead fist at the now-exposed head. Body head, body head, just like he had been taught in the textbooks.

'Haven't you heard?' Barq huffed between Roth's shots. 'Inquisitor Joaquim is dead. Three weeks ago, Archenemy mechanised forces made a concerted push for the outer shelf continents on Kholpesh.' Barq paused briefly as a crisp hook cracked his ribs. 'The Cantican 4th and 12th division were routed. Joaquim was amongst those killed.'

Roth was shocked. The grave news startled him so much he didn't even see Barq's takedown. Roth was slammed around the midriff. His feet cleared the air before his body came crunching down hard on the packed earth below. Momentarily dazed, the air stunned out of his lungs, Roth blinked. The equilibrium in his ears swirled with vertigo. Celeminé shrieked something in the background, but Roth couldn't make it out.

Then he began to choke. Barq was applying a forearm across the side of Roth's neck, jamming his weight behind the blade of his ulna. The chokehold was cutting off his carotid arteries. Blood pressurised in his head, thrumming so hard Roth could feel the tremor behind his sinus passages. He was blacking out.

'One for me,' growled Barq with laboured breaths. 'That's an Ezekiel choke. The Kasrkin taught me that one.'

Abruptly the pressure eased. Barq eased his hand off Roth's neck and the blood seeped back into circulation. Rolling off him, Barq slumped onto his back, breathing hard.

'Joaquim is dead?' Roth croaked. Propping himself up by on an elbow, he coughed.

Nodding, Barq gestured to Celeminé. 'The three of us are all that Gurion has at his disposal. As far as the Conclave goes anyway.'

'When do we leave for Kholpesh?'

'As swiftly as possible. Tomorrow I will be travelling by sauropod train into the Eridu Marches and linking up with the xeno-archaeologist. You can accompany me if you're feeling better.'

As she heard this, Celeminé stood up from the pommel horse she had been leaning against. 'Sauropod train? I've never been on one of those,' she said.

Roth shook his head. 'I need you to stay here and keep close scrutiny on Captain Pradal.'

Celeminé looked decidedly crestfallen, but acquiesced.

'Vandus, can we not travel by locomotive? I've heard Aridun has an excellent overland transit rail,' asked Roth.

Inquisitor Barq's mood darkened several shades. 'The steam locomotives have been decommissioned. The railways are far too susceptible to Archenemy attacks.'

'Aren't the Ironclad forces stalled beyond the demarcation line beyond the Cage Isles and western wastelands?' asked Celeminé.

What she said was true. The heavy concentration of lassilos and other anti-air defences had driven enemy deployment out beyond the Cage Isles. By reconnaissance reports, the fragmented islands were now teeming with Archenemy nautical forces. Shoals of iron submersibles, sea-barges and plated galleys filled the Cage Isle channels, their bellies swollen with cargo and enemy troops. Imperial outposts on the demarcation line harassed them with heavy ordnance, but the vessels sailed largely unchallenged, deploying forces freely across Aridun.

'Most of them. But the Ironclad are raiders. Rogue bands have continually harassed Imperial supply lines. At least by sauropod we won't be immobilised by a destroyed section of track. Since the outbreak of invasion, the Archenemy have detonated twelve hundred kilometres' worth of locomotive railway.'

Roth nodded grimly. They were dealing with a different sort of enemy. The Ironclad were raiders first and soldiers second. Even when they did not have the advantage of numerical superiority, as was the case on Aridun, they inflicted disproportionate damage on civic and military infrastructure.

'So, armoured and armed for the trip then?' Roth asked.

'I wouldn't leave the southern belt without anything short of serious firepower,' Vandus answered flatly.

Roth was about to laugh until he realised that his old friend was very serious.

CHAPTER TWELVE

THEY DESCENDED FROM off-world in their holding pen, transferred onto a brig-lander and escorted by a squadron of Archenemy interceptors for landfall. On board the brig, they were guarded by a hundred veteran Ironclad – scarred, knotted fighters bedecked in the collected trophies of war. As prisoners went, they were a valued prize indeed.

When their captors herded them off the landing ramp, Silverstein winced at the unaccustomed glare of searing sunlight. He had lost count of how many days he had been caged, and his augmetics reacted badly. Lens shutters flared for low-light reception; the sudden flood of sun almost blinded him.

When the apertures of his bioptics recalibrated and his vision flickered back, Silverstein almost wished he had been blinded permanently. He found himself in a war camp of the Archenemy.

The scene before him was a vivid nightmare in flesh. A vast gridwork of parked vehicles covered the scorched

and salted earth. They had laid waste to a square kilometre of ground, burning the land into a blackened
wound. Amongst wheels and tracks of their vehicles,
bivouacs and camouflage netting were erected as shelter.
It was a muster yard of mechanised machinery – Scavenger light tanks, Chimeras, Hellhounds, FPVs and
eight-wheelers, dormant like sleeping predators. They
marshalled under the watchful gaze of sentry towers
erected on skeleton girders.

A pall of chemical smoke, fuel and burning plastek cut
the air. Presiding over the encampment were two crude
wooden idols, seven metres in height. Carved with
rough, blunt strokes, the idols depicted a leering daemon, its tongue hanging past its waist, carving an infant
from the belly of a pregnant woman. In their own crude,
supernatural way, the idols were the most deeply disturbing things Silverstein had ever seen.

THE PRISONERS WERE frog-marched around the perimeter
of the camp, a snaking earthen embankment raised to
chest height. Soldiers of the Archenemy stared at them.
Just the thought of so many tainted eyes boring into his
back coated Silverstein in a film of cold sweat. Some of
the Ironclad chuckled, in evil, delighted little burbles,
running a finger against their throats.

To ignore them would have been impossible. He
feigned disinterest, indignantly straightening the gold
piping on his filthy, decaying jacket. When he had been
a gunbearer for his father's hunting trips, he had often
thought that by closing his eyes and not seeing the prey,
then perhaps the prey would not see him. He reverted
back to his childhood instincts and squeezed his eyes
shut. It wasn't that Silverstein was a coward, no; he was
just trying to keep his sanity intact.

'Uhup uhup,' an Ironclad snarled into Silverstein's ear.
He was shoved as his tormentor pointed at the back of

an armoured transport truck. Silverstein smoothed his collar and levelled his gaze at the Ironclad. For his defiance, the Ironclad punched him hard in the kidney and hurled him up onto the back of the truck by his lapels. Doubled over in shock, Silverstein felt rather than saw his fellow captives pile onto the truck after him, crushing him with their weight.

The hatch of the panelled truck was shut, eclipsing the light like a closet door. Cloyingly hot, suffocating and pitch-black, Silverstein strained to hear the low rumble of other engines grumbling to life. A convoy escort, he surmised. They were being transported elsewhere, to whatever fate awaited them. Outside, someone pounded the side of their truck with hard, reverberating slaps. It was followed by a peal of muffled laughter as the truck kicked into gear.

There was nothing Silverstein could do but wait and see what became of him.

IT WAS, AS expected, a bright, humid dawn as the two inquisitors tramped through the reef-lands. Roth placed a hand to shield his eyes against the suns as he peered at the rather peculiar mode of transport that awaited him. Despite his travels, he had never seen anything like it.

The sauropod train was saddling up on the humid mud flats, beyond the outskirts of Aridun Civic. The reptilian beasts were great and grey, some of the male bulls growing to six metres tall at shoulder height. Down the cabled length of their long swaying necks ran a plume of dull feathery spines.

Roth counted eight of the beasts tethered by harness, seating platforms swaying from their backs. When they brayed, they emitted a sonorous trumpet from the hollows of their cranial crests. Roth found the sound at once both eerie and majestic, like a suite of brass horns resonating from some deep ocean.

Fussing around the stomping pillars of their feet, caravaneers adjusted caparisons of gaudy beaded fabric, tassels and jingling silver discs. Shaded wicker sedans swayed upon their backs, some beasts already carrying a dozen handlers, musterers and guards. On the decorative platform of the lead caravan beast, Roth recognised the distinctive outline of a belt-fed heavy stubber.

'Vandus, you always did remember to travel with elegance,' Roth said sarcastically as he plugged the polished boots of his fighting-plate deep into mud.

'You can always walk if you wish,' Barq retorted as he hauled himself up a hemp ladder that dangled down a sauropod flank.

Inquisitor Barq, ever the eccentric, was clad in wargear of a sort Roth had never seen before. It was, in a way, typical of the Ordo Xenos. Barq was suited in an olive-drab bodyglove, but from the abdomen up he was shod in a hulking armoured rig. His torso, shoulders and arms flexed with thick, cabled plating. The pugnacious outline was reinforced with sledgehammer fists and piston banks along both arms. Multiple heavy-calibre barrels arrayed in racks of eight lined the back of each armoured fist. Despite its armament, it was the milky green of the enamel and the oddly organic curves of Barq's rig that caught Roth's attention.

'Xenos-tech?' said Roth as he scaled the ladder.

Barq laughed breezily. 'Not quite. I procured this suit from a pompous house of a particular upper-tier hive.'

'Would it be prudent of me not to ask you which noble house this was?'

Barq winked. 'It would be for the best. I had suspicions that they may have had limited dealings with the xenos tau – but benign enough for me to let it slide. They were very grateful and gifted me this marvellous suit.'

'You're getting soft.'

'And you're getting stiff in your old age,' retorted Barq.

Roth shook his head as he settled in the creaking wicker of their sedan. 'You're dancing with devils, Vandus. I could have you martialled before the ordos for that act alone.'

'Not if I silence you first,' chortled Vandus, flexing his segmented paws.

Roth was poised to riposte but the crack of the musterer's whip and the resonant bellow of sauropods drowned his words. With a lurching, lolling rhythm the great beasts began to move and the winding rampart of the Fortress Chains receded into the distance.

BY STEAM LOCOMOTIVE, the trip would have taken less than three hours but conflict had forced the decommissioning of locomotive rail. By sauropod it took the better part of a day. But Roth didn't mind the time spent. After the catastrophes of the preceding weeks, he appreciated the open country.

Everywhere, Roth experienced the new era of a planet in evolution. They plodded through biotic reefs that purportedly sprawled out to the coastal basins – endless kilometres of whispering horsetail fern, cycads and clustered conifer. But he saw too the vestiges of a past ecosystem. Monolithic salt flats, once thermal oceans, lined the horizon with bars of crystalline white. Shale rifts, red bed sandstone and calcite plains marked the graves of a former environment.

Most startling of all were the abandoned city-states that kept silent sentry on their trail. When the suns shifted axis, thousands of years ago, Aridun had been besieged by hurricanes, floods and temperatures that had boiled the moisture from the earth. Long since abandoned, these cities crested the horizon as hollow skeletons, black with age and neglect.

At least twice during their trek they encountered packs of dog-sized carnivores. Attracted by the warm musk of humans and the ground tremor of sauropods, the reptiles paralleled the caravan at a cautious distance. Caravan guards fired lasguns over their heads to scatter them.

'Those are just heel-biting scavengers. It's the Talon Squalls you should be afraid of,' said Barq. He handed Roth a gilded telescope with his ponderous hands and gestured to the distance.

Roth had indeed heard of them already. The animals had quite a reputation amongst those inclined to study fauna. Naturally, Roth was a curious and learned individual, although the biological sketches did not invoke the true ferocity of such animals. Peering into the telescope, Roth spied gangs of flightless birds powering across the southern horizon on long loping strides. Even at a distance they appeared large, far larger than any avian had the right to be.

'And what of the Archenemy?' Roth enquired.

'The aerial defences have driven enemy deployment far out beyond the wastelands. Splinter raiding parties, however, are a real threat,' Barq said.

Roth could understand how Aridun had escaped the worst of the Archenemy attentions, at least for now. The environment was not exactly conducive in supporting the large-scale movement of troops, especially raiders with poor supply lines. It was hot, it was barren and it was open ground.

Roth sat back, wiping his brow. By late afternoon the air was dry and quiet. Even under the shaded pagoda of their sedan the temperature was in the low forties. He was not acclimatised, and what's more he was beginning to seriously regret wearing his Spathaen fighting-plate. The metal was incubating him in a cocoon of prickling heat.

'This xeno-archaeologist, what ungodly effort would draw him out here, to a desolate warzone?' Roth muttered, mostly to himself.

'Actually, as part of the bargain in aiding us I've promised her a secure transport out of the Medina conflict zone. She came to Aridun in order to study the new cycle of history and was trapped by the initial Archenemy offensive.'

'A she?'

'Oh yes. Professor Madeline de Medici of the Katon-Rouge Universitariat.'

At the mention of her name, Roth clucked his tongue. He was entirely familiar with the works of Professor de Medici. She was a prominent xeno-archaeologist, a leading scholar in her field within the star system if not the entire subsector. Her works were prolific, including *A Treatise on Pre-Imperial Man* and *Reflective Studies of an Early Eastern Fringe*. Roth admired her dedicated approach to field research as much as her eloquence in script.

Had Roth not been a servant of the Imperium, he had often fancied that he would have become a scholar. Indeed, he took his academic fascination past an amateur hobby, and his large estate on Arlona was more of a dedicated library than a manor. To Roth, study was a compulsion. He had been smitten by the concept of the warrior-scholar ever since he read of the Gojoseon Kingdom on ancient Terra, and their caste of Flower Knights or Flower 'youths'. Such youths were socialised from a young age in the arts of calligraphy, archery, theatre and horsemanship. They were the symbiosis of martial and mental prowess, and a symbol of spiritual balance amongst the ancient Asiatic realms. Roth had long held a romantic fascination for these knights and despite being older now, a part of him continued to extol those virtues.

THE PETRIFIED FOREST of 0Eridu lay eight hundred kilometres from the Archenemy demarcation line. The

wilderness was located exactly half-way between the
southern savannah of Aridun Civic and the Archenemy
amassing beyond the wasteland rim. Roth and Barq dismounted the sauropods at the edge of the woods and
proceeded on foot.

The geosite resembled a sculpture garden of melted,
wrinkling rock. Pillars of argon cobalt and organic mineral rose like titanic chess pieces. Everywhere Roth
looked, he caught fleeting glimpses of frozen time, the
fossilised imprint of a leaf on a stone, fronds and whorls
against bedrock, the spinal column of some extinct beast
surfacing above the sediment.

Overhead, wilting, leafless trees some sixty metres tall
created an arterial web with their frail, feathery branches.
Some of the trees had been opalised, trailing glistening
seams of pearlescent gem. Sun dappled through the
bowers, cutting stark patterns on the mosaic floor.

Under the bowers of bearded wood fungus, Roth
found Madeline de Medici's excavation team toiling in a
narrow little gorge. The labourers were local, bronzed
from constant sun exposure. They must have been desperately poor rural workers, considering most other
Aridunians had refused to stray far from the southern
belt since the invasion.

As the inquisitors approached the excavation site, half
a dozen men rushed to intercept them. Instead of the
khaki overalls of the excavation crew, these men wore
dark linen morning coats with black three-piece suits.
Instead of hauling picks and shovels, gilded hand-las pis-
tolletes were suspended by gold chain from their belts.
Pinned to their lapels was the crest of administrative
office on Aridun – the Governor's seal.

'Halt! Stop where you are!' they shouted.

It almost made Roth burst out laughing. The armed
group were a pompous bunch – svelte, mincing men
completely out of their element. They tried to look

intimidating and professional, but were far too sunburnt and miserable to be taken seriously. They were little more than technocrats playing soldier.

Putting his hands up in mock surrender, Roth cast a sidelong grin at Barq. His old friend shrugged his power-armoured shoulders with a mechanical whir. They were alike in many ways, in mischief especially.

'Disarm yourselves. Lay your weapons on the ground and lie face down. Immediately!' ordered one of the armed men, levelling his pistol at Roth. He appeared to be their leader, a tall man with the long, haughty face of an Administratum clerk. This clerk, however, had obviously chem-nourished the muscles of his arms to be more aesthetically intimidating. Neither of the inquisitors were overly impressed.

'You're joking, right?' snorted Barq. He held up the heavy-gauge bolt-racks on the back of his hands. Roth wasn't sure whether Barq was indicating the idiocy of their request, or whether it was a subtle threat. Either way, Roth found it immensely entertaining.

'I don't know who you think you're talking to, but I am Lorenzo Miaz Hieron, envoy and security specialist of Madame de Medici,' he trilled with a measure of shrill indignation.

'I'll talk to you however I please,' Roth goaded, stringing the man along.

'Do you want to die? Are you stupid? Do you know Aridun is at war? State your purpose or suffer the consequences!' Hieron cried. His fellows agreed, heads bobbing like token birds.

'Lorenzo! Laslett, Hamil, Piotr, the rest of you! Mind your manners!' came a voice from behind Hieron. It was a woman's voice, imperious and stately without even having to shout.

Roth did not immediately recognise the esteemed Madame de Medici. She was far younger than he had

expected. He had envisaged a wizened, perhaps moth-
erly academic; instead the woman before him had the
porcelain skin, high cheekbones and delicate figure of a
well-bred noble's daughter.

Madeline de Medici ducked out from the flap of her
canvas tent. She balanced a lace parasol delicately in
gloved hands. Given the climate, her attire was entirely
inappropriate: a modest pencil skirt and double-breasted
coat of twill. Her face was blushed with subtle rouge and
her hair curled into loose chestnut ringlets so fashion-
able amongst the upper-spire aristocrats. Anywhere else
but on an archaeological site within the heart of a warzone, Roth would have mistaken her as a spire heiress.

'Madame de Medici?' said Roth, still unsure if it were
truly she.

'Madeline Rebequin Louise de Medici. But please, do
call me Madeline,' she said, curtsying.

The inquisitors both bowed graciously.

'Madame Madeline, I am Obodiah Roth. I must admit
I am a great admirer of your works. *On the Natural Cycles
of War and Conflict* was an impeccably researched collection of essays.'

Madeline tilted her nose up. 'Inquisitors, you flatter
me,' she said.

'Inquisitors?' spluttered Hieron, backing away. He ushered his colleagues aside like chastised children.

When the guards were out of the earshot, Madeline
strolled closer to the inquisitor. 'Excuse them. I am sincerely embarrassed by their behaviour.'

'Call this a casual observation, but those men are not
fighters,' Roth said.

'No indeed they are not. But they claim to be. So let
them. The Governor of Aridun provided me with some
of his household custodians. The Governor insisted.'

'Was the Governor trying to get you killed? The Archenemy are held at bay less than a day's travel from here.

You should not come out this far with those fools as protection.'

'Don't tie yourself in knots, inquisitor, I can look after myself,' she sniffed.

She was perhaps correct, thought Roth. Of all her texts, the one which stood out to Roth was her recently documented field study of ancient pylons scattered across rimward planets of the Eastern Fringe. The book was in limited circulation and included woodcut illustrations of an eldar attack on her excavation team. She had evidently escaped, and her resultant accounts of the tale caused quite a stir, even amongst the ordos.

'Be as it may,' Barq interjected, 'it is time for you to send those fops back to the Governor's estates and come with us. We are pressed for time.'

'I've got several trunks of field equipment and research I will be needing,' Madeline called over her shoulder as she twirled away. 'Have my crew load them onto your vehicles.'

'We don't have vehicles, madame. Only sauropods,' Roth called after her.

She halted, turning slowly. Her lips pursed, her heart-shaped face florid. 'I cannot ride by sauropod! A lady does not travel by pack beast!' she implored.

'You can always walk,' chuckled Roth.

CHAPTER THIRTEEN

LORD MARSHAL KHMER plucked a pistol from the tiered cabinet. It was a heavy hammerlock pistol of dark wood, as long as his forearm and fluted with a sweeping grip. Acorns and leaves of crisp topaz inlaid the pistol grip while vines of silver filigree chased the barrel. A weapon of its calibre had not been used since the Hadrian Emergency in the Bastion Stars, circa 762.M41.

Khmer had collected this particular hammerlock as the trophy of a duel many years ago. The Naval admiral who had lost his pistol had also lost several fingers to Khmer's sabre. It was fortunate, Khmer mused, that one of those severed digits had been the officer's trigger finger.

Inserting a cartridge into the breech, Khmer sauntered over to his shooting gallery. It was his own gallery, his very own on board the *Carthage*. The hall had once been a troops barracks, which could have housed two platoons of sixty. Now it was a lead-lined hall, latticed shooting booths facing a target gallery at varying ranges of twenty to two hundred paces. One entire wall of the gallery was devoted to the magnificent vault of Khmer's antique weapons display. It had glass-paned racks containing fusils, flak muskets, hand-crafted solid sluggers and ancient rifles as long as a man was tall. There was even a sleek assembly of military-grade lasgun variants.

The marshal squared up in a double-handed shooting stance and took aim at a painted canvas target at eighty paces. The canvas was painted with an almost child-like caricature of a daemon, eyes bulging, teeth gnashing. He drilled three rounds into the target, the kinetic impacts whipping the target pad like a kite in high wind. The hammering snap of shots was echoed by the lead-lined acoustics of the hall. For Khmer there could be no better sound.

'Clean this for me,' said Khmer as he tossed the pistol into the waiting hands of a junior officer. 'If I find a lick of carbon in the working parts, I'll have your hide for guncloth.'

The marshal strode over to his antique arsenal and selected an autogun. The piece was nondescript as far as his collection went, an obsolete rifle of stamped metal and ageing wood. Well over a metre in length, its characteristic iron sights, scythe-shaped magazine and hardwood stock bespoke of its age and previous owners. The autogun was crude but it had history.

Khmer was a great appreciator of history. Each of the weapons had a different tale to tell, a different war front experienced, from the up-armoured lasgun of the Bastion Ward Interior Guard, to the revolving hand cannon plundered from the techno-barbarians of the deeper Shoal Clusters. History was written by those who shot fast, and shot true.

'Lord marshal! A word, please.'

Khmer placed the autogun back in its velvet cradle and looked up to see Forde Gurion storming into his chambers. Judging by the galloping clank of his augmetic legs, the inquisitor had not come for personal reasons.

'Forde Gurion,' Khmer acknowledged with an air of nonchalance. He turned back to inspecting his weapons.

'I must speak with you, lord marshal, now if you please,' Gurion said through clenched teeth.

Almost wearily, Marshal Khmer looked at Gurion. The inquisitor lord stood before him, the muscles in his jaw twitching, a document brief viced hard in his mechanical hand. Khmer dismissed his attendee with a wave.

'Gurion, what seems to be troubling you?'

The inquisitor shook the parchment in front of him. 'This. This states that as of 06:00 yesterday, Imperial reinforcements from the Lupina chain-worlds were re-routed away from the Medina war zone. Seventy-six thousand riflemen of the Lupinee 102nd were diverted to shore up defences for the Bastion Stars.'

'I don't see the problem,' said Khmer, as he began to polish a flak-musket with the sleeve of his dress uniform.

'The problem, lord marshal, is that you authorised this diversion.' Gurion spat the last few words like venom.

'That is true. I did what would be best for the long-term objectives of the campaign.'

'Need I remind you that the Council of Conclusions has decreed our objectives? We are to hold the line at the Medina Worlds until such time as the enigma of the Old Kings can be dealt with.'

Finally, Khmer put down his musket and turned to face Gurion. He cleared his throat.

'Those are your objectives, Gurion. My military objective is simple – to deny Chaos forces the space, coordination and ability to conquer the subsector. In this context, a concentrated defence in the Bastion Stars is how I will achieve this.'

'That decision is not yours to make. My Conclave has conclusive evidence that suggests the Old Kings myth is of threat-level alpha.'

'You are not a soldier.' Khmer said, sincerely lamenting. 'You do not understand war. We do not win wars by suggestive evidence. We win wars by logic and strategy. Can you not understand that?'

Gurion shook his head, not because he could not understand, but because he realised that Khmer was too hardened in his ways. Peeling aside the lapel of his coat, Gurion let his Inquisitorial rosette tumble from its chain. 'Lord marshal, the Inquisition works in its own ways.'

If Khmer understood the symbolism, he paid it no heed. Instead the lord marshal wandered down the aisle of gun racks until he found what he was looking for. He took up a lasgun, peered down its scope and balanced the rifle in his hands.

'Do you see this rifle, Gurion?' he asked. It was a soft gun-metal grey all over, with a collapsible stock and a shortened muzzle that gave the weapon a squat, brutal profile.

'Yes. That is a lasgun. Evidently, I am not as well versed in the specifics as you,' replied Gurion, clearly uninterested.

'This is not just any lasgun. See this picatinny rail here?' said Khmer, pointing to the grooved carry handle. 'And the shorter length of the barrel and handguard? Modified for airborne deployment?' he continued, indicating towards the polished barrel and the smooth grey polymer of the body.

'I see it,' Gurion answered cautiously.

'This is a Guard-issue weapon of the Bravanda Centennial regiments. But more than that, this weapon saw action during the reclamation of the Bravanda Provincial Palaces. In 870.M41, the elite wealth-barons, a dissident faction known as the Revolutionists, imprisoned the Regent of Bravanda in his own palace. The ruling elite and the landed gentry established their own governance, and the rural masses of Bravanda lamented but could do nothing.'

'I am familiar with the Revolutionist uprising on Bravanda. Please continue.'

Khmer shouldered the rifle to aim at a phantom enemy in the distance.

'You have to understand, the Imperial Guard, we represent the people. And the Regent was the people's Regent. On the first day of the revolution, without specific orders, a small group of loyalist Guardsmen stormed the Provincial Palace.'

Lowering the weapon, Khmer racked the charger bolt and stripped the barrel in one liquid motion.

'This very gun was in the possession of a Sergeant Natum Quarry, 7/7th Centennial. He held the gates alone for forty-five minutes against Revolutionists. He was one of five brothers, all of them Guardsmen, and the son of a manufactorum father who often worked through his rest shifts in order to feed his boys as they were growing up. Sergeant Quarry cost the dissidents some forty casualties. Do you know what the Revolutionists did to him once they got him? Many of the dissidents were convicts, condemned men that the wealth-barons had freed from the penal colonies. When they finally got him they mutilated him and paraded parts of him on pict. His posthumous Medal of Valorous Citation was awarded to an empty grave.'

'That is a stirring tale,' Gurion admitted. 'But I fail to see the connection to our issue at hand.'

'The point I'm trying to make should be self-evident. War is conducted by guns and behind every gun, a man. Medina is of no strategic value and I will not waste the lives of my soldiers here, when we could make a stand on the Bastion Stars, alongside the Lupi-nee Rifles, the Bastion Ward regiments, Montaigh, Arpadis Mortant.'

Gurion sighed deeply. This was Lord Marshal Khmer at his best. For all his egomania, his political viciousness and his pomp and flair, the man was a brilliant leader of men. He would not be wearing his rank if he were any-thing less. It wounded Gurion to think that he might have to resort to Inquisitorial authority and dethrone the lord marshal. The Medina Campaign was demor-alised as it was without the loss of its highest-ranking officer.

'Lord marshal. Let us, for a second, forget about the Old Kings of Medina. Even then, you would be aban-doning the Medina Corridor, and leaving billions of Imperial citizens to die at the hands of Chaos.'

'You may think me a monster. But I do what I must to deny the Archenemy. It takes a monster to do what I do. I am a lord marshal. I command killers in the act of killing. You stick to what you know,' bellowed Khmer. His introspective persona fell away like a curtain and his face seeped with veiny red. Khmer's legendary temper was building pressure.

'I understand. But I have my reasons and I would not be here if I did not think it was crucial. My Conclave is hard at work in achieving the same objectives you do. The forces of Chaos are not irrational, why do they want Medina if you don't? Why?'

'I don't know. I don't need to know. We choose to fight our battle in the Bastion Stars. Not here!' snarled Khmer. He threw Sergeant Quarry's lasgun across the chamber. The gun skipped across the marble floor and crashed into a display stand of long-arms, bringing down a forest of muskets.

Unflappable, Gurion betrayed no emotion. 'You can rage all you wish, Khmer. But I am the Inquisition. Do not force me to wrest control of the campaign and your Canticans away from you. You are a fine general and it would be a tremendous loss to the campaign.'

Teeth bared, his face utterly bestial, Khmer leaned in close on Gurion. The inquisitor lord remained stony faced, his augmetic hand hovering over his Lugos. Gurion knew he could not be complacent: Khmer was far too unpredictable. A raging lord marshal with an arsenal of weapons in arm's reach made for a volatile combination.

'It doesn't matter,' Khmer spat. 'Your Task Groups on Aridun are finished.'

It was the only thing Khmer had said so far that elicited a tremor of shock in Gurion. No one was supposed to know his Task Groups were on Aridun but the Conclave. Gurion had kept no written data of their status, had discussed their situation with no one. Yet the inquisitor said nothing. Gurion had been at this game too long to betray his emotions. In his time serving the Inquisition, he had lost sixty per cent of his body to conflict. A man so scarred became honed to a rough edge. He had learned to keep his face passive, his mouth shut and his eyes open. He would watch the lord marshal, because that was what he did best.

Recoiling, as if he had said too much, the sudden change in Khmer's demeanour was startling. Loosening out his shoulders, the lord marshal turned away from Gurion as if they had not spoken at all. He loaded a fresh power cell into the lasgun and drifted almost absent-mindedly towards his gallery booths.

'Before I go,' Khmer called to Gurion over his shoulder, 'I would like to remind you that I am the last piece of sinew holding this entire campaign together. Take me away, and Medina will come crashing down around your ears, inquisitor.'

* * *

NIGHT WAS ALWAYS a time of calm at the temple. But tonight, an unexpected visitor stalked through its empty corridors.

Ghostly and swathed in shadow, her long limbs moved so fast, so awkwardly, that she seemed to flit between positions. Not really walking, but almost flickering between the alcoves to the columns, from column to underneath the stairs.

The priests had taken their evening supper. The patients had returned to their wards and infirmaries. The arterial corridors were lambent with the monochrome light of the moon. In the central prayer hall, a single shaft of moon slanted from the atrium ceiling, the translucent pillar swimming with motes of dust.

Everything was so utterly still that the spectral shifting of the shadow seemed brutally intrusive. She had entered through the atrium, detaching from the vaulted ceiling like a liquid droplet. Then she had darted her way from shadow to shadow, hugging the inky depths of architecture.

As she skimmed past the light, she revealed glimpses of her form. Sweeping, corded limbs shod in vambraces and greaves of hardened leather binding. The flash and flicker of naked blades.

The intruder scaled the walls with effortless ease, limbs rippling like an arachnid. Vaulting over the lip of a third-storey landing, she prowled down into what appeared to be a temple kitchen.

It was lighter here. Flat stone benches and clay ovens dominated the open space. Cauldrons, copper pots and ranks of clay jugs arranged in neat rows like an army of terracotta.

Three priests in their vestments of stark white hospitalier tunics were scrubbing clay platters at a water trough. They were deep in murmurs of conversation and did not see the shadow that crept in behind them.

She slid out three throwing needles and flicked them casually at a distance of fifteen metres. The piercing slivers entered the base of the victim's skull, between the second and third vertebrae. Two of the priests collapsed, their nervous systems shutting down, their legs folding. The third priest spun around, in time to have a throwing needle enter the hollow beneath his sternum.

As he died the last thing he saw was the face of his murderer, the stylised mask of a grinning jester – its teeth long and leering, its eyes slitted in perpetual laughter.

The assassin whispered away from the murder scene and drifted down a tight, winding ribbon of steps. She emerged in the northern ward. It was a long hall where the mentally infirm would spend their daylight hours, wandering absent-mindedly and conversing in a sporadic fashion.

It was almost empty, the narrow arched windows casting long strips of alternating light and darkness into the hall. At the far end, sunk into a rocking chair, was the still form of a patient who never moved from his perch. A veteran of the Guard, the man now spent his waking hours staring blankly at the wall, his nails digging crescents into the armrests of his chair.

The assassin dispatched him quickly with a narrow blade and moved on.

The northern ward opened into the infirmary. A line of brass-plated doors were set into the clay walls that housed the individual dormitories of the psychiatric patients. The windows that banked the corridor were barred.

Drawing a spine-saw, the assassin entered the dorms in methodical succession. She worked quickly, flickering in and out of the rooms, attending to each patient. Twice, the night-shift priests accidentally came upon her. Twice, she garrotted them, dragging the corpses into the dorms and locking the doors.

The assassin emerged from the last door at the end of the corridor. Her spine-saw was feathered with long strings of blood. The jester's mask of black and white was now contrasted with perfect droplets of red.

Unlatching a pouch from her utility belt, the assassin checked her chron. She was dead on schedule. Sheathing her spine-saw, the assassin ghosted into the western ward. By dawn, the Temple of the Tooth would be truly empty.

CHAPTER FOURTEEN

ROTH WAS AWAKENED by a scream.

Even through the hazy fog of sleep, the cry was unmistakeably chilling. The timbre was shrill, agonised, and almost plaintive. He could recognise the sound of death anywhere.

Kicking himself off the bed in a tangle of linen, Roth groped for his plasma pistol. The candles in his room had thawed to sludge as he slept, and it was pitch black. His palm grazed the cold, heavy metal of a pistol grip and his frantic heartbeat slowed to a controlled feather. The ascending hum of gas fusion as he powered the Sunfury off safety made him feel secure, like a torch in the night.

Then came another scream, closer this time, a long drawn-out warble that ended abruptly in a hacking gasp.

Roth briefly considered suiting up in the fighting-plate, scattered in pieces across his dormitory floor. Once he steeled his resolve, his realised the idiocy of such a notion. Instead, he slid into the blue silk robe that he had shed at the foot of his bed. He made for the door, but doubled back and donned his tabard of reactive obsidian. Just to be safe.

He burst out of his room, pistol leading, but stopped short at the threshold. Roth was not sure if what he was seeing was real. The scene before him pulsed from his pupils to his retina and into his visual cortex, but part of his brain refused to accept it. It was all too ludicrous.

The door opened into the atrium, an open-air tiled courtyard. From the arched columns and tympanums, several corpses were hung. In the centre of the atrium, where a stone fountain babbled gently, the water was crimson. Propped up around the fountain, four dead priests sat upright. One was missing his hands, another his mouth gaped without a tongue, the third had no ears and the last one seemed to stare at Roth with raw, empty eye sockets.

The symbolism was not lost on Roth. It was the closing scene from Methuselah's tragedy *The Four Hells of a Heretic King*. The fourth act of the piece traditionally involved the hubris of King Messanine and his final punishment in the one hundred and nine layers of hell. It was, for lack of a better interpretation, a warning against the impious and unfaithful. Back on his home world of Sancti Petri, Roth had seasonal passes to all the local theatre companies, and this piece had been his favourite. But any previous rendition he had seen could not compare to the visceral horror of the vision before him.

'Heretic…' a voice whispered, almost into his ear. The voice was silky, smoky and shrouded in shadow.

A lesser man would have hesitated, perhaps even turned to find the source of that voice. Roth knew better.

He launched himself into a headlong tumble as something cord-sharp and whisper-fast sliced the air above his head. Rolling into a crouch, Roth pivoted and took aim with his plasma pistol.

His assailant kicked the weapon cleanly from his grasp. It was, Roth thought with self-admonishment, too easy.

'Be still heretic, we'll make this quick.'

Roth rolled onto his arse in a backwards tumble to create distance. The assassin stalked him into the courtyard. Out there, under the watery light of the moon, Roth saw his killer clearly.

She wore a black-grey bodyglove, the polymer fabric swirling like iridescent petroleum, blending in and out of the shadows. Roth estimated at least a dozen various types of blade, hook and shuriken were attached to her various slings and harnesses although he couldn't be sure – his head was pounding with adrenaline.

The assassin stalked towards him, hunching like a coiled feline. Her face was an inscrutable mask painted in the macabre form of a laughing jester. Roth recognised a death cult assassin when he saw one. She did not possess the techno-wizardry of a temple trained Assassinorum agent, but what she lacked she made up for with ferocity. For a death cult assassin, it was not a matter of eliminating a target; she was less calculating, less programmed than a Culexus or a Callidus assassin. Instead, she used her rudimentary arsenal of blades with a creative splendour that heightened murder into the realm of theatrics.

Kicking backwards across the tiles, Roth sprung up onto his feet, adopting a fist-fencer's orthodox stance. He would not lie to himself: unarmed, he was as good as dead.

The assassin flicked something at him.

A throwing needle pierced his forearm, sinking deep into his muscle spindles. The pain sent sparks of shock down into his elbow.

'No poison?' Roth mused, trying to maintain his wavering composure.

'I said keep still. You didn't. So we can make this slow and painful,' she replied.

Slowly, purposefully, the Assassin unsheathed a razor's edge from her back. It was not a murder implement; this was a weapon for close-quarter combat. A slivered oblong of metal, the wafer-thin slice of monofilament blade was exactly a metre in length and a uniform one finger's width wide. In the night, it somewhat resembled a broken sword with a two-handed rubberised grip.

As the Assassin slashed the air with it, the razor emitted a shrill humming resonance. It was so sharp it was splitting the air, Roth mused.

'At least humour me, tell me who sent you,' said Roth, backing away and biding for time.

'I am doing the Emperor's work,' she hissed. Without telegraphing her movements, in a single mercurial surge of energy, the Assassin aimed her razor at the gaps between the tessellating panes of his obsidian tabard. The blow was so fast, so precise, without an iota of wasted effort. One stroke, one kill.

Roth moved forwards on his opponent, his fist-fencing instincts possessing him. Had he tried to slip backwards, the razor's edge would have surely taken off his trunk, cleanly above the hip. As it was, he moved inside of her blow. The razor teethed into the black glass, glittering fragments exploding into the air. The tabard was not armour, not against physical attacks anyway, but it was enough to deflect the weapon's finite edge.

Roth would not get another chance like that. He seized on his fleeting advantage, grabbing the hand that wielded the razor's edge. It was all he could do to delay her. Like a coordinated chess game, the Assassin somersaulted out of his grip, landing four or five paces away.

Then the air erupted with the hammering report of gunfire, sparking and roaring into the still night air. Both Roth and his assassin went to ground as tracers lit up the atrium. The shots almost seemed indiscriminate in nature.

On his stomach, Roth peered up at the muzzle flash. He saw Madeline de Medici, under the atrium arches, standing in her chiffon nightgown, firing away with a greasy machine pistol. Her marksmanship was enthusiastic yet poor, the gun bucking under her barely contained grip.

Judging by her frantic rate of fire, her gun would be spent in several seconds. Roth had to act quickly. Shimmying on his hands and knees, he retrieved his Sunfury from the base of the fountain.

He gripped the pistol just as Madeline's weapon clicked empty. The Assassin was already up, sprinting towards Madeline with long, floating strides. Her razor's edge was raised like a scorpion's sting, coiled to strike.

'I am Inquisition!' Roth bellowed, emphasising his announcement with a shudder of psychic will.

He could not see the reaction beneath her jester's mask. But judging by the slight shift in her shoulders, the tiny recoil of her step, it was not something she had known. The Assassin halted, her mask peering impassively at Roth.

It was her mistake. Roth fired four successive shots, a steady draw of the trigger – *tap tap tap tap*. It unleashed a pillar of incandescent energy, trailing threads of atomic afterburn. The Assassin was vaporised, her constituent atoms dispersing into the curtain of heat and steam. Within seconds, all that remained were the molten puddles of metal blades, cooling rapidly on the atrium tiles. The wall of consecrated mud behind her was now a crackling web of burnt, flaking clay.

Madeline dropped her gun, her hands and expression frozen in a mixture of terror and shock. A door swung open. Vandus Barq, a sheet wrapped around his naked self, stumbled from his room.

'Where in Throne's name were you?' growled Roth, adrenaline still glanding hot through his veins.

'Sweet merciful…' Barq gasped, his eyes wide as he took in the carnage.

The others of the Task Group rushed into the atrium in their sleepwear, evidently roused by the skirmish. Celeminé and Pradal stopped as they neared Roth, wordless. Neither could do anything but stare at the meticulous arranged corpses. Celeminé's shoulders began to tremble. Pradal hugged his lasrifle close to his chest.

'Where were you?' Roth repeated, shouting this time.

Barq shook his head slowly. 'I'm sorry, Roth. I must have slept through it,' he admitted guiltily.

'Look around,' Roth snarled, pointing at the dead, at the jagged seams of bullet-holes, the blood that laced the tiles in glistening starburst patterns. 'You slept through this?'

'Yes. I did. What happened?'

Roth shook his head. He didn't know who to trust any more. Someone close to him had marked him for death, marked his Task Group for elimination. Someone with tremendous Imperial authority. He wished his old mentor, Inquisitor Liszt, were with him to soothe his fears, to tell him what to do. Or even Gurion, to lend him guidance. For the first time in his career, Roth thought he might have been too young for a task of such magnitude. For the first time, he realised there were those who did not fear the Inquisition.

'Vandus. I'll be making for Kholpesh come dawn. Do not follow me.'

'Obodiah, please, tell me what's happening?'

'I can't. But I think it would be best if you did not accompany me to Kholpesh. I fear betrayal.'

Barq blinked in disbelief. 'You do not trust me?'

Roth steadied his breath and levelled his gaze first on Celeminé, then Pradal and finally locked eyes with Barq. 'There is a betrayer amongst us. It's not that I think it is you, Vandus. But that I do not want to kill you if you are. I'm sorry, old friend.'

CHAPTER FIFTEEN

THE TRUCK ROLLED to a shuddering stop. Trapped though he was, Silverstein felt the lurch of deceleration and heard the squealing protest of the brakes. He did not know how long they had been travelling for. Perhaps two hours, perhaps eight. It was impossible to tell.

'No, Silverstein, don't try,' Asingh-nu pleaded in the dark. Silverstein couldn't see him but he could recognise the drawling Cantican vowels of a former rural labourer.

'Perhaps, if we wait a while, we will have a better chance for escape,' Temughan stuttered. He did not sound so sure. For a former clocksmith with steady hands, steady rifle-firing hands, the guerrilla fighter lacked a steadiness of nerve, Silverstein noted. He would be a liability in the event of escape.

'Silverstein, you decide what to do, I will follow you,' said Apartan. He was a former soldier, a sergeant in the CantiCol 2nd Division. Despite the over-enunciation of his syllables in the Cantican accent, his terse staccato speech was unmistakeably military. Nerseh, a dust-hunter and trapper from the Outbounds of Cantica, nodded in agreement. In their time together, Silverstein knew both men to be coarsely dependable and he was glad that of everyone, those two were with him.

'You do what you want. I have no intentions of meeting the warlord. I don't think it sounds particularly pleasant. Do you?' Silverstein said, addressing the others.

Aghdish, the oldest of the captives, a coarse labourer with heavy hands from the ports of Cape Cantica, made the decision for all of them. 'Do what we said we'd do, Silverstein. It's that, or we die,' he said flatly.

The hatch swung open on its hinges. Unrelenting sunlight streamed into their temporary prison. Silverstein shuttered his augmetics and went over the plan in his head for the hundredth time, visualising it in minute detail.

An Ironclad leaned into the lorry. 'Aram gadal, aram! Aram!'

Silverstein replied by slamming his jackboot into the throat of the Ironclad. He aimed his heel into the soft point between the soldier's gorge plate and his facebindings. The Ironclad gurgled wetly behind his mask, stumbling with rearward steps as he clutched at his crushed windpipe.

Without a second thought, Silverstein hurled himself out of the truck. It would be his only chance. His fellow captives piled off after him. The huntsman landed awkwardly on his shoulder, his hands still bound. He looked up, assessing the situation.

They were in dense wilderness. Colossal trees with thick craggy trunks like inverted mountains branched up around him. Banks of gingko and fern clustered in tiered shelves amongst the tremendous root systems. Silverstein was huntsman and the wilderness was his trade, but he did not recognise this place.

Around the disorientated captives, the vehicle convoy had stopped to refuel. Ironclad hauling battered jerry canisters of fuel stared at him. They saw him. He saw them. In the scramble to draw weapons, several of the Ironclad dropped their fuel containers. Shots, angry and hissing, snapped at the edges of his clothes. A las-round dropped Aghdish, puncturing the Cantican as he made a dash for the trees. Another shot punched clean through Nerseh's abdomen, folding him over. Now there were three.

Silverstein dived for the fallen Ironclad, still writhing on the ground, blood and froth seeping from his face-bindings. He wrenched a laspistol from the Ironclad's hip holster.

The huntsman aimed as he steadied his entangled wrists. Las-shots fizzled next to Silverstein's ear, so close he could feel the prickling heat of its afterburn. He aligned the shot at the toppled jerry cans, gurgling fuel onto the hard-packed earth. One precise round was all he needed.

The tightly focused beam of las sparked into the fuel. The effect was instantaneous. Swooning fire rose into multiple growths of searing gas clouds blossoming into the air. There was a low crump of pressurised oxygen, an expanding shell of corrosive heat. It ignited a chain reaction.

Smoke, solid and black boiled in gagging clouds. Fire washed on the wind, sheeting in orange swirls. Men staggered about, blinded and choking. It was exactly what Silverstein needed. With a click, his augmetic shutters opened and his low-visibility vision revealed the scene before him in shades of monochrome green.

He locked onto an Ironclad outrider, astride his bike, pawing at the air with blind, groping hands. Silverstein dispatched him with a snap of his laspistol. One after another, in vivid two-dimensional optics, Silverstein searched out the outriders, took aimed and killed them with headshots. He put down six of them in about as many seconds.

Turning to his fellow captives, Silverstein pushed them in the direction of the fallen outriders. 'Seize the bikes, grab as much fuel as you can!'

Rendered senseless by the inferno, the guerrillas fumbled against the heat and fumes. 'Go! Faster!' Silverstein urged, pushing them along. A las-shot fizzed over his shoulder, dangerously close.

The huntsman rolled the corpse of an outrider off his mount. It was a quad-bike, with deeply treaded all-terrain wheels. Silverstein slid onto the seat and gunned the throttle, his wrists still bound. The quad-bike snarled in response.

'Follow my lead,' Silverstein called out. With a sharp lurch, the bike shot off into the rocky wilderness, weaving between the ossified trees. He looked behind to see the bikes of his guerrillas storming out of the oily smoke, tracer and las chasing them.

THE HEATING GRATE in Gurion's stateroom fluttered low, exuding its dim murky warmth. The tittering woodwind symphony of Cavaleri's *Summer Garden Allegro* drifted softly in the background. The old inquisitor was asleep at his desk, pillowed by mounds of tactical readouts and war reports. The last weeks had been hellish; the campaign was faltering. Intel reported that the invasion had begun on faraway Sinope. His nights were marked by endless war conferences and urgent debriefs as the High Command agonised over their successive defeats. Gurion snatched irregular naps when he could. At two hundred, he was not the young man he used to be.

It was during his slumber that Roth came to him. Or rather, an astropath appeared in the eye of his mind in the visage of Inquisitor Roth, a mere mouthpiece of psychic conveyance. The astral projection broke through a physical distance of three hundred thousand kilometres, painted directly into his frontal lobe.

'Lord Gurion,' said the ghost image, his voice reverberating with mind echoes.

Gurion's subconscious woke with a start, although his physical body sunk into deeper sleep.

'Roth. What time is it?'

'Late. Is that Cavaleri I hear?'

'Oh yes. Of course. Music is the only thing that keeps me sane these days,' Gurion chuckled gently.

'Then I think I must be already mad, Gurion. Things are very bad here. Soured up, as you would say.'

'Is anything the matter?'

'Where do I start?' Roth uttered with a watery sigh. 'There is a betrayer within my ranks. There have been too many close attempts on my life so far.'

'How do you know it is betrayal? You are, after all, in a warzone that is nothing if not on the edge of conquest.'

'Because my murderers are Imperial agents. A death cult assassin, local mercenaries last under the employ of the Medina war effort. The nicest kinds.'

'I see,' Gurion reflected thoughtfully. When he was thoughtful, he rolled the words on his tongue like he was evaluating a complex wine.

'I can only assume that the location and the activities of my Task Group remain a secret of the Conclave?'

'Yes of course. Only I know the status of the Conclavial Task Groups–'

'Which would mean I have an infiltrator in my ranks, leaking out my intelligence and keeping two steps ahead of the game grid,' Roth finished.

'Are you safe now?'

Roth's astro-vision shrugged its wispy, translucent shoulders. 'I will continue on to Kholpesh tomorrow.

But I will not be leaving with Inquisitor Barq's team. I cannot afford to…'

'I understand. You are caught in a vice. Transiting between battlefields with a betrayer at your side warrants a special kind of caution,' Gurion mused.

'I suspect Varuda,' Roth admitted bluntly.

'Well then you are not alone. He does everything short of admitting foul play. But I cannot act without premise. Not at a time like this. The campaign hangs by a thread and summary punishment of its highest-ranking general is a risk I cannot take. Not without solid cause.'

'Of course. Do one thing for me, Lord Gurion.'

'Anything.'

'Follow Varuda, and you'll find the rat.'

Gurion nodded thoughtfully. 'I won't let him out of my sight.'

CHAPTER SIXTEEN

KHOLPESH, GEOGRAPHICALLY AND architecturally, had much in common with Cantica and the grapevine worlds of Medina. Civilisation clustered on a dispersed chain of archipelagos, mid-ocean ridges immersed in a churning sea of milk. The triangle suns of Medina pivoted constantly in the bleached sky. As a consequence, the protein-rich water that covered much of the planet was subject to mass condensation and the formation of attendant thunderstorms. There was no night or day on Kholpesh, only the searing glare of sun and the boiling black clouds of tempest.

It was for this geographic reason that the Archenemy conducted war on Kholpesh in a different way. Through the absence of open ground to facilitate mass aerial deployment, the Ironclad heralded the invasion with aerial bombardment. Squadrons of Archenemy interceptors and bombers skimmed on the shrieking turbines of slam-propulsion engines. They slashed through the sky like bats in formation. Archenemy escort cruisers, ones that had slipped through the Imperial Navy picket, lurked in the sky like ghostly floating continents.

The bombing had laid waste to Kholpesh. It left a trail of blast-flattened destruction from the citrus groves of the sandy coastal plains to the tiered domes and minarets of the Kholpeshi city-states.

The enemy strategy had been to disrupt, disorder and wound. It had achieved this objective within just three days of sustained bombing. Roads and transit systems were destroyed, rural districts were isolated, cities were burning and four million citizens became displaced and homeless. The death toll reached one hundred and twenty thousand.

In a way, the initial bombardment fortified the morale and spirit of the Kholpeshi people. In Mantilla, the axial city of Kholpesh, the streets became congested with citizens rushing to donate blood and food to the outlying regions. So thick was the congestion that the Governate issued an unprecedented mandate for citizens to return to their homes, lest they hamper the organised relief efforts.

Unable to wait idle, isolated companies of CantiCol infantry marched seventy kilometres in one day, in order to initiate a rescue effort to the ravaged southern rural districts of Astur and Valadura. The Kholpeshi Governate was in disarray and senior officers of the Cantican Colonials organised independent rescue efforts.

Twenty-four hours later, a column of sixty thousand Guardsmen, shovels on their rucksacks, banners of the Kholpeshi Garrison fluttering, began the long trek to the outer provinces.

Military trucks with supplies attempted to cross the burst dams and irrigation systems between shallow archipelagos with a cavalier disregard for their own safety. Many made it through to the refugees stranded amongst the ruins of their villages, delivering much-needed medical and food supplies. But dozens of trucks, along with their occupants, were lost to mud sinks and landslides.

Further from the city reaches, in the provinces, settlements became isolated in their own little pockets of suffering. A husband bound the body of his wife to his back with string, as he rode his bicycle thirty-five kilometres to the funereal caves.

In the cities themselves, many wandered amongst the rubble and smoke in a daze. In Orissa Minor, a young mother and father shrieking with distress flagged down and pleaded with a passing industrial dirt-miner to find their son, lost underneath the collapsed folds of their tenement building. The parents had been on manufactorum shift when it happened. Despite a death toll that reached the hundreds of thousands, a crowd gathered in breathless silence as the sheets of rockcrete were lifted. For many hours they dug, passers-by joining in with shovels, pails, even bare hands.

When the debris cleared inside, they found three bodies. A young child, two months shy of six. He was cradled in the arms of his grandfather, his grandmother holding her husband from behind. Even amongst the destruction, the crowd wept openly.

AXIAL MANTILLA, THE ruling seat of Kholpesh, had always been the domain of the aristocrats, oligarchs and upper tier of Kholpesh. It was thus the only city-state sheathed in the semi-sphere of a void shield. Like a shimmering bubble of oil-slick water, the shield dissipated the worst of the Archenemy bombardment. It was precisely because of this that Mantilla became the focus of the Ironclad's major ground offensive. Having secured a deployment site following their brutal aerial campaign, the Archenemy besieged the city-state with the entirety of its Kholpeshi invasion force – fifty deca-legions of Ironclad, five hundred thousand strong, supported by the motorised and mechanised battalions so prevalent amongst Ironclad doctrine.

By the fourth month of the siege of Mantilla, the battle had mired into a grinding trench war of attrition. The Imperial trench networks were three hundred metres deep, the high mosaic walls and shield pylons of Mantilla rearing up behind them. Entire sections of the sand-bagged entrenchment were within grenade-throwing distance of Archenemy trenches. It was vicious, it was close and the firing never stopped.

It was here that the Task Group made their descent. The stratocraft scraped an evasive landing into the defensive bulwark, tailed by enemy flak and tracer. It was the welcome they had all expected.

Once on land, the Task Group understood their obligations and they went about them with determined efficacy.

Liaising with Cantican senior officers through Captain Pradal, Inquisitor Roth made a thorough assessment of the siege. He inspected the flak-board trenches, ankle-deep in sour filth, slogging through kilometres of zigzagging fortifications. The Cantican Guardsmen on Kholpesh were the most desolate body of fighting men he had ever seen. Their uniforms were ragged and worn thin; many were wounded and indiscriminately bandaged. Disintegration seeped into the very eyes of those men.

Madeline de Medici, escorted by Inquisitor Celeminé entered the city of Mantilla proper. They were to establish communications with one of Madeline's contacts, a minor broker of the underground and often very elite network of private collectors.

The atmosphere within the capital was like nothing they could have imagined. Two million refugees crowded the streets, shuddering in blankets and bundles of their last possessions. They clustered in throngs, sleeping openly on the pavements, in alcoves and crevices, and congregating in miserable huddles down side lanes and one-ways.

Under the protective veil of the void shield, the aristocrats and wealthy bourgeois flaunted their position with a defeatist debauchery. They revelled as the planet burned. In their pavilions and theatre-houses, they saluted endless rounds of liquor with the cry, 'They are coming!'

There was no rationing. No sense of responsibility or inhibition amongst the elite. Mantilla had accepted its fate. It was only a matter of living as much as they could with the time they had left.

THE AUTO-SEDAN, CIGAR-NOSED and open-topped, was chauffeured by a young transport corps lieutenant. The Cantican officers, in their peculiarly cavalier fashion, had insisted that Madeline and Celeminé travel into Mantilla by staff car.

Mantilla was an old and powerful city-state. Tall terraces of soft pastel – pinks, jades and powdery blue – lined the slab stone roads. The city grew in tiers, and to Madeline, it reminded her of an ancient pre-Imperial text documenting the Tower of Babel. Plum minarets and flaking, gilded domes dominated the skyline. In all, Mantilla had a haughty cosmopolitan charm that was unmatched by any other city-state on Kholpesh.

Not too far into the hab districts, their staff car became mired in refugee congestion. The desperate and the hungry tapped at their tinted windows, hands held out, pleading. The young lieutenant blasted his horn as he eased the vehicle forwards. Behind the soundproofed windows and armoured chassis, Madeline felt strangely distant from their distress. Their voices were muffled. The air in the staff car was cold and recycled. It made the outside world seem surreal. Unbearably so.

Madeline and Celeminé alighted from the vehicle, much to the protests of their escort. The two ladies, both dressed in the demure cultural garb of Medinian women, proceeded through the city on foot.

They cut across the municipal park of the district. The neat lawns and geometric footpaths had become a designated refugee camp. Makeshift tents strung up from ration sacks lined the square in densely packed rows. People resorted to using the sculptural fountains as drinking water, and disease spread rapidly. Everywhere they looked were the jaundiced faces of cholera and dysentery.

Beneath the columned arches, Madeline noticed small malnourished children track her with dark, sunken eyes as she went by. They lolled in the arms of their parents, too tired and too sickly to move.

'This is horrible. This place is so wretchedly filthy. And the smell. Is this what all wars are like?' Madeline asked.

'These are the lucky ones. Millions of refugees, some coming on barges from across the archipelagos, some trekking for days on foot. For every one refugee you see here, they shut the gates on a dozen. Hundreds of thousands of people were caught out in the open as the Archenemy mounted their initial ground offensive,' Celeminé said.

'Oh please. Stop!' Madeline said, not wanting to hear the rest.

The pair of them walked on in silence for some time.

They followed the pedestrian bridges that would take them into the commercial district. The four-storey terraces that faced onto the streets, with their painted railings and tiled steeples, were shut off from the world. Only the very privileged lived here. The refugees huddled for shelter at their doorstep, foraging through their debris bins for edible scraps.

Many times during their walk, Madeline saw the sled-chariots of minor dignitaries or bourgeoisie rattle past. Their occupants were more often than not blind drunk, sometimes yelling obscenities at the refugees who did not scurry fast enough away from the path of their horses. Once, a bodyguard riding on the running board even began unleashing a lasgun into the air to scatter the people before him.

As they walked closer to the upper tiers of Mantilla, the atmosphere began to gradually change. In the exclusive commercial and administrative quarters, the refugees began to thin out. Ape-faced private house guards stood sentry outside the gates of estates and manor houses. Women with painted faces, probably aristocrats by virtue of their tall hair and suggestive bodices, cavorted openly in the streets. Dishevelled noblemen mingled amongst them, their breath sour with alcohol, laughing the laugh of the mentally diminished. All were wreathed in beads and dry, wilting flowers.

Madeline was disgusted.

A soft-middled aristocrat grabbed her from behind, cackling as he buried his face into her neck. 'Please, where are your manners?' Madeline protested, trying to shrug him away.

The man was persistent. Still snorting his intoxicated laugh, he encircled Madeline with sweat-slick arms.

Celeminé put him out with a palm to the base of the skull. She moved fast and Madeline barely had time to register the movement. With a grunt, the man sagged to his knees, cupping the base of his neck.

The pair trotted away quickly, melting into the lascivious crowd.

THE TEA-HOUSE WAS created as a splendid aviary.

It was a fan-brimmed pavilion, its wrought-iron scroll-work and railings painted sea-green. Tripod tables and chess stools clustered under the veranda and meandered down the sidewalk. In the centre of the tea-house, a bird-house crafted as a fenced palace contained hundreds of songbirds, flickering flashes of emerald, sapphire and magenta.

Here, the Mantillan elite could go about their daily business of trade, politics and social obligation without the unsightly distraction of war or refugees. A dozen private guards shouldering flechette shotguns saw to that.

It was also where Madeline would rendezvous with her broker. She recognised him immediately. He had no name of course, brokers worked on a strictly need-to-know basis; the black market of relic smuggling was an exclusive network and the patrons took this very seriously. But Madeline had acquired his services enough times to recognise him by face.

The broker was a mad bear of a man, shaggy and genial. Yet on occasion he wore periwigs of absurd pomp, flowing, curled and beribboned. A tiny waistcoat was stretched to splitting point across his shoulders and a lace cravat adorned his bullish neck. Combined with his looping pencilled eyebrows and white-painted face, he was once the most curious yet repellent individual Madeline had ever been acquainted with.

'The client is always right,' Madeline said as she took a seat at his table.

'Oh, the client is never wrong,' answered the broker with the prearranged cue.

'This is a friend of mine, Lady Felyce Celeminé. She is the client interested in purchasing.'

The broker extended a heavy paw gloved in lace. 'Pleasure to meet you, Lady Celeminé. You can call me Little Cadiz.'

'Oh of course, Little, what a delightful name!' squealed Celeminé, feigning interest. Madeline could see the repulsion that threatened to manifest as a gag reflex well up in Celeminé. But the inquisitor kept her poise.

Little Cadiz promptly ordered a round of herbal infusion before discussing business, as was the etiquette.

'At your behest, I have devoted a good deal of time and energy to thinking of the patron. To this date you have not identified any of these patrons specifically, nor have you outlined the content of their character, forcing me to draw certain conclusions about them from your tone of voice,' tittered Cadiz in his strained alto.

'I refer to the patron Hiam Golias. A collector, I believe, who is offering a relic from the Age of Apostasy?'

'I have inferred from your confident tone that these relics are at the very least quite important, as you seem to be in a hurry to locate them. Were these relics of a more mundane nature, say a rather expensive clock or xenos jewellery, I believe you would sound more relaxed.'

+Is he mad?+ Celeminé projected into Madeline.

Madeline nodded slowly, biting her lip.

'But no, your tone has been one of abstract concern, and seemed to be directed at the wellbeing of yourselves. I can certainly sympathise with your point. We live in a dangerous world and at a dangerous time. I would be hard pressed to come up with a group of people more at risk in this world than us, other than perhaps smaller children.'

+This has got to be a ruse to throw people off,+ Celeminé sighed.

'If it is, he does his job well,' Madeline whispered under her breath. 'When can you arrange for us to meet with Master Golias?' she inquired, jotting down a tidy sum on a paper napkin as her broker's fee.

Little Cadiz slid the napkin over to himself and peeked at the numerals. He appeared satisfied.

'For the sake of the completeness of our deal, I would say – imagine a grand social gathering for recreational purposes, to be held on the Golias Estate. A celebration of liberation! That is where you shall find Master Golias.'

+Ten seconds. I'll give him ten seconds before I cross this table and put him to sleep,+ Celeminé commented with a searing tinge of half-hearted aggression.

Madeline laughed out loud without realising.

'I'm sorry, was it something I said?' Cadiz enquired, clearly concerned.

'No no, not at all. When is this celebration to be held?'

'Every night of course! They are coming, there is no time left to squander,' he cawed theatrically.

'Of course,' said Madeline flatly.

'But tonight is when Golias is willing to see you. The both of you. He is very eager to do so.'

Slipping a vellum fold from his breast pocket, Cadiz daintily slid it across the table. 'Invitations to the Golias Estate. I wish you all the best with your purchasing ventures.'

With that, Madeline and Celeminé rose from the table, curtsied and left the madman.

CHAPTER SEVENTEEN

ROTH STALKED UP to the observation deck of the command post bunker. A flock of staff officers trailed him, ghosting him so hard they trod on his heels.

The bunker was set at the foot of Mantilla's fortress walls, ringed by the apron of trenches that spiderwebbed the terrain around it. An ugly structure of prefab boarding and sandbags, it resembled a fat-bellied urn, piled high with kev-netting and hessian sacks. Yet from the observation tower, the bunker afforded a clear enough view of the battlefield.

At first survey, the terrain was barren and undulating. What little vegetation that might have clustered in that sandy soil had long been churned away by artillery. The Imperial trenches encircled the city with a twelve kilometre stretch of razor wire, tank traps and gun nests. Facing them, almost interlocking amongst them, were the trenches of the Archenemy. Tactically speaking, the enemy held the higher undulating hills. It was a bad position for the Imperium, as the Ironclad artillery in those hills had been able to rain down ordnance with almost clear line of sight.

'This is terrible,' Roth said. 'Absolutely untenable.'

'What right have you to say that?' growled one of the officers.

The man who had spoken was Major General Sihan Cabales, commanding officer of the Mantillan siege. He had been caustic with Roth since the inquisitor had made landfall. He was a tall gentleman in his late seventies, with a broad, imposing frame that stretched the shoulders of his cavalry jacket.

'Major general, why, is it not an elementary mistake to allow the enemy to claim their high ground unopposed?'

Cabales joined Roth at the sandbagged ledge. The field before him was smoking, like the soil itself had soaked up the heat of the bombs that pounded it. 'Because,' he began, 'these men are the most demoralised troops I have ever had under my command. Absolutely useless.'

'General, wars are not lost by men, they are lost by officers. I'm not a military man, but even I know that,' Roth said. The inquisitor couldn't help himself, he realised he was being entirely too pompous, but the general could do with some unwinding.

'Then you do it,' Cabales grinned wolfishly. 'You can take command of that far section of the Magdalah trenches.'

The general snapped his fingers and a young lieutenant bearing his snuff box and a handful of maps stepped forwards. Cabales slid one of the map tubes from the pile and unfurled its flapping corners across the ledge. 'Here, the Magdalah foothills. If you think you can claim any of these hills, claim that one.'

Roth found the foothills on the map, and then made a sweep with his telescope. It was not a good area. He adjusted the mag-scope and zoomed in on a blast-withered patch of flat, rocky ground. A lattice-work of trenches covered most of the low-lying ground. That in itself was a military blunder.

What's more, the Archenemy to their front had claimed the Magdalah hills. They rose up half a kilometre away, a series of hump-backed ridges, wrinkled with crevices, crannies and the natural cover of rock and gorse. The enemy had established static firing positions from up on high, shelling and pounding the flat, open trenches below. It was, in Roth's opinion, the worst possible tactical plight.

'Will you accept?' Cabales said, loud enough for all the assembled officers to hear.

It was a ploy of course, for Cabales to regain face and knock the upstart young inquisitor off his pedestal. Cabales knew this. Roth knew this. An older, reserved commander, perhaps a veteran with less to prove, would have thought it folly. The voice of his mentor Inquisitor Liszt would have been lecturing him. But Roth's mind was already made.

'I accept,' Roth shrugged. 'Take me down to the Magdalah section and allow me to meet these fellows.'

THE DEFENSIVE LINES around the Magdalah foothills were called the 'The Pit' for good reason.

Casualty percentage rates here were in the low forties. Elements of the 9th and 16th Infantry, 7th Light Horse and 22nd Lancers who had been deployed here were known as those who 'drew the backend straw' amongst comrades.

Roth stepped down into the trenches and his boots immediately settled into five centimetres of gluey scum. It was a thoroughly wretched mixture of mostly mud, precipitation, human waste and no small amount of blood. He waded through the trenches with Pradal close behind, following an escort of NCOs.

It was humid here, the moisture clinging to his sinuses like a steaming film. The temperature in the low thirties did not bode well for the corpses, some of which were stacked stiffly horizontal to the sandbags and flakboards that reinforced the trench walls.

Roth stepped carefully, resisting the temptation to bring a hand to his nose and mouth. It would not lend a good impression to the troops he would have to command. The inquisitor moved amongst them, giving them curt nods when they caught his eye. But they rarely did. Many of the Guardsmen sat blank, with the glazed stare of exhaustion and some measure of shell shock.

Altogether, they were some of the most demoralised soldiers Roth had ever encountered. They had shed their proud brown jackets, squatting about in breeches and braces. Most huddled on crates, muttering darkly and smoking. Many others still wore their rebreathers, as the threat of poison gas was constant.

It was perhaps a slight detail, but what concerned Roth the most was the way they carried their rifles. One could always discern the morale and training of a soldier by the way they carried their arms. Well-trained troops had good trigger discipline, fingers coiled loosely outside the guard ready to fire, or straight by their shoulders like spears. Others still, carried them close to their chests, cradled in their arms as if about to rear. The variations were many, but the intentions were the same – the guns were always ready to discharge at the enemy.

The men of the Magdalah defences settled on their lasguns like crutches, leaning on them with weary resignation. It seemed they had given up the thought of fighting, they just wanted the time to pass less painfully.

Roth crouched down next to a bearded soldier whittling sticks with a bayonet. He couldn't tell what rank the man held, as his rank sash was soiled and bloodied beyond recognition. 'Soldier, where can I find Colonel Paustus?'

The man didn't respond. Roth repeated himself twice before he realised the man was deaf from shelling.

Captain Pradal caught the man's attention by placing a hand on his bayonet. The man looked up and Captain Pradal signed up a deft series of field signals. Something in the order of 'look for the colonel'.

The man spoke, his voice unconsciously loud. 'The colonel is dead. Mortared yesterday. Major Arvust commands this section now. He should be in the comms station if he's not dead already.'

Pradal signed his acknowledgment and Roth moved on, trying to step on the duckboard path laid over the worst of the collected filth.

They found Major Arvust in a hollowed section of the first-line trench, under an improvised command post. A vox set was mounted over a stack of ammunition pallets and a plastek groundsheet was pitched overhead to keep the rain from damaging the comms system. The major hunched over the arrays bay, staring blankly as a tabac stick melted down to grey ash in his hands.

Major Arvust was a Guard-lifer. Roth could tell by the set of his jaw and the way the index finger of his free hand was constantly flexed, as if coiled to squeeze over an invisible trigger. The man was rough-edged, his face handsome in that rugged, sun-battered way. Looking to be in his late forties, Roth knew a career in the Guard was severely ageing. Most likely the man was no more than mid-thirties.

'Sir, Captain Pradal, military liaison of the Medina High Command, sir.' Captain Pradal snapped a stiff salute.

The major's eyes never left the vox array. He flung his hand up to his head in the most half-hearted salute short of being a fly swat and took a draw of his tabac.

'Major General Cabales already voxed through your arrival. You and the inquisitor. What do you need here?'

Arvust said, not bothering to look at either of them.

'To bolster command staff in this area. From what we've heard the casualties among officers have been appalling, sir,' Pradal said.

The major shrugged. 'Be my guest.'

Roth took one carefully placed step forwards. 'Let's cut to the point, major. This section is dying; I've never seen Guardsmen in such a state of disrepair. I don't want to tread on your toes. Either you'll help us reclaim this section, or you can leave.'

Startled by Roth's candour, Major Arvust ashed his tabac and turned to regard Roth with a slow, appraising eye. Roth knew immediately that the major was a solid officer, a good navigator placed into a sinking ship.

'I've tried. HQ staff want us to sit tight in a static defence. My hands are tied,' the major said with resignation.

Roth squatted down in the mud next to Arvust and studied the officer's notes and tactical spreadsheets. 'My hands are not tied. I have authority to command the defences here as *we* see fit. Provided you wish to facilitate this arrangement.'

'We'll see.' A genuine smile twitched at the corners of the major's forlorn scowl. 'If you mean to do what you mean to do, then I hope you have some sort of plan.'

'Let's see what we can hammer out,' Roth said, tracing the grid map with his finger.

THE GOLIAS ESTATE was a four-storey villa daubed in powder-pink pigment. It was a villa of Kholpeshi design, taller than it was wide and severely asymmetrical. It teetered above a mezzanine gallery with long winding stairs that speared fifty metres to the commercial district below. Six hundred-odd steps was no easy climb, and Madeline had to fuss about her face with a kerchief, lest her sweat dampen her cosmetics. Perched so high up on the tiers of Mantilla, the Golias Estate was decidedly impressive with its haughty, antiquated air.

'This place is marvellous!' shouted Celeminé as she bounded up the steps. She was dressed in a petal frock of cream linen with a hooded scarf of soft wool, an outfit Madeline had personally selected. The inquisitor spun on her heels, the long tails of her scarf dancing with her. The heights did not seem to bother her at all.

But the heights bothered Madeline. The steps were narrow and of worn, uneven stone that spiralled down into the dizzying depths below. On stiletto-heeled buckle boots, she precariously edged up, pausing ever so briefly between each step. Like Celeminé, Madeline had dressed for the occasion in a chemise.

'This Hiam Golias, what sort of character is he?' Celeminé called down.

'He's a minor game piece. See these workshops and boutiques along the commercial galleries? He owns quite a few of them.'

'Uh huh. And you know him how?'

'We… have history,' Madeline concluded and left it at that. It was no fault of her own that in the two times she had dealt with Master Golias, he had exuded a blasé, dispassionate charisma that she had not been able to resist. It was better to let Celeminé find out about Golias herself.

'And how does the network operate?'

'Well, the relic trade is a mix of enthusiasts. Historians, investors, collectors…'

'Cultists?' Celeminé added.

'I suppose, if the right item was on offer. But it's clandestine – don't ask, don't tell. Everything is based on word of mouth and reputation. If your dealings aren't clean no one will operate with you.'

'And what would that mean?' Celeminé asked, bounding three or four steps closer in one leap.

'You lose your network. Your source, the smugglers, the brokers, the clients. Everyone meshes together on a need-to-know basis. It's a fraternity to keep away the undesirables.'

'What do you mean by undesirables?' asked Celeminé, although she already knew.

'The Inquisition of course,' laughed Madeline.

THE CELEBRATIONS HAD already begun by the time they had arrived. Or perhaps the previous night's festivities just hadn't ended. Either way, Golias's guests lounged about the antechamber. Many had the slack, sweaty faces of surge-heads and the rest were evidently drunk. They lazed about in various stages of undress, lost in a fugue of self-indulgence.

It was a shame, since the chamber itself was breathtakingly beautiful. Hand-woven Cantican rugs and cushions were strewn about the floor. The walls were red velvet, floral detailing picked out in gold thread. Exotic stuffed beasts, off-world felines and horned, hairy herbivores were locked in a stiff pantomime in the corners of the chamber, their out-stretched paws draped with lingerie. It was a beautiful house and a shame that it had to be despoiled by those with no appreciation for it, thought Madeline.

As they trotted past the antechamber, sleepy, whispery voices called out to them, yearning for them to join the writhing limbs. Others called out the Mantillan toast of the hour – 'They're coming!'

'Go frag yourself,' Celeminé muttered under her breath.

A porter in servant's robes led them into the dining area. Divans were set around a marble table so that the guests could recline as they ate. On the table were platters of raw shellfish, aquatic delicacies and gelatinous desserts. Without a doubt, these were not the rations decreed by governing mandate.

'I appreciate the hospitality, but we have already eaten. Would you be able to lead me to Master Golias?' Madeline asked.

'Master Golias is occupied at the moment. If you will help yourself to refreshments, he will attend to your needs as soon as he is able,' the porter recited.

+Tell him if he doesn't drag Golias out here, this little birdie will start blasting a heavy-cal pistol into the ceiling,+ Celeminé whispered into her mind.

'My client has an appointment with Master Golias and she is in a terrible hurry,' Madeline interpreted smoothly.

'Is my presence required?'

They all turned to see Hiam Golias stride out of an adjacent chamber, his house robes unashamedly open. Two females, aristocrats judging by their pouty cos-implant lips and heavy eye make-up, followed him guiltily, clad in boned corsets.

'Master Golias. It is I, Professor de Medici, and this is Lady Felyce Celeminé.'

'Of course, how could I forget such a delicious face!' laughed Golias, stepping under the light of the chandeliers.

He was a distinguished gentleman in his late seventies who had aged immensely well, on account of his pampered lifestyle and no small amount of juvenat treatments. He was tall and broad, with chem-nourished muscles and a long mane of silver hair. His face was greasily confident if not handsome, with a tall, prominent forehead and a sternly set jaw. Although he was not a fighter, he had an aristocrat's fascination with adventure and had tattooed the emblem of an obscure Guard regiment onto his abdominal muscles. Of course, Golias had never served, a man of his status did not, but it certainly sparked conversation with females.

'I'm surprised you remember me, Master Golias,' said Madeline. She found herself hating him yet flushed in the cheeks at the same time.

'I'm surprised you believed I'd forget. And this, this is Felyce? She has a wonderful curve in the small of her back. If only all my prospective buyers were so athletic,' Golias said. He appraised the girls as he would a fine piece of antiquity, or perhaps stock in an auction yard.

+Revolting. Absolutely revolting.+

Madeline started, subconsciously putting a hand to her florid cheeks in embarrassment. She hadn't intended her surface thoughts to be so obvious. Such transparent behaviour was quite beyond the bounds of etiquette.

+It's fine. I can see what you mean. If only I didn't hate him for his confidence, his wealth, his tastes, his fine mane of hair…+

With a single clap of his hands, Golias dismissed his guests from the dining chamber. They drew away sheepishly to seek other vices.

'Shall we find more private arrangements to conduct business?' Celeminé said coyly, playing every bit into the persona that Golias wanted her to be.

'That all depends, my lady, on what sort of business you would like to conduct,' Golias laughed with an unsettling silkiness.

ROTH AND HIS officers worked long into the days and nights. There was much to be done. Battle plans were drawn and scrapped, timings were coordinated and many tabac stubs were collected in the ashtray. Roth had never realised the minute details that contributed to a strategy, even down to the order in which his men would march.

The triple suns never set on Kholpesh and their time was marked by the regularity of gas attacks.

Almost on the hour, the tin whistles would relay down the trenches. Men would tug goggled rebreathers out of musette bags, pressing cumbersome masks over their faces. Rolling banks of ochre and creeping tendrils of mustard would wash over the trench systems, billowing in a slight easterly. The gas was a dense respiratory irritant, and movement only worsened its effects. Instead the men would stand up on the firing steps or parapets, allowing the dense fumes to sink and settle. It happened so often that the men often continued to play cards or clean weapons, almost unperturbed.

Admittedly, Roth found it difficult to plan tactical strategy and discuss battle plans through the filmed lens and filtration hoses, but he managed. Roth managed because he had known his strategy the minute he laid eyes on the men under his command. To him, they were thoroughly demoralised Guardsmen, sitting about withering under constant enemy aggression. What was needed was an offensive, an all-out push into the enemy-held Magdalah hills. Roth would give them what the overly cautious HQ staff had denied them for so long. He'd try to give them the good fight. On a personal level, it was what Roth needed to occupy his mind while the Task Group went about their networking. It gave him purpose after the events on Cantica.

The fight itself would be an uphill battle. According to the readouts provided by Major Arvust, the geography, enemy disposition and their own resources did not leave them with many choices. The Archenemy were dug in amongst the foothills, roughly four hundred metres across no-man's-land.

From his magnoculars Roth could spot the Ironclad's large number of static armour: light tanks, tankettes, bombards and Basilisks, mostly hulled down in static firing pits. The silvery glint of their turrets buried under camo-netting resembled studs riveted into the soil. They would be hard to dislodge and the Ironclad would not expect the besieged Imperial forces to mount any form of counter-attack. It was an assumption that Roth intended to exploit to its fullest.

These vehicles had been devastatingly effective from their high vantage points but Arvust and Pradal firmly believed they would be vulnerable to a well organised infantry advance. Roth was inclined to agree if only by dint of their sheer confidence.

To this end, Roth had rallied the combined companies of the 7th Light Horse and 22nd Lancers, leaving the 9th and 16th infantry in reserve to hold the trenches. Numerically, with less than four hundred Guardsmen for the offensive, the numbers did not favour them. Yet these Guardsmen were the elite Cantican Horse Cavalry. The lancers especially were fighting men of no small repute. The Cantican Colonials lacked heavy armour prevalent amongst other Guard formations, and the lancers bridged the gap between infantry and vehicle. While the primary role of the light horse was to escort the few precious tanks in the Cantican arsenal as mounted infantry, the lancers were the shock troops.

In particular, the lancers wore chest bandoleers clustered with fuse bombs. Mounted on nine-hundred kilogram destriers, the lancers would even charge headlong into enemy formations, leaving a trail of fuse bombs in their wake.

Unfortunately, having been relegated to trench warfare, the Cantican cavalry had parted with their steeds in Mantilla. Roth commandeered what horses he could. He voxed for the reacquisition of their steeds but was informed that of the several thousand well-trained horses left inside the city of Mantilla, hundreds had been slaughtered for food in order to fuel the aristocratic celebrations. Roth met this news with a series of choice expletives and very real threats to the well-being of the entire Mantillan upper class.

After his temper had simmered down, they re-adapted. The Magdalah offensive would become a mixed mounted infantry advance. Under the cover of rain, the 7th and 22nd would storm the Magdalah foothills, each man loaded with as many explosive charges as he could carry. Their targets would be the ponderous beasts of static armour, the very same engines that had rained down tonnes of ammunition onto their lines for the past months. Lacking the proper supplies, many Guardsmen even resorted to creating their own improvised trench-fighting devices with what equipment they had at hand.

Given two days to prepare, the Canticans proved the inventiveness of Guardsmen in the art of dealing death. Stick grenades were defused and studded with nails to make hand clubs, knotted balls of rope were embedded with .68 calibre rounds to make studded flails. The simplest weapon Roth noticed during his final inspection was the sharpened entrenching tool. Even the thin metal plates supplied to reinforce firing steps in the trenches were hammered roughly into tin sheet breastplates. The process of industry and the preparation of war infused the Canticans with a vigour they had not felt since the beginning of the conflict.

The charge would be straightforward. It was a simple plan but was by no means flawless. But for the Guardsmen, it was better than waiting in the trenches for the unseen shell with their name on it.

CHAPTER EIGHTEEN

THE ATRIUM CEILING captured a shaft of sunlight in a single slanting pillar of gold. Motes of light, soft and dancing, coalesced across the surface of the impluvium pond below it.

The indoor atrium garden of the Golias Estate was by no means large, but what it lacked in grandiose scale it far exceeded with Neo-Medinian design. The atrium was three times taller than it was wide, the soaring heights allowing for a cradling canopy of imported trees, mostly tall finger palms and fern-tailed fronds. Trellises of carnivorous flower vines and potted succulents in poisonous colours jostled for attention in a vivid display of off-world flora. To complete the interior, a stone bench and upright harp were arranged at an angle from the central pond, a pocket of ambience beneath the subtropical surroundings.

'This is impressive, Master Golias,' Celeminé whistled. A mechanical nectar bee crafted from golden clockwork buzzed onto her shoulder and misted the air with an artificial fragrance before darting away.

'Oh this? This is nothing. It's all worthless once the Archenemy take this city,' Golias shrugged. He plucked several permellos from an overhanging bower swollen with fruit and handed one to Madeline.

'This is why you need to offload your item in such a hurry?' Madeline asked.

'Offload is an inaccurate term. I have plenty of prospective buyers for this item. Particularly from the Imperium, if the rumours are to be believed,' said Golias as he shed his robes and slipped into the pond.

'Rumours?' said Celeminé, her face suddenly serious.

'Indeed. Rumours abound. Have you ever heard of the Old Kings of Medina?'

'In passing.'

'You know the children's tales. Artefacts from the War of Reclamation, something like the Emperor's own balls or what have you. Either way, I have something valuable in my hands.'

'You have the Old Kings in your possession?' Madeline exclaimed, loudly enough to lose any pretence of bargaining power.

Golias snorted as he floated on his back. 'Perhaps not. But what I have is a relic that reveals much about the nature of the Old Kings, most likely sourced from the same origins.'

Celeminé dared to press. 'Master Golias. The Imperium could have much to benefit from that. Especially during such a time of war. Is it right for you to keep it?'

'Who are you, the Inquisition?' he cackled crisply. 'It's exactly because they want it so badly that a private collector from the Alypsia Subsector offered me half a continent worth of holdings for it.'

Golias waded to the edge of the pond and licked the water of his lips with a predatory smirk. 'If you have what the Imperium wants, that is power.'

'That's treason,' Celeminé said flatly.

'Who is this bitch and why is she in my house?' snapped Golias, pointing at Celeminé. His demeanour changed with a volatile reaction, on no small amount of alcohol and residual narcotics.

'Please, Master Golias,' Madeline stepped in. 'She means no offence by it.'

Golias glared dangerously at Celeminé, his pupils dilated and his breath snorting his nostrils in ragged jags.

'We can surpass your highest offer. What Lady Celeminé means is, why you would wish to sell such a valuable item so hurriedly?'

That seemed to placate Golias somewhat. For a moment Golias's temper wavered before his features softened. 'Because I enjoy a fine life. Kholpesh will not live forever and I have something the Imperium may find very valuable.'

Golias hauled himself out of the impluvium, shaking down his wetted mane from side to side. 'Better I take what I can now and live than die waiting for the highest bidder. Let me show you this.'

Naked, Golias crossed over to them and parted the waxy folds of vegetation. He led them through the garden, rustling through the curtain of fronds and leaves until they reached an alcove in the atrium, previously obscured. Beyond the alcove window on a rooftop landing pad could be seen the hook-nosed beak of a military flyer.

'This is why I need to liquidate my assets,' Golias proclaimed proudly. He led them outside to his landing pad, so high up that they could see the pulsating flashes of war in the horizon.

Outside, like an eagle in its roost, wings folded and landing struts clawing the ground was a Golem-pattern cargo flier. Thirty metres long, it was turbine-nosed and round-bellied, ugly in the utilitarian way that only military logistics equipment could be. The Golem was a supply craft, ferrying cargo within fleet cruisers and more than capable of short-distance space flight. Madeline was not the least bit surprised that Golias had been able to procure one.

'I take it I should not ask you how you obtained this?' Madeline said.

'You wouldn't believe the things I had to do to pilfer one of these from the Governor's facilities,' Golias laughed as he patted the cannon-mouthed propulsion thrusters on the Golem's wing. Where Golias's hands rested, Madeline could clearly see the scraped-off paint scars of a Munitorum serial number.

Madeline and Celeminé circled around the craft, prodding at the fuselage pretending to be impressed. Golias had balls, they gave him that. Since the Medina Campaign, Imperial mandate had decreed a ban on all non-Imperial military fliers. Refugee barges transiting off-world were few in number and even then, most placements were allotted to Imperial authorities and military chieftains. Most on Kholpesh simply did not have the means to escape.

'As you can see, I am well prepared once the void shields come down. I have a chartered trade frigate waiting to ferry me beyond the Bastion Stars. What you choose to do with the artefact once I am gone is no concern of me. Most of my prospective buyers will probably want to sell it for magnified profits to the Imperial war machine.'

'If you could lever a greater price from the Imperium, why do you sell to private buyers knowing they will sell on?' Madeline questioned warily.

'Because I have no desire to deal with the Imperium. None. You can do whatever you want. I'll be on my vineyard several subsectors away by then,' Golias grinned.

'Can we see this relic?' Celeminé asked.

Golias looked at her incredulously before a burble of laughter snorted from his nose. 'Absolutely not. Are you an amateur at this business?'

'How do I know what I am paying for?' Celeminé protested indignantly.

'Again, who is this bitch? Does she know nothing of the network? Who was your broker?' snapped Golias.

Celeminé pushed Madeline aside.

'I have rank and authority,' she said, before Madeline could restrain her.

Golias looked incredulous. 'Who are you?' He snapped. 'Military? Ecclesiarch? What in Throne is going on?'

Madeline tried to mediate, cupping her hands in supplication. It was no use. Celeminé had said too much. Golias was heading towards the door. Madeline gripped the inquisitor by the arm and pulled her away.

'Guards! Guards!' Golias began to shout.

Madeline and Celeminé turned and fled. They clattered through Golias's finely appointed home, shoving aside his many dismayed house guests. Hiam Golias chased after them. His guards were with him now, toting shotguns that they dared not fire into the clusters of house guests.

'Seize them!' Golias called from the upper-storey landing of his staircase as Madeline and Celeminé reached his entrance foyer. A noble in an avian mask and costume made a clumsy swipe to grab them as the two reached the door. Celeminé struck him on the side of the neck, digging her wrist into his carotid artery. The bird-faced man crumpled, and with that they dashed out the grand double doors of the Golias Estate.

THE RAIN SWEPT in horizontal sheets.

It was some time in the haze of afternoon, and pre-dusk always brought rain on Kholpesh. Like pressurised steam, the whirling pattern of storm clouds would build up throughout the day until finally the sky would burst into a torrential downpour.

The 7th and 22nd advanced at a despondent trot, their horses drooping under the downpour. Out here, the poison gas remained active in the soil for several days given the constantly humid weather conditions, and the ground was a solvent yellow. Rebreathers were a necessity in order to move through the tainted soil. Men and horse alike had faces shod in the bug-eyed sheathing of Cantican MK02 gas filters.

Before them, the open mud flats that separated the warring trenches had become a morass of sink soil. The dragon's teeth of tank traps and coils of concertina wire rose out of the mustard-grey bog. In some places, half-submerged corpses lolled like hump-backed marine life.

Roth and Captain Pradal, along with a platoon of lancers, moved ahead of the main line of advance. They dismounted and crawled forwards on their stomachs, cutting breaches in the cordons of concertina wire, of which there were many. It was a slow and arduous process, probing the soil around the barbed coils for mined explosives before signing the all-clear for the battalion advance.

Roth slithered close to an Archenemy trench. It was so close, Roth could have spat into it had he wished to. A lone sentry stood on the firing steps, squinting into the grey curtain of rain. He was manning a drum-fed autocannon; both he and his weapon were draped underneath a pattering plastek sheet.

Once the way was clear, the forward advance party slithered back towards the main line of advance. Four hundred horsemen mounted on slab-muscled destriers were waiting patiently in the rain. Their horses pawed at the soil, snorting and shaking their heads. Of the men, some were praying while others stared in silence at the enemy lines they could not see. Their sabres were drawn and their lances were steadied. They had been briefed by their commanders to ride in a staggered line. Upon contact with the enemy trenches, the 7th Light Horse would dismount and engage the Archenemy positions. The Lancers would continue on using their momentum, their speed and the shock of cavalry to seize upon the undefended rear-echelon armour. It was simple enough, and the Archenemy would not expect such aggressiveness from the thus far soundly defensive Imperial positions.

Roth's steed was a fine specimen of war horse, twenty-five hands tall with rolling, mountainous muscle. The horse shifted its bulk underneath Roth's legs, teetering him precariously. Roth had been a fine leisure rider but of combat riding he knew little. Besides, it had been many years since he had ridden.

Roth looked up into the sky. The clouds were a solid ashen grey and he could barely see the riders to either side of him. It was not, he reflected, the best way to reacquaint himself with the equestrian arts.

Major Arvust trotted over to Roth. 'We're all in place, signal the charge,' he whispered as he handed him a tin officer's whistle.

Roth shook his head. 'No. They're your men, you do it.'

They waited breathlessly for several more seconds, savouring the heavy staccato of rainfall. Then the major blasted the whistle.

With a tidal roar, the CantiCols rose from the mud flats and charged towards the enemy trenches. They charged into the heavy fog of grey mist, seeming for all the world to be charging at phantoms.

The Archenemy fired blindly at them. Rods of las-fire hissed from the murky mist to their front. A spear of light hit a lancer to Roth's left. Rider and horse bucked backwards, their forward momentum suddenly arrested.

The last Roth saw of them as he galloped past was the silhouette of hooves flailing in the air.

They were close now. If Roth squinted against the lashing raindrops he could see the ominous silhouettes of Archenemy soldiers, prowling on the firing steps of their trenches. At fifty metres out, the enemy saw them and the fire became accurate. Thudding tracers began to bowl over the Cantican cavalry. But by then, the horsemen were already on them.

Abruptly, the foggy grey was lit up by flashes of searing orange. The Guardsmen announced their presence by lobbing grenades into the unwary trenches. A fluttering chain of detonations pounded Roth's ear drums into a tinnitus ring.

To the credit of the Lancers, they executed their battle plan to the letter. The first wave of cavalry, once having unleashed their explosives, dismounted and assaulted the trenches on foot. The second wave continued on mounted, clearing the trenches with jarring crunches of hooves on soil, galloping for the secondary defences.

Roth stood up on his stirrups, screaming as he ignited his power fist. His horse sprinted the last few metres into the enemy lines, and Roth rolled off the saddle into an ungainly dismount. Grenade flashes hazed his vision, and the inquisitor half-charged, half-fell into the enemy trench.

It was utterly disorientating.

Dirt and debris swirled about him. Detonations sprayed the entrenchments with feathery streaks of gore and shrapnel. Archenemy soldiers reeling from the aftershock of explosives were struggling to fight back. Looking up, Roth spied a Cantican Guardsman teetering above him on the edge of the trench, his face collapsed by a lasshot. The man was dead but still sat upright in his saddle.

Roth struck out with his fist on instinct, rendered senseless by smoke, rain, blood and the sheer aural assault of close combat. They could not use firearms for fear of friendly fire, and the cramped confines did not allow for the use of fixed bayonets. They fought with whatever was at hand.

An Ironclad wielding a rectangular cleaver circled around to Roth's left, hacking at his thigh. The blade sparked off trauma-plate as they connected. Another enemy soldier swung a barbed trench pike into the back of Roth's head. Blunt, brutal pain spread in the back of his skull. Roth bit his tongue and blood began to drool from his chin.

Dazed, Roth leaned down and threw out his hand in a backfist. It was a wild, desperate technique but the enemy were too close, too pressed to avoid it. The back of his power fist clipped into his unseen assailant's jaw and catapulted the entire head clean out of the trench. Still snorting like a wounded bull, Roth hammered his palm down on the cleaver-wielding Ironclad. The Arch-enemy folded at a crisp ninety degree angle and hit the mud without further movement.

Roth looked around, blood cascading from a gash at the top of his head into his eyes. It was a deep cut, he could feel it by the way it was numb instead of painful. He only hoped his skull was intact. Blinking the oily crimson from his eyes, Roth tried to gather his senses.

Captain Pradal lurched into his field of vision, slashing the air with his trench club. His right hand hung at his side, blood soaking the sleeve up to the elbow. He was missing two fingers from that hand.

'What happened to your hand?' Roth yelled above the rattling clamour.

Pradal looked and his mangled fist and laughed, almost surprised. 'Didn't even notice,' he cackled.

Their rage was up now. That was dangerous, Roth knew. They could not become mired in a protracted engagement in the trenches. It would not be long before the Archenemy began to filter in through the trench networks and overwhelm them with numbers. They had to keep moving.

'Keep advancing, targets on our axis of advance,' Roth screamed. He pointed up the undulating slopes and the enemy armour that dotted them.

Major Arvust blasted his whistle. 'Fuses! Fuses!' he cried, ordering them to disengage with more grenades.

To their credit, the Cantican discipline held and they broke away from their staggered enemy. Leaving their horses panicking on the other side of the trenches, they surged up the hill on foot. The Guardsmen tossed delay-charged fuse bombs in their wake to deter pursuit. Having cleared the first line of trenches, the Cantican cavalry moved to join the second wave in the skirmish on Magdalah.

ROTH POUNCED ONTO the front cowling of a KL5 Scavenger.

He climbed onto the tank, boots slipping against the smooth plating as he fought for purchase. His power fist gouged deep molten holes into the sloping frontal hull as he hauled himself up.

The turret hatch swung out and an Ironclad writhed out. Roth backhanded him back into the vehicle. A Cantican Guardsman climbed atop the turret and dropped a frag grenade into the opening. It clattered into the cab with a metallic echo. Roth slammed the hatch shut and both men leapt off as a muffled crump shook the tankette.

All around, the men of the 7th and 22nd swarmed over the Archenemy war machines. The hull-down vehicles snarled back with thunderous 105mm shells and the chain rips of cyclical cannon fire. Many of the Canticans had dismounted, weaving amongst the vehicles and sowing explosives.

The fuse bombs and frag grenades cut through the downpour of rain as miniature claps of thunder – incessant, sparking up like water being poured onto electric circuits. The most devastating were the PK-12 drill-charges. A small clamp mine, the drill charges could be magnetised to the side of a vehicle. Upon ignition, the charge propelled a molten core of copper with an armour penetration of ten centimetres. Each Cantican carried at least three or four.

Roth circled around to the periphery of a Leman Russ. The behemoth was a ransacked Guard vehicle, its old camouflage blistered and scraped down to a burnished metal hide. The Leman Russ was hull-down in a wide earthen pit, the monstrous snout of its turret cannon trying to track its sprinting human targets. PK-12 in hand, Roth slapped the charge onto the gap between turret and chassis. He was moving again before the heavy guns could track him. Behind him, an expanding shockwave chased his heels and a sheet of flaming wreckage slashed overhead.

It was a brief, brutal clash. The Ironclad infantry were in disarray and many abandoned their positions as the cavalry penetrated their front-line trenches. The wave of flashing hooves and incendiary explosives were too much for them. These were not the same broken Guardsmen who held the Magdalah trenches by the skin of their teeth. The Ironclad were not prepared for it.

Roth saw a light horseman land behind the mantlet of a Basilisk. The Cantican laid into the Ironclad crew with lance and sabre, killing two before being dragged off his steed. To Roth's immediate right, a lancer Guardsman unleashed his rocket tube at an oncoming FPV. The hood of the Ironclad vehicle peeled back like blistering skin. It ran over the lancer and kept going, a fireball carried on by wheels of melting rubber.

A tankette went up in a star of exploding pieces. Spikes of las sizzled past Roth, so close he could feel the steam of rain drops as the rounds punched through them. A grenade went off close by.

'Regroup! Regroup!' Roth ordered, pulling hard on his reins. In their fury, the cavalry charge had dispersed, chasing individual targets and scattering the enemy. It was to be their undoing.

The momentum of the cavalry charge was faltering. Ironclad infantry were regrouping and fighting back. Fast-moving FPVs were converging on them, making their presence known with pintle-mounted heavy stubbers.

'Tighten the formation!' Roth screamed, his voice stolen by the wash of rain storm.

A cone of flame rippled across his front, consuming several horsemen and the wreck of a KL5. Like a ghost, the sinister form of a Hellhound flame tank emerged from the rain curtain. Its turret was licking with tendrils of fire.

Roth turned his horse and spurred it into a gallop. He had to find a vox-operator before the Archenemy, clashing their war drums and howling for blood, managed to encircle and overwhelm them all.

He found a vox-caster, but the operator was no longer alive. His horse was nowhere to be seen, and his body was laid out on the soil, stiff and jawless. The vox system was submerged in mud several metres away.

Vaulting off the horse, Roth sunk to his knees and scrabbled for the handset. A line of tracer stitched the mud in front of him, kicking up plumes of grit. Roth forced himself to steady his pulse and hands before dialling in on all vox frequencies.

'This is the 7th and 22nd Magdalah Cavalry. Request immediate reinforcements in the Magdalah foothills, we are pinned by anchor fire. Over!'

'Magdalah Cav, this is command HQ. Reinforcements denied. Magdalah hills is red zone, what in the Emperor's name are you doing out there?'

Roth fired several plasma rounds from his pistol in the general direction of enemy muzzle flashes. He doubted he hit anything.

'HQ Command, we are reclaiming the foothills. Request immediate assistance to consolidate captured ground.'

The voice on the other end, despite being fuzzed with static, was clearly incredulous. 'Consolidate captured ground?'

'Are you stupid? We've shaken the Ironclad loose. I am–'

Roth was cut off as a solid slug punctured the vox-caster. The next shot slammed into Roth's chest just below his ribs, putting him straight onto his arse. The kinetic force was so great that he sunk slightly into the mud. Roth wheezed for constricted breath. Beneath the trauma plates, he could feel the small bones of his floating ribs popping and grinding.

A second shot hit him at the armoured strong-point below the sternum. A rounded segment of abdominal sheathing just above his breastbone collapsed inwards. At best, it would be a hairline fracture and severe bruising. But Roth feared the worst – deep internal haemorrhaging.

He tried to roll onto his knees but the hot brittle pain flickered his consciousness. Blacking out repeatedly, the next few moments became a stuttered series of events as Roth slipped in and out.

He saw Ironclad troopers march out of the enshrouding smoke – a long line, their silhouettes bladed and sharp.

He saw the corded pillars of equine limbs appear around him. The Canticans must be regrouping.

A shell ploughed into the cavalry. He didn't know how close. But it was close enough for him to see at least one horse and rider thrown five metres into the air, limbs skewed in impossible angles.

There was a lot of shooting. Many of his men were dying.

When he finally came to, rainwater had collected in the gaps of his armour. The cold seepage on his bare skin brought him some clarity. Looking around, he saw some of the 7th and 22nd still fighting, the riders standing high on their stirrups as they fired their lasguns. But most were casualties. The bodies of horses, upended, their legs in the air like in a slaughterhouse, littered the battlefield. Guardsmen hunkered down behind the bulk of fallen steeds, firing sporadic shots as they tended to wounded comrades.

There was no real cover. The Ironclad went to ground, firing from prone positions. Visibility was almost non-existent.

'Can you hear me?' a voice lanced through the wall of gunfire, and a heavy hand gripped the back of Roth's shoulder rig.

Roth rolled his head back and saw Major Arvust. A gash had opened over the officer's eyebrow and diluted blood leaked down his face. Roth managed a weak nod.

Arvust began to drag him back towards the defensive position. Cantican Guardsmen, probably less than company-strength, were huddled down behind the broad flanks of dead horses. They faced outwards in a ring taking single well-aimed shots to conserve ammunition.

Of the remaining Imperial force, they had one heavy weapon at their disposal. It was a wheeled rotary gun – a heavy stubber with multiple repeating chambers towed by Cantican cavalry. It was not much but it was all they had.

Connecting a wedge of coiled ammunition into the cartridge cylinder, Major Arvust set down behind its butterfly trigger, peering over the brass gun-shield.

'How many spitters do we have for this thing?' Arvust called to his troopers.

'Six hundred jacketed lead and about four hundred boat-tails and tracers, sir,' a young corporal replied in between shots.

'Get rid of the tracers, I don't want to give away position. How many do we have then?'

The corporal immediately began to slot out the interspersed tracer rounds from a wedge of ammunition with the tip of his bayonet. 'No more than nine hundred rounds all up, sir.'

Major Arvust cranked the rotary handle. 'Well then, we better make these count.'

Rocking back on its spoked wheels, the heavy weapon began hammering out a steady *cham cham cham*. Spent cartridges, steaming in the downpour, ejected from the side port. Roth counted them as they spun, arcing through the air.

CHAPTER NINETEEN

THE SCARLET LETTER was the most basic of Inquisitorial methods. But throughout the centuries it was always one of the most effective. Gurion had used it to great effect throughout his career and it had never once failed him.

It was the most rudimentary method to reveal infiltration. False intelligence, or the bait, was deliberately slipped off to the enemy. In this case, Roth had specified Lord Marshal Khmer.

From then on, it was a mechanism of human manipulation. The enemy would pass the bait on to the infiltrator. The infiltrator would act on false intelligence, thereby revealing himself to possess knowledge that no one unaffiliated with the enemy should know. It was a simple trap and one of the core tenets of Inquisitorial method.

It was simple, but its complexity lay within the artistry of execution. A perfectly orchestrated scarlet letter was a trap of subtlety.

Gurion had delighted in the pantomime. He had even agonised many days over it. Something special and particularly intricate would be reserved for Khmer.

First, he had selected the corpse of a crewman from the morgue. The man had died of natural causes; as natural as could be when a hawser cable in the docking hangar had snapped loose, whipping eighty kilograms of tension cable into his chest.

Gurion had dressed the body in a grey storm coat and tactical vest, and even holstered a bolt pistol to the hip. Most crucially, he slipped an Inquisitorial rosette around the corpse's neck and ordained him 'Inquisitor Gable'.

The bait, in this case, was documentation placed in the pocket of Inquisitor Gable. It simply stated that the Conclave suspected an infiltrator in Roth's Overwatch Task Group. Further, it stated that Delahunt's encrypted rosette contained the identity of the infiltrator and that Roth was working to decrypt the rosette. Of course, it was conveyed in code, but it was a basic code that Gurion had purposely made sure Naval Intelligence could analyse.

The irony was that Gurion had no concept of what was contained within Delahunt's log beside his contact with Celeminé. But Khmer was not to know that. The seed would already be planted.

The corpse of Inquisitor Gable was placed onto inbound cargo, left specifically for subordinate officers of High Command to discover. Gurion did not doubt that High Command would examine the corpse and secretly pilfer any intelligence before tasking the body to Gurion's care.

It happened exactly as Gurion predicted. The corpse was repatriated to the Conclave, minus the documentation on its person. It would be in the military bureaucracy's hands now. To have attempted to directly feed the false intelligence to Khmer would have been far too obtuse. Instead he let events take their natural course. Without a doubt, Lord Marshal Khmer would be briefed on the corpse if he did not directly search the body himself.

As the finishing touch to his scarlet letter, Gurion wrote a post-mortem report on Inquisitor Gable. He reported that the inquisitor had been killed on Kholpesh by subversive elements. At the following Council of Conclusions, Gurion debriefed the war council with great solemnity. Inquisitor Gable had died in the service of the Conclave, and the officers, including Khmer, had participated in a minute's silence.

The trap was laid. The rest, he knew, was up to Khmer.

A TANK SHELL landed in the midst of the Imperial ground assault.

It was a splintered sabot projectile. The way it skimmed low across the terrain, screaming like an unleashed banshee, was unmistakeable.

The shell exploded on impact, its bursting charge expelling shrapnel in a streamlined forward direction. The effect on troops in the open was terrible, shredding uniform from flesh and flaying flesh from bones.

Most likely, Roth thought, it was fired from a Leman Russ. He had to move before the Archenemy gunners could realign and reload.

Roth rolled out from behind the cover of a fallen horse and began to crawl through the mud towards where the 7th and 22nd were reforming. His ribs throbbed with a deep bone pain and his dented sternum plate dug into him, but he kept moving. The lancers and light horse were a disciplined lot, and they kept movement constant, firing and reforming before the Archenemy could draw an accurate bead. Disciplined fire and movement was the only thing that kept them alive.

That and the rain. Precipitation continued to shaft down in whickering grey pillars, hard enough that Roth could barely see twenty metres in any direction. If it abated, they were as good as done.

Major Arvust dived into the mud slick next to Roth. His kepi hat was gone and mud was on his cheeks. 'Inquisitor! We have to withdraw! I can't afford any more casualties,' he shouted.

To reiterate his point a high-powered las-round, more than likely from a lascannon, scorched the ground ten paces away. The sudden pillar of energy left a vacuum in its wake that refilled with a thunderclap.

Roth was torn. To withdraw now would relinquish all the gains they had made in the foothills. Although they left a trail of burning vehicles in their path, the enemy would reclaim the high ground and they would be strategically in the same situation as before. It would turn their tactical victory into nothing more than a fleeting act of defiance.

'Withdraw then, while we still can,' Roth said. He would have liked to believe that his injuries played no part in his decision, but he was not so sure.

'Listen for my signal. We'll veer to our east and circumvent the Ironclad's frontline trenches in the event they've regrouped to cut us off.'

'Clear enough!' Roth cried, rainwater and blood trickling into his mouth.

Major Arvust rose into a crouch and took two steps. A solid round punched through the back of his head. The exit wound sprayed Roth with a sudden, shocking burst of steaming blood.

Arvust froze. He looked at Roth, his eyes wide. The major's mouth was moving, trying to work words but nothing came out. His brain was no longer connected to his spine. In a slow, syrupy motion, the major toppled backwards at an angle.

Then the Ironclad exploded out from the mist curtain.

They came, shrieking down on them, materialising out of the threshing rain like smoking ghosts. Water vapour curled off their scrappy, plated silhouettes. Their combat instruments were brandished. Maces, flails, warhammers and cleavers glistened with the sheen of wet metal.

For the first time, Roth found himself face to face with the raiders of Khorsabad Maw. He saw their masked, faceless faces and their crudely barbarous attire. He felt outraged that such savages could threaten the fabric of civilisation. Roth realised he hated them. It was not fear or adrenaline, but a bland baseline hatred. He hated them for the inconvenience it caused him. It was absurd that he was squaring up with the Archenemy, but was driven by a cavalier disregard for his own life. He didn't care, he was just angry.

The Ironclad splashed through the mud. The first Canticans they met were still crouched, firing lasguns over the ribcages of fallen steeds. Their forceful, brutal instruments of war clove into yielding flesh and brittle bone. The impact of the Ironclad charge threw up vertical sheets of blood. Guardsmen toppled as heavy pieces of metal broke them apart.

Roth rose to his feet, his rage overriding his pain. 'Up! Form up and at them!' he bellowed. 'Fix bayonets and at them!'

There was no real direction in attack any more. Roth could not distinguish forwards, nor rear or flank. The battle was a clashing mess. An Ironclad with bulky shoulder pads forged from tank-treads slid in front of Roth. Roth pressed his plasma pistol against the Ironclad's hulking shoulder rig and blew it off. At point-blank range, the Ironclad fell aside, his upper torso incinerated. The superheated gases blistered Roth's face with steaming backwash, but he was glanding on far too much adrenaline to notice.

Roth fired more shots. The fusion-boosted trails of energy ruptured three more Ironclad. Solid matter was rendered into gas, forming dense fountains of bloody steam. Roth drained his entire cell and reloaded.

Captain Pradal floated in Roth's peripheral vision, his lasgun chopping away on semi-auto. Roth had thought he was dead too. The sight of him urged Roth to fight on.

'Getting us all killed wasn't part of the original plan, captain, I apologise,' Roth yelled as he fired at targets no more than striking distance away.

'We did what we came to do and we're doing it well!' Pradal shouted back. He nailed an Ironclad through the vision slit in his text-book shooting stance.

'Nonetheless, I sometimes think I put myself in unnecessary danger,' Roth yelled as he side-stepped a flanged mace.

'You really think so?' replied Captain Pradal. Roth couldn't tell whether the captain was being sarcastic. A mace slashing across his field of vision warranted most of his attention.

One of the Guardsmen close by fell to his knees, his forehead stoved in by a ball-socketed hammer. Roth lunged with his power fist, splitting weapons and pounding aside the Ironclad who pressed in around him.

He was so lost in the frenzy of punching, bobbing, weaving and tearing that he didn't see the sledgemaul that slammed into his lower back. Electric agony shot up his spine and his legs buckled. The pain was so real he could taste it in his mouth, harsh, bitter and sulphuric. He was hit again but this time he didn't feel it. He only found himself laid out on his back, staring at the sky.

The world around him seemed to shut off. Scenes of fighting became stilted and fragmented. He remembered thinking that pain was a good thing. Pain meant his body was still working the way it was meant to. No pain at all was never good.

He saw the sledgemaul swing up like pendulum. Roth watched its trajectory. He waited for it to come down on his head. He wondered if he would feel anything.

But he never did.

The sledgemaul never came down. A round poleaxed its wielder away, in a direction that Roth couldn't see.

Other shots followed the first. Clean, precise shots. Glowing white, las-rounds like rays from the Emperor's halo. Several Ironclad close by were hit. They went down soundlessly.

Dimly, as if very, very far away, Roth could hear the sound of tin whistles. At first he thought it was the sound of pressurised blood escaping his ears but it was not the case. The sound of CantiCol command whistles was distinct. It was the most beautiful sound Roth had ever heard.

Captain Pradal's face fell across his vision of the sky. 'Keep breathing, Roth, keep breathing. Can you move?'

Roth shook his head, not knowing if he could. Then he realised his foolishness and raised a leg. He could.

'Are they here?' Roth said as Captain Pradal shouldered his arm and guided him back to his feet. The captain fired several more shots from his lasgun, one-handed.

'They're here. They're here in force,' Pradal replied.

The rain was abating now. Across the mudflats, advancing across their flank, churning on segmented treads, came a full squadron of Leman Russes. The smooth-plated hulls were painted in the brown, grey and gold of the Cantican regiments. Their pintle mounts were spitting tracers with overlapping regularity.

Advancing between the rare Cantican tanks came six, eight, perhaps ten companies of Cantican infantry. Arrayed in close-order march ranks, they fired as they advanced, a withering lattice of enfilade fire that scythed down the enemy's exposed flank. Drummers rolled out a strident percussion, officers conveyed orders on their tin whistles and regimental banners fluttered.

'They answered the call then,' Roth muttered.

Pradal didn't answer. He fired several parting shots one-handed as the Ironclad broke away. The impetus of their counter-attack was gone, chased down by las and solid shot. The torrent of fire stitched up the Magdalah hills, following the Archenemy over the crest. Firepower like thousands of glowing darts following the fleeing enemy, tagging and dropping them face-down into the terrain.

Someone shouted 'Magdalah is ours!'

The survivors of the 7th and 22nd did not cheer. They simply collapsed into the mud, exhausted, their faces mute. Many closed their eyes and just went to sleep. They knew, for now, they were safe.

THE MAGDALAH FOOTHILLS had been the first real Imperial victory for many months.

Elements of the CantiCol field artillery and other infantry battalions reinforced the 7th and 22nd on the Magdalah. Wading through the after-smoke of defeat, the Ironclad retreated, losing a two kilometre stretch of defences. The Imperial standard was raised on the hills.

News spilled onto the streets of Mantilla, and for a while even the refugees danced and laughed. A hasty artist's rendition of the Imperial standard being raised on Magdalah, borne aloft by a noble-chinned officer, was plastered all over the city walls. Although no such officer existed, the image became the prevailing face of Imperial resistance for many weeks after.

CHAPTER TWENTY

SILVERSTEIN WATCHED THE Ironclad from concealment.

He was coated in red earth, a sandy film of dust that grazed even the lenses of his bioptics. He stayed low, splayed out against the rim of a dry riverbed. His breathing had been regulated, slow and shallow. A layered cloak, mantle and shawl of matted taproot, tangle stem and other stringy desert foliage splayed from his figure. Like him, the guerrillas were also shambling with camouflage. Had it not been for Silverstein's expertise, the Ironclad patrols, which had hounded them for the past five days, might have already found them. Bone dust and salt had been rubbed into the camouflage to conceal his smell. It had thrown the Archenemy attack dogs off their scent during their initial escape, and Silverstein had insisted on maintaining the ritual. The guerrillas did not argue. Under the cover of night, they were just another wrinkle in the ridges and ribs of the rock basin.

Less than twenty metres away from them, three fuel tankers, caterpillar-tracked beasts with snaking carriage bays, were draped in camouflage netting. In the dark, the eighteen-metre long vehicles formed swollen silhouettes, but Silverstein knew from experience that aerial reconnaissance would only discern three long banks of shrubbery.

Apartan, the ex-sergeant, rustled over to Silverstein, the shrubbery of camo-shawl nodding gently. 'That's the eleventh fuel cache we've come across in the past three days,' he hissed urgently into Silverstein's ear.

'This one is a source depot,' Silverstein said to the guerrillas spread out around him. 'See the extraction tower?'

Asingh-nu shook his head. The rural Cantican had never seen an extraction tower before. The skeletal structure of steel girders before him looked awkward and vague. 'What is it used for?'

'Plumbing fossil fuel from the shale deposits. The Archenemy are collecting resources for a massive campaign, discreetly I might add. Spreading out their caches and amassing their forces in the wilderness, far away from Imperial auspices.'

'Why? Why don't they just attack and claim it like they have with Orphrates, Tarsis, Ninvevah...' Apartan paused and swallowed. 'And Cantica.'

Silverstein had no answer.

The Ironclad had been operating this way for some time. They were amassing resources, rearing their supplies for invasion, all the while carefully concealing their movements from Imperial reconnaissance. Silverstein's optics had picked up the distinct outline of Naval scout Lightning soaring high overhead, no doubt on aerial surveillance. The Archenemy were going to great lengths in order to hide themselves. It was a most methodically clandestine preparation, distinctly removed from the Ironclad's mass aerial deployments. It was too unusual to ignore.

'Get low!' Apartan hissed.

They all went low, pressing their faces into the rock. The stone was still warm from the residual heat of the previous day. Silverstein counted backwards from ten, slowly, clutching his looted laspistol. He looked at his hands and saw that white spots of discoloration dotted the back of his hand. Then he realised it was the other way around. The tiny white specks were the colour of his natural skin, otherwise caked in a scabby bark of dirt, grease and too much dried blood. His hands were mauve and so too was his face. It had been weeks, if not months since water had cleansed his skin. Five days since their escape, and for how long before that?

'Enemy, down below,' Temughan whispered to them as he peered over the ridge with a rifle scope.

Silverstein looked and affirmed that fact with his bioptics. Ironclad sentries were posted around the petro-extraction tower. More Archenemy soldiers were stripped to the waist, hauling barrels and connecting clamp hoses to the waiting caterpillar carriers. It was a bizarre contrast between scarred, pallid torsos and the faceless iron masks. Until now, Silverstein had often doubted whether they were truly human beneath the jagged sheets of metal.

+++ **Distance: horizontal 17 metres – vertical depression 6 metres.**
Heat/Movement Signatures: 8 Human/Sub-Human (85% Variation)
Temp: 31 degrees
Visibility: Low +++

'Eight hostiles in view,' Silverstein said, relaying the information to his companions as he processed the data. 'This is how we're going to play, I want the ex-Guardsman and the farm boy with me,' Silverstein said, indicating to Apartan and Asingh-nu. 'Temughan, hold this ridge and cover us, pick them off if anything goes… awry.'

Temughan, the clocksmith with his steady hands, nodded in acknowledgment. He racked the lasgun, the only real weapon they had managed to salvage since their escape five days ago. The others slithered over the ridge line on their hands and knees, clutching looted weapons and braces of munitions and improvised explosives.

They moved with agonising slowness, sometimes not appearing to move at all, creeping forwards with small, controlled shifts of muscle fibre. They moved in a wide circle around the encampment, sweeping out to come in the flank. The silhouettes of Ironclad flickered everpresent in their periphery. Silverstein tried not to look at them. It was an old hunter's myth that looking at your quarry would give them the kindling, warn them they were being encroached on. It was like children who believed if they covered their eyes they could not be seen. There was some truth in that. A good huntsman was guided by other senses.

It took them twelve minutes to sweep around to the side, and a further ten minutes to close the distance towards the extraction tower.

'Stop!' Apartan hissed urgently at Silverstein.

The huntsman was already still. With his left foot, Silverstein quivered the camouflaged reeds around his ankle softly, to match nodding movements of the dry rush grass that he had crawled over.

An Ironclad staggered into the darkness towards them. It was dark and Silverstein could see only the silhouette of broad, boxy shoulder guards. The huntsman chose not to analyse the trooper in any greater detail. He did, however, notice that the Ironclad had the unmistakeable outline of a heavy stubber yoked across his shoulders.

The three of them lay very still. The Ironclad came closer. A metal-shod boot complete with bolted ankle plates stamped onto the ground a mere five metres or so from Silverstein's face. The Archenemy trooper began to prod the strip of dry rush grass with his foot, as if searching for something.

Slowly, Silverstein's hand slid towards the trigger of his EN-Scar autogun. The Ironclad stepped closer, prodding the grass with one boot. Silverstein placed a hair of pressure over the gun's trigger.

With a grunt of satisfaction, the Ironclad found what he was looking for. The trooper fumbled with his chainmail tabard, muttering under his breath. Silverstein heard the drizzle of hot liquid hissing against dry grass and breathed a sigh of relief. The trooper had been searching for the latrines.

They waited until the trooper was finished, then for several minutes after that. Finally, Silverstein flashed the hand sign for them to continue.

Bellying forwards on their elbows, they crept on to the Archenemy fuel depot. Here, the enemy's need for concealment meant the camp was unlit except for the light of the moon. The darkness was to Silverstein's advantage.

The huntsman made one more scan of his area with his bioptics. He counted eight Ironclad, no more. Rising onto one knee, he signalled for the others to take aim at targets to his far left. Looking down his own iron-sights, Silverstein sighted the six others. He searched for a fluid pattern of fire that would carry him seamlessly from one target to the next. He considered firing at the sentry by the base of the extractor, but realised that by the angle of his position, it would leave the furthest target, lounging by the cab of a fuel carrier, open to escape. He could begin firing from the middle outwards, at the two Ironclad smoking tabac at the centre of the camp, but the variance of visibility might alert the enemy to the angle of his muzzle a fraction of a second too early.

After much deliberation, Silverstein settled on a linear pattern of fire, from right to left, darting from one target to the next. If the wind did not affect his aim, which it probably would not, he could put down all six of them in under three seconds.

There was a crackle of shots. Frantic and urgent. The guerrillas reared up, firing on full auto.

'Hit the trucks!' Silverstein shouted.

There was another stutter of barking muzzles followed by a tremendous explosion. For a brief second, night became harsh white day. A roaring mushroom of angry red gas erupted from the ruptured tankers.

Under the belching smoke and confusion, Silverstein rushed towards the drilling rig and hurled a single fragmentation grenade down the drill pump. The huntsman then ran and did not turn back. The resultant explosion would likely have scorched the hair from his face.

Silverstein and the guerrillas exited the area swiftly, their quad-bikes long gone before Ironclad units could be alerted. As they fled, the horizon fluttered a satisfactory yellow against the deepwater sky. It was the ninth oil well that they had set fire to in just five days.

ROTH WAS RETIRED to the officers' infirmary, kept quite separate from the hospice tents of the enlisted men. In the aftermath of Magdalah, combat medics tied him to a horse and led him back into Mantilla for treatment. Had he not been numbed by metadine and hyproxl, the shuddering trot of horseback would have been agony to his battered body. The inquisitor was billeted in Bocob House, an orphanage within Mantilla and far away from the fighting outside its walls, and there he was allowed to rest.

Bocob House was a large, double-winged Imperial building, as austere as Kholpeshi design would allow. Despite this, the structure was still a domed collaboration of glazed tile, mosaic and coloured glass inlay. The clay earth court which surrounded the orphanage was scattered with wooden structures of children's play.

There were slides, teeter-saws and climbing rings, structures that resembled the skeletal carcasses of animals picked clean by scavengers and bleached by sun. Of the children, there was no sign. No one seemed to know where they had gone.

No one thought to ask.

Wounded officers were cycled through here quickly. They didn't have enough beds, and the frontline combat exacted a heavy toll on the officer cadre. Officers with anything short of a grade-two injury were sent back to the front after a maximum of three days at Bocob House. Those who died were taken to the cellars that had once been used for food stores. The pallets they had vacated were hosed down with water and new occupants assigned to them. Blood and waste collected in the sheets and soggy mattresses. It was the reason why Bocob House now smelt of decay.

Roth was a grade-four injury.

The pain was probably at least a grade three. He had sustained blunt force trauma to his sternum and chest, enough to cause minor internal bleeding. The medics had also braced his spine with iron rods to limit movement in his back. The sledgemaul had slipped a disc and almost herniated a fluid sac in his seventh vertebrae. His collection of injuries most likely warranted more than a grade four, but the medics had deemed his injuries 'non-life threatening/absence of bodily severage'.

Rather, Roth had languished for the past twenty-four hours in a semi-comatose fever. He had developed an infection that was more likely the result of poor infirmary hygiene. The medics hooked him up to a fluid drip with a halo of tubes. Amongst the inflow of war casualties, no one noticed he was an inquisitor. In Bocob House he was simply a grade-four patient and they let him ride it out.

'This is just an opinion. But I think you want to get yourself killed.' A voice roused Roth from his heavy slumber.

Roth woke with the heated flushness of a man on the tail-end of sickness. Groggily, Celeminé swam into his vision. She was still clad in her petal dress. Heavy eye shadow of iridescent green gave her eyes a feline slant. She was also wearing long fluttering faux eyelashes and had removed her lip ring. Roth barely recognised her.

'What in Throne's name are you wearing?' Roth murmured weakly.

Celeminé crossed her arms and pretended to be angry. 'This was for the Golias meet. But you wouldn't know because you were too busy trying to make a name for yourself amongst the Guard,' Celeminé chided.

'I think she looks quite pretty,' Madeline said, drifting to his bedside. Likewise, she too was clad in her festive garb. Her chestnut hair was worn long and straight with a blunt, severely fashionably fringe. Her lips were ruby-red.

'You both look like street walk–'

Roth was cut off in mid-sentence by a hard cuff to his shoulder.

'That's no way to talk to a lady,' Madeline admonished.

'Maybe you both should go back to the Golias Estate. He seems to know what a lady should be,' Roth said, still juddering with a delighted burble.

'I don't think we are welcome there any more,' said Celeminé.

Roth stifled his humour. 'How did the meeting play out?'

'Bad,' Madeline said. She shot a look at Celeminé, but said nothing.

'How bad?'

'He tried to have us killed,' Celeminé replied.

Roth shot up. His spine brace was awkward and cut into him but Roth didn't care. 'He did what?'

'Tried to kill us both when the transaction went sour. He's playing the deal cautious. I didn't think he was going to let us even examine the merchandise.'

'But you know the relic is genuine?'

'I don't see why he'd try to kill us over it, if it wasn't,' Madeline concluded.

Roth began to tear out the tubes from his wrist, unplugging them from his flesh with a frantic fury and then unbuckling his spine brace. The exiting needles left puckered welts of purple.

'Roth, what are you doing?' Celeminé cried out in protest. They tried to push him back down onto the pallet.

But Roth's temper was up. He brushed their fussing hands away and tore off the last of his bandages. 'Find me Captain Pradal. I want him to hand-pick a platoon of Cantica's best. We're going to pay that bastard Golias a visit. Tonight.'

THE LANCERS WERE one of the founding units of the Cantican Colonials. They were an elite formation that had been a Regiment of Origin, amalgamated from the fractious colonies of Medina. Even during the Reclamation Wars the Lancers had fought with sword and halberd as the loyalist Frontier Auxilia. That had been six thousand five hundred years ago.

As a poorly equipped force, Cantican Guardsmen were defined by the quality of their men not the superiority of their equipment, and the Lancers were the apogee of this philosophy. Much like the Kasrkin of Cadia or the Commandos of Kurass, selection into the Lancers was limited and highly selective.

A minimum height of one hundred and eighty-five centimetres was enforced and physical demands were high. The regiment largely selected its own. Candidates could be drawn from any unit within the Cantican Colonial regiments and thus selection was egalitarian in a rough, uncompromising way. They were a hard bunch and the company, not the officers, decided who was permitted to wear the Lancer pin.

Recruits, referred to as 'Ponies', were hazed mercilessly regardless of background. They were constantly beaten by up to five fully fledged Lancers at once in a ritual called 'Callusing'. Ponies were mentally and physically broken. It was a process much like the sharpening of a stick. Stripped down to nothing but a jagged mess, the real mettle of a man could be seen and judged by his peers. Those who did not break were welcomed into the fold. For those who did, the Lancers joked, they could always join the Mounted Infantry.

Roth could not have asked for a better selection of soldiers for his raid on the Golias Estate. Captain Pradal had taken him to the Lancer billet, a commandeered building known as the House of Jealous Lovers. It was a courtesan's hall on the fringe districts of Mantilla, illicit and since the war, closed. The House's front façade cascaded with silk drapes of a red and the interior was much the same. Expensive off-world textiles in shades of red, black and tan rippled down the walls, fanned by the open-framed windows.

He found the Lancer reserves cleaning weapons and making kit checks beneath the voluminous gauze curtains. It was a strange visual composition – lean, hard-faced Guardsmen, clacking and snapping rifles with focus, while silk drapes billowed around them. Most of them sat on large oval beds, their gun parts and kit laid out on the linen in greasy black lines.

'This is Captain Almeida, he will be the commanding officer of Two Platoon. Call sign Jackal,' Pradal introduced proudly. Although they were of equal rank, it was evident that the younger Pradal was in awe of the Lancer officer.

The captain shook Roth's hand. The skin of his palm was hard and horned and Roth noticed the skin of his knuckles was coloured dusty white. It was the sign of a bare-knuckle fighter.

'Inquisitor. Your command of the Magdalah offensive was magnificently daring, I applaud you and so does my camp. But I hope your reputation does not give you the wrong ideas. We're Lancers, and these are my Lancers. You work with us, understood?'

So Almeida was the archetypal special duties officer, Roth thought. He warmed to his gruff candour immediately. It was not every day a field officer spoke so openly with a member of the Inquisition.

'Perfectly understood, captain. We storm the Golias Estate and we're done. In and out,' Roth said.

Almeida didn't look at him. His face was creased with focus as he strapped the trademark bandoleer of fuse-bombs and frag grenades across his chest. The explosives clustered in their leather harnesses like swollen metal fruit.

'Captain Pradal has already briefed me on the operation. There will be civvies on the estate so my boys and I will be using low-calibre submachine rifles. I don't want any stray las going through walls and killing mothers, elders and loud children. Any questions?' Almeida asked.

He brandished a T20 Stem autogun, gummed with grease and probably more than several centuries old. The weapon was of stamped and pressed metal, its profile spidery, resembling nothing more than a pipe with a metal T-bar for a stock. Its magazine was distinctly side-fed and horizontal. Without a doubt, it was the most awkward and unimpressive gun Roth had ever seen.

'A Stem T20, captain? Is that weapon going to suffice?'

Almeida clicked a magazine into its side-feed and released the cocking handle with a metallic snap. 'What difference does it make whether the round is .75 cal from a bolter, or a 10mm slug from an autogun? If I drill you between the eyes, it's all the same.'

The captain made a valid point. The Cantican Colonials certainly were not a highly equipped regiment, but if forty angry Lancers could not storm the estate, then they might as well not try, thought Roth.

TACTICAL ENTRY OF the Golias Estate was a delicate matter. The quaint charm of the terrace lent it a certain measure of tactical advantage. Being perched high above street level denied the platoon any option for multi-point entry. The winding stone steps created a natural bottleneck so a frontal assault was out of the question. According to Madeline and Celeminé, the terrace's multiple bay windows housed an overlapping array of alarm systems.

To make matters more precarious, the triple suns cast their light indiscriminately, chasing away shadows and betraying their presence. Stealth would not be an option.

Rather, Almeida ordered a shock raid on the estate. Roth did not object. Jackal One, a team consisting of twelve Lancers, would storm the main entrance, breaching the brass entry door with explosives. Jackal Two, a twelve-man fire-team led by Celeminé and seconded by Pradal, would enter through the roof-top garden by way of Vulture flier.

That left Jackal Three, led by Almeida and Roth who would enter the terrace through the courtyard at the rear. It was straightforward and uncompromising in execution, just the way Roth preferred.

THE WIND WAS coarse and heavy, carrying grains of sand on its warm current.

The outside wall of the courtyard was of smooth terracotta. Roth hugged it, harnessed to a climbing cable that bumped him rhythmically against the walls with every gust of wind. They were high up, on the highest residential tier of Mantilla, a cluster of fabulously wealthy estates reserved for those who had the creds to invest.

Roth checked his wrist chron. According to the winking digitised display it would be starting soon.

On cue, his vox headset spluttered with static. 'All call signs, this is Jackal One, entry team in place. Stand by for countdown. Over.'

Almeida squeezed the bead of his wraparound vox between thumb and forefinger. 'One, this is Jackal Three. Rear entry team in place. Over.'

Digitised, Celeminé's voice echoed his call over the vox system. 'One, this is Two. Jackal Two ready for descent. Over.'

Roth looked up to check. Indeed, the speck of a Vulture gunship was sweeping in, the thumping howl of its turbine thrusters still quiet enough to go un-noticed.

'Fuses ready!' Almeida commanded, his voice amplified by the gusting wind.

Like the Guardsmen in his fire-team, Roth selected a frag grenade from his borrowed bandoleer. He tested the grenade in his hand, rolling the weight on his palm. As one, the fire-team twisted the pins out and squeezed the grenades hard, holding the catch release in place. They waited.

There was no mistaking the signal when it came. A deep earthly tremor of multiple explosions, travelling from the front of the terrace. Even muffled by walls, Roth felt the energy pass through the back of his spine like a wallop of solid wind. Jackal One had breached the entrance.

'Breaching now!' Almeida bellowed as Jackal Three tossed a volley of grenades over the wall. There was a shuddering blast that sent up puffs of dusty debris along the edge of the wall.

Roth was the first to scramble over the courtyard. His T20 Stem was already cradled in his hands, aimed across the tiled garden at the terrace house. The aching joints and injuries of the previous days were forgotten as adrenaline pumped hard through his system. Lancers dropped down around him, crouched with their weapons ready. They met no resistance.

There was no one in sight.

They had come over the wall expecting a fight. Household guards at the very least, but nothing. The fire-team seemed stunned, as if momentarily at a loss with what to do with the weapons they held if not to kill.

'It's clear. Where the hell is everyone?' Roth hissed to Almeida.

The captain shook his head, clicking his vox headset. 'Jackal One, this is Three. Report status, over.'

Silence over the channel.

Some of the Lancers looked at each other uneasily. They realised there were no sounds of gun-fighting in the house. Just an eerie calm and the tittering of clockwork insects in the garden.

'Jackal One, this is Three. Report status, over,' Almeida repeated.

Then, with a shriek of static, Jackal One flooded all channels with their report. It was so loud that several of the Lancers close to Roth winced and tore at their headsets.

'Emperor! Oh damn, oh damn, oh damn–'

There was a rush of static.

'I'm bleeding everywhere! I'm spilling out–'

The vox abruptly cut out. It had been the voice of Sergeant Chanchyn, leader of Jackal One. The frantic terror in his voice burned itself into Roth's memory. Several Lancers tore off their headsets, swearing blackly.

Then Jackal Three was hit.

Trigger mines buried in the subtropical plants went off with a searing flash of white. Roth never heard the explosion, just an overwhelming ring in his ears. Anti-personnel shrapnel shredded the garden, whipping up a blizzard of scrapped vegetation and human meat.

It took some time for his senses to return. For a while, he saw only white and heard only the ringing in his ears. When his senses flooded back like a vacuum he took in the scene before him. Almost half of the fire-team lay on the ground, their limbs twisted and split, their blood pouring out in gulping spillages. The explosives had evidently been hidden beneath the roots of a knot-bole cycad and those closest to the tree had been the worst hit. Bodies lay around the splintered stump.

'Are you good?' Almeida shouted directly into Roth's ear. The captain was bleeding from a split in his right cheek, a deep cut that revealed the whiteness of bone beneath.

Roth checked himself over, patting his limbs. His fighting-plate had absorbed the damage. Pock-marked dents showered up his left calf and torso, small and multitudinous like a galaxy of stars. The anti-personnel mines would have pulped his flesh otherwise.

'I'm good, I'm good,' Roth said.

'Fraggers pre-empted us. Who the hell told them we were coming?' spat Almeida.

We were betrayed, Roth wanted to say. But now was not the time. Instead he looked around and made a quick assessment of the situation. Of Jackal Three, four of the Lancers were evidently dead and two of the wounded would be in no shape to fight. One wounded Lancer was cupping his upper arm, the entire bicep muscle having been stripped away. Another was screaming horribly, his face scoured away by gravel and woodchips into one large graze.

That left seven of them including Roth and Almeida. It might not have been enough, but there was no turning back. Almeida was already up and running, signalling for the others to follow.

Roth crossed the courtyard, kicking over a bird-fountain out of spite on the way. Almeida reached the back door, a lattice screen of fragrant wood. He kicked it in with a boot and hurled a grenade into the dark interior.

Roth sprinted after Almeida. Adrenaline pulsated through his temples. He fired his T20 Stem. The weapon shuddered as he released a burst of semi-automatic fire. It lacked the wrist-jarring recoil of his plasma pistol, but the streak of orange tracer was strangely satisfying. Roth stopped at the threshold of the house, firing a three second burst into the smoke-filled room before hurtling in after the captain.

Golias's private guns waited for him on the other side. They all looked to be ex-gang muscle. The elites of Mantilla had a patronising fondness for hiring slummers as their private guards and escort. There seemed to be an impressive fascination with the chem-nourished biceps and tattoos of a ganger. It made the bourgeois feel like they were flirting with danger. It injected some edge into their otherwise pampered lifestyles. These men were no different. They were all pug-faced and shaven-headed. Tattoos crawled up their necks.

Hiding behind divans, settees and overturned book-cases, the Golias militia handled their street weapons with amateur bravado. They fired wildly, not so much concerned about aim as with laying down an inordinate spray of firepower.

It was in this close-range firefight that Roth truly noticed the difference between well-trained Guardsmen and street gunners. The Lancers went to ground, calm, some even hand-signalling for targets. Their return fire was precise. A house guard was struck in the sternum, spinning him around. The next shot caught him in the back and sprawled him out. Another guard clutched at his throat, frothing at the mouth. The Lancers played well-aimed squeezes of the T20s, rounds hitting the centre of mass.

Within a handful of seconds, the Lancers had cleared the room. Five Golias militia sprawled on the fine carpet under the clearing haze of smoke.

'Clear!' Almeida yelled.

'Clear!' his men echoed.

Then they were up and moving again.

A FUNCTION HALL took up most of the first-storey building plan. Private guards of the Golias household were waiting in ambush there.

Roth felt their minds, crouched behind pieces of ornate neo-colonist furniture. He smelt their anticipatory fear like sour musk in the air. He could sense their lethal intent.

Halting the fire-team before the function hall's sliding lattice doors, Roth warned them of the enemy in wait. Almeida did not question it. He punched a wide, ragged dent into the latticework and the fire-team lobbed a series of grenades underhand into the room.

There was the detonation. They waited for an exact two-count before storming into the function room, the muzzles of their T20s flashing spears of flame into the coiling smoke.

Roth chased the fire-team into the room, weapon raised. The grenade fog was lifting, and the Golias guards were fighting back. The heavy period furnishings of ivory, ebon and solid, well-made wood had protected them from the worst of the fragmentation. They answered back with shotguns and loud solid sluggers.

The sheer volume of projectile and trace fyceline in the room was a tangible smog. They were firing at men less than ten paces away. Roth staggered behind an upturned armoire, seeking cover behind the dense ebon-wood furnishing.

No more than arm's reach away, a Golias gunman rose up from behind the other side of the armoire. He fired a loose shot and missed, his aim thrown as he hastened to duck. The shotgun perforated a bookshelf behind Roth.

'Frag it,' Roth swore. He dropped his T20 and tugged his Sunfury from its holster. Exhaustion was robbing Roth of his momentum, and he could feel the pain from his previous injuries ebb like a creeping tide. He needed to end it quickly. Roth's first plasma shot melted a perfect hemisphere over the lip of the cabinet. The next shot bisected the offending gunman on the other side.

'Jackal Three, this is Jackal Two,' Celeminé's voice crackled over the frequency.

'Two, this is Three, come in, over,' Almeida reported. His command was punctuated by a raking volley from his T20.

'Our entry point is denied. Repeat, entry point for Jackal Two denied. Our craft scanners have picked up heavy weapons and explosive traps on the rooftop. This is going to be harder than we thought,' she yelled.

'Two, this is Three. Abort entry,' Almeida said. He fired another burping burst from behind a divan. Turning to Roth he shouted, 'It's done. We're playing on our own now.'

Roth tucked his head as shotguns barked over him. They were alone, that much was true. But these were the Cantican Lancers, and their enemy were nothing more than hired muscle. Roth wasn't the least bit fazed.

'Fire pattern Ordnance,' Almeida instructed over the squad-link.

It was the one training drill that the Lancers had run through with Roth before the operation. They had only shown him the rudiments in passing but it was a simple enough drill. Everyone in the fire-team had been assigned an odd or even number.

On Almeida's command, the evens rose and lay down a screen of covering fire forcing the enemy down. Roth was one of them. He rolled to his knees and hammered a series of plasma shots down the length of the chamber. The shots atomised fabric and calcified wood on contact, laying out fist-sized holes of destruction at the far end of the function room.

The odds primed grenades, and as the evens ceased fire, they uncoiled into a semi-crouch, hurling the grenades across the chamber with a leaning wind-up. The explosives bounced off the walls, landing behind the makeshift barricade of the enemy.

Sheets of sparking explosions engulfed the furthest end of the room. The walls shook and loose plaster drizzled from the ceiling. A bookcase collapsed.

The heated exchange of fire died away. The enemy were screaming, moaning. They were street scrappers, young ganger braves with enough scars to impress the closeted aristocracy into employment. Some knew the business end of a knife or pistol, but they were no match for trained soldiers.

The survivors emerged from behind their barricade, hands raised in surrender. Almeida rose too, picking them off with one clean shot each. There was not enough time and too much at stake to process prisoners.

Roth rested for a moment, breathing hard against the battered, splintered and scorched remnants of the heavy armoire. He looked at the dispatched gunmen, their bodies draped across the barricade. Despite himself, Roth pitied the corpses. They had simply been desperate men, men who found themselves in a business way over their heads.

'All call signs, this is Jackal Three, first storey is clear. Proceeding to second level. Over,' Almeida broadcasted into his vox headset. In all likelihood, Jackal One were all dead and Jackal Two would be a long time coming. He might as well not have used the link at all.

They were moving again. Almeida and his sergeant ran point. They ran with a synchronised efficiency, Almeida bent double in a running crouch, his sergeant aiming a T20 over the captain's hunched back. Together, the seven men of Jackal Three made for the railed, corkscrew staircase to the upper levels.

THEY MET DOGGED resistance at the connecting corridor of the second storey, with Corporal Aturk being downed by a headshot on entry. There was a ferocious exchange of fire but the Lancers pushed the house guard back. Private Aman, the fire-team's surviving assault specialist, took to the fore with a flamer. His weapon unleashed a tornado of fire down the corridor, incinerating a twenty metre stretch of hall. It was over in a matter of seconds.

They found Golias's house guests, herded together like frightened sheep in some of the upstairs guest rooms. Perhaps fifty or sixty Mantillan elites, huddled in the chambers, crying and frightened to the point of hysteria. The black rouge ran down the faces of women in dripping rivulets and the men were even worse, their shoulders racked by uncontrollable sobs. Some were still crashing on narcotics, their delirious terror amplified by opiates.

At one point, Sergeant Calcheed gripped the silk lapel of a wealthy oligarch and pulled him close. The man was obviously under the influence of obscura, spurse, alcohol or some combination of the three.

The sergeant leaned in until they were nose to nose, and grinned. 'So you want to ignore the war by revelling hard, huh? How about ignoring this?' Sergeant Calcheed pressed the barrel of his T20 to the man's head. The merchant audibly soiled himself and his knees buckled. Calcheed dropped him, disgusted.

Roth looked to Almeida but the captain did not reprimand his sergeant or tell him to stop. The captain said nothing. In a way, Calcheed was only acting out how they all felt. For too long the nobles had gone about their business, ignoring the war at the expense of all others. It felt good; it felt like the Emperor's justice to snuff their debauchery.

They locked the panicked guests in their rooms, barring the doors with heavy antique chairs to prevent any interference, before pressing on.

It was not until they cleared the second storey that they heard the Vulture gunship of Jackal Two overhead, pounding the rooftop garden with autocannons. It sounded like an industrial drill dismantling the upper storeys.

'Jackal Three, this is Two. Permission granted from Central Command to use aerial weapons in a civilian zone. Neutralising rooftop obstacles. We'll be down to play shortly. Out,' Celeminé reported.

GOLIAS WAS TRAPPED between Jackal Three storming up the corkscrew staircase from the lower levels, and Jackal Two sweeping down from the rooftops. Golias militia attempted to intervene in the rooftop garden, but soon learned that their street-fighting held no credibility up there either.

'Two, come in Two. Third storey all clear except for the atrium and his launch hangar. Report status?' Almeida growled. The fire-team was crouching low now, wary. Their guns flickered from corner to corner. Golias would be close.

'This is Two. Rooftop all clear. No place left to run. Over.'

'Loud and clear. Stay sharp on the rooftop and be ready. We might flush him out yet. Out.'

This was when Golias would be at his most dangerous. Roth knew it all too well, that when the quarry was cornered, he was the most unpredictable.

Jackal Three found Hiam Golias in his atrium. The man was not armed. He did not appear to be. He was naked, lounging silkily by his impluvium pond.

The fire-team fanned out, training their submachine weapons on him while auspexes scanned for trip-wires, trigger bombs and motion sensors. Golias didn't seem to care much for them. He splashed the pond surface with his palm, watching the wrinkles in the surface ripple outwards.

Roth approached the collector, slowly.

'Hiam Golias. This is Inquisitor Obodiah Roth. I have heard a lot about you. I thought you would have put up more of a fight, considering.'

The collector looked up lazily, pushing his silver mane upwards and away from his face. He shrugged, nonchalant. 'And I thought you would all be dead by now. Sometimes plans don't go our way.'

'You're a bastard, do you know that?' Roth remarked.

'I was just protecting my interests. No one told you to come looking for me,' Golias shrugged.

'And who told you that we would come looking for you, Golias? Who told you?' asked Roth, standing over Golias.

Golias didn't look at him.

'Someone with my interests in mind. Someone who doesn't like you, inquisitor.'

Roth decided to change tack. He brandished his plasma pistol, and drew it across Golias's field of vision.

'This is a Sunfury MKIII plasma pistol. Its fusion reactor core fires an ionised gas nova that will melt ten centimetres of plasteel. Do you have any idea what this will do to your face?'

Golias said nothing.

'Let's start with some questions,' Roth said, evening his tone. 'Who told you I would be coming for you?'

Finally Golias levelled with Roth's gaze. 'I don't know. I was warned by a Cantican officer. He did not indulge me with who sourced to him. Don't ask, don't tell. It's how we operate.'

Roth probed him with a gentle mind spike, intruding on the man and making him startle visibly. Roth was perhaps more forceful than he could have been. He simply rifled through his emotional receptors, roughly. Golias was telling the truth.

'Next question. Where is this relic?' Roth asked.

'What will you pay me?' Golias replied brazenly.

'I have three choices for you, Golias. We can kill you now, if you're stupid enough. Or you can work with us, and live. Third option, you play me the fool, and we airevac you and drop you into Archenemy territory.'

'You won't kill me, you need me for the relic,' Golias said confidently.

Roth slapped the haughty merchant on the back of the head. He dealt him a second humiliating slap. 'Are you stupid, man? Auto-séance. Heard of that? I'd love nothing more than to put a round through your skull and drag your soul kicking and screaming from the abyss for answers.'

Golias was less confident now. There was a tremor in his lip, slight but noticeable.

'Be a good man. Show us where it is,' said Roth, crouching down next to Golias in an almost benign manner. 'I don't want to have to waste a shot on your stupid head.'

CHAPTER TWENTY-ONE

'I'VE NEVER SEEN anything of such scale and preservation,' Madeline said.

She had joined Roth's fire-teams via escorted Vulture gunship. Her expert opinion had, in Roth's words, been warranted out of utter necessity. The Task Group, steering Golias with the muzzles of T20 autoguns, were led down a mineshaft. That was what it appeared to be at first glance, once Golias had opened a vaulted blast door concealed behind an oil portrait of a Golias ancestor.

'This place is a mine in every sense of the word,' Madeline continued breathlessly.

The elevator trolley, a wire mesh cage of flaking red oxide, clattered as it lowered the team. Its keening metallic screech echoed down the abyssal depths, screaming back up at them from below. Down and down they went, for six thousand metres until they hit the bottom.

'Holy Throne,' Roth muttered, as the phos-lamps of the conveyance trolley illuminated the subterranean dark.

'Yes, every bit as majestic as you expected,' Golias said.

In truth the collector's relic was not what Roth, or indeed what any of the Task Group, had expected.

At first it appeared to be a mining seam, at least eight thousand metres in length. Striations of ore and red ironstone ran the length of its sheer, scoured face. Anchor bolts buttressed the monstrously cavernous heights where rock had been sheared away in precisely cut horizontal and vertical sheers.

Yet as they approached, they could make out finer details. Crenulations and fleche spires melded from the rock-face like unfinished sculptures. In some parts, repeating pointed arches seemed to be carved into the geo-strata, long orderly rows that played the entire length of the mining cut.

'This is Imperial Gothic architecture, Ecclesiarch design, perhaps?' Madeline murmured.

'No. Dictator-class design,' Roth said.

'Dictator? I'm not familiar with that era of architecture. Is it of Fringe cultural origin?' Madeline asked.

'What he means,' Celeminé began, 'is that this is a Dictator-class cruiser. Can you see the lance-decks there? The gargoyle steeples there?'

Golias's relic was a fossilised Imperial cruiser. A patina of mineral growth sheathed its exposed parts, simple salts and silicate deposits glittering like a rime of gritty ice. Geo-forms clustered across the ship's flank like a hide of barnacles. It was as if the cruiser itself had become a part of the planet's mantle, a tectonic wedge of quartz, mica, calcium and ironstone sediment.

Golias guided them up a ramp that led into a blast-cut opening in the ship's broadside. The wound in the ship resembled a mining tunnel. Support beams created a framework beneath the sagging rock where demolitions and mining drills had punctured its surface.

'This is the *Decisive*, a Dictator-class cruiser of the 2nd Naval Expeditionary Fleet,' Golias proclaimed proudly. 'The ship itself was downed on Aridun at some point during the War of Reclamation in Medina. There was nothing in the ship's data to reveal the cause of the ship's demise but judging by this entry wound in the ship's hull, it had not been primitive barbarians that the Imperium had been fighting.'

Roth paused at the threshold of the cruiser's wound. The jagged cross-section of the ship revealed a hull that was almost five metres thick. Whatever had damaged the *Decisive* had been powerful indeed.

'Golias, if you've got any more aces up your sleeve, forget it. I want nothing more than to finish you, so don't give me a reason. Understand?' Roth growled.

The collector nodded mutely as Roth vented his plasma pistol with a vaporous hiss. Celeminé lit the ignition on her hand flamer. Captain Pradal slid the bolt of his T20 to semi-automatic. Even Madeline cocked the hammer of a slim, revolving stub-pistol.

'You first,' said Roth, waving Golias into the shaft.

Slowly, the Overwatch Task Group entered the ossified cruiser.

THE VAST INTERIOR of the cruiser was barely recognisable.

Over the millennia, beards of stalactite drip from the upper gantry formed an undulating warpage of ground rock across the surface flooring of the vessel. Roth led the way, the beam of his stab-light probing over broken shapes of ship instruments and cavernous corridors.

House Golias had strung up dim, phosphorescent lamps to light the way. Under the pallid light, Roth could see that age had changed the ship in strange ways. The belly of the vessel was vast, painted in hues of rotting teal, brown and mostly black. Many interior walls had collapsed, or had melted seamlessly with stone. Veins of opal glimmered in fissures. Thermal springs had formed in some corridors, vomiting intermittent geysers of toxic gas. The air was bad, and the wet, humid fumes cultivated bacterial strains of fungus on the walls.

'Don't touch anything, some of the microbials here are quite infectious,' Golias said as he expertly led them down a path he had obviously trodden many times. The ship had been the sole reason that the ancestral patriarchs of the Golias house had levied their estates in its location. They knew its worth, and invested in it. An investment that spanned forty-five generations.

'Slow down, Golias.' Roth commanded. 'Where are you leading us?'

'To the ship's bridge, where else? Unless cave exploration is what you were after,' Golias said in an irritatingly off-hand manner.

'Golias, I'm very close to headbutting your nose inwards,' Roth said flatly.

They climbed rather than walked for some time until finally emerging in a communications hall. Thirty metres to their front, the blast doors to the bridge yawned open like the ruptured shell of a rotting crustacean.

'There's the bridge, undisturbed since the Reclamation Wars,' Golias said, suddenly rushing forwards over a crest of calcite deposit that might have once been a broken support strut.

Roth tightened the grip on his pistol and signalled for several of their CantiCol escorts to stay guard outside the command bridge.

Unlike the rest of the cruiser, the reinforced vault of the cruiser's bridge was remarkably well preserved. It was like a piece of history, crystallised in time. A tactical spreadsheet was still spread on the tact-altar, its small chess-like pieces still pinned in place. The ship's command throne was untouched, its neural plugs placed in a neat row on the leather seat.

'Servitors?' asked Madeline, pointing to the trio of frail cogitate-logicians standing around the command throne. They were strange creatures, with despondent human faces and ornate box-shaped torsos. Keys and wires spilled from a hatchway in their abdomen.

Golias nodded. 'We purchased them to maintain this vault. They can power up the ship's main databanks.'

Roth waved his pistol at Golias. 'Be a good man, and power up the databanks.'

Golias, for once, was obedient. The servitors began their work, their bald heads bobbing up and down in rhythmic unison as their fingers trotted across the ivory keystrokes. Some of the cogitator screens had been damaged during the initial crash-landing six thousand years ago. Many of them had also fallen into disrepair despite the efforts of the House Golias servitors.

'Over the course of several thousands years the computers had lost physical memory,' Golias explained. 'Disintegrating logic-engines and withering circuitry have corrupted much key data, but what I have here is invaluable. You'll be so pleased, inquisitor.'

With a mechanical groan, the cruiser's banks started. The monitors that still functioned flickered a lambent green as the servitors dredged up the ageing data.

IT HAD BEEN there the whole time.

When the hololithic map of the Medina Corridor was projected, the six-thousand-year-old image reviewed Medina as it was – a cluster of globes each marked with clearly visible orbit lines and equatorial ley-lines across the planet's surface. As the three-dimensional map made its orrery revolution and the planets shifted, the puzzle, for Roth at least, fell into place.

It was a moment of fleeting clarity, the exact breath between accepting reality and the blindness of not knowing.

The Medina Corridor was, in the old proverbial, a treasure map. The equatorial ley-lines formed linear markings across the globes. They appeared as thin razor scratchings visible from orbit. The alignment of planets in the Medina Corridor formed a stellar map, and the equator lines formed patterns. Patterns that were complex and interlocking yet primitively minimalist in concept.

Roth was dumbfounded that they hadn't seen this earlier. It had been so evident, literally before their eyes. The Medina Corridor formed a series of links with the axis of the equatorial planar lines all meeting at a central location.

The centre of the Old Kings.

'Chaos isn't digging blindly at all…' Roth began.

'No. They're forming the old equator lines and schematics required to awaken the Old Kings,' Madeline said.

'Awaken?' Pradal asked, taking off his cap and running a hand nervously through his hair. The young captain was obviously confused.

'I'm not sure. But ley-lines have existed for as long as human civilisation. Geodesy was an old Terran discipline of studying a planet's magnetic fields, polar motion, tides and so forth. Early man postulated that such lines were extraterrestrial in nature, along with a heavy dose of geomancy. What I am sure of is that these lines across the Medina Worlds are related to the Old Kings.'

As the map spun on its three-dimensional axis again, dense blocks of script scrolled up the length of the monitors, revealing the extent of Imperial war-making intelligence during the Reclamation campaigns. It seemed even during the Reclamation, the Imperial military machine had given some focus on the existence of these Old Kings and their potential for changing the course of the campaign.

According to the sources, the origins of the Old Kings began far back in the antiquity of Pre-Imperial Medina. What the ship's data described as 'Early Sentients' had come to Medina, bearing with them the influences of a highly advanced xenos culture as well as their worship of the stars and constellations. This Roth already knew from Gurion's briefings, but there was much more lodged in these databanks.

When the Early Sentients finally left the Medina Worlds, they left for their subjects a parting gift. They bequeathed them an embryonic star. Through their worship of the stars, in effect, the Sentients had gifted Medina a god. It was the Old Kings or the Star Ancient or the myriad other names that had passed through the generations. The star was held in a form of dormant stasis described as a *Tomb Bell*, to forever watch over the people of Medina. Or so the databanks would have Roth believe. There was so much detail, so much scripture. So much to take in.

The intelligence report continued, 'During a great time of strife, at the precise alignment of the magnetic conduits of the ley-lines with the astronomical bodies, the star could be released from its stasis and unleashed. The star within the Tomb Bell can be thus removed from its resting place and unleashed where strife is greatest.' The report became vague thereafter, postulating various theories as to the significance of the ley-lines and the destructive magnitude of an expanding star.

'A star kept in stasis?' asked Roth.

'This worship of astronomical bodies has happened for all time since the history of man,' Madeline said.

Roth understood. On Terra, he knew of lost tribes that
had carved similar lines visible from orbit. These lines
were the geological conduits of magnetic energy. Roth
had read about these before, although the true meanings
and practices soon became lost to ritual and symbolism.
Man did not truly understand the teachings of the Early
Sentients. But they trusted themselves to a blind following of the schematics ordained by the elder races. They
carved great helio-lines, swathes of geometric markings
across the surface of their planets. The data did not elaborate any more as to the nature of these xenos or their
practices. Roth humbly conferred with Madeline for
answers.

'Early Sentients, madame?'

The professor shook her head as she read. 'Probably a
disambiguation of the term. It would not be the first
time that an alien race has played its hand during the
early formative years of human development.'

'And these lines? These ley-lines, have you studied
them at length?'

'I've seen them before. The composition of globe lines
was called "*Pedj Shes*" in the earliest languages. It literally
means "stretching of the cord". It's a process of marking
long linear geometry across the surface mantle of planets, so that during a specified point of the astronomical
revolution, the equator lines would align and create
shifts in magnetic polar energy.'

'And the early Medinians understood all of this?'

'Probably not. An isolated society's first contact with
others often results in attempts to emulate and mimic
without reason or understanding. According to anthro-
pologists, symbology and fetishisation became more
important than knowledge.

Roth had known that primitive civilisations when
contacted by the Imperium often resulted in such
behaviour. Primitives had constructed canoes in the

shape of Imperial ships. The Tukaro culture of the Mephius subsector even shaped spears in the crude outline of lasguns, and made their warriors brand themselves with a stylised aquila, in order to mimic the power of the Imperial Guard.

Indeed during the Tukaro Civil Wars, the Imperium had deployed onto the primitive planet with a great deal of unknown equipment. The vast amounts of war materiel that were airdropped onto these archipelagos during the subsector campaign necessarily meant drastic influences to the Tukaro people, who had never seen the Imperium before. Manufactured clothing, medicine, canned food, textiles, weapons and other cargo arrived in vast quantities to equip soldiers. Some of it was shared with the Tukaro indigenous. Following the resolution of civil strife, the Imperium abandoned the primitive planet. It had no strategic or resource value to the Imperium, and planetary governance was ceded to the Ecclesiarchy. The cargo lifters no longer visited.

In attempts to receive cargo, the indigenous Tukaro imitated the same practices they had seen the soldiers use. They carved headphones from wood and wore them while sitting in fabricated control stations. They waved dried-leaf landing paddles while standing on the runways. They lit signal fires and torches in the abandoned starports.

The difference here was that the Early Sentients ordained mankind to worship the stars. They promised that during the proper alignment, the Old Kings would wake from their dormant slumber and strike their enemies down with wrath should their civilisation ever be threatened.

Suddenly it all made sense to Roth. He did not require the rest of the databank history to connect the remaining pieces. The insurrectionists who had fought the Imperial Fleet during the Reclamation Wars had attempted to release their embryonic star. Of that there was no doubt.

The Medina Corridor's unique stellar alignment, orrery orbit and axis angles, and most importantly the constant shifting of its axial cycles, meant that the helio-lines that had once marked the planets would shift into alignment. But they had failed. Evidently, the Imperium had reclaimed the Medina Worlds.

'Do you think that the natives tried to release the embryonic star? Do you think that is what caused the mass extinction on Aridun?'

'I've never thought of that,' Madeline admitted. 'But it would make sense. If the star was still dormant, releasing it from stasis would at least have caused a radioactive flare.'

'Which would mean…'

'Which would mean an erosion of the planet's atmosphere, causing turbulent climate changes.'

Roth breathed out with the weight of revelation. He realised the only difference between the six-thousand-year-old projection before him, and the cartographer's charts he had studied in his pre-operation briefings, was the absence of those global markings. As the millennia worn on, Cantica and Kholpesh built their cities on cities and the lines were buried under civilisation. The same geodetic lines that the Archenemy were unearthing. It was a matter of filling in the gaps, retracing the zenith, the nadir, the azimuth points. Measuring for elevation and meridian planes and thus rebuilding the schematics of these Early Sentients.

'These scratchings, these ley-lines, how do they awaken the Old Kings?' Roth asked.

'I can only answer in terms of pre-history. It was common amongst the prehistoric tribes of Terra to believe such lines channelled the magnetic energy of planets. There must be some correlation between magnetic equator lines, the alignment of astronomy and the stasis field of the Old Kings. The timing seems key here,' Madeline surmised. 'Once the stasis field is disrupted, I'm guessing this violent star can then be transported within its Tomb Bell to *wherever the strife is greatest*, as this scripture suggests. The Archenemy have timed this well.'

And indeed it was all executed with impeccable timing. According to the orrery of the hololithic map, the constellations were already in perfect alignment. The Old Kings would be active now, roused from their dormant sleep and thrumming with the magnetic sustenance channelled by the conduit ley-lines spanning an entire star system.

But the worst, the very worst was the revelation that they had all deceived themselves. They had underestimated the enemy. Khorsabad Maw's vanguard assault had not been a blindly roving treasure hunt. It had not been the sporadic plundering of planets. Rather, it had been a methodical process of preparation.

They had not, as Imperial intelligence believed, been using the slaves to excavate in some vain attempt to locate the Old Kings. The quarries, so visible from orbital reconnaissance, had been the geodetic constructs.

What terrified Roth even more, the one thing that was most horrifying, was that the Archenemy had known where the Old Kings slept all along. They had simply chosen not to play their hand too soon and reveal it to the Imperium. Instead they prepared their conduits, leaving the Old Kings on Aridun untouched.

The Archenemy had been waiting until the lines had been laid across Medina from Naga to Tarsis, and the embryonic star was ripe to release from stasis. From there on, the Archenemy could remove the star contained within its vessel, and utilise its destructive potential at any strategic location within the Imperium. Lord Marshal Khmer had been wrong. Very wrong.

Chaos had not been irrational. They had been so entirely logical that the Imperium had missed it.

WITH THE REVELATION of the Old Kings, the Task Force moved quickly. Preparations were made to transit off planet immediately. Mantilla was crumbling and the minor victory at Magdalah, although morale-lifting, did not abate the inevitable. The void shield was stuttering in places, and Ironclad gas artillery was beginning to pound on the city proper. Of Hiam Golias, the collector, Roth made sure to confiscate his cargo-flier for the war effort. The collector, under the auspices of Cantican military provosts, was then sent to the front-line trenches as an auxiliary labourer. Of his fate, Roth knew not.

The inquisitor was already preoccupied with the next phase of his mission and his mind was elsewhere. As pressing as it was to act swiftly on Aridun, Roth was a man of priorities and he could not leave Kholpesh without flushing the traitor from within his ranks.

THE SCARLET LETTER was a trap of two folds.

Once the quarry took the bait, it was up to him to reveal himself through error. An error that an innocent man would never have made.

The error here would be Delahunt's log. The jewel of his signet ring was plugged to a decryption machine like a crumb of food in a spring-loaded rodent trap.

Roth had made it clear, in no uncertain terms, that he had found something of interest on Delahunt's log that the previous encryption scan had not relinquished. He'd put it down to poor system function; the device used in the tunnels of the Barbican had been rudimentarily crude.

It was all a ploy.

Now Roth lay in wait, sequestered within the panelled walls of their military billet. His room had been purposefully left in a state of disarray. He had informed the Overwatch Task Group that Major General Cabales had requested his immediate assistance regarding an issue of tactical significance. Roth had ordered the Task Group to prepare their equipment for transit to Aridun in his absence.

Now he, and ten hand-picked Canticans, men he had personally drawn from the trenches with no prior contact to his staff, lay in wait.

He had even left the linen on his pallet bed unmade, and the drawers of his dresser ajar, as if he'd left in haste. The decryptor was in the corner of the room, beneath a glass-shaded lamp, its gilded keys chattering quietly.

THE FIGURE PADDED down the barrack's billet. It was late in the evening and although the Kholpeshi suns were still searing, the rest shutters had been drawn along the corridor. Slatted bars of fiery amber sun played along the plyboard walls, bending the shadows into exaggerated shapes of black on a canvas of fiery orange. The figure slinked along the shadows, veiled in inky blackness.

Roth's room was easy to find. It was the only room along the corridor with the door ajar. Evidently, Roth had left in a hurry.

There was no need for stealth. It carried with it unwarranted suspicion. Rather, a hand pushed the door open, brazenly.

'Roth, Roth are you here?' called the voice.

The figure stepped into the empty room. Their billets were spartan, the sleeping quarters of a gas mill where the workers were allowed their daily six hours of rest shift. That had been before the war.

Roth's room contained nothing more than a single iron-framed bed. Gas canisters in rusted cylinders lined the plyboard partition walls, towering over the bed in a way that suggested utility room rather than sleeping quarters. A single ventilation fan stuttered overhead. It squeaked on its wiring, its blades lashing fast-running shadows continuously across the room. These quarters were not known for their comfort.

In a far corner of the room, nestled between a gas cylinder and a sheet-metal spit bucket, a decryptor was at work. The machine looked at odds with its surroundings, its ivory keys tapping, sinking and releasing of their own accord. Mother-of-pearl panelled the casing and a series of whirling gyroscopes timed the rhythm of its work. A golden cherub's face mounted at the centre of the console released a paper tongue of readouts, its decrypted data collected in a spool of loose parchment.

The figure locked the door and stalked towards the decryptor. Delahunt's ring was attached to a pulse data link, the cord winking a cold blue light. The figure knelt down before the machine and halted its process with a few deft strokes of its ivory keys. The decryptor gunned down with a reluctant groan of cogs, the paper tongue ceasing to lengthen.

Unfolding a flask from beneath a belt, the figure began to douse the machine with a slick, oily liquid. The stale, humid air of the room was suddenly cut with the sharp sting of naphtha. Particular attention was paid to the signet ring; that had to burn first.

Producing a small book of paper tinders, the figure struck one. A small flame guttered into being, producing a small halo of light around the hand that held it.

Something was not quite right.

Under the light of the teetering little flame, the decryptor's data slips could be read clearly. They did not say anything of worth. Rather they said nothing at all. The signet ring had been emptied of its data cache and replaced with a sequence of scramble patterns and sequenced nonsense.

Scarlet letter caught – caught scarlet as now – letter spilling scarlet – caught now –

'Oh Throne,' said the shadowy figure.

ROTH HAD SEEN enough.

He laid open the plyboard with a kick of his metal-shod feet, sending the partition board flying in separated parts. Gas canisters toppled, collapsing in a domino chain with hollow metallic rings. Cantican Guardsmen, their lasguns held up to shoulders, came barging in from all sides, kicking down the dormitory partitions.

'Cease and surrender! Inquisition!' Roth yelled.

He lined up the target kneeling in front of the decryptor with his pistol. He steadied his aim and stopped.

He froze, his mind stalled as it struggled for rationality.

Celeminé stared back at him. Her eyes were so far open her pupils were surrounded by white.

Roth hesitated. His mind tried to invoke some logic into what he saw. He tried to find some way to explain what was happening that did not lead to confrontation. Roth's mouth was so dry, and his mind was so blank. Fumbling for reasoning, he found none except that it had been Celeminé all along.

The hesitation was all she needed.

An expanding ring of psychic energy fluttered from Celeminé. It was partly powered by her mind, partly driven by her intense instinct to fight back. The wall of solid force hit the Cantican Colonials closing in on her, striking with the impact of a fast-moving freight vehicle. The last of the partition walls and gas banks were bowled over like loose skittles. Guardsmen were poleaxed off their feet, their entire skeletal structures rendered into splintered fragments on impact.

Roth was blown half-way back across the adjoining dormitory, sliding across the floor before his momentum was arrested by a storage locker. His psi-reactive tabard calcified, some of the obsidian panes around the hem turning to a dusty, brittle white. It was a forceful mind blow, but Roth had taken worse. He staggered back onto his knees.

Celeminé stalked towards him. The sudden explosion of psychic force left her weak and off balance. She lurched drunkenly towards him, a thread of blood running down her nose. 'I should have known, Roth, you can't work a decryption to save your life.'

'I just did,' Roth said. He reached for his pistol and realised it had spun out of his grasp. He bided for time. 'Why did you betray us?'

Celeminé almost smiled. 'Come on, Roth, you sound hurt. You should have seen this coming. I'm surprised it took you as long as it did. Aren't I ambitious enough for you?'

'What did Khmer give you? How did he turn you?'

'I am a woman, Roth. The ordos, it's a patriarchal game. Khmer gave me something you wouldn't understand. He promised me he had the pull to give me greater authority.'

'You had authority. You were an inquisitor.'

Celeminé laughed. Even now, Roth found it a pretty laugh; she curled the corners of her lips up like a broken bow.

'Not like that. He would have given me things you wouldn't have.'

'Me? What are you–' Roth began.

'You insensitive ass,' she laughed. Roth flinched at her stinging words. 'You still don't understand. I would have the opportunity to advance more rapidly as an inquisitor.'

'He lied.'

'Everybody lies,' Celeminé shrugged.

Roth squeezed the trigger.

She beat him to it. Her psychic form, a rushing bow-wave of tidal energy, surged up and towards him like a tsunami.

Roth's psychic power could not hope to match her strength for strength. He played the intellect's game. He shifted his mind into an empty bubble, allowing the crashing tide to carry him.

Celeminé's attack swept them away, taking them high above the Mantillan skyline within the span of half a second. Roth knew he was in deep now. He was playing her game.

Celeminé attacked hard and furiously. Sea serpents, wide of jaw and many-headed, uncoiled from her mind's eye. Seven, seventy, eventually seven hundred sea serpents like tendrils of hair writhed and intertwined as they reached out with snapping, translucent maws.

He wasn't strong enough to counter anything like that. Roth refused to play her game. He curled up into an abstract shape, too many corners to be a triangle, far too multi-dimensional to be a polygon. The lashing serpents hammered him, knocking him about. It hurt Roth, threatened to break him, but it confused Celeminé, denying her a tangible target.

But her intellect directly correlated with her psychic ability. She adapted quickly, fusing her hundreds of serpents into a single horned fish, its grinning maw bristling with spikes. The leviathan engulfed Roth, swallowing him whole. Roth dispersed himself like droplets of water just as the maw snapped shut. He survived, but barely. The fish blew out every shingle of the gas mill roof like a storm of broken teeth in its psychic backlash.

Roth was tiring now. His mind wasn't sharp. Part of him was still in disbelief, and the doubt had a tangible effect on his psychic ability. Sluggish, he crawled away, seeking escape. He fled in the only direction he could go – out beyond the trenches towards the Archenemy.

Taking the form of a streamlined bolt, Roth streaked out
across Mantilla. The Imperial trenches, throbbing with
small-arms fire blurred beneath him. Celeminé pursued.
He could feel her mind-snare, reaching out for him.
Several times she almost touched him, the whispering
fingers of her pursuant form sending shocks of fright
through him.

+Celeminé. Why?+

+Shut up, Roth. I'm tired of explaining already. Let's
just finish this.+

She chased him far from Mantilla into the battlefields.
Out beyond, in the fields of the enemy, the psychic
planescape was different. The sky was darker there, the
light filtered and silty. The plague of Archenemy minds
below him seethed like a pit of violence, aggression and
ignorance. The things he could see there, the ambient
memories of so many murderers, were strong enough to
completely destroy his sanity.

Roth dived in amongst it.

It was akin to plunging into a cauldron of boiling
water. The shock almost killed him. His physical body,
many kilometres away, convulsed with enough force to
cause hair-line fractures in his spine. He tried to shut out
the minds of the Archenemy but they were all around
him. He suddenly knew what it was like to kill a child.
He knew the wild elation of watching others die from
slow poisoning. He knew what it was like to slide a razor
into the belly of a sleeping man.

Worst still were the ghosts. They were vaguely
humanoid shapes, smoke-black and faceless, they
clutched onto the Ironclad, hugging their backs, riding
on their shoulders, holding their legs with a tortured,
vengeful grasp. They were the dead – souls of murder vic-
tims, unable to leave the world. The followers of the
Ruinous Powers had an ability to blur the line between
the warp and the world, allowing the spirits of the dead

to manifest in strange ways. Here, they clung to those who wronged them, hanging over them like a dark aura.

Roth tried to shut it out, throwing up layers and layers of mind blank. He reduced his psychic signature and buried his face in the soil.

Celeminé swept in after him, trailing psychic magnificence. She took the form of a kingfisher, wings flared. Her confidence was to be her undoing.

The spirits, if not the resonance of the warp, then the angry ghosts of those the Ironclad had killed followed their armies like an aura of vengeful suffering. They were attracted to Celeminé's psychic brilliance.

The sudden swarming of despairing spirits snared Celeminé. She fought back, the wild lashes of her psychic will actually haemorrhaged the brains of several Ironclad sentries in a nearby tent. The ghosts leered at her, clawed at her, pulled and pleaded for her to stay with them. To join them in their suffering.

Roth seized his moment. He would not have another like it.

He surged back into his body. A fraction of a second before Celeminé realised he had gone.

Roth awoke back in the gas mill. The metaphysical shift was disorientating. The room spun in helical spirals. He staggered and righted himself. The room was covered in a thick crust of frost and the temperature was well below zero. Roth pawed through the ice, clawing at a T20 autogun on the frozen corpse of Guardsman. It dislodged, sleeting panes of thin ice as Roth picked it up.

Celeminé returned to her body as Roth's bearings returned. Her psychic discipline was good despite the distraction Roth had inflicted upon her. Celeminé's eyes tore open, immediately ready.

But Roth's trigger discipline was better. He squeezed the trigger. The first shot hit Celeminé below the ribs, buckling her onto her knees. His next round entered her below the chin, jetting a thin stream of crimson onto the white ice.

Inquisitor Felyce Celeminé lay, face-down in the snow. Strings of blood stained her yellow bodyglove orange.

Roth stared at her. His laboured breathing spiralled up in frosty plumes. A tension headache constricted his cerebellum, sending nerve tingles into his right elbow. He felt intoxicated, his mind dulled in what psychic-duellists termed *post-duel stupor*. It was his brain trying to recuperate from the confrontation. Blood pounded in his temple, its beat irregular.

As he sat, he thought about the vengeful ghosts that latched onto the Ironclad, following their killers into eternity. It was an unsettling thought. He could still feel the tortured thirst for revenge that those spirits had for their murderers. Roth wondered if Celeminé would follow him, her ghost latched onto his back for all eternity. A part of him hoped she would, to absolve him of guilt. And although he should not have felt guilt, try as he might, he did.

CHAPTER TWENTY-TWO

'I WILL NOT commit my soldiers to Aridun. I will not commit my soldiers to this war,' Lord Marshal Khmer announced to the assembly of senior commanders.

Those were the historic first words for the last Council of Conclusions of the Medina Campaign.

There was a stir of unease but none of the officers objected.

The lord marshal, naked of his medals and ceremonial trappings, wearing the starched uniform of a Cantican rank-and-file, stalked across the podium, playing his audience like a grand thespian.

'As Aridun has fallen quiet, the last of the core worlds of Medina are potentially lost.' He paused, allowing this fact to sink and settle.

He continued imperiously. 'There is nothing left for us here. Gentlemen, let us not forget the first rule of military engagement. Fight with objective. We have lost any and all objective in Medina.'

Polished boots clapping across the grated decking, Khmer walked to where Forde Gurion sat in the front bench. He levelled his gaze on the inquisitor and said with great clarity, 'For us to stay, we would be fighting out of emotional ties, out of moral obligation. We would not be fighting as military architects, but rather men blinded by loyalty to our home. We would not be generals, we would be guilty of being *civilians*.'

The last words were twisted and spat at Forde Gurion. The implication was clear.

There was some truth to Khmer's words. The silence of Aridun had been brutally abrupt.

The last message, received by long-range vox, was transmitted from a listening station in the Cage Isles of Northern Aridun directly to the 9th Route Fleet. That had been at 13:00 hours, on the first day of the new Medinian moon. The transmission had reported low-level enemy activity across the demarcation line, nothing out of the ordinary.

By 14:00 hours that day, communications ceased. All vox systems were down and astropathic signatures in the Governor's palace on Aridun were dreadfully cold and empty.

General Cypus Tanbull of the CantiCol 12th Division remarked that the planet had, for lack of a better term, 'fallen quiet by providence of the God-Emperor.' It was a sanguine way of saying something sickeningly dreadful had occurred on Aridun, and High Command had no intelligence to go by.

The Council of Conclusions was called, but conclusions had been the antithesis of what they had achieved. They had no intelligence to align their debate. Orbital reconnaissance showed nothing across the continental plates. Nothing at all, not even the twinkling constellation of lights that illuminated a city at night. Just blackness. It was as if Aridun had been wholly abandoned in the span of several hours.

That had been four days ago. Ironically, and truly by the providence of the God-Emperor, the situation had changed.

With a hydraulic hiss of his legs, Gurion rose from his seat.

'Lord marshal, there is logic in your words,' he mused. 'But the situation, I believe, has changed dramatically. I have come as swiftly as time would allow, to report to the Command a critical piece of intelligence unearthed by my Task Group.'

Something hardened behind Khmer's eyes but he allowed the inquisitor to continue.

'The Old Kings have been discovered.' It was Gurion's turn to play the theatrical role. He even sharpened his words with a touch of his mind so it reverberated in the minds of those seated around him.

'The Medina Corridor, the very star system, forms the fabric of the Old Kings. It has been before our eyes the whole time if we had bothered to see it.'

Gurion pushed past Khmer, ignoring him and addressing the assembly as he touched the hololithic projector. An orrery orbit of the Medina System flickered into grainy translucence, the image hovering like an inverted pyramid from the projector lens.

'If we study the equator lines and surface markings of the planets, we can see wide globe-spanning lines on most of the planet clusters,' Gurion said, indicating each of the planets in turn with his finger.

'Now, if we allow the planets to shift through their cyclical rotations, the equator lines form distinct patterns.'

Steadily, the planets spun on their heliocentric axis. The equator lines, like scars across the planets' surfaces, shifted until finally Gurion paused the projection. The projection showed the planets in the first moon cycle, with the triple suns at contrasting angles.

There was a rustle of discussion amongst the officers.

Although some of the equator lines were broken, and some planets bore none, a lattice of overlapping lines, oddly abstract but startlingly apparent, seemed to link the planets of the Medina Corridor. There was a symmetry and order to them, but at the same time there was a fluid yet alien regularity to the planetary markings. Gurion had already taken measuring instruments to them and the angles were razor edge in precision. It was extraordinary considering the true scale of those planets. Almost like a series of curving script had been sliced into the skin of each planet, overlapping and dancing.

'Mathematics and patterns, inquisitor?' Khmer snapped impatiently.

'Let him speak,' the Space Marine envoy said, his bass voice rolling with thunderous authority.

Gurion remained placid. 'This was an orbital map of pre-invasion Medina. I now invite you to study an orbital surveillance of the star system, after the Archenemy conquest.'

An orrery projection replaced the first. There was little difference, except the monolithic excavations and quarries of the Ironclad were clearly visible. In their new context, the massive quarries and excavation sites lined up with the pre-existing ley-lines seamlessly. On the planets of Ninvevah, Baybel and Cantica, where no lines had existed before, the excavations surfaced new ones, at exact angles with the old.

At the centre of the symmetry, during the first day of the moon cycle, was the planet of Aridun.

This was, perhaps, the greatest revelation to High Command since the conflict had begun. The assembly erupted. There was a tumultuous babble of shock. Even a two-hundred-year-old admiral of the fleet, a veteran who had seen everything in his centuries of campaigning, held a hand over his mouth.

Gurion did not need to explain it, the orbital picts said everything. The Archenemy had never been conducting a blind treasure hunt of the relics. They had never been acting with the irrationality that Khmer and many officers had predicted.

No. Rather, they had been re-creating the broken equator lines, and finishing the perfect symmetry of new ones. It was a monumental task that spanned the star system. They were recreating the ritual of the Star Ancients with chilling precision and the Imperium had never even known.

Chaos had been acting with logic and precision. That was what frightened the assembly of warriors so much.

For the first time, Khmer relented. 'What does this forebode?'

'Let me explain this precisely. The Old Kings, or rather the Old King, is an embryonic star held in stasis. Aridun marks the central axis. That is where the Old King lies. It has been placed there in line with astronomical and magnetic properties. We believe that is what the old tales refer to when they say the stars will rouse them from dormant slumber. The old mathematical geodesists of Terra would suggest that the magnetic fields and polar motions have disrupted the dormant star's stasis field,' Gurion replied.

'And so the Old King has been, in a way, activated...' a Naval officer from the assembly murmured, loud enough for all to hear.

'Perhaps. Perhaps not. The only way to know is if we deploy an expedition force onto the planet,' Gurion declared.

'What if they are activated? Then what?' Khmer pressed.

'Although we do not know what form this star exists as, more than likely, the Archenemy will not unleash an embryonic star on Medina. It's strategically insignificant.

From all our sources, this star seems to be dormant within some sort of a containment vessel. Now we don't know what this is, but it's intuitive enough. Once activated by the ley-lines it would suggest that this vesselled container can then be removed and utilised elsewhere.'

'I don't follow you,' Khmer said stubbornly.

'Let me put this in terms you will understand. This is a star within a vessel. Think of it as a bomb. Except this bomb, when unleashed, will likely consume an entire star system and expand outwards with radiation and enough kinetic energy to rend rifts in the warp,' said Gurion. 'As an example of course. We won't know until we send an investigative team to Aridun.'

'Out of the question. I will not send soldiers as sacrificial lambs. You said yourself, the Old Kings may already be roused from their dormant state,' Khmer interjected. 'This does not change our strategy to reinforce the Bastion Stars.'

'Logical, lord marshal, logical,' Gurion conceded. 'Which is why I volunteer to deploy my last remaining Task Group to Aridun.'

Khmer ground his teeth, ready to speak again when Gurion halted his words with a mechanical hand. 'As I speak, Inquisitor Obodiah Roth and his task force are en route to Aridun. Once they make landfall, they have forty-eight hours to contact us by long-range vox.'

'And then what?' Khmer asked.

'If they are able to contact High Command, we will deploy all available military resources to secure Aridun. I do this by mandate of Inquisitorial authority. If they do not, then you can have your withdrawal, lord marshal.'

Above the piped collar of his uniform, Khmer's carotid arteries throbbed like hose-pipes. The scarred skin of his face turned a pressurised red. The lord marshal nodded once, very slowly. 'Excellently played, inquisitor.'

Gurion snapped the CantiCol salute to the assembly of commanders, clashing a mechanical fist to his chest in the gesture of solidarity. 'This is the one chance you have to fight for your birth worlds. Have the fleet and the Guard prepare for rapid deployment. You have forty-eight hours, followed by a six-hour notice for mobilisation.'

Gurion strode out of the war vault, halted at the blast doors, then turned to regard the assembly one last time. 'This is our time, gentlemen. If we fail now, you will be remembered for it, regardless of the victories and triumphs you have already bled for.'

CHAPTER TWENTY-THREE

THE ORBITAL RECONNAISSANCE of Aridun had been accurate regarding the abandonment.

There were no signs of life, at least in the human sense. The stratocraft skimmed low across the southern savannah belt of Aridun Civic, to avoid radar detection and to survey the city. The maze of streets was empty, and although it was only a bruising dawn, no lights were visible along the skyline.

What the reconnaissance had revealed were the burning pyres that smoked into blackened embers out in the thousand kilometre reefs of cycad and gingko that surrounded Aridun Civic.

The pyres were monuments, some as high as sixty, seventy metres tall. The pyres resembled gas nebulae, blackened and swollen and crowned with gaseous flame. The stratocraft had veered in, trying to snatch close observation.

As they flew through the pillars of smoke, Roth had ordered the pilot servitor to vent atmospheric oxygen and allow air into the cabin. The sour, acrid stench of burning flesh and hair that seeped into the vessel confirmed Roth's suspicion. It was indeed corpses of Aridun out there in those fields, heaped up and burning. The smell was so pervasive, Captain Pradal had vomited three times before the stratocraft's venting systems repurified the oxygen and locked down the atmospheric seals.

But the oily taste still lingered at the backs of their throats.

'I've seen the Archenemy do this before but never on such a scale,' Roth admitted. 'Once on a mining station in Helm's Outreach, the Juventist Cult there had murdered almost everyone. They had been desperate enough for the people not to contact the Imperium. The desperation had tallied almost thirty thousand lives.'

'That's obscene,' Madeline said, looking out the starboard ports, the flames of the evening light reflecting dancing shades across her face.

'Mmm,' murmured Roth listlessly.

'Something is eating away at you, Roth. You look morose.'

'I'm fine about Celeminé.'

'I didn't say anything about Celeminé...' she said, letting the statement hang in the air.

'Madeline, don't start. Celeminé and I, we had a working partnership. We were inquisitors. At best we would have stayed together in cooperation for maybe several years, who knows maybe several decades. But eventually the Inquisitorial calling would take us apart from each other. By ideology or by personality we would eventually go our separate ways. For Celeminé, this happened much sooner... and much more regrettably.'

'Very detached perspective, Roth. It's not like you.'

'That's because now is not the time to have my head between my legs, figuratively speaking.'

In truth, Roth had not been well. Most times he kept it together, but at times Celeminé and Silverstein seemed to haunt him. He thought he heard them talking sometimes, but reminded himself it could not be. Yet it was also a time when he could not afford to be anything less than mentally precise, and it was only the fortitude of an inquisitor that had allowed him to go on. Inquisitorial fortitude and chems. He had glanded endorphin pills, dopamine injections and had not eaten properly in months. He barely recognised the blackened hollows around his eyes and pale, gaunt cheeks that sulked at him in the mirror.

The peals of a tri-tone over the intercom system shook Roth from his contemplation. 'Preparation for landing in six hundred seconds,' the servitor pilot announced in his monotone voice over the speakers.

It was time.

Roth led Madeline to the shuttered landing ramp where Captain Pradal was securing a vox array to his backpack with locking straps. His lasrifle was slung muzzle-up across his shoulder and a bolt pistol from the stratocraft's arsenal bay was tucked into a thigh holster.

'You look ready to start a war, captain,' Roth smiled.

'I'm ready to end one, inquisitor. Do you think this could really be the end game?' the junior officer asked. He struggled to shoulder the bulk of his equipment.

'No doubt,' Roth said, helping the captain weave his arms under the straps of his load-bearing pack.

'Once we touch down, this craft is moving off-world. I don't want it to betray our presence. Either we make contact with High Command and initiate the grand offensive, or we die here.'

Captain Pradal nodded contentedly; he jumped up and down to test for loose equipment before flipping his white kepi onto his head. 'Either way, I'll die on my home world.' He moved to the landing ramp ponderously under the bulk of a vox array and webbing, his musette bags of ammunition, magnoculars, rebreathers and water bottles clustered from his hips and thighs.

'Are you sure you're ready for this, Madeline? This is your last chance, the offer to ferry you off-world still stands. It's not too late to stay on this craft,' Roth asked Madeline.

The xeno-archaeologist had eschewed her finery for more climate-appropriate gear. A frock coat of loom-woven ceramic polyfibre cascaded down her narrow shoulders, winking like fish-scales of opaline green. A scarf of fine chainmail was wound about her neck and head like a coif.

'I've made up my mind, Roth, it's my scholarly duty to see this through,' she said as she pulled on a pair of kid-skin gloves.

'In that case, get rid of that irritant,' Roth said, pointing to the revolving stubber holstered at her waist belt. 'It will just annoy the enemy.'

Roth crossed over to the stratocraft's arsenal bay and popped open a locked trunk. He retrieved a compact carbine, matt-black with a ribbed foregrip and blunt-muzzled profile. Silverstein used to call it a shard carbine, but the common name was simply ripper pistol. He reversed the weapon and handed it pistol-grip first to Madeline.

Roth then dumped a brace belt of magazine cartridges into her arms. 'This gun belonged to an old friend of mine. It fires a concentrated coil of metal shards at a target, highly accurate up to eighty metres. The recoil is smooth but it can dispatch a tusked mammoth with one shot.'

Madeline tested the weapon awkwardly, wedging a magazine into place. She looped the belt of spare mags over her arm like a swinging satchel.

'Good enough?' she asked.

'More or less.'

The stratocraft made a sharp descent, its steep, curving flight taking them across the reef plains. The insertion point was a matter of mathematical formula. The axis of a stellar map, despite its star-spanning length, had been calculated down to a variance of several degrees. The pilot would land them eight kilometres west from where the Old Kings were believed to rest in buried dormancy.

Roth nodded to Pradal and Madeline. 'Whatever happens, know we were doing the Emperor's work.'

ANGKHORA WAS NOT an Imperial name.

Like the names of all Medina Worlds, administrative protectorates and city-states, the name was a vestige of the early Medinian tongue. The language had long been suppressed, by dictate of Imperial decree, but names were all-pervasive. Names bespoke history, recognition, a single word that conjured the sentience of a place.

Angkhora was a place of abandonment. It was one of the forgotten cities of the previous dynasty, a broken link of the Fortress Chain after the millennia-long drought and flood cycles of M36. The rampart wall, which connected Angkhora to the Fortress Chains, was sagging and moss-eaten.

Perhaps its desolation was fitting. For as long as man could remember, Angkhora, the axial centre of the Fortress Chains, was a place for burial. The unique reverence of ancestors had devoted an entire city to the interment and rest for those who had passed.

In the early tongue, Angkhora literally translated as 'The house that the first creators built'. It had been built to represent the island in the sky that deities of pre-Imperial Medina had come from, an early myth of creation.

On the horizon, Angkhora appeared to levitate above the earth on a shimmering mirage of heat, although that was an illusion. Its profile was dominated by a quincunx of sandstone towers, ogival in shape like tightly furled buds of flowers. Stairs were a dominant feature; the city had no walls, only ziggurat steps that tiered the outer cruciform terraces. The design gave Angkhora a harmonious symmetry that seemed strangely inhuman in the precision of its arrangement.

Roth's insertion point was exactly eight kilometres out from Angkhora, the minimum distance in the event of signature detection. They made landfall on an apron of reef mangrove that sprawled out before Angkhora's monument gates. The region was a glistening plain of muddy water and bulbous, shallow-rooted hydrophytes.

Slogging under the weight of thirty kilograms of surveillance, survival and military equipment each, the trio waded through the shin-deep mangrove. Their weapons were cautiously shouldered as they advanced, scanning the surroundings for signs of enemy or natural predation. Madeline had warned them the primordial creatures that inhabited the low lands were small but they could be quick, darting out of mud burrows with snapping, lashing jaws.

Moving at a stealthy, wary creep, the task group reached the three-hundred-metre tall gates of Angkhora in just under four hours. They halted several times during the advance, allowing Pradal to make intermittent signal burps on his vox, broadcasting to low-frequency Imperial channels across the southern belt. There was a chance the frequencies had already been compromised, but it was a gambit Roth was willing to make. Yet they received no answer by the time they reached the monument gates.

Up close, Roth could see the narrative scenes etched into the stonework. Each dancing character – animal, flower or astronomical body – was no bigger than Roth's thumb, yet the cavorting figures were carved across the entire surface of the gate pylons.

'These gates here, they depict the interment of the dead in their final resting place – the garden in the sky. Angkhora was never a place of domestic living, it was an extensive tomb-city,' Madeline said, reaching out to touch the stone with her gloved fingertips for protection. It was a Medinian superstition she had acquired in her studies.

'They built this place for the dead? All of it?' Roth asked.

'Yes they did, but that was a long time ago. For the past several centuries, the climate has become more habitable, temperatures here have lowered and a substantial part of this city had been converted to urban hab, mostly for the destitute, the poor, the ones less missed, so they lived here amongst the dead. The population for this city should be at least eight thousand,' she said but then checked herself. '*Should be…* eight thousand.'

'That's a bad omen,' Captain Pradal said, making the sign of the aquila before thrice tapping the stone with his knuckles. Cradling the lasrifle slung across his chest for comfort, his other hand resting on the bolt pistol at his thigh, he crossed the threshold into the dead city.

Within, the streets were a rambling maze. The flagstones were worn smooth by flood and silt deposits, and then baked into a cracked finish by the searing heat. Black run-off like dried tears ran down every surface of stone, what Roth could only imagine as being the evaporated essence of time itself. From what Roth had seen, ancient structures were often blackened through sheer dint of age.

Of the population of eight thousand, there was no sign.

'No life signs at all,' said Pradal, reading an auspex that was attached by a wire cord to his hip webbing. 'Not in proximity at least.'

'Signal-burp again,' Roth bade him.

'Sir, I've been transmitting on sustained long-range frequency for the better part of four hours, emitting contact to listening stations across the entire southern belt. If anything, we'll bring every Archenemy within the southern savannah on our tracks.'

'I know, captain, but we need this,' Roth said.

They went down into cover, moving towards a line of stone apartments. Whatever purpose the terraces served in the city of the dead, it had been converted to a tenement block. They entered one of the small habs, noting that all the apartments were missing their doors.

Inside, they could see signs of recent habitation. A stone pallet bed was unceremoniously upended, its thin mattress half-thrown across the apartment. Tables and lockers of a cheap mass-produced alloy were dented and ransacked, the meagre possessions strewn across the floor. If Roth's forensic reasoning was anything to go by, it seemed that the occupant had been dragged out of bed as they had slept.

'Sustained signal-burps, captain, keep them brief and clear,' Roth ordered.

The inquisitor moved to one of the low square windows cut into the thick sandstone. He surveyed the city quietly as the captain went about his work. The tightly coiled streets were empty and heavily shadowed by the ogival towers at their cardinal points above.

'So this is where the Old Kings sleep,' Roth whispered under his breath.

A GIANT, LURKING within the deep folds of stone that formed the architecture of Angkhora, watched the three little humans.

It watched them with the same malevolent interest that a predator would regard its frail, cumbersome prey.

As the giant moved, the shadow of late afternoon rippled across its glossy hide. Where the sun shone, its hide was a hard black enamel, so glossy it was slick with a film of red. Like blood on the surface of black oil.

And how it moved! As overwhelming as the tide, it surged on plated limbs through the crumbling masonry. The brutal speed and controlled power with which it cut across the rooftops and streets was terrifying.

It could, if it chose to, warn the others of its kind. But the giant chose not to disturb them. It lived by the rhythm of killing and eating and it would be better not to share its prey.

Leaping from roof to roof with a simian lope, the giant paralleled the movements of its prey, constantly keeping them under its watchful eye.

ACCORDING TO THE complex geometry of the equator lines and if their mathematics were anything to go by, the Old Kings of Medina would be buried in the central tomb complex, deep within the womb of Angkhora's central ziggurat.

'At least another twelve kilometres to our north-east unless we can find some way to circumvent these dead-end avenues and maze stair-wells,' Pradal said as he checked his auspex.

Referring to his map-sleeve, Roth traced the route with his finger. It was an imperfect map, an old piece they had acquired from Madeline's own scholarly collection. In the time since its making, the galleries and step-mazes of Angkhora had been subject to collapse. Even conservative estimates put them half a day's trek from the site.

Roth shrugged off his canvas bergen and rolled his neck, easing out the acidic knots along the muscles of his shoulders. 'Drink some water and grab some tiff while you can, we've got a long way to go yet.'

With a sigh of relief, Captain Pradal sunk down under the shade of a mausoleum and unlocked the strap of his webbing and equipment, keeping them within easy reach. He stretched out his leg and began to unwrap a block of compressed grain ration.

'We're being followed,' Madeline said, moving to join the others under the alcove of balustrades. She turned and played her carbine across the garlands of stone flowers that uniformly edged the pediment rooftops.

Roth looked up from his map and swore quietly under his breath. 'I thought so. I've known for some time but I didn't want to cause distress until someone else concurred.'

Roth looked across the silhouette of Angkhora. The city of the dead stared back at home, utterly quiet, refusing to give up its secrets. For the first time, Roth noticed that not even the leather-winged lizards roosted here, nor flocked to the skies.

'What do we do?' Madeline groaned, suddenly despairing.

'We wait,' Captain Pradal said confidently. 'Let's find a defensible position and bait him out.'

'Elementary bait ambush. What could go wrong?' Roth winked. With delicate care, Roth folded the map into its plastek sleeve and folded that into a side-pocket in his bergen.

'THIS WILL DO,' Roth said.

The chosen site of their ambush was not ideal but it would suffice. It was a stair pillar, or rather that was what Roth called it; Madeline assured him they were called *gopurams* in ancient Terran Anglo. Its foundations were a rectangular slab of sandstone, likely more than some fifty tonnes. The structure tapered up, each stepped tier diminishing in size as they swept upwards, in acquiescence to the heavens. The song birds, chariots and horned animals that dancing along the bas-reliefs of each tier represented the sky gardens of the dead, a reminder that Angkhora was a cemetery for the past.

Song birds and horned animals had not danced on Aridun for thousands of years.

'Whatever it is, it's coming closer,' Madeline whispered without turning to look.

Roth nodded softly. He too had seen a ghost of movement in his periphery, just a vast and very sudden shadow that was no longer there when he turned. Their hunter was getting careless – either that, or it was getting bolder.

'I've seen the hostile too, several times now,' Pradal said. He stopped plodding up the ziggurat and checked on the course of the suns. It would be dusk soon, one sun was already dipping along the horizon as an amber rind, another sun making a heliodonic arc over the first, turning the deepwater sky from blue to black. In Pradal's military training, dusk was the most opportune time to attack, when the mind was hard-wired to rest at the break of light.

'Don't look down, but I think it's slinking at the base of the ziggurat,' Madeline said, hurrying up the last few steps to the shrine at the top of the gopuram.

If what Madeline said was correct, it meant that the hostile was no longer tracking them; it was simply stalking them in the open. It meant the hostile had no need for stealth, perhaps even deliberately induced the fear of attack by flitting in and out of view. Roth gritted his teeth, resisted the temptation to look down the steps and followed Madeline.

'Pradal, cover the north, Madeline, cover the south, I'll take the east. The suns are coming down west so keep your backs to them,' Roth commanded.

The top of the gopuram was a flat square about twenty metres wide along each side. The three of them crouched down, back to back, their weapons pointed directly ahead. Their position afforded them a magnificent view of Angkhora; as the suns set, they chased the yawning shadows. The sunlight gleam of sunstone fading to a dim purple.

The hostile did not need to wait for dusk.

Roth heard steps, dulled and quietly menacing. The sound of grit and loose earth crunched underfoot.

'Here it comes, up the north face,' Pradal said, thumbing his lasrifle to its highest setting.

Roth spun on his coiled crouch to face the approach. He felt the familiar surge of adrenaline, building like a spring coil in his bladder.

The slow, deliberate steps sounded like war drums. The Tong cannibals of the Punic subcontinents used war drums to psychologically assault the enemy, Roth remembered. A deep, almost ritualistic rhythm that put the 'fears in the bellies of their foe'. Roth imagined it would be quite similar – he certainly felt the fears.

'Throne, I hate this, I hate this,' Madeline hissed under her breath.

The steps stopped.

Pradal slid a frag grenade from his belt loop, tensing to hook the pin with his thumb and throw one-handed.

Vandus Barq surfaced over the edge of the ziggurat. He looked a mess. His armoured rig was blackened with ash and his face was marred with speckled bruising. In his steel-gloved hands, he clutched a vox-signaller, the tracking array guiding him up.

'Roth! You bastard! When I snagged those vox transmissions I knew it was you.' The inquisitor was trembling, quaking.

Roth rose to his feet and placed a hand on one of Barq's heavy shoulder guards. 'Look at you, Vandus. Calm down, you look a mess.'

Barq shrugged off Roth's hand, his shaking head. 'Not now, not now. You're being hunted.'

'Hunted? By whom?' Captain Pradal said, still aiming his rifle along the northern edge.

'I said not now!' Inquisitor Barq snapped, almost irritably.

Barq's breathing was irregular and laboured; a nervous tic was seizing the entire left side of his face. Roth recognised the latent stage of shock when he saw it. Something was terrifying an Imperial inquisitor, terrifying him enough to send an inquisitor's formidable mental faculties into neural overload. The fear in his belly, as the Tong cannibals would have said.

'Barq, you have to explain what is happening. Intelligence before action, the first preamble of the Inquisition. Come on now, old friend, breathe, breathe,' Roth said.

'Roth. I'm coherent,' Barq jagged through gritted teeth. 'I've got a vehicle waiting in the causeway. We have to get out of this region, you don't understand. We have to go – if the vehicle is still there.'

Roth was reluctant. Travelling at night in the dead city did not appeal to his sensibilities. He looked at the horizon; the suns were sinking into hazy crescents and tinting the city a murky purple.

But then he saw it again. The silhouette of a giant, rising across the rooftops. It was backlit by the twilight, like a shadow puppet. It was there and then it wasn't.

This time they all saw it. Madeline exhaled sharply.

Roth made up his mind. 'Okay, Vandus, show us to your vehicle.'

Quickly, before night falls, Roth thought to himself silently.

Barq's vehicle, thankfully, remained where he left it, underneath the lengthening shadows of a lotus shrine.

It was a V-8 Centaur, a small military tractor. Its square-framed, boxy hull was painted in the russet-brown of the Cantican Colonials. The 'rearing horse, sabre and cog' crest of the CantiCol 6th Logistics and Supply dominated the welded frontal plates.

Clambering into the Centaur's open-topped cab, the Task Group nested amongst the neatly stacked rows of ammunition and the disassembled parts of a 75mm mortar.

Barq snuggled down into the operator's seat, hunching his shoulders so he could lean forwards and peer through the narrow, visored vision slit.

'Are you fit to drive?' Roth asked.

'Oh please…'

Barq fumbled at the ignition. Finally, with a guttering metallic chain rip, the Centaur coughed into shuddering wakefulness. The Centaur rolled forwards, picking up speed, little by little.

It wasn't fast enough.

The stalker exploded from the shadows. He was enormous. From the plated pillars of his legs to the towering turret of his torso, he throbbed with primal power. His armour was of the deepest red, so red it was almost black. In metal-shod hands he swung a double-handed chainsword, the venting pipes at the hilt grumbling with exhaust.

Captain Pradal screamed. It was the first time Roth had heard a trained soldier scream with such fervent, almost plaintive panic. It was a horrifying sound and Roth did not ever wish to experience the organic fear again. He looked to see what Pradal saw and froze.

It was an Astartes of the Chaos Legions.

'Blood Gorgon!' Barq roared, without turning to look. He gunned the Centaur, taking its engine to protesting limits.

Roth was the first to react. He leaned over the edge of the vehicle and let loose a plasma shot. The Traitor Marine took the hit on the tower of his shoulder plate, before accelerating fast towards them. It was so explosive, like the gliding footwork of a champion fist-fencer, utterly in control of his body, thought Roth. Except this monster weighed half a tonne.

'Throne's sake, come to your senses!' Roth bellowed at Madeline and Pradal. His shouts seemed to rouse them from their paralysis of shock. Captain Pradal, still screaming in wide-eyed panic, began to hose his weapon in a rearward direction on full auto. Madeline fired her carbine double-handed; the first torrent of shrapnel went wide as their vehicle thumped over a loose flagstone. The second expanding coil of splintered metal hit the Blood Gorgon across the thick slab of his chest. It barely arrested his sprint.

The Blood Gorgon closed the distance. How fast were they going? Perhaps forty kilometres an hour? And still the Traitor Marine was gaining on them, pumping his armoured legs with seismic force, blading his arms as he closed in. Like the pirahnagator, he was utterly explosive in a single direction.

'Turn! Keep jinking!' Roth called to Barq.

The Centaur peeled off from the causeway down a walled viaduct. The evasive manoeuvre left the Blood Gorgon careening away, albeit briefly, at a perpendicular direction.

A plasma shot ate a broken, calcified puncture in the Blood Gorgon's upper thigh sheathing. Las-rounds bubbled the waxy enamel of his ceramite. Flechette shells puffed like smoke against his hide. The Blood Gorgon pounded down on them, undaunted.

Barq turned them down a broad boulevard, ornate headstones flanking the avenue like cathedral pews. It was difficult to navigate in the dark, the headlamps bobbing and shaking, revealing only a blurred path of illuminated ground that streaked by beneath them. Roth didn't know if Barq knew where they were going.

The Blood Gorgon was close enough that one of his enormous, armour-shod gauntlets could almost grace the tow bar of their Centaur. Close enough that Roth could see the Traitor Marine's face plate, snouted and equine with flared nostrils and a shrieking mouth grille.

In his desperation, Roth seized one of the mortar rounds from the stack. He banged the percussion cap against the plating of the Centaur and lobbed it over-hand from the back of the vehicle. The round clattered, bounced and skipped against the cloven boots of the Traitor Marine and exploded.

The Blood Gorgon actually staggered, briefly. He growled through the bassinet grille of his helmet. The sound amplified through his chest speakers, wet and tremulous.

'Mortars, use the mortars!' Roth yelled to his team. They didn't need his coercion. Both of them were hurl-ing mortar rounds at the Blood Gorgon with a reckless desperation. A chain of explosions crackled in the wake of the Centaur, blowing fragments of stone from the road. They aimed the mortars low, banging them against the vehicle plating and skipping them at the Blood Gor-gon's legs.

By the time Vandus careened the vehicle down Angkhora's gate causeway, the pillars of the Blood Gor-gon's legs were blackened and scorched. Fluid sprayed from fissures in the ceramite with each thundering step, either blood or machine fluid.

'Keep him off us, this is going to be a tight stretch!' Barq shouted from up front. Roth turned to see for him-self and swore. The causeway was a broad and unbroken ribbon that snaked down two kilometres. There was nowhere to turn.

The Blood Gorgon caught them. He closed the dis-tance with one last spur and then leapt into the air with monumental effort. He swung the double-handed chainsword down in an executioner's arc and took the entire rear plating off the Centaur in one crumpled sheet. Without pause, his next strike, a horizontal backhand, sheared the roll-cage off the Centaur with a rending shriek of metal and buzzing chain teeth, throwing out a fan of orange sparks.

Roth rolled backwards onto his arse and kicked away lamely. The Blood Gorgon punched at Roth, a downwards hammer-fist. Roth managed to shrimp away from the ceramite fist as it bashed a crater into cab decking.

Roth would never forget what happened next. He would owe his life to it.

Captain Pradal rose before the Traitor Marine. He stood between Roth and the towering, armoured giant. The junior officer drew the bolt pistol and fired, two shots, point-blank into the Blood Gorgon's helmet. The grille dented and warped under the impact of the shots. The force was enough to whip the Marine's head backwards.

The staggering giant lurched, turning his head away. A gauntlet swung out, seizing the captain's head between the vice of his segmented digits. Pradal didn't even scream as the Blood Gorgon squeezed with iron-grinding strength. The good captain died without a word.

Pradal's blood washed over Roth in a blinding mist of red.

Roth knew he had perhaps one heartbeat, perhaps two, before the opening was gone. The inquisitor stopped thinking – thinking would slow him down. He drove himself forwards and threw the single most important punch of his life, a lunging, overhand right. His Tang-War power fist impacted into the Blood Gorgon's sternum, at the point where the buttressing cables of his abdomen met the ceramite of his lower pectoral slabs.

There was a snap of negatively charged atoms colliding as Roth drove his fist into the giant's chest. The Blood Gorgon screamed. The decibels actually blew out his chest speakers. Roth doubted he would ever have full hearing in his right ear again. The power fist splintered the fused calcium growth of the giant's ribcage and parted dense cables of muscle. It wouldn't be enough to kill him.

Roth drove his glove upwards, sharply and to the right. He ruptured the Blood Gorgon's secondary heart before spearing for the primary.

Finally, with a tectonic shudder, the Blood Gorgon died. He slid like an avalanche off the gaping rear of the Centaur.

Roth sagged to his knees, blinking the blood back from his eyes. It was getting into his nose, his mouth, sinking into his teeth. None of it was his own. As the V-8 Centaur pulled out of the final stretch of causeway from Angkhora, Roth keeled over onto his side, completely and utterly spent.

CHAPTER TWENTY-FOUR

'THE ARCHENEMY KNEW. They knew all along. They were just waiting for their time,' Inquisitor Barq murmured listlessly.

'They tricked us then. They outplayed us,' Roth agreed, staring vacantly into the distance.

They sat on a mesa, sixty kilometres north of Aridun Civic. Far enough from the savannah and deep enough into the wasteland to be surrounded on all sides by undulating dust plains. It was early dawn, and the sands gleamed a bone-polished ivory, the ridgelines ribbed by morning shadow. The V-8 Centaur, or rather the mangled remains of it, was parked some metres away, empty of fuel. They had ridden the vehicle as far it would go, as far as it would carry them from the southern belt. The body of Captain Pradal lay close by covered in a plastek sheet, his arms folded over his chest and rifle.

'Tell me,' Roth began. 'Tell me again, how this came to be.'

Barq flexed his fists and closed his eyes, as if shutting out memories he didn't want to relive. 'Five days. Five days ago, they hit Aridun. Damn, were they good. They took out the communications first, took out the listening stations, comms towers, broadcast ports. Everything. Completely shut this place down.'

Roth scooped up another handful of sand and rubbed it into the dried blood on his armour, scouring away the red-tinged flecks. 'Then the Guard?'

'Yes. Without communications, isolated garrisons can't muster much defence.'

'Then the southern belt?'

'Yes. Before cleaning up what isolated settlements lay outside the savannah region,' Barq said, irritably. They were all feeling volatile. Roth felt the same way, the urge to curl up and sleep, and never to wake up, was overwhelming.

'One company of Traitor Legionnaires, you say?' Roth pressed again.

'In my opinion, at least one company, no more than two. Any more than two hundred Space Marines and there wouldn't have been much of Aridun left.'

It was evident in retrospect. It was always evident in retrospect. The Archenemy had been meticulous in planning. They had seized Medina, one planet after another, preparing to wake the Old Kings, staying one step ahead of the Imperial resistance. Meanwhile, they had gathered mounting forces on Aridun, beyond the demarcation line, waiting. Lulling High Command, drawing resources away from Aridun onto other war fronts. Waiting until the alignments of the planets were true and proper before dispensing the Traitor Legions to cleanse the entire inhabitable stretch of Aridun.

'Is everyone dead?' Roth hazarded to ask.

'Some fled into the wastelands, but without water, I doubt they would have lasted long. For those who do, I have no doubt that they'll run into Ironclad land forces coming across the subcontinent.'

'That's very bad indeed,' Roth said. It was quite the understatement.

Barq opened his eyes and levelled his gaze at Roth. 'It was nice of you to come back for me. It's good to know that my friends do not think I'm trying to kill them any more.'

Roth looked away, suddenly aware of his friend's inference. 'I'm sorry, Vandus. I had no choice.'

'I'll beat you thoroughly when this is all over,' Barq said, breaking into a slight smile.

Roth opened his arms and chortled softly. 'Vandus, if this is ever over, I'll gladly give you a free shot. You'll need the handicap if we spar again.'

'What do we do now?' Madeline said suddenly. They were the first words she had spoken for several hours. Since she had seen Pradal killed.

'As strange as it may sound, by the God-Emperor's providence, we are fortunate,' Roth announced confidently.

Madeline and Barq both looked at him as if he had gone entirely insane.

'I will contact Gurion by vox, and request the immediate deployment of standby forces from the 9th Route Fleet. Our first priority is to reclaim Angkhora from the Blood Gorgons, before the Ironclad can consolidate their grip on the region.'

'How do you know the Archenemy do not have the Old Kings in their possession already?' Madeline asked.

'My dear,' Roth began, 'do you think any of us would still be alive if they did?'

THE IRONCLAD ON Aridun were mobilising. Across the Punic subcontinent, two thousand kilometres across the fossil plains, the armoured and motorised columns of

Archenemy trawled across the desert. Beyond the Cage Isles, a fleet of iron submersibles and propeller-driven barges set sail across the saline channels. From the furthest salt flats of west Aridun, to the endorheic basins in the continental tip, the Ironclad emerged from hiding, converging on the Fortress Chains.

Four figures, small and inconsequential, watched the mobilisation from the crest of a sand dune. The bone dust clung to their shaggy reed camouflage in powdery white. They looked to be nothing more than a bank of mossy taproot.

'We're moving out with them,' Silverstein declared.

'What, with them?' Temughan asked, pointing into the horizon with a dirty finger. Before them, the Ironclad were deploying in force. There was no need for camouflage netting or concealment any more. Even if they did, it would not have concealed the thousands of vehicles amassing on the continental sand sheets. Bone dust rose in solid, expanding walls.

'Surely not,' Asingh-nu echoed.

'It would not be possible, we'd all be killed,' Apartan argued. 'How would we even follow their advance across the salt pans?'

'Come on, men, where is your sense of adventure? The calling of Imperial endeavour? Plains to be conquered, worlds to be liberated,' grinned Silverstein half-jokingly.

The huntsman shimmied back on his stomach, away from the ridgeline, before rising to his feet. He noticed his boots were dirty, and he remembered he had not taken them off since leaving the *Carthage* for Cantica, all those months ago. How long had it been? Silverstein couldn't remember.

He crossed over to his quad-bike. The bare metal had been baking under the suns and was hot to the touch. Silverstein secured the jerry cans of fuel and water on the saddle-pouches, checking the locking straps for friction.

The bullpup autogun he had liberated from the Ironclad Naik was buttoned down, running parallel to the bike's rear chain and sprocket for quick access. Silverstein hadn't stolen the bullpup at all; the weapon still bore the Munitorum script and serial of a Bastion Ward regiment weapon. Silverstein was simply returning the weapon to the Imperium.

Silverstein smoothed out his cloak of desert taproots and tied it over his head. 'In all seriousness, gentlemen, the Ironclad are on the move. We can hide, but there will soon be nowhere to go. Have you thought about that?'

Apartan plodded through the bone dust and tugged the netting of xerophyte moss and tangle root from his bike. He too secured the camo shawl over his shoulders. 'If the Archenemy are getting ready for a fight, I don't want to miss it.'

Temughan and Asingh-nu crossed over to join them with some trepidation.

'If we must,' they chorused.

Silverstein laughed. 'Follow my lead. We'll make it fun, like tracking big game. Really big game.'

THE CALL TO deployment reached Gurion by long-range vox just minutes before his arrest.

Lord Gurion placed down the long-range ear horn as the door to his stateroom was breached by provost marshals. Six provosts stormed into Gurion's room, racking shotguns and barking at him. Following them at an unhurried pace was Lord Marshal Khmer, a cape thrown casually over one shoulder. At his heels came a trio of black-coated political commissars, clutching sheaves of edict warrants.

Gurion simply raised his hands.

'Lord marshal, you've come for me, I see?' Gurion said.

'We'll be asking the questions now, inquisitor,' Khmer sniffed haughtily.

'Oh I see. Can we do this after we deploy the forces onto Aridun? I have just received word from my Task Force that the situation has become most dire.'

'No. Gurion, never. You are under arrest by power of military law,' Khmer said. He clicked his fingers at a waiting commissar. The political officer clopped one step forwards with his polished jackboots and read from the warrant in his hands.

'Inquisitor Forde Gurion. You are hereby charged with conspiracy to impede sound military strategy. Until your date of hearing, you are to be confined to the brig with temporary suspension of any and all powers. By written rule of Section 22 of the 599 Military Charter.'

'I'm an inquisitor,' laughed Gurion. 'Your military laws do not apply to me.'

Khmer smiled. 'That may or may not be true. It will be up to a council of sufficient authority to decide. Until then, you are to be confined for your own good, and the good of the Medina Campaign. I'm terribly sorry, but you will not be able to use your Imperial authority to deploy any of my troops until this matter is cleared.'

'Well played, Khmer,' said Gurion, nodding slowly.

The lord marshal dipped his head. 'I am mobilising all resources to transit for the Bastion Stars as we speak. When and *if* this matter is decided by council, then you can feel free to pull my troops back from the Bastion and return here to Medina, in your own time.'

Gurion drummed his mechanical hand on his desk impatiently. 'Are you finished, lord marshal?'

Khmer narrowed his eyes warily. The change in Gurion's tone foreshadowed something else. Suddenly, the half-dozen provosts he had brought with him didn't seem quite enough.

Gurion rose from his seat. 'You don't challenge me, Khmer. That is your flaw. I had long predicted you would try something like this. But it doesn't really matter.'

In the corridor outside the stateroom, there was the sound of a scuffle – harsh, angry voices followed by the muffled grunts of men. There was a smacking sound and the thump of something hitting the carpet.

Khmer suddenly looked uncomfortable. He wasn't sneering any more.

'Don't mind them. Those are just Inquisitorial stormtroopers overpowering the provost marshals you posted outside. Don't worry, my men are very well trained and wouldn't hurt yours unnecessarily.'

'Is this a mutiny?' Khmer snorted.

'Of course not. It's a denouement.' Gurion pointed at the lord marshal with his mechanical hand. 'Varuda Khmer. I have evidence beyond doubt that you have used your rank and authority in the perversion of Inquisitorial duties.'

The provosts and commissars in the stateroom edged away from the lord marshal. The uncertainty slackened their faces. Shotguns aimed at Gurion listed slowly towards the floor.

'You infiltrated my Conclave with a compromised inquisitor. Whether you blackmailed her or what you offered her is beyond my care. You have tried several times to murder my staff. I've had enough, Khmer. The campaign will be better off without you.'

The lord marshal began to back towards the door. 'We will see what the council has to say after they've heard your evidence.'

'I don't need anyone to hear my evidence. I am the Inquisition. The only reason I kept you alive was because I did not want to needlessly kill a veteran officer in the middle of war. I kept you alive, Khmer, remember that.'

The lord marshal snatched for the Lugos autopistol at his gun belt.

But Gurion was already armed. The brass tip of his index finger – the finger pointed squarely at Khmer the whole time – hinged upwards. A monofilament thread shot out and penetrated his chest, barely disturbing the fibres of Khmer's jacket. The monofilament uncoiled inside the lord marshal's ribcage. Massive internal bleeding and trauma to his internal organs sent him down immediately. Lord Marshal Khmer fell onto his face and never moved again. With a flick, the monofilament fibre retracted, leaving a pin-prick wound that resealed airtight. Not a drop of blood was spilled.

'Put down your guns,' Gurion said to the provosts. The men hurled their shotguns down obediently.

'Khmer is done. Temporary authority of the 9th Route fleet is ceded to me. Does that conflict with military law, commissars?'

The political officers shook their heads. 'No, sir, it does not.'

'Good. In that case, give order for the chief of staff to mobilise and deploy to Aridun, according to the contingency plan. Don't stand there nodding, go!' shouted Gurion.

The commissars clicked their heels sharply, saluted and ushered each other from Gurion's stateroom.

CHAPTER TWENTY-FIVE

THE LAST WAR began six days after the helical-lunar cycle. When the fringe world of Naga aligned precisely with the equator of Baybel, and the helio-lines of the core worlds drew a straight plane across the Medina Corridor.

All Imperial military power in the system was committed. Every last fighting man.

A quick-reaction force of one hundred and twenty thousand Cantican Colonials on standby in orbit above Aridun was immediately deployed. Lord General Faisal, operations commander, wrote, 'In the event of a full-scale defensive, Angkhora would be the target for this war of attrition but holding the Fortress Chain would be the key to victory.'

In the days preceding the reactional deployment, a further sixteen divisions of CantiCol Guardsmen hurtled down from the sky in a storm of troop carriers, braving the lashing storm of aerial defence across the Fortress Chains. Artillery, horse cavalry and, above all, infantry landed in masses. The Hasdrubel 5th, heavy infantry from the neighbouring Seleucid subsector and elements of the famed Aegina Prestige regiment were committed to the Last War. Four hundred and sixty thousand men, all told.

The company of Traitor Marines holding Angkhora was dislodged only after a relentless campaign of aerial superiority. Imperial Marauder bombers of the 9th Route Fleet strafed the dead city, pounding the prehistoric structures with kilotonnes of incendiary explosives. Even then, it took the combined strength of the standby reaction force to besiege and reclaim Angkhora and the site of the Old Kings. Casualties, even during the formative stages of the war, were very high.

Imperial scholars would later attribute the initial deployment of the Last War to air superiority; air superiority provided by the 9th Route that the Archenemy did not have. Without it, the landing forces could not have been inserted directly onto the Fortress Chain. They could not have threatened the Traitor Marines with ground forces alone. Certainly, they could not have consolidated their position in the face of Ironclad deca-legions advancing across the subcontinent.

It was the greatest providence of the God-Emperor. Lord General Faisal highly commended the work of Inquisitor Obodiah Roth, Inquisitor Vandus Barq and Professor Madeline de Medici for the intelligence, which facilitated the Imperial deployment to Aridun before the Fortress Chains could be consolidated by Ironclad forces manoeuvring inland. Inquisitor Felyce Celeminé was posthumously awarded the High Lord's Order of Gallantry for her work and remembered for her death at the hands of the Archenemy, so that others could live.

Orbital reconnaissance from above Aridun revealed the advancing thrust of the Ironclad legions. Scouting elements sent to probe against the advancing enemy returned in terrified states. The Archenemy numbered, even by conservative estimates, in the region of perhaps seven million. Tanks and fighting vehicles and marching legions. Imperial Marauders sallied forth to harass their advance. Pilot remarked it was like dropping stones into water. There was no effect on the tide.

It took High Command some time to realise that the Archenemy were in no hurry to consolidate the Fortress Chains or the Old Kings. It made no difference to them whether the Imperial armies dislodged the Blood Gorgons to claim the city of the dead... They had no strategic need for time. The Archenemy since the Medina Campaign fought a slow, methodical war, preparing the trap and closing it like a steady vice. Seven million Archenemy did not hasten.

General, commander of 5th Division made the most resounding quote of the war. He remarked that, 'They were dead men, dead men defending dead things.'

At 04:57, three days after the Imperial deployment and nine days of the lunar cycle, the Ironclad rose within view of the southern savannah. The banners of Chaos thrashed in the hot wind, the legions marched, the crash of their boots like a sonorous, continuous scarp of thunder. They pounded war drums, sounded braying, plaintive war horns. Columns of armour advanced in the fore, winding like rivers of glistening steel.

The Guard had known the numbers of the enemy, but they had not been prepared for the sight of them. They flooded the open plains. Artillery observers from the upper tiers of the cities reported that the thousand kilometre reefs surrounding the chain had been churned into a marsh of smeared mud in their wake. On the ramparts, Guardsmen penned their last thoughts to paper and cast them into the wind. They hoped the Emperor's cherubs would deliver their prayers to their loved ones. It was even reported, though unconfirmed, that there were incidences of

Guardsmen throwing themselves off the city walls at the sight of the advancing Chaos legions.

Thirteen minutes past the hour of five, batteries of the 11th Colonial Artillery fired the first shell. The Ironclad exchanged siege fire from advancing tank columns. Sabot shells pounded the city-chains with colossal plumes of dust.

These shots heralded the Last War.

'Sɪʀ, ᴛʜᴇ Oʟᴅ Kings are interred deeply, of that there is no doubt.'

The man who spoke was a Cantican corporal, his brown felt jacket matted with salt and grit dust. He leaned heavily on a shovel, panting, sweat plastering his hair in greasy whorls across his forehead. The pale blue rank sash denoted him as a corporal of the Cantican 1st Combat Engineers, but until the excavations were complete, he was relegated to shovel digger.

'I propose that we utilise the explosives, at least until we break the silt layers,' Roth said. He shielded his eyes from the sun with his hand and cast an appraising eye over the excavation site.

'Heavens no! No more demolitions,' Madeline called as she climbed over a loose mound of dug-up shale. 'It's too much to risk triggering something unexpected. From now on, manual digging only.'

Roth shrugged reluctantly. 'You heard the lady. No demo, corporal.'

The Guardsman breathed heavily, shouldered his shovel and ran back down the excavation slope, barking out commands.

The dormant site of the Old Kings, as calculated, rested in the centre of Angkhora, exactly ninety degrees from either hemisphere and at balanced angles with the three suns, and with the Medinian moon at the zenith of the lunar cycle.

Unfortunately, that had placed the site directly underneath a tomb stack in the eastern quarter of the city. It was a vaulted, multi-segmented mausoleum of carved stone sixty metres high, its slightly sloping walls resembling a lotus bud with six hundred thousand tightly coiled petals. Each petal was an individual tomb wreathed with bas-reliefs depicting the character and deed of the deceased within.

In the words of Madeline, it made for a 'delicate endeavour'. Military engineers cratered an opening at the base of the tomb stack, a dry, jagged wound in the ground that led into a steep artificial canyon. Controlled demolitions and pneumatic drills had shattered through eight stratum of sediment, limestone, shale and mineral.

'We just need more time to extract the ironstone layers,' Madeline said. 'If it were so simple to excavate, then even the Traitor Marines would have completed the task already.'

The layers she referred to were the hard seams of clay and iron ore deposit that had collected during many tumultuous climatic changes. The ironstone formed a porous lattice of dense, rust-red stone. Iron ore was not easily broken by pneumatic drills.

'Time is something we do not have at the moment,' Roth replied. To punctuate his words, the sky throbbed with the pyrotechnic light of nearby explosions. The crump of shelling could be heard seconds later, low and ominous.

'The Archenemy are pounding at the gates of Angkhora,' Roth said. 'Thirty minutes ago, the eastern wall district was lost. The 22nd Battalion were routed, and the 9th suffered forty per cent casualties by last report. The enemy are no more than sixteen kilometres from this very point.'

Madeline rubbed her temples. 'I know what I'm doing, Roth. Four or five days. Give me that and I'll have reached the Old Kings.' She paused as another crackle of shelling flooded out all sound before resuming. 'I've never been wrong in all my academic career.'

Just then, an aide wearing the rank sash of lieutenant appeared at the rim of the crater. He had come by horse. Judging by the grit on his cheeks and the scorched, blackened muzzle of his lasrifle, he had just ridden from the front lines.

'Inquisitor, sir, your counsel is requested by the lord general,' the junior officer gasped, struggling to rein in his horse as it pawed at the flak board laid out around the excavation site. In his other hand, the officer led a riderless steed, saddled and ready for Roth.

Roth nodded and turned, his obsidian tabard winking with a sharp snap of his heels. Before climbing up the shale slope, Roth turned back to Madeline.

'I don't know if you have four or five days. The Archenemy are already in amongst us, street to street, house to house.'

'Five days or nothing, Roth,' Madeline called after him.

THE FIRST EIGHT hours of fighting were the worst. The white, searing sky of morning could not be seen under the pall of smoke that hung like swollen storm clouds over the southern belt. Throbbing outbursts of fire raged along the Fortress Chains. Manes of flame licked along the connective ramparts and swirled into the urban strongholds. The shockwave of shells that shook the ground became incessant.

Most of the cities along the chain lacked truly defensive walls. The fortifications had been built for an era when war was made with lance and mace, and the walls had since then crumbled into worn stubs of bas-relief and historic friezes. The vast ocean of Archenemy hit them like a tide, crashing into the boundary walls, spilling onto the causeways, saturating the arterial streets. The Ironclad foot-soldiers did not, at first, use their firearms. They came in a seething horde brandishing the brutally pugnacious instruments of close combat, the implements of the raider. They clambered over the low walls, face first into the firepower of CantiCol defence lines, seven million voices thrumming as one.

Within minutes, the frontline battalions were pushed back by the sheer magnitude of the Archenemy offensive. The CantiCol's close order drill collapsed as punctures opened up across the lines defending the major causeways and connective ramparts. Cantican field officers withdrew from the outlying districts, turtling their forces into civilian housing or anywhere with cover.

The initial trauma of assault was demoralising for the Guard. Despite the tactical firing lanes set up along the causeways, the defensive bottlenecks along the outer perimeters, the overlapping firing arcs, gun nests and wire cordons, despite every tactical advantage, they were swept aside. Across the Fortress Chain, entire brigade positions were perforated and dismantled by the spearing advance of Ironclad. Companies and platoons became isolated and encircled. H company of the 46th CantiCol Battalion took shelter in a textiles mill on the outer districts of Chindar City. Cut off and besieged, the company held out for almost an hour before they ran dry of ammunition. Their bodies were chained and dragged through the streets by Ironclad FPVs. Several kilometres east, in the chain city of Barcid, a platoon of CantiCol led by an inexperienced lieutenant actually tried to surrender as their temple was overrun. The captive platoon was marched within view of the 19th Battalion, holding a static defence across the eastern Barcid viaduct. In view of their comrades, each man in the platoon was strangled by an Ironclad Elteber, by hand, until dead. Their bodies were rolled unceremoniously into the canal.

By the sixth hour of fighting, there was very little semblance of a war front. The Archenemy were
out-manoeuvring the beleaguered Imperial positions.
Units were constantly ordered to withdraw in order to
protect their rear-line artillery and command positions.

In the roiling mass of street fighting, Imperial Navy
aircraft were unable to pin-point enemy targets. The
Archenemy pressed hard, fighting in and around the
Imperial defences. It was a tactic that the Imperial High
Command coined 'hugging' and it robbed them of their
one advantage in air superiority. Marauder bombers
were relegated to strafing runs of the rear Archenemy
lines, bridging the role of mobile artillery.

Angkhora, the resting place of the Old Kings and the
concentration of the heaviest fighting, was the most
firmly held. The plazial causeway from Angkhora's monument gates was heavily contested; its stone-slabbed
thoroughfare would allow the conveyance of Ironclad
heavy-tracked vehicles into the city, five abreast. The
Imperial Command could not allow that.

Colonel Isa Batam had been given charge of holding
the central causeway, an assignment he considered a forlorn hope. He nestled his men down behind the animal
statues that flanked the overpass, creating a firing lane
bristling with cannons, rockets and serried ranks of las.
They had waited as the constant stream of vox reports
crackled over their comms channel, relaying the enemy
advance as they broke through the struggling defences of
the outlying Angkhora region. The muffled screams and
stilted report of gunfire washed with static unnerved his
men. They chewed tabac to relieve the tension – jaws set,
eyes wide, breathing hard through their nostrils.

The advance of the Ironclad was pre-announced by the
vox-broadcast death screams of the commanding officer
assigned to the defences of a neighbouring district to
Batam's direct east. The Ironclad burst through the

ceremonial gates, a full deca-legion of foot-soldiers in a sweeping phalanx of ten thousand. Batam had exactly six hundred and ninety men under his command.

Although the approach was heavily mined, the advance of the Ironclad was undeterred, unhurried, marching to the rhythm of a sonorous war drum. At the front of the column, an Ironclad Naik brandished the paper lanterns of Khorsabad Maw.

His men fired shots. Batam almost wondered if the Archenemy realised they were there, and if they did, whether they even cared.

But care they did. The Archenemy broke ranks, surging apart to assail Batam's flanking positions. Threads of las-fire connected his thin lines of Guardsmen to the swell of Archenemy fighters. They managed three seconds of unopposed fire before the Ironclad swarmed over their positions.

An Ironclad trooper wearing a wedged breastplate leapt over the hippocampus statue that Batam had crouched behind, slashing the air with a palm razor. Batam plunged his spike bayonet into the Ironclad's hip, at the seam where his breastplate met the fauld petals. The spearing strike arrested the Ironclad's airborne momentum, jarring Batam's shoulder sockets. Batam fired a burst of las into the Archenemy, point-blank, and stomped him off the end of his rifle.

'Hold now, die where you stand!' the colonel shouted. He looked around at the heaving scrum of flashing blades and desperate bodies. One of his company captains, Siem, appeared by his shoulder, draining his clip on auto.

'Sir, I think it's time. We're doing less than we expected,' Siem shouted above the clash.

It was indeed time. Colonel Batam could see the twin pylons of the Angkhora gate, about a kilometre down the causeway. The monolithic tines were wreathed in gun-smoke, solid and unaffected by the carnage below.

Captain Siem was right. They could not hope to hold the causeway. As a pillar of Guard doctrine, when position becomes untenable, deny all strategic utility for the enemy.

'Trigger the charges, captain. Damn it, man!' Batam called. The colonel turned and realised the captain was already dead, his jostling corpse held upright by the press of bodies. A razor slashed at Batam's head and the colonel ducked under. The blade took his right ear and part of his scalp clean off. Batam, clutching the bleeding ruin of his head, fumbled for the wired detonator around his belt webbing. He grabbed it and frantically scrunched the charge receiver with his palm.

Demolition charges secured around the base of the gates blew out in an expanding ring of smoke and fragments. The three hundred metre tall pylons buckled and began to topple with ponderous speed. Thousands of tonnes of carved stone – with the cavorting animals that revered the dead – came crashing down onto the causeway. The avalanche tremors could be felt by the men fighting at the furthest chain cities, even above the shock of shelling. Six thousand tonnes of limestone falling from a height of several hundred metres was a sound one did not hear often.

Colonel Batam and all his men died instantly. The central Angkhoran causeway was reduced to a broke back ridge of rubble. Dust debris thrown up by the force of collision continued to rain back down in a deluge for many minutes after. Across the Fortress Chain, the fighting resumed unabated as if nothing of great significance had occurred at all.

INQUISITOR ROTH RODE to Joint Command as fast as he dared to press his horse.

In an unassuming crypt, vaulted in one of the oldest burial districts of central Angkhora, Lord General Murat

Faisal presided over the Last War. Incidentally, the crypt was also the family tomb of Aridun's first post-Reclamation Governor. Roth thought it was a poetically fitting place to orchestrate the Last War.

The war room was much more orderly than Roth had expected. General Faisal had dismissed most of the staff aides, junior officers and non-essential personnel from clogging the dark confines of the crypt. Bays of vox and communications equipment surrounded the circular, vaulted chamber. In the centre of the tomb, the stone coffin of First Governor Faribault had been converted into a makeshift chart table. Amid a hunched ring of staff chiefs, General Faisal received incoming reports of the collapsing front with a level stoicism.

Faisal was a native Cantican by birth, with fierce angular features mantled by dark wing-like eyebrows and skin the colour of sand-blasted wood. He wore a lengthy ceremonial coat of brown Cantican felt with simple, hand-painted shoes of cerulean silk that gave way to leather bindings up his calves. His ivory rank sash, wound around his waist and diagonally across his shoulder, denoted the deeds of his ancestors, and his long martial bloodline. Roth knew little of his reputation except that he was a fastidious, efficient yet altogether uninspiring commander. Having known that, anything was better than his predecessor Khmer.

'I was requested, lord general,' Roth said, bowing slightly but making no military salute. Although he had not meant to, Roth's mind could read Faisal's red-hot panic beneath his facial wall of weary calm. He noticed that Faisal's top collar buttons were popped open, and his laspistol sat loosely in an unbuttoned holster.

'Inquisitor, what news of the Old Kings?' Faisal asked. The terminology, or rather the acknowledgement of the relics, coming from the mouth of a high-ranking commander seemed awkward, like his tongue was reluctant.

'We have located them but it will be some time before we can excavate to the required depths.'

'The entire western flank of the Fortress Chain is collapsing. We lost contact with 5th Division Command in the city of Argentum. Gone. Overall casualty reports estimate anywhere between sixty thousand to one hundred thousand in losses.'

Faisal let his report hang in the stale tomb air.

'Sir, are you… attributing such losses to the Conclave?' Roth tested.

'Should I be?' Faisal asked wearily. 'I don't truly blame you inquisitor, rationally I shouldn't. But it's hard to send these men to their deaths. Show me something of substance, inquisitor.'

'Angkhora is of substance. We need five days, lord general.'

'And what of the Old Kings? What will you do once you have them?'

'If circumstances allow, we will ferry them off-world. Hell, sir, I'll eat them with a knife and fork if I have to, as long as the Archenemy does not reach them.'

Faisal nodded sagely, concentrating on the map before him. 'How do you propose my armies bide the time required?'

Roth crossed over to the map of southern Aridun. It was a good map, military-grade, with precise grid referencing and good aerial outlay. Tapping the eastern-most tip of the Fortress Chain, Roth indicated to the city of Bacaw. 'Start a fighting withdrawal from here, contract our defensive lines,' Roth traced the Fortress Chain down with his finger towards the middle, 'and concentrate our defences on Angkhora.'

'I agree, sir,' said Major General Ashwan. 'Our only hope of defending Angkhora is if we initiate a fighting withdrawal. We can't hold a four-hundred kilometre stretch of city. Ours lines are too thin. We have some sectors where one or two kilometre stretches are being held by a single platoon and one support weapon.'

'If we withdraw ourselves to Angkhora,' Faisal mused, 'then we have nowhere left to turn. We will have conceded ground to the enemy and run ourselves into a grave.'

'It won't do, sir, the Ironclad are raiders first and foremost. We need to weather their initial storm, and storm they will,' Roth said.

General Faisal shook his head bitterly. 'I agree but this just seems to go against all my military logic. We are the Guard, we hold ground, we seize ground and we fight for position. I agree with you, Roth, I really do, but it's hard when this is all so abstract.'

'Let me put this in a more sequential manner. The Archenemy need Angkhora. Deny them,' Roth said, plucking up the force counters representing Imperial battalions, and placing them in a ring around the cartographer's sketch of Angkhora.

The lord general loosened his collar. 'Let me tell you a story, inquisitor. I fought during the Petro-Wars of 836, very long ago. I was a captain of infantry then. I still remember, on the cotton fields of Baybel I lost my entire company to an ambush. We were shot to pieces by an unruly mob of agri-combine workers. Why? Because I deviated from my patrol route. Do you know what a Baybelite cotton field looks like when it is covered with the blood of your men? It weighs heavily on your conscience, inquisitor. As an officer, you do not forgive yourself for something like that. Forty years later, and it still keeps me up at night.'

'Do you know what would happen to the Bastion Stars, hell, what would happen to holy Terra if the Archenemy had the capability to unleash an embryonic star into the system?'

Faisal shook his head. In truth, Roth did not either. But the tactical implications of such a weapon would be convincing enough to any military man.

'We can do this,' General Ashwan concluded, jabbing at the map with an index. 'Collapse the ramparts, causeways and arterial routes as we withdraw. Leapfrog the battalions towards the centre. If we keep moving, we can dull their numerical superiority.'

Roth looked to Faisal. 'They're your men, lord general. What say you?'

'I think this operation speaks for itself,' Faisal said. 'We'll fight from house to house and make them bleed for every inch of ground they take.'

CHAPTER TWENTY-SIX

DOWN BELOW, IN the narrow defile of a laneway, a platoon of metal-shod troops picked their way through the skeleton of a commercial bazaar. Behind them, a Scavenger-pattern light tank idled at a walking pace, its eight wheels grinding over the brittle remains of canvas tents.

The light tank was an ominous beast, the sloped, hard angles of its hog-faced hull painted in chipped white. A flat turret mounting a 55mm autocannon traversed slowly, like an animal snout sniffing for scents.

Barq waited in the upper-storey miradors, watching the tanks intently. The Last War required the efforts of every available man, and Barq did not think an inquisitor was any exception. Much to the chagrin of the Conclave, Barq had volunteered as an attachment officer to the 76th Battalion. Gurion had reckoned the battlefield no place for an inquisitor, but Roth was on the front and Barq could not let his old friend do it alone. Besides, he did not wish to be outdone.

From his ambush point, Barq allowed the Ironclad below him to prowl their way down the laneway. Behind the advancing platoon, a column of heavier-armoured vehicles brought up the advance. Some of the tanks, mostly squat heavy-weapon platforms, barely manoeuvred down the thoroughfare, their sponsons gouging against the crumbling brickwork on either side. Barq waited until the last battle tank had edged its bulk into the throat of the alley before he tapped three pips on his vox headset.

A domino-ripple of explosions tore down the lane. The light tank directly below Barq's position seemed to unfurl as if the bolts that held the tightly hammered plating had sprung loose. Sheets of metal blistered and peeled away as the Scavenger's chassis caught fire.

From high up, along the miradors and rooftops, CantiCol Guardsmen volleyed down stabbing beams of las-fire and pelted grenades. The backwash of heat was furious enough that Barq could see it – a warped, shimmering curtain of steam, smoke and tangible high temperature.

Barq leaned over the galleried balcony and unracked his plated gloves. The multi-barrelled systems – fed by two belts of .50 cal winding around to an ammunition cache on Barq's back – kicked into gear. Barq swung his fists in wide arcs, an almost liquid coil of tracer unwinding from his rig. Ejection ports set near his thumbs bubbled forth with spent cartridges like copper foam, hundreds of steaming casings cascading onto the streets below.

The sustained fire from Barq's glove-guns raked into the reeling platoon of Ironclad. If it were not for the piston banks and stabiliser cables of Barq's plated arms, the recoil alone would have detached muscle from bone. Five hundred rounds of .50 cal gouged deep punctures. Five hundred rounds in five seconds, and then the feeder belts clicked empty.

'Inquisitor, division command has ordered a regional withdrawal, effective immediately.'

Barq turned to see Private Haunen, the vox-operator of Alpha Company, 76th Battalion, stepping into the plasterboard ruin of the upper gallery. The private proffered the vox-speaker in one hand, and in the other held his smoking lasrifle upright.

Barq waved the handset away. 'Withdraw to where?'

'High Command is retracting our battle lines and pulling our forces towards Angkhora and redrawing the fronts to Iopiea and Sumerabi, both three links along the chain from Angkhora, east and west. The further links of the chain, Chult and Methual have already been abandoned with more to follow.'

The withdrawal had certainly been overdue, thought Barq. Since the initial battle, the Imperial army had been pummelled into disarray. Barq barely knew which way was forwards and which way was back any more. Twice in the last eight hours they had almost triggered ambushes upon their own retreating forces.

'Echo Company of 76th will be falling back behind our positions now, directly to our rear. We are to pull back immediately under cover of their fire.'

'Let's get moving then,' Barq agreed.

Further down the laneway, CantiCol began to retreat from their firing posts. Flitting figures in white kepi hats darted along the rooftops and disappeared. Their withering blitz of fire softened to sporadic parting shots.

'Go on then! Move!' Barq ushered Private Haunen across the room and down the stairs. Behind him, the mirador he had occupied was obliterated by a tank shell in a blossoming cloud of sandstone. The Archenemy were staggering back from the shock of their trap.

Barq's company melted down into the winding stair-streets and circulatory laneways, weaving into the old city where vehicles could not.

* * *

'FIFTEEN DEGREES EAST, adjust one mil vertical,' Silverstein instructed as he peered into the distance.

Apartan, nestled down behind the length of his auto-gun, adjusted his aim and fired. The round cracked down from his position at the embrasure of a prayer tower, disappearing amongst the fire and smoke of battle below.

'Hit,' Silverstein reported.

The huntsman clambered up the ziggurat to Asingh-nu. Like Apartan, the Cantican was crouched over an autogun, the foregrip of the rifle resting on the statue of a six-limbed dancer. From here, Silverstein was afforded a different vantage point of the battle, a different target. Since the Ironclad had besieged the Fortress Chains, the guerrillas had stolen amongst the confusion, shooting and running. It was not much, but every Archenemy downed gave them a certain measure of victory.

'Six hundred metres to your eleven o'clock,' the hunts-man said, reaching out a hand to correct Asingh-nu's aim. 'Adjust minus two mils vertical, steady the breath-ing now, your aim is terrible, shaking all over the place.'

Asingh-nu fired, without even looking.

'Hit,' Silverstein said. He clapped Asingh-nu on the back.

From behind the Archenemy advance in the fallen city of Chult, Silverstein's guerrillas could see the battle that was heaving out to their front. The Imperium had with-drawn in ragged, wounded swathes and the Ironclad had pressed forwards, leaving a trail of corpses and fire in the suddenly empty city of Chult. Several kilometres away they could see the muzzle flares of distant artillery duels, the luminous pulse of explosions they could barely hear.

It gave Silverstein the perfect opportunity to stalk his quarry. They had ghosted at the tail of the Ironclad war front, harassing them. By Silverstein's count they had killed thirty-nine Ironclad Eltebers, Naiks and other field-grade commanders, as well as a handful of regular troops, although those were less valuable as targets. Given that they had tailed on the dust plumes of the Ironclad advance for days, thirty-nine was a fair number.

Dancing precariously close to the edge of the gopuram stair-tower, Silverstein edged along the painted steps to where Asingh-nu's rifle was facing towards the connective ramparts of the chain. Settling into a comfortable crouch, Silverstein began to scope for targets with his eyes.

'Let's see if we can get our fortieth kill,' he said to himself.

THE LEGIONS OF the Archenemy pressed their advance relentlessly throughout the coming night.

As Aridun slipped into evening, they split their advance into several concentrated spearheads aimed at breaching fractures in the Imperial cordon. At Iopiea, the newly drawn-up defensive front, a column of fast-moving fighters – mostly fighting patrol vehicles and outriders – rolled in fast to hit the Iopiean central causeway. The CantiCol 112th Battalion and 5th Lancers were fighting with their backs against the wall, drummed into flat-footed submission by the sudden speed of the assault. It took twelve minutes of heavy fighting before they were relieved by elements of the Hasdrubel 5th Founding.

The second attack pressed in along the western front of Sumerabi, hooking in like horned pincers. Motorised bikes and single-engine quads shrieked through the tightly wound streets of the Sumerab manufactory district, penetrating into and amongst the company-strength forces there. They forced the Imperial forces to scramble for cover, scattering into the many blockhouses and production mills. For a long while, the mounted raiders of the Archenemy ruled the night. They gunned their bikes in circles around the cowering Canti-Col, firing machine pistols into the sky, hooting and screaming in the dark tongue.

These were all diversionary attacks to preoccupy Faisal's senior commanders. The main thrust of the attack occurred in Angkhora. Unable to utilise the central causeway, an armoured formation of seven hundred tanks rolled through the outlying cemetery districts that ringed the upper tiers of Angkhora. Their tracks crushed thousands of headstones. In regions of thin topsoil the tanks even churned up shrouded corpses and stiff, buried limbs.

Brigadier General Matani Gaul mustered a staunch defence along the threatened regions with a combined brigade-level counter-attack of artillery and well-placed infantry positioning. Unfortunately, General Gaul himself was dispatched by a stray shot from a Vanquisher cannon in the first ten minutes of fighting. His second, Colonel Shedu, could not regain the general's momentum.

Hesitant and indecisive, Shedu adopted a raggedly ad hoc approach, committing piece-meal companies to the offensive, splitting his forces and feeding them part by part to the advancing tanks. Within six minutes, Shedu had lost the equivalent of two thousand men.

It took the arrival of the Aegina Prestige regiments to prevent total collapse along a three-kilometre stretch of the cemetery district. Resplendent in their armour of wire and carbon-diamond plate, the Aegina heavy infantry hit the flank column of the Ironclad armour. Mortar and lascannon lit up the night as the Aegina moved in to insulate the defences. Ironclad tanks were reduced to ruptured ruin as the Aegina moved in close, their heavy weapon fire-teams funnelling 'murder lanes' with their mortars and laying down a fan of lascannon into the channelled groups.

So fiercely methodical was the Aegina counter-offensive that the inevitable infantry advance never came. Four deca-legions of Ironclad faltered at the rubble-strewn plains of the cemetery district, milling into a confused halt. In the darkness, the four hundred Aegina troops lay down enough sustained fire to convince the enemy there were at least ten thousand Imperial troops holding the lines there.

CHAPTER TWENTY-SEVEN

THERE WERE RUMOURS, all across the front, that Khorsabad Maw himself was leading the Archenemy on this final offensive.

Vox relays from the field officers and brief reports from divisional command eventually filtered their way up to the Joint Command at Angkhora. These reports all adhered to a certain theme – Khorsabad Maw or someone believed to be him had been sighted leading the Archenemy invasion.

As the first night drew to a close, both sides withdrew to lick their wounds. Although the fighting didn't stop, the murderous storm ebbed into sporadic exchanges of fire from buildings and street corners.

The toll, according to Imperial intelligence, was severe. Of the four hundred and sixty thousand men who had manned the defences of the Fortress Chain that day, ninety thousand were dead and twenty thousand lay within the infirmaries that had been established in the green zones. A further sixteen thousand men were unaccounted for, swallowed up in the confusion of fighting.

The Imperial Guard had, in the span of twenty-one hours, abandoned thirteen of the Fortress Chain cities, thickening and bolstering their war-front around Angkhora and six cities on both western and eastern flanks. Already, they had lost two-thirds of their defensive position, an inordinate amount by anyone's standards. In the wake of the fighting, those desolate strongholds barely resembled the great tiered cities of Aridun. Artillery had eroded them into molars and stumps of foundation, the tracks of heavy vehicles grinding the rubble into dust.

As dawn prepared to break on the second day of fighting, the Guardsmen were roused into activity by tin whistles. They smoked tabac vacantly, trying to shake some feeling back into trigger-numbed fingers. Others broke open ration tins, scooping the contents out with their hands and into their mouths hungrily. Ash blackened the faces of the men and dulled the light of their eyes. They were resigned to the knowledge that the second day of fighting would be worse than the first. Fatigue had already set in, and the killing had become rhythmic.

Lord General Faisal and Inquisitor Roth toured the frontlines on horseback. The war, Faisal decided, could no longer be waged from behind tactical spreadsheets and sheltered bunkers. The Archenemy were at the gates and it was time for even the senior officers to commit themselves to fighting. The troops would need the morale if they were to see out the day.

Roth attached himself to the 10th Brigade, holding a strategic point across the eastern face of the Angkhoran canal, a boundary moat on which funeral pyres had once been set adrift. Brigadier Sasanian of the 10th and most of his staff had been killed in the early hours of the day before. The 10th would need leadership if they were to prevent the Archenemy from using the canal. It was now a strategic crossing, a bridge into the central heart of Angkhora. Roth decided, with his usual clarity, that this was very much like Tamburlaine's theatrical *Crossing of the Medes*. It would be a place to die a good Imperial death, if the Emperor willed it.

Fighting re-erupted before the suns had even cleared the horizon. At 02:58, Inquisitor Barq, leading a forward patrol company on the ramparts of Iopiea, voxed a frantic request for reinforcement. Archenemy troops, of a disposition not yet encountered before, had engaged them with brutal efficiency. The distress was soon echoed by commanders across the first-line fronts. A new troop-type was leading the advance, running roughshod over the CantiCol. A company commander of Alpha Company, 66th Battalion at the Iopiean defence voxed in that it was, 'too damn early in the morning for this,' before his vox-line went dead.

The Archenemy were bringing their most potent weapons to bear.

'The 101st and 104th Battalions are being pushed back across the canal. The 99th Battalion, as far as I'm aware, are all routed,' reported Major Cymil. He hunched down next to Roth, one hand holding his kepi in place as if he were trying to push his own head as low behind the broken wall as he could.

'And what of the 102nd?' Roth said, naming the fourth and last battalion in his command.

'Advancing across the canal bridge to cover the 101st and 104th from pursuit,' Major Cymil shouted back above the percussive thrum of shelling.

'Dammit no! Vox the 102nd to hold the line at the bridge, I don't want battalions advancing to support retreating units, we don't have the damn numbers!' Roth bellowed. The brigade major scrambled away, holding his hat the entire time.

Roth turned his attention back on the scene before him. The boundary canal was a wide irrigation ditch that was more dam than canal, running from Angkhora into the mangrove wetlands of the surrounding region. It stretched five hundred metres across, from bank to bank, as old superstition believed that would be too far for restless ghosts to cross from the burial city and escape into the Fortress Chains. The ribbons of two pontoon bridges had once provided pedestrian thoroughfare for the living. These very bridges were now the source of Roth's despair.

The four battalions in his command were bunkered down on the Angkhoran side of the canal – almost four thousand men, foraging for cover in the broken teeth ruins of rubble, trading shots with the Archenemy on the opposing bank. Many of the shots landed short of target, drumming into the water and walking frothy plumes across its entire surface.

Across the algae-rich water, a line of Ironclad were drawn in a two-kilometre battle line on the bank, at least one hundred men deep – judging by the sheer volume of enemy fire that was tearing the brigade into constituent companies, it was a conservative estimate.

'The enemy are advancing!' came the relaying cry across the banks of the canal.

Roth peered over the wedge of masonry and saw the Ironclad legions navigate onto the bridges. The war-drums were sounding their inevitable beat, the enemy marching in an extended column with banners fluttering like the Dark Age spearmen of Terra.

Roth darted from cover. He was sprinting towards a depressed ridge of scree where fifty or more CantiCol Guardsmen were taking cover. He hurled himself across the open stretch of ground as plumes of enemy shot chased his heels. Roth landed amongst the huddled press of Guardsmen.

'Major Cymil, where are you?' Roth called.

'Sir!' came the resounding reply. Cymil rose into a half-crouch and hurried over to the inquisitor.

'We don't have long, so make sure this message is voxed to all battalion commanders in the brigade. I want them to allow the enemy to cross the bridge–'

Cymil cut the inquisitor off mid-sentence. 'Sir? Allow the Archenemy to cross the canal?'

'Yes!' Roth shouted, juicing some extra clarity into his words with a touch of psychic resonance. 'I want half of the march column to be allowed to penetrate our lines here.'

The look that Major Cymil afforded Roth implied he was clearly, and beyond all doubt – mad.

Roth continued, 'Once the Archenemy have formed more than half of their numbers on our side of the canal, I want the battalions to bring down the pontoon bridges and split the enemy forces from mutual support. Once we've cut them in half, I need the 7th Artillery to be on standby to flatten those bastards on our side of the canal. Understood?'

Major Cymil swallowed. 'This could become a right mess, sir.'

Roth gripped the major's lapel and pointed to the marching enemy. 'That is a right mess. Once they get to grips with us, that will become a right mess.'

The brigade major saluted and scrambled away, howling for the primary vox.

BARQ SAW THE vibro-pike slash in and shoulder-rolled away, the blade humming over his head. The Archenemy trooper retracted his lunge and squatted down into a flare-legged fighting stance. The enemy trooper didn't move, daring Barq to come forwards.

'Vox to Bravo Company, tell them we're falling back and have them cover our tails!' Barq shouted to his adjutant. But the assault had been so fast, his adjutant was in all likelihood dead.

The Archenemy warrior shuffled one step forwards, prescribing a slow circle in the air with his vibro-pike. He was one of those in the Archenemy formation who had led the assault since morning, rolling over the forward CantiCol formations. Having been privy to intelligence documents that the line Guardsmen obviously did not, Barq recognised them as the Iron Ghasts. These 'Ghasts' were the elite ship-boarding raiders of Khorsabad's armies, and also his personal retinue. Wherever they went, Khorsabad was sure to be. Already the CantiCol were referring to them as 'Guard-fraggers' in vox reports. It was an appropriate name given the ease with which these troopers dispatched other fighting men, making the post-mortem look more like a homicide than a fight.

The Iron Ghast before him was insulated in steel, sets of small iron plates laced together by cord. It had a box-like appearance, with large oblong shoulder guards. He was broad, excessively armoured and monstrously imposing. The iron cuirass that gave them their name resembled a belly-wrap of thick girded metal that fell into a plated apron. The antlered helm and iron mask were forged as one. The iron that shod the wearer's face resembled a burial mask with long, smiling, stylised teeth. Unlike the scrap-heap arsenal of the Ironclad raiders, there was a disciplined and therefore dangerous uniformity to their battledress.

Barq back-pedalled, almost losing his balance on the rubble spill. His glove-guns were dry of munitions and he had only the plated fists. Those, and the autopistol at his hip. Around him, his company was in disarray. Lieutenant Pencak's platoon was cut off, presumed lost during their retreat. Barq's other three platoons were engaged in a fight that spilled out between the ruins of a tenement block and the surrounding streets around it. His men were everywhere. They were running, not retreating, running in all directions.

The flood of vox from the first-line defences was much of the same. The loose array of infantry companies sent into the bombed-out ruins ahead of the Imperial battle lines as spotters and forward observation teams were being butchered. They had all been hit hard since the early hours of morning. Guard-fraggers, these devils truly were. The dismembered remains of Guardsmen littered the streets, their flesh, pulverised by vibro-pikes, attested to that fact.

The Ironclad shot forwards with his pike again, two metres of violently oscillating steel spearing for Barq's sternum. The strike was so fluid that Barq had no time to react. He simply watched the pike plunge. It was a killing strike, of that there was no doubt; the sonic tremors would likely separate the fibres of his upper chest and overload his heart. But the strike never impacted.

Barq's force generators kicked in, throwing up a minor bubble of anti-gravitational force. It blunted the pike's force with a syrupy envelope of friction. The force generators were not strong enough to stop the pike completely, but it was enough to slow it down before impact. Barq seized the chance to swim around and under the polearm with his upper body. He weaved upwards with a short, snapping uppercut inside the Ironclad's guard. The bank of pistons powering his arms provided Barq the mechanical leverage he needed to pound a concave into the Ironclad's face plate. The chin dented, warping the long, smiling teeth. Three months training with the Cadian Kasrkin had taught Barq to chain his strikes, and chain them he did. He stomped his heel down onto his opponent's knee. As the armoured form began to buckle, Barq slammed a forearm down in the gap between the Ironclad's cuirass and the semi-circular lamé of the helmet's neckguard. The piston-driven strike shattered the vertebrae.

Barq did not pause to savour victory over his fallen foe. A squad of the Ghasts, a bristling wall of vibro-pikes and lasguns, were storming down a narrow stair-street to his front. More were emerging from the surrounding streets and tenements, the blood of Barq's company skidding off their humming weapons like water off a hot surface. A beam of las punched into the force field, pushing it to its limits, sending kinetic ripples across the air. Residual heat scorched a neat little hole in the enamel of his armour. Tau-tech was good, but it was not indestructible. The adrenaline and temple-hammering panic of closing death impelled him into action.

'Company withdraw. On me!' Barq turned and slipped behind the blasted stump of a public fountain as las-shots drilled smoking holes where he stood. The scattered parts of the company, in limping, scrambling handfuls, fled down the street.

Barq, drawing his autopistol, crouched behind the fountain waving his men down the street, hoping that Bravo Company were still holding the east quadrant and that he was not shepherding his men into the enemy. It had gone to the point where he was not sure any more.

'Sir, you have to move,' a Guardsman said as he staggered by. Corporal Tumas was perhaps his name, Barq thought, but he could barely recognise him. Ash turned the corporal's face into nothing more visible than a set of teeth and eyes.

'Is that all of us?' Barq asked.

'The ones we could carry, sir,' the corporal admitted painfully.

The inquisitor fired several pitiful, defiant shots down the street, in the direction of the enemy. The dull crack-ing report told him he did not hit anything. Keeping his head low, Barq joined the remains of Alpha Company of the 76th Battalion in full, panicked retreat.

MADELINE WAS LOSING her excavation team.

In the first morning, an enemy shell had landed amongst the mountain of loose earth adjacent to the excavation basin, the shower of grit getting into their eyes, mouth, nose and clothing. Madeline had thought that was bad enough.

On the second day however, the shells were beginning to find their mark. Two had landed into the quarried basin itself, killing thirteen Guardsmen who had been hauling wagons of rock from the shafts below. Within four hours, she lost another twenty men, all to shelling above ground.

It was deemed too dangerous for her, and Captain Silat, operations commander of the 1st Combat Engineers, had confined Madeline to the digging shaft that had burrowed six hundred metres below ground.

At first Madeline had been thoroughly displeased. She had wanted to oversee the excavations from above ground. That and the fact she had always been horribly claustrophobic. But now she was sure her aggravations were unfounded. It was amazing to see the Guardsmen unearth the chamber seal of the Old Kings, scraping the dirt and earth away from the ancient structure with careful reverence. It was still half-obscured by ironstone and loose earth but already it was the most wonderful thing Madeline had ever seen in all her academic endeavours.

It was the sealed entrance. She was sure of it. She could read the curving script, or at least bits of it. Some of it was written in stylised Old Terran Anglo, one of the root linguistics of High Gothic. The rest was finely engraved lines of script in Oceania Terran, a pre-Imperial language she had dealt with but never specialised in. The language was thirty-nine thousand years old and originated from the south-eastern archipelagos of very early Terra.

It proclaimed, in rough translation, of the dormant star that slept within, and of the alignment of the constellation that would awaken it. There was more, but Madeline could not translate it.

The seal itself, although still largely buried, was undeniably disc-shaped, with a radius of around sixty metres. Blocks of script and engravings depicting the flora and fauna of Aridun in relation to the constellations and galaxy covered millimetres of its exposed surface. Madeline could only see the carvings when viewed under the lens of a jeweller's scope – the birds, flowers, insects and traipsing mammalians were only millimetres big, and the largest carvings of a trunked mammoth was no bigger than her pinky nail. She could not imagine the tools required to create artwork of such a scale to such finite precision. As a rough estimate, there must have been tens of millions of figurines on the seal.

'Ma'am, one of my men has found something you have to see,' said Captain Silat.

'What is it, captain?'

'I have no idea, that was the question I wanted to ask you.'

They picked their way up a steep scarp of ironstone that encrusted the lower half of the seal. Silat led her past a long section of narrative depicting thousands of dancing humans worshipping constellations until he found a slab of inscription. The carvings there seemed out of place. They were crude, with chipped chisel markings where none existed on the rest of the seal. Most importantly, however, it was written in Low Gothic.

'It's right here,' Captain Silat said, pointing to the patch of ironstone that Madeline was almost standing directly over.

She startled, almost slipping on the scarp. Half-exposed by pick and shovel, the mummified remains of a man gazed up at her, its jawbone gaping open. Much of the skin was immaculately preserved, the waxy brown rind sagging over a skeletal structure that had been flattened by the rock deposits.

'It's holding a chisel and flint,' said Captain Silat.

Madeline crouched down to examine the body. Indeed, gripped by the leathery fingers was a head of flint and a chisel. The man, or woman, had obviously been drowned by the avalanche of clay and silt in the act of adding the cruder inscriptions to the seal.

'May I point out that he is wearing the period dress of a pre-Imperial Medinian warrior?' she said.

'You can tell?'

Madeline nodded. Although the cloth on the body was stiff and soiled, like the body it was well preserved by the mixture of clay and ore. The corpse wore a hauberk of knotted rope, armour of finely woven hemp designed to turn the point of a blade. On its skull, a layered headscarf was embroidered with the Oceania Terran word for 'resistance'.

'The helmet is a giveaway. It is from the Reclamation Wars. This is one of the insurrectionists who fought Governor-General Fulton and his campaign to bring Medina back into the Imperium, six thousand years ago.'

'And of the inscription, does it mean what I think it means?' Captain Silat said, catching the block of text under the beam of his phosphor lamp.

Madeline squinted at the writing and began to read aloud. 'So ends the chapter of freedom. We tried to awaken our Lord, our Star, but the constellations were not aligned for his coming. Our Lord awoke, yawned and returned to slumber but with his brief release, he took this world from us. The floods and storms are our doing, let the Imperials know this.'

Madeline stopped reading. She heard Captain Silat's exhalation, sharp and breathless. In all likelihood Silat had little concept of what that meant, but Madeline knew all too well. According to the inscription, the insurrectionists had attempted to release their embryonic star during the War of Reclamation, that much she could gather. But the helio-lines had been undrawn, and their planet's alignments had been incorrect. The star had been released, but the incorrect schematics had led the star to 'yawn and return to slumber'. Astronomy and cosmology had never held her interest, she had preferred to study humanity and history's place within the universe rather than the universe itself. In retrospect, those dreary cosmology lectures were coming to fruition now. In her opinion, it could only mean the star had flared, but likely collapsed back into a stable proto-state.

The flare. The flare would have been enough to release enough radiation to deplete Aridun's ozone and atmosphere, bringing with it flood, drought and mass extinction. The Old King had been the reason that Aridun died the first time.

If the embryonic star was to be released at the height of its power, Madeline had no doubt that it would consume the entire Medina Corridor and project enough radiation to reach the nearby Tetrapylon and Manticore subsectors. The energy released from an expanding star would be enormous. The dense molecular expansion of a formative star would destroy entire worlds, star systems, subsectors.

'What this means,' said Madeline slowly, 'is that beyond this seal exists an entity which can consume everything. It means that we cannot allow the Archenemy to reach it.'

High above them, the quaking of shells reminded her of the war that raged above the surface. 'Captain, hurry please, we have to double-shift the work teams. We don't have time to squander,' she implored him.

CHAPTER TWENTY-EIGHT

'FORM A LINE!' Roth cried, and his orders were relayed
along the bank of the eastern canal with shrill blasts of
the drill whistle.

The 102nd Battalion were to hold their position at the
mouth of the bridge. The 101st and 104th Battalions
were to fall back, goading the Ironclad to press forwards.
In any event, that was Roth's plan.

The 102nd were veteran soldiers, hardened by over a
decade of bandit insurgency in the Sumlayit mountains
of Cantica. If any battalion had the mettle to hold their
front against a tidal assault of the Archenemy, it would
be them. On the other hand, the 101st and 104th were
garrison battalions, unblooded troops who had never
experienced anything more taxing than border patrol.
Roth only hoped they would make an orderly withdrawal and steer the enemy into the proper artillery
zones. The 99th and 105th of 10th Brigade had already
been decimated in the first day of fighting, their remnants attached to the surviving battalions.

As the Archenemy column marched past the middle of the bridge, they broke into a shuffling jog. The porous stone and rope of the pontoon began to sag under the weight of so many troops. Their war-drums began to pound faster, louder. The Archenemy broke into a stampede.

Along the bank, the 10th Brigade unleashed a volley of las in staggered firing lines, the second rank firing over the crouching heads of the Guardsmen in front. Although the enemy possessed long-barrelled firearms, they fired back with pistols and carbines and brandished melee weapons. The choice of armament was largely important in an urban context, and mated an aggressive mobility with tactical organisation. Roth did not have much faith in static bayonet defences against the devastating impact of mauls, hammers, flanged maces and machetes.

'Guardsmen of Cantica! These are the men who burnt the houses of your ancestors! To arms! To arms!' Roth bellowed.

The 101st and 104th were strung out in a thin line, anchored at the bridge by a defensive wedge of the veteran 102nd. As the Ironclad closed on the bank, the raiders began to surge off the narrow pontoon into the waist-deep water. The enemy spread into frothing waters like scuds of piranhas, kicking the water into foam. Roth did not doubt that hundreds of them drowned in the stampede, but thousands more charged up onto the bank within seconds, shrieking and baying in their dark tongue.

Roth stood at the fore of the 102nd, the battalion holding a wedge adjacent to the bridge. He walked purposely upright against the unnerving whine of incoming fire. It would do no good for his battalion to see him cowering for cover. He blew on a tin whistle at one-second intervals, directing a steady volley of fire. Support weapons pounded larger, heavier rounds into the water, spewing up geysers that were ten metres high. They kept firing even as the Ironclad were an arm's length away, close enough for them to see the intent in their enemy's posture, the lowered heads, the raised weapons. Some of the Ironclad reached out for them as they scaled the bank, grasping with their dirty fingers.

When the Ironclad charge hit them, it hit them with all the force of seventy thousand troops behind the surging scrum. The first wave of Ironclad did not even have room to fight; they simply crashed into the line of bayonets, going under as the next wave of Ironclad trampled over the top of them. It was hell. Everywhere Roth looked was killing, odd and bizarre in its reality.

He saw a Cantican Guardsman spear an Ironclad with his bayonet. The Ironclad slid down the length of the spike and began to gouge the Guardsman's eyes with both hands. He saw a monstrously thick-necked Cantican cave in the face-binding of an Ironclad with the butt of his rifle, and stab a second and a third. The next time Roth looked back, the same Guardsmen was strangling an Ironclad by the neck even though he was bleeding out from a dozen gunshot wounds. The true mettle of a man was laid bare, often in the minutes preceding his death. It was a horrible revelation.

Roth thrashed his power fist as if he was threshing wheat. There was simply no room for footwork, for slipping his hips into the punch, for pivoting on the balls of his feet. He lashed back and forth, left, right, forwards – left, right, forwards, as fast as he could drive his arm. His shoulder ached with the act of killing. Something glanced off his head and Roth felt his skin split. Blood pressed down on his eyelashes and blinked into his eyes. He laughed. He laughed at the mess he had got himself into as blood streamed down his face. His nose was broken too; he could see the bridge of it, on the edge of his vision. Laughing hurt his nose, but he couldn't stop.

As expected the 101st and 104th began to collapse, falling away from the bank. The Archenemy pushed after them, swarming onto dry land. To their credit, the battalions peeled away with some semblance of a line, segmenting into companies and drawing the Archenemy in their thousands across the rubble-strewn district beyond.

'Advance, in formation, advance!' Roth bellowed, amplifying his voice with psychic resonance to be heard above the caustic crash of weaponry.

The 102nd, in their V-formation, drove a wedge into the horde of Archenemy, pushing closer towards the bridge. CantiCol Guardsmen waded into the water, fighting their way towards the pontoon bridge.

Roth blew his whistle and, as he had instructed, any Guardsmen within throwing distance began to hurl krak grenades and demo charges at the bridge. The water exploded in shattering columns of steam, rocking the pontoon. The tension cables holding the bridge snapped under a barrage of explosives. Section by section, like a drowning serpent the bridge rolled and submerged. Freed of support, sections of the pontoon twisted and flipped, shedding hundreds of Ironclad into the water. The winding column of Ironclad was swallowed in the aquatic murk, thirty metres deep at the canal's centre. Armoured as they were, Roth imagined they would sink quite quickly.

Suddenly cut off, the Ironclad on the rubbled plains of the bank stopped engaging the 101st and 104th. Perhaps they even realised it was a trap as some of the Archenemy troops turned around, heading back towards the water. It did not save them from the pre-designated ordnance zones as artillery began to fall amongst them. Those that escaped the artillery were rooted out of hiding and mopped up by the remainders of 10th Brigade.

* * *

BITTER FIGHTING RAGED in every street, every temple, every house, every basement and every staircase. Fire-fights even trickled down to the underground burial systems.

However, as a pale, hollow dusk began to settle on the second day of the Last War, the fighting began to fade with the light. The suns sunk, the haze of twilight quickly diluted by the ink of purple. The darkness was too treacherous for the conduct of fighting.

As night fell, shelling on both sides intensified and the CantiCol withdrew from the wingward cities of Iopiea and Sumerabi. Swathes of the city, entire acres were nothing more than an undulating desert of rubble. In some narrow streets and connective stairwells the corpses piled so high that the retreating Guardsmen had to kick them down in order to go over them. Iopiea and Sumerabi had become untenable. Quite simply, there was little left of the cities to defend.

Intelligence reports at dusk estimated there were less than one hundred thousand fighting men defending Aridun. The trauma of such high casualties on the psyche of the troops would be a telling factor in their disposition in the final efforts to come.

Against the backdrop of pulsating shell explosions in the night horizon, the frontline receded to reinforce the defenders at the central-axis cities of the Fortress Chain – the cities of Phthia and Archeh. Broken remains of retreating brigades were merged with the beleaguered forces at the new front. Where the officers had all been killed, command was given to the most senior ranking Guardsman. It was rumoured that the nine thousand men amalgamated into the 5th/8th Brigade was led by a junior lieutenant newly graduated from staff academy.

There was now no place left to retreat. A collapse at either Phthia or Archeh would allow Archenemy legions to launch unopposed offensives against the exposed eastern and western flanks of Angkhora. During the retreat, someone had scraped onto a passing wall, 'There is no ground for us, not beyond here.' Regardless of who had written it, the wry scrawl was picked up and relayed across the Imperial vox-networks as a catch-cry of the last efforts.

AT THE NEWLY established Imperial front, in the late hours of evening, Lord General Faisal himself toured the dug-in CantiCol lines, at the fringe districts of Phthia. Against the advice of his chief of staff, he was still dressed in his ceremonial coat of brown Cantican felt, complete with neat rows of medals that began at the chest and ended well below his thighs. Crossed over his belt were a pair of Cantican cavalry sabres, and over these, a twin pair of curved daggers, the quartet of blades sweeping from his waist like an impressive set of tusks. Unarmoured, and almost unarmed, Faisal was determined to tour the lines in traditional regalia. It was a subtle message to his troops – that everything was as it should be.

The lord general was genuinely impressed with the way his men had fortified the district. They were strung out in mutually supporting companies, holding positions in the tenement halls and storage-houses which faced the bombed-out ruins of the eastern approach. The barrels of guns bristled from the broken windows and rooftops of almost every building he saw. The line stretched for thirty kilometres around the city limits, interposed by strong-points of support weapon batteries. Beyond them, along the rampart walls that connected the cities of Phthia and Iopiea, the 22nd/12th Brigade held the winding stretch of brickwork. Mortars and bombast platforms trundled on rail tracks along the battlements. In some parts, enemy artillery had collapsed the rampart into a sagging slope of rubble spill, scorching the limestone a dense, streaky black, but the troops still held the position.

The lord general dismissed his cadre guard of Lancers and walked, unescorted, to the frame of what had once been a chariot shed. The stables were now fire-blackened columns of stone, and the clay tile roofs had shed broken-teeth gaps to reveal the support structure beneath.

Inside the chariot shed was a sentry team of Cantican Colonials. Three Guardsmen huddled around the embers of a hexi-block ration fire. Two more had set up bipod lasguns on the low stable walls overlooking the rubble plains of the east, observing the direction of the Archenemy approach.

As Faisal stepped into the chariot shed, the Guardsmen abruptly stood to attention. Their senior, a sergeant with a curling beard, snapped him a quick salute.

'Sergeant Sulas – sentry post 11/A, 55th Battalion of the 7/15th Brigade, sir,' bellowed the sergeant in his loudest marching voice.

'At ease soldiers, at ease,' Faisal said, waving them down. The lord general looked at the Guardsmen of sentry post 11/A. They were haggard-looking men, badly bandaged and languishing. Most of the sentry posters, Faisal knew, were wounded men who the medics simply did not have the supplies to treat. Knowing that the injured would hamper the fighting efficiency of a platoon, these men were left as sentry posts along the front lines as forward observation teams. In all likelihood, these men would be dead by morning.

Faisal crouched down next to the sergeant by the glowing fire and warmed his hands a little. 'What is the order of the day?' Faisal asked.

'Grabbing some tiff, sir,' replied Sergeant Sulas.

The sergeant was stoking a tin of ubiquitous 'Meat C-Grade' that he had thrown into the ashy embers. He jabbed at the little canister with the tip of his bayonet, warming it up whole.

'You could join us, sir, that is, if you'd like to, sir,' a young private offered.

Faisal realised he had not eaten properly since landfall, and he was ravenously hungry. 'Of course, I would love to, that is if you have the rations to spare,' said the lord general.

With expert hands, Sergeant Sulas snatched the Meat C-Grade from the fire and doused the tin into a pot of cold water and ration tea leaves. The hot tin heated the water, drawing a cloud of steepage from the tea leaves. Without pause, the sergeant pinch-gripped the tin out of the hot water and peeled it open with the flat of an eating knife. The opened can revealed a surprisingly wholesome-looking round of marbled meat.

'The trick is, sir, to eat this meat without tasting too much of it,' Sergeant Sulas said. He scraped the meat out into the sheet of rehydrated rice and began to douse it with condiments, his fingers darting from ration packs like some sleight of hand.

'Pepper and pickled bell chilli are the key to good tiff. Masks the chems they use to preserve this meat,' said the sergeant as he scooped some of the rations into a cup canteen and offered it to the lord general.

The tin of gelatinous meat melted into the dehyd rice. Small pods of angry-looking chilli bells were mixed into the steaming container. Tugging off his gloves and using his hands, the lord general unceremoniously pushed the rice into his mouth, making muffled, appreciative sounds. It was salty and oily without being greasy. The spicy sourness of the pickled chilli made him inhale the meal. Within seconds, Faisal was teasing the last scraps of chilli and rice from his cup canteen.

Faisal waited for the Guardsmen to finish eating in contemplative silence. Once the meal was done and tea was shared, Faisal gestured to the sergeant. 'What is it that has confined you to sentry duty, sergeant?'

Without a word, Sulas unbuckled the gaiter around his calf and slid his boot off, slowly and smoothly. His sock, sticky with blood, was plastered to the boot and peeled off, along with several strips of skin. It was a las-wound, partially cauterised and seeping tears of blood and pus. Faisal was shocked to see a hole in the top of the sergeant's foot, moist with infection and blistering with white skin cells.

'Doesn't hurt, sir. Can't feel a thing but I sure as frag can't run like I used to,' Sulas shrugged.

'And you, private, what is your name and why are you here?' Faisal said to the young man squatting next to Sulas.

'Private Kabau, sir. Las-shot to the upper arm. Tore away my upper bicep down to the bone,' said the young man. He wormed a finger into the loose, yellowing bandages around his arm to reveal the top of his wound. Faisal could see the puckered mass of melted skin and even the whiteness of bone. Las-wounds were a horrible thing to behold. They cauterised the wound, deadened the nerves and were crippling. Men didn't die immediately from blood loss, instead, they lingered for days in agony until infection set in. It would drain the platoon of resources and limit the unit's field effectiveness. One wounded soldier could be expected to take a further three or four men to carry and care for him. It was, in effect, the perfect weapon of mass war.

'Have they given you fentanyl for it?' Faisal asked.

Private Kabau with the sheared arm shook his head mutely.

Faisal popped the gold buttons of his coat and drew out a foiled sleeve of tablets. It was the plus-grade chems that all high-ranking officers were issued with – pure opiate analgesic. Faisal handed the packet to Sergeant Sulas, who took them with a mixture of relief and dismay.

'Distribute them accordingly, sergeant.'

* * *

DAWN CAME, BUT the suns did not. Intensified shelling
had diffused the sky to a husky graphite-grey. The suns
did not penetrate the pall of smoke and everywhere
Guardsmen whispered of dark Chaos magic.

In the twisted remains of Iopiea, the streets were
empty. The Imperium had vacated the city during the
night and now the Archenemy marched in unopposed.
All of the Imperial Guard had retreated, all but Watcher
Platoon of Bravo Company, 45th Battalion. Somehow,
somewhere during the hurried mess of mass withdrawal,
the Watchers had been left behind and cut off by the
sweeping Ironclad advance.

As the pale deepwater-blue of dawn began to light the
courtyard of a grain mill, Watcher Platoon spread out to
cover the main avenues of approach. Lieutenant Almyra
pulled security at the gates of the courtyard with half a
dozen able-bodied Guardsmen. On the north side of the
courtyard, where the terracotta walls had been demolished,
Sergeant Cepat curled up behind the rubble line with six or
seven men, pointing their weapons into the maze of stair-
case-streets and sloping laneways that bordered the mill.

The enemy, they knew, were fast approaching. They could
follow the movements by the flutter of distant war drums.
But try as he might, Sergeant Cepat could not focus on the
danger of their circumstances. His mind kept wandering to
stupid, inconsequential things. He remembered that
tomorrow, the date would fall on his annual medical examination. As a fifty-year-old infantry dog, Cepat was required
to pass an annual clearance run on brigade orders or else be
retired to administrative duties. Cepat wanted to know if
the exam would still be required. He shouted to Almyra.

'Sir! Am I still scheduled for that damn yearly medical?'

The lieutenant turned to regard his sergeant with a
confused look. He shrugged, motioning for the sergeant
to stay quiet.

Cepat was still thinking about the cold, intrusive medical instruments they used when the first round sent up a clod of dust in front of him. The first shot was followed by a sharp brittle volley. In under a second, the courtyard was deafened with the popping of rounds, grenade bangs and the urgent shouts of Guardsmen calling out targeting sectors.

Ironclad troops began to clatter down the stairs, firing as they came. Cepat put six rounds downwind, then another two for good measure before weaving back behind cover.

Cursing, the sergeant hunched down behind the wooden stock of his lasrifle and began to pick steady shots. He was angry because the damn lieutenant never did tell him whether he needed to take that damn examination.

UNDER THE RUDDY half-dark of dawn, Silverstein led his guerrillas on foot through the unmapped maze of Phthia. They moved slowly, feeling their way through heaps of rubble some eight metres high.

They were no longer simply following in the wake of the Ironclad advance, now they were amongst them. The guerrillas and their huntsman picked their way carefully along through city blocks. In the streets they found nothing but corpses, broken vox-sets, torn bits of clothing, stains of blood. Over all of this was a blanketing deluge of spent ammunition, millions upon millions of brass cartridges, las-cells and discarded magazines. Silverstein could not put his foot down without stepping on one of them.

They avoided the main columns of advance, but occasionally, they would come across a roaming murder squad, or some other flanking company-sized formation. During these times, Silverstein's expertise in camouflage and concealment saved their lives. Shadow reflection, seam blending and natural curvatures were all part of the huntsman instinct. They navigated the shadows well.

'This is the spot,' Silverstein proclaimed. He was looking up at the collapsed shell of a tenement building. It was a recent addition to the city, judging by its rockcrete support and probably only centuries old compared to the crumbling millennial sandstone around it. All the windows had been blown out and a good third of it had caved inwards like a rotting shipwreck.

The guerrillas scraped up the scorch-blackened hole in the tenement's side and moved to the upper galleries overlooking an uneven tier of ground-down city.

'What I'd give for a wedge of smoked cheese and a snifter of wine,' Silverstein said as he stabilised his bullpup autogun on its bipod.

Asingh-nu sniffed. 'I was never an appreciator of cheese myself.'

'That's because Asingh is a rural plebe. He wouldn't tell cheese from cattle groin,' Temughan taunted. Apartan laughed his harsh, barking military laugh.

Silverstein shook his head. 'That's because you've never had a good cheese. Balance of sharp saltiness and mellow sweet, well aged and earthy, cured from Odessian goat's milk. Have you ever imported a Stilt-On-Haystack smoked from the Narbound Subsector, smoked with hay-twig? Gorgeous, I have a round sitting in my cellar… back home on one of my estates…'

He trailed off, suddenly weary. It became clear to him that he was very far from the comforts of home. It occurred to him that if he made it out of this mess alive, he would discharge from the service of the Inquisition. Then, pondering more, he remembered the forty-three kills he had amassed, and reconsidered. Where else would he be able to hunt game like this?

'Fire as many good shots as you can get off in under one minute, then we move. Clear?' Silverstein said.

The others nodded. They were working in teams of two now, each shooter with a spotter. Temughan, with his artisan's hands, lay behind the wooden stock of a Garlans-pattern autogun. Its slender, bottle-nosed profile was of fine-grained wood and the straight-grip stock fitted smoothly in the his hands. Apartan the ex-Guardsmen hunched next to him with a pair of magnoculars, not seeming to mind that the diminutive clocksmith was making the shots.

Silverstein allowed Asingh-nu to fire the bullpup. Although the huntsman was an immaculate shooter, his optic augmentations made him an even better spotter. Asingh-nu simply had to squeeze the trigger and breathe when Silverstein told him to.

Even with the poor visibility, they could see a defiant line of tall chimney mills intact despite being surrounded by broken lumps of rubble. Several hundred metres away, Ironclad scouting parties would be picking their way through the city in preparation for another mass offensive by morning. Silverstein would make sure the way was not clear for them.

Suddenly, the smooth dome of a steel head bobbed into view less than two hundred metres away.

'Sighted,' Apartan called from their position.

'Be my guest, gentlemen,' Silverstein said as he watched the top of the head move along a crest of jagged sandstone. The target moved unevenly, almost staggering. Something about it made Silverstein nervous. It dawned on him.

'No! Cease fire!' he hissed urgently.

It was too late. Temughan's shot rang out. The round struck the top of the bobbing head and it went flying. The target had been nothing more than a shaped hub of metal propped up on a rifle.

'Damn it,' Silverstein managed as he threw himself flat.

Return shots flashed from the crest line. Out there, someone opened up with a heavy support weapon, hammering the tenement shell with fat-calibre rounds. Temughan rolled violently off his rifle, blasted into three distinct parts. Apartan jerked backwards, shuddering as a round exited out of his back. The support weapon stopped firing and just like that, the dawn was quiet again.

Silverstein, swearing repeatedly under his breath, rolled onto his knees in a cloud of brick dust. 'Are you fine?' he asked Asingh-nu.

The guerrilla patted himself down. He nodded with wide, terrified eyes.

The huntsman, still swearing, pointed to Temughan's rifle.

'Take that, fire once from the fifth window when I tell you to, then get away from there. Perfectly clear?'

Asingh-nu shot him a puzzled look but nonetheless nodded and timidly crawled over to the blood-burst stains of Temughan and Apartan.

The huntsman seized his bullpup and crept to the edge of the tenement, where the wall ended like the broken pieces of a jigsaw. He leaned out and scanned the area with his bioptics. By eye, he gauged wind current, temperature and visibility. Satisfied, Silverstein gave Asingh-nu the thumbs-up.

The guerrilla fired and threw himself away from the window. Out on the crestline, the muzzle of a heavy bolter was lifted into position and the silhouettes of three Ironclad – appearing as grainy monochrome shapes to Silverstein's eyes – raised themselves.

Silverstein snapped off a trio of fluid shots, dropping two of them. The third round missed, fragmenting off the heavy gun's hand rail. Re-aligning with pause, Silverstein banged off a fourth shot that might have clipped the Ironclad as he disappeared behind the crest.

'I think it's time to move, we've been here too long.' Silverstein gestured for Asingh-nu to follow him. The huntsman turned towards the remains of his comrades sprayed out across the apartment floor. He spared them one last glance and headed down the staircase.

SOMETIME DURING THE night, the remains of Barq's company, just nineteen men, staggered upon the outpost of Zulu Company, patrolling the city grid beyond the ramparts of Phthia.

Zulu Company had bunked down in a gatehouse overlooking the main western causeway that linked the outskirts of Iopiea. It was a solidly strategic post. The gatehouse itself was a squat tower of ancient stone blocks. Barq was sure that beautiful carvings must have once run up the gate-tower, but the stones had gathered several thousand years of moss, clumping together in thick, rotting beards of green.

Captain Bahasa was the leader of Zulu Company. His men did not call him sir, they called him boss because that was the kind of officer he was. Dour, stern and as broad as he was tall, Bahasa stalked the battlements with a T20 Stem autogun looped across his chest and a stub of tabac winking out of his mouth. It was common knowledge that Bahasa had nothing left to lose, like most; none of his family had managed to board a refugee barge during the opening months of the campaign. He went about the defence of the gatehouse with a reckless abandon borne of vengeance. He laughed, he barked and he joked in the face of death.

As morning came, Zulu Company dug in. The railed bombast platforms were wheeled into position to face the east, thick-rimmed bronze barrels turned skywards. Industrial trolleys of ammunition were sent along the rampart rail-line to the gatehouse, re-supplying the heavy stubbers that lurked in the murder-holes and gun loops. The grated portcullis was welded shut and the stone gates were barred.

On the battlements, Inquisitor Barq surveyed the teams of mortar-men. He walked between them, offering words of encouragement and envelopes of opiate pain-killers. It was little more than a gesture of assurance. For the company of over one hundred men, they had only been spared one combat medic – Corporal Rwal. He was young, inexperienced as far as Barq knew, and had been promoted in rank yesterday after their medic sergeant had been hit by a stray round.

'Corporal, do we have the supplies on hand to tend to these men?' Barq asked.

Corporal Rwal was standing at the edge of the parapet. He was nervous. Barq could tell by the whites of his eyes, and the way he chewed his tabac, clenching his jaws.

'Corporal, supplies?' Barq repeated.

Rwal turned suddenly from his thoughts. 'I have the supplies. But I don't have enough hands, sir.'

'I'll stay with you during this fight. Tell me what needs doing, corporal, yes?' Barq said, moving to join him by the parapets.

Corporal Rwal didn't answer. He was off again, chewing and gazing into the distance. Plumes of smoke rose like bubbling black pillars across the ancient city. Even now, in the early quiet of dawn, Barq knew that the foot spotters and Ironclad scouts were prowling through those streets. The attack, he knew, would not be long in coming.

He was right. At 03:55, as the suns rose against their eyes, the Archenemy attacked. They kept the glinting glare of sunrise behind them. Against the suns, the Iron-clad rose like haloed silhouettes – dark figures, horned and plated against a liquid orange horizon.

Small-arms fire trotted along the brick embrasures. The Ironclad broke across the band of wetland bordering the gatehouse, sloshing across the soupy reed paddies. Packs of fast-moving outriders and treaded FPVs preceded the main assault, blasting up at the gatehouse with automatic fire. Behind them, a battle line of Ironclad foot-soldiers almost a kilometre wide closed in on the gatehouse in a flanking sweep.

Barq and Corporal Rwal rushed to the top of the battlements where two platoons of Zulu Company were manning the mortars and unleashing las-volleys over the walls. There was so much activity happening in such a confined space. Company commander Captain Bahasa was standing upright over the battlements, changing magazines from a T20 Stem autogun. Barq screamed for him to get down, but the captain didn't hear, working the mag into his weapon. A round hit Bahasa in the chest and the captain collapsed. Barq thought he was dead for sure but the captain picked himself up, laughing. The bullet had pierced the compass he clipped to his webbing strap, lodging itself in the metal dial face.

To their front, a stub gunner slumped over his weapon and slid limply down. Barq and Rwal rushed over to the gunner but were stopped short by a cry for help across the other side of the battlements.

'Medic! Medic!'

The cry echoed from various points across the battlement, plaintive and loud even above the roar of gunfire. It came from all directions as casualties mounted.

Corporal Rwal did what he could. Those mortally wounded, such as a mortar loader who had taken shrapnel underneath the chin, were jabbed with the painkillers Barq had distributed earlier. There was no saving those ones, especially when their skin was greying and their eyes were rolling back to white. Those who could fight again – injured limbs, bleeding wounds – Rwal would work on frantically, holding a drip-bag high in one hand. Barq followed the young corporal with a leather case, handing him the surgical instruments as the corporal shouted himself hoarse.

Below, the enemy were banging on the gates. Rockets and heavy support weapons pummelled the walls relentlessly. A private on his knee, firing over the lip of an embrasure, was hit. The shot snapped his head back and sent him straight down. Another Guardsman of Zulu Company sprinted forwards, dragging him by the webbing straps away from the wall and swung his body towards a pile of dead and wounded, collecting in the centre of the turreted rooftop. Another Guardsman would take his place. The scene was repeated again and again like a maddening loop. Dying, firing, reloading and dying again.

Blood covered Barq's gauntlets in a red sheen, trailing fine threads up his forearms. He stopped thinking and let his hands do the work, pinching down on sutures or administering chems as Rwal directed. The faces of the Guardsmen, sometimes mouths open in mute pain, would stay with Barq for the rest of his life. These were fighting men, the warriors of the Imperium, screaming violently, their muscles hanging open in bloody flaps. Barq vomited twice, and the third time was retching bile as he worked. He dared not vomit onto the wounded, so he vomited onto the wall merlons, ducking his head below the crenels.

Sickness threatened to overwhelm him for the fourth time while powdering the shredded thigh of a Guard sergeant. The inquisitor leaned towards the parapet and heard a hollow pop. He opened his eyes and saw a grenade hit the edge of an embrasure. It bounced up off the edge and rolled off the block of stone. Then it went off.

The embrasure absorbed the flak and explosion of the blast but disintegrated. It threw out a disc of gravel, tight and compact. The storm of grit hit Barq full in the face. Barq went to his knees, his face transformed into a raw, bleeding graze. He had never even had time to activate his force generators.

'I can't see a damn thing,' Barq spat, teetering along the parapet, his hands groping blindly. 'Can't see a damn thing!' he said again, this time tinged with a wail of urgency.

Captain Bahasa, firing from the wall, ran to the inquisitor's aide. Corporal Rwal rushed over as well. Barq was screaming.

The medic took one look at Barq's face and shook his head at Captain Bahasa. It wasn't good. Grit and rock filled Barq's open eyes, like a lens of densely packed sand.

'Are my eyes fine?' Barq said, pawing at the corporal.

'You'll be fine. A temporary side effect,' he lied.

The inquisitor brushed him away, suddenly wailing. 'Don't lie to me. Am I blind?'

'Yes,' said Bahasa.

'Holy Throne, not now,' Barq hissed through gritted teeth. He staggered along the parapet, driving his plated fists into the crenels. Ageing limestone crumbled like chalk beneath his frustration.

Bahasa and Rwal both urged the inquisitor to get down. Barq did not wish to hear them. The enemy below fired up at his exposed upper body.

A solid slug punched into Barq's shoulder, spinning him around. Another shot entered upwards through his lower back, where the upper-body rig offered no protection. The round pierced his heart and exited through his upper chest. A small convex puckered outwards on the plate there.

Inquisitor Barq was dead before he hit the ground. Rwal hoped the wound, through his heart, had caused him very little pain.

CHAPTER TWENTY-NINE

The Ironclad were wrestling the Fortress Chains out of Imperial control. By the third day of the Last War, seams were fracturing along the encircled Imperial front.

The locomotive railheads at Phthia across the central-eastern canal changed hands twelve times in five hours. At some places, the firing was so dense and constant that troops were reduced to raking blindly around corners and over ledges with the barrels of their weapons.

Facing the enemy assault towards the west at Archeh, the Canticans could not hold any longer. For many of the Guardsmen, there was simply nothing left to give. After the adrenaline, after the terror, after fifty-six hours of close-quarter combat, there were erratic reports of men dying from exhaustion.

Throughout the day, Imperial Vulture gunships and snarling, fat-bellied bombers made low strafing runs over Archenemy positions. They flew against snagging flak curtains thrown up by tracked, super-heavy anti-aircraft decks and even the vectoring fire of portable rocket tubes. Despite the high casualties, pilots flew sorties throughout the daylight hours, pausing only to refuel their craft.

The chief of staff predicted that total, absolute collapse would occur within twenty-four hours, perhaps forty-eight at the greatest. At the excavation site of the Old Kings, engineers wired thermal charges along the basin and shaft tunnel. If the Archenemy came upon them before the Old Kings could be unearthed, they would bring down the site. It would not deter the enemy, but it would be a last act of defiance. Captain Silat of the 1st Combat Engineers vowed that the Archenemy would not finish the work he started.

The defeat began at exactly high noon on the third day. At the cargo station district of Archeh, the combined 2/15th Brigade under the command of Brigadier General Dreas Dershwan were broken. Their dead littered the cargo bays amid rotting boxes of vegetation and spoiled meat. Brigadier Dershwan was hung from the highest temple spire, suspended by a thread of spool wire. It was rumoured, although unconfirmed, that the remaining elements of Blood Gorgon Traitor Marines punched their way through the turtled Guardsmen. In this way, the 2/15th were soundly defeated, leaving a wide puncture wound to the heart of the held Imperial positions.

The end, as predicted by High Command, came much sooner than they expected.

'KEEP IN FORMATION! Advance in platoon order!' Roth barked at the men around him. They were struggling. He could tell. Nearby, a Guardsmen fell to his knees and slid against a slope of jagged wall. The soldier leaned on his rifle, with his head down. He would not be getting up again.

Discipline, the foundation of military efficiency, was eroding.

Roth stomped about the formation, dressing the ranks of his men. Behind their ragged line of advance, the cardinal tomb-towers of Angkhora rose up, their sloping apexes swathed in a swirl of smoke.

Roth no longer commanded the 10th Brigade. He was not sure who he commanded. Throughout the night, the remnants of withdrawing CantiCol had filtered through his position without any semblance of command structure. Companies, platoons and even lone, wounded soldiers trickled towards the 10th.

Within an hour of daybreak, Roth was despairing. He estimated he had at least six thousand men, ten thousand at the most, under his faltering command. Infantry, Lancers, gun crewmen, even transport and ordnance had gravitated under his jurisdiction. Many had no idea who their immediate seniors were, or who had overall command of a platoon or company, let alone the battalions.

As they advanced, the Lancers consistently moved ahead of the brigade, deftly picking their way through the rubble landscape. With their distinct grenadier belts and drawn sabres, the elite Guardsmen almost showed an abject contempt for their lagging comrades. They communicated with deft hand signals while the officers and NCOs had to shout orders at the non-Lancer troops around them. The younger and more inexperienced Guardsmen drifted away from their platoons and followed the Lancers, huddling close. There was no sense of order to the advance. It seemed with the impending final days of war, the Guard had no fear of military punishment. They were in hell already.

When the fighting began in early morning, it came as no surprise to Roth when the diluted 10th Brigade dissolved into disarray.

The fire-fight started abruptly. Ironclad tanks – heavy-tracked weapon platforms with splayed hulls – crunched through the remaining partitions of upright masonry.

Ironclad foot-soldiers moved amongst them, their muzzles flashing from wall-less door frames, roofless windows and scattered foundation blocks. The result was panic.

The Lancers charged ahead, brandishing their cavalry sabres. The rest of Roth's brigade lingered, headless and without a functioning command system. Some units made no attempt to advance, they simply sank down and returned weak, uncoordinated fire. Officers stormed about in an attempt to rouse their men but the men had no fight left in them. Others units routed, fleeing deeper into the Imperial lines.

'Major! Major! Rally the men with me, we are to withdraw and regroup!' Roth shouted at the closest ranking officer. The major was standing in the open, with his back to the enemy. Serene, almost complacent, he was readjusting the straps of his webbing as small-arms fire kicked up clods of dirt around him.

Roth had seen it before. Neural overload. There was too much noise, too much fear to the point where the brain was ignoring it. The major stood in the open as tracer zipped around him. A round thudded into the back of his head. He went down face-first and didn't move any more.

Roth shimmied behind a stone coffin. The heavy casket had been thrown from a bombed-out mausoleum some thirty metres away. Evidently the force of the blast had deposited the coffin neatly in the middle of the road, upended but intact.

'Excuse me, I can't see anything. Would you point me in the right direction?'

Roth spun about to see a Cantican trooper pawing at his shoulder. The man's eyes were bandaged and he was crawling amongst the sharp stones on his hands and knees.

'Towards the enemy, or towards our main lines?' Roth said, easing the man behind cover with him.

'Whichever one will give me a quicker death,' answered the blinded private.

'I remember the grand poet Huerta once wrote the only thing that matters in death is permanency. We're all as good as done – today, tomorrow or the day after. Die with a rifle in your hand,' Roth said.

As if to reiterate his point, the husk of a chariot shed under which a platoon of CantiCol were taking cover went up in a vertical cloud of fire and grit. The building had been close by, and rained ashy detritus down on Roth and the blind Guardsmen. The tank that flattened the building rolled over its remains, the snouted turret traversing slowly from left to right, no more than twenty metres to Roth's left.

'Can you hear tanks?' said the Guardsman, sitting with his back to the wall.

'Oh yes. I can definitely hear tanks,' Roth agreed. The sprawl-hulled tank trundled past him.

'No, not the enemy tanks. I can hear Imperial tanks,' the blind Guardsman said.

'You can tell?'

'Yes, because I hear horses too. I can hear their hooves trembling the stones.'

Roth tried to focus yet he heard nothing. Nothing other than the deafening fury of a short-range firefight. Perhaps the Guardsman's loss of vision allowed him to focus his sensory faculties on things he otherwise would not.

And indeed the Guardsman was right. The Archenemy tank that had creaked past exploded as a shell erupted against the flank of its armour.

'Yes, I definitely hear horses,' the Guardsman agreed. He stood up, craning his head as if he could still see.

Tanks in the reverent brown of the Canticans were cutting across the enemy flank. Between their thickly armoured bulks, mounted CantiCol Guardsmen fired upright from the stirrups of charging horses. Their angle of approach allowed them to spear at the softer flank of the Ironclad armour. Detonations erupted everywhere. Turrets began smoking.

'It's our cavalry,' muttered the Guardsman.

The squadrons powering across the rubble were mostly ancient, obsolete tanks. Siegfried siege-tanks, Centaurs, several Leman Russes. The Canticans did not possess many armoured vehicles at the beginning of the war and they did not now. What cavalry, motorised or organic, they had, they assembled it into a motley armoured regiment. Roth saw before him now – the Cantican 1st Mech-Cavalry Regiment.

Ancient engines of war, their plates held together with bolts and reverence rumbled alongside the thunderous hooves of Lancer cavalry. Yet as they blazed through the enemy attack, clashing steel on steel, it was the most beautiful sight Roth had ever seen.

'BE ADVISED, COMMAND element is dead. Be advised, command element is dead. Over.'

The same message was relayed a thousand times over the Imperial vox-net. The channels buzzed with the frantic chatter of news. Lord General Faisal was dead.

Doctrine should have warranted a restriction of information. No one, especially not demoralised rank-and-file, should have learnt of their general's death. Yet a corporal who had witnessed the event had released the word and now it spread like an incendiary bomb.

Corporal Bacinda had been the closest one when it happened. He was also the vox-operator of Echo Company of the 46th. The lord general had been touring the lines, resplendent on his horse and his traditional dress, and standing high in the stirrup on his painted shoes.

The troops had been dug in behind a breastwork of rubble and furniture, their rifles pointed towards the smoking western front. The morning's engagement had been predictably brutal and Bacinda's platoon had been cycled back to the secondary lines in order to rest briefly. The men had been eating what food they could forage and slumping asleep while leaning on rifles. Then Faisal had come and they had all staggered to attention. Bacinda remembered seeing the throbbing glow of explosives in the horizon and the lord general ride against it, administering words and stern, knowing looks to his men. It almost made Bacinda forget his hunger as he watched.

No one saw it coming. The artillery shell landed thirty metres away, exploding in a mushroom of dust.

Faisal was killed by a small piece of shrapnel that entered his ear. The shrapnel exited the forehead and Bacinda remembered looking up at the general's face. It was serene. Faisal never knew what killed him. Perhaps he never knew he had died.

The general's blood, hot and arterial, spurted into Bacinda's face. It fell into the mess tin he was cradling in his hands. His meal of boiled grains was ruined. It came as a great surprise to him that the sudden shower of blood into his meal upset the corporal so much more. He tried to cover the tin with his hands. It had been his first meal in three days. Ludicrously, Bacinda even considered whether the meal was still edible.

Faisal's horse panicked, carrying the general's body away down the breastwork. In a final show of the macabre, the general's body stayed upright in its saddle. The platoon line didn't react. They didn't know how. Even old Sergeant Habuel looked shockingly still. Of all Echo Company, it was Bacinda who put down his tin of bloodied grains with weary resignation. He sighed, lamenting the loss of his rations, then picked up the handset of his vox-caster.

* * *

THE TOWERS OF Angkhora. Or so Asingh-nu told Silverstein.

The burial-centre of Aridun, placed at the axial centre of the Fortress Chain. From their vantage point on the scorched tin of a production mill roof, they could see the skyline of Angkhora. It was hazed by a shimmering screen of heat – heat emanating from the embers and hot, molten rubble of shattered cities.

Although the rural labourer had never been there, he had heard stories of the Fortress Chain from a wealthy cousin. The man had coveted a finely woven rug that depicted the lotus-bud towers where the ancestors of Aridun rested forever. It had made Asingh-nu very jealous.

'The enemy have been pressing towards that central stronghold ever since the first shot. Why?' Silverstein asked as his bioptics clicked and whirred, capturing still images for photo-analysis.

'A man of my education is not meant to know these things. But anyone can tell you it's bad luck. Places where the dead go are not places for the living,' Asingh-nu said, tightening the grip on his autogun.

'Do you hunt, Asingh-nu?' Silverstein said, changing the subject smoothly. He turned to regard the guerrilla with his sutured yellow eyes.

'I was a rural. Of course we did. My sons and I did often. At night we'd walk through our lagoon paddies with a good blunderbuss and track swamp pigs. They were small, but very fat and very delicious with good vinegar.'

'Did you ever lure them, bait them to ensure the fattest, largest bull-swine would appear for the show?'

'Small clumps of stale grain would do the trick. The staler, the yeastier, the better. Sometimes we'd lure three or four of them together at once, fighting over the bait.'

'Well, look at it this way, Asingh-nu. Angkhora is the bait for the Archenemy. It's something they want. That usually means the big game is there, the bull-swine, if you will, of the den.'

'You mean their leader? I'm rural, not stupid,' Asingh-nu shrugged.

Silverstein laughed. 'Of course. But we can really hurt them there. Maybe tag ourselves a few Chaos generals. Would that not be grand?'

Asingh-nu surreptitiously made the sign of the aquila at Silverstein's mention of Chaos. He tapped the map-wood stock of his Garlan auto for good measure.

'I'll go,' he said. 'Maybe I'll find the one who killed my sons.'

THE FIGHTING WAS so close that if Madeline was at certain points of amplification in the cavity tunnel, she swore she could hear the individual gunshots from the city above.

'Captain Silat, have your men prepare the thermal charges. If we – if I – am unable to decipher the text on this entrance seal–'

The captain snapped his heels in salute. 'Already executed, ma'am. I've posted a section of my men around the excavation perimeter. We'll be ready to do it if the Archenemy comes.'

'Thank you, captain, your aid has been invaluable.'

Satisfied, Madeline turned back to trawling the disc-seal with her jeweller's lens. It was a monumental effort as the inscriptions were minuscule and her lens, which fitted over one eye, was no larger than the circle formed by her thumb and forefinger. She had not slept or eaten since the Last War had begun. Climbing the scaffolding to study the disc was all she had done.

The disc itself, once unearthed, was exactly seventy seven point seven metres in diameter, and geometrically perfect. The surveyance laser, when it measured the size of the disc, had displayed a mathematical constant. What was more alarming was that the disc was formed entirely out of one solid medallion of bone. In her years of archeotech knowledge, Madeline knew when to recognise bone when she saw it. A well-aged bone was neither dense nor brittle. Soaking up the terroir of its surrounding earth, bone tended to become a waxy, matured ivory that deepened in colour with age. The colour of this bone was tarred brown. She couldn't fathom what kind of creature had bones of such gargantuan width.

'One more thing, ma'am.'

Madeline turned reluctantly from her work and looked down the scaffolding to see Captain Silat standing to attention below.

Madeline rubbed the bridge of her nose. 'Yes, captain?' She said wearily.

'My company. We've been working on this excavation for days and now – well now I've sent most of them upside to defend it. They'll probably die doing so. What I'm trying to say is, ma'am, could you tell us what this is? My boys want to know what they're dying for.'

'Of course, captain,' Madeline said softly. She began to edge her way down the scaffolding.

'What the inscriptions say, and there are many, is that the Old King sleeps within. He will only be awakened at the proper alignment of the ancient planetary schematics and their relation to the stars. It's all very ritualistic. They worshipped the stars here, before Him on Earth, these people worshipped stars like the very old tribes of Terra.'

'Are the stars aligned?'

Madeline bit her lip. She was not sure how much intelligence she should share with a field officer. As she debated with herself, she heard the clatter of bombs through the thick stone overhead. It sounded like a truck had dumped a cargo of anvils onto rockcrete. She concluded that they would not have long anyway. The captain and his men had a right to know.

'Yes. They have. It's what the Archenemy have been planning since the beginning of their invasion. They were marking out the lines of ritual on each conquered planet and waiting for the proper orbits. They were fighting this war on a schedule.'

Silat was stunned. His face was evidently trying to understand. 'They knew?'

Madeline nodded.

'So, if we break the seal, will we wake him – it?' the captain asked.

'That's what I've been trying to decipher. Much of this is written in an old Terran language I have not been properly schooled in. It seems to be recurring that the Old King is captured within some sort of containment vessel beyond this disc. If my translations are accurate, some kind of a "bell" within this tomb.'

'So we should set demo charges to it then?'

'Gosh no!' Madeline said. 'We do not know what is on the other side. We could damage, or worse, somehow wake the Old King. No, no demo!'

'Well what then, ma'am?'

'Give me one or two hours, there is some more text I would like to examine before we attempt to open this seal.'

'What should I prepare then?'

'Prepare a drill. An orthodontic bone drill would be perfect,' Madeline said.

'We're engineers. We have a powered drill-tractor,' the captain offered.

'That'll do, captain. And also, if you could spare at least twenty of your best men. I want them to be here when this disc is breached. Just to be sure…'

The captain saluted with a renewed sense of purpose. 'Of course, ma'am. I'll bring forty.'

CHAPTER THIRTY

THE FINAL OFFENSIVE was mustered at the crematorium district. It was the only sizeable tract of land on which Imperial forces could consolidate without the presence of heavy enemy fire and the threat of repeated ground assault. The intense heat and clamour of war raged in the surrounding districts, but this area was still and quiet.

It was a square plaza, dotted with funereal kilns, arrayed in a pattern that mathematically matched the major constellations overhead. Most of the kilns had been rendered to dust by shelling, and those which had been unscathed were crushed by the heavy tracks of the assembled vehicles.

The assault of the 1st Mech-Cav had broken the main spear of the enemy advance not ninety minutes past, allowing the infantry battalions enough respite to regroup. Now, as the street-to-street fighting renewed, Cantica's only armoured division ranked together for one final assault. It would be all they'd have left.

The soldiers of the 1st Mech-Cav sat on the hulls of their tanks, the Lancers nursed their steeds. All stood to attention as Inquisitor Obodiah Roth clambered atop the turret of a Siegfried siege-tank. Standing up there, Roth looked as hardened and tattered as any of those Canticans before him. The inquisitor, they all knew, had bled and fought hard to save their home. He had given them the chance to use all of their training to inflict as much punishment on the Archenemy as possible. As far as the Guardsmen were concerned, the inquisitor was one of theirs now.

Roth still wore his fighting-plate and his black scale tabard. The plate was battered, scorched and rashed with pock-marks, and the obsidian was broken-toothed. Over that, he wore the ceremonial longcoat of a Cantican officer. Intelligence staff had instructed him to wear it unbuttoned, so it streamed in the wind like a ragged cape of brown felt. His right hand was loosely viced under the segments of his Tang-War power fist and the Sunfury MKIII in a shoulder rig under his coat. To everyone else, he appeared unarmed, utterly in command of himself. It was a time when these men needed the morale, and the intelligence staff had executed their job perfectly.

Roth pulled his long, lupine frame up to full height, standing atop the turret. The suns glinted off his wiry shoulders and made his armour gleam silver. He surveyed the mustered regiment before him. All of the machine-powered war engines that the CantiCol ever had at their disposal, even before the Medina Campaign, had been assigned to the 1st Mech-Cavalry Regiment. The tanks were exceedingly rare and the months of fighting had drained them to their limits. Every tank showed the scars of on-the-run repairs. In all, there were over six hundred tanks – a majority of Leman Russes, a solid lance of Siegfrieds, a scattering of ageing Salamanders,

Kurtis tanks and even Centaurs. Escorting them were two battalions of mounted Lancers. Roth knew not all of those were true Lancers; some were Guardsmen who had adopted a spare horse in the heat of battle. But they would suffice, thought Roth. If the last several days of fighting were anything to go by, Roth was sure they would not fail him.

In view of the assembled Guardsmen, an officer of the Aegina Prestige hoisted himself onto the frontal hull of the Siegfried. He snapped up his face visor of diamond polyfibre, in the way of an Aegina salute.

'Major Sebastion Glass of the 7th Muster, Aegina Prestige, sir.'

'Inquisitor Roth of the Ordo Hereticus.' Roth shook the major's hand and bowed low.

Major Glass, like others of the Prestige, was clad in the bulky accoutrement of urban combat. Grey fatigues, flame retardant boots, thigh holsters, dump pouches, chest harnesses, all made the standard-issue CantiCol canvas satchel look positively spartan. Over this, he wore an outer tactical vest of hand-sewn diamond inserts, complete with throat and groin plates. The vest of diamond sheets had a frosty sheen that showed a subtle contempt for enemy fire.

'Inquisitor Roth. With the fatal wounding of Lord General Faisal, command is granted to you on request of Inquisitorial authority. The Aegina accepts this, and I pledge all the men and arms I have remaining under your command structure.'

Roth bowed formally. 'Thank you, major. How many men do you have?'

'Only two platoons, sir.'

The major gestured to four slate-grey Chimeras. The Aegina Guardsmen were making final weapons checks in two neat rows. Even their standard-issue lasguns were complicated pieces with additional scopes, bipods, folding stocks and even underslung grenade launchers. Others were cleaning and greasing mortars and lascannons. The Aegina were motorised heavy infantry who worked in organic fire-teams. Their platoon-level support weapons and their combination of precision ordnance and lascannon had been invaluable during the last three days of urban fighting. Despite their techno-finery, Roth knew they were good soldiers who had suffered badly. Two full battalions of them had made landfall on Aridun, just four days past.

'You must have suffered heavy casualties in this war, major. The Emperor appreciates the sacrifice the mothers and wives of Aegina have made.'

Major Glass nodded and snapped the clear visor down. As he descended from the tank, Roth turned to address his men.

'Gentlemen. I am not of worth to address you for this coming battle. You have all been soldiers far longer than I ever will. There is nothing I can tell you that you will not already know. Rather, I will tell you intelligence has pin-pointed the location of the Chaos commander, by the preceding movement of his elite retinue. It is a chance to clash our iron against theirs. That is all. Go to your vehicles, gentlemen, and grace be with you.'

Roth hopped down into the turret of the Siegfried as the crew of 1st Mech-Cav scrambled to their stations. The plaza flooded with the harsh, throaty burble of gunning engines. The air was cut by the sweetly toxic stink of petrol. As one, the entire fleet of Cantican armour rolled out to the fighting in a three-pronged column.

THE ADVANCE RUMBLED through the streets at full power, hurtling over rubble and pounding through walls. Their tracks churned through the ruins of mausoleums, throwing up a cloying storm of corpse dust and limestone. The Siegfrieds – a hybrid armoured bulldozer and light tank

– forged a path at the front of the column, their dozer blades ploughing through the rubble.

At sectors they encountered unorganised resistance, but speed and combined firepower pushed the Ironclad infantry on the back foot. Their battle cannons, pintle-mounted weapons and auxiliary support guns threw out a wide, branching chain of fire before them. Their advance could be tracked by the streams of tracer, las and shell smoke that latticed the air as the column weaved through the old city.

'Command, this is call-sign Starlight. Repeat Big Game's location. Over,' Roth shouted into the radio speaker over the creaking and thrumming in the tank's confines. 'Big Game' was the code for the Chaos commander, a code Roth was sure that Silverstein would have used had he been with him.

'Starlight, this is command. Our trackers show you are on course, keep moving north, about half a kilometre out. Expect thickening resistance as you near designated zone,' crackled the anonymous intelligence officer over the vox-net.

Roth thought he heard gunfire in the background of the vox, but he could not be sure over the roar of his tank. 'Loud and clear. Can you give us a vox warning as we move within one city block of Big Game? Over,' Roth shouted with one hand to his ear.

There was a tinny but audible sigh on the other end.

'That's a no, sir. Command base is being overrun as we speak. I'll stay on the line for as long as I can.'

Roth dropped the handset from his mouth and swore softly. 'Command, save yourself. I'll keep sharp for Big Game. Keep one round for yourself, soldier. Good luck.'

'Thank you, sir. Out.' The message was said with great finality. The command vox-net clicked out for the last time.

* * *

THE HUNTSMAN STOLE amongst them. Up until that point he had laid low during the day and shadowed them during the night. Now he scampered above the eaves and rooftops, penetrating deep into the ten kilometre long marching column of Ironclad troopers.

Like any good hunter, Silverstein had learnt by watching the behaviour of his quarry.

Silverstein slid over the ridged guttering of a mausoleum roof. He made sure the stair-street was clear before dropping down and slipping deeper into the warren of lanes. Asingh-nu dropped down and followed him.

No more than one city block away, perhaps closer, they could hear the marching orders of the Ironclad and the brief fire-fights that would erupt as Imperial elements harassed them.

Silverstein halted at a corner, peered around the bend and nodded to Asingh-nu. 'He is close. I can see banners, I see his own men.'

Asingh-nu breathed deeply. 'Back when I was tilling my paddies, I never had to kill a Chaos warlord,' he pronounced insightfully.

'This can be your first,' said Silverstein, and with that the huntsman disappeared around the corner.

'ENEMY BLOCKADE AT intersection ahead. Sight confirmed?'

'Confirmed.'

The backwash chatter of Roth's vox headset was drowned out by the echoing thump of weapons on cyclical fire. Leaning waist up from the Siegfried's turret, Roth sighted the Ironclad blockade from his magnoculars.

There was perhaps a company-sized formation of enemy infantry at the intersection. They were still uncoiling razor wire and attempting to forge together a hasty defence as the front of the 1st Mech-Cav column closed within firing distance. The enemy fired at them from rooftops, windows and side-alleys. A rocket streaked in front of Roth's tank on a plume of unwinding smoke. As Ironclad troopers appeared in the mouth of laneways, pintle-mounted stubbers from the column spat tracer at them until they disappeared from view. Roth saw the turret gunner from the Leman Russ in front kneecap an Ironclad with a sustained drag of his stubber. As the Chaos raider buckled in two, the gunner yelped in triumph. A shot from an adjacent balcony took his head off and he slid lifelessly back down the turret. The drumming of small-arms fire on armour plate became a deafening rain.

'Spear Three, this is Spear Two. Enemy blockade sighted at right of advance, engaging – over.'

'Received. Out,' Roth shouted into his wraparound vox-mic.

As promised, Spear Two, the second prong of the advance, cut through the Ironclad blockade in a perpendicular direction. They lit up the enemy to their front with a salvo of flanking fire. There was a shattering report and the explosive bark of cannons. One second Roth saw through his magnoculars the running shapes of Ironclad, scarpering behind a makeshift roadblock of rubble and tin sheets. The next he saw the blockade shred in all directions and the running shapes break and bounce into chunks of meat.

'Two to all spears, the intersection is clear of hostiles.'

'Loud and clear, Two, good job,' Roth voxed.

The two prongs merged at the intersection before splitting into opposing pincers around a cemetery block. Paralleling their route, the third column rumbled their way alongside the viaduct, throwing tracer and shell out across the canal. They continued, trading shots with heavy resistance, towards their objective.

* * *

THE BANDIT INSURGENCY had never been this bad. Bombardier Krusa had been stationed for eight years at Mon Sumlayit in Cantica, fighting the bandit kings. It had been bad then, patrolling those harsh, windy hinterlands. It was not uncommon for bandits to trap lone patrols of Cantican Guardsmen, surrounding them during the night and butchering them with stick bombs and machete. The war had raged there for thirty years and was as bitter the whole time Krusa served there. Roadside bombs, night raids, close-quarter skirmishes – taking the mountains had been hell. For every one and a half bandits killed, they lost the life of one Guardsman and still the insurgency swelled with the influx of rural, poverty-stricken men. It had been a mean fight and Krusa had lost many friends there, yet this war made the insurgency feel like a comfort tour.

Bombardier Salai Krusa served with the 5th Cantican Colonial Artillery, and they held position on a demolished plateau of an upper-tier burial stack. Up until eight hours previously, their front had been defended by several battalions of CantiCol infantry, allowing the battery to work their Griffons, Basilisks and field guns against the Archenemy. But now the Archenemy had penetrated to the rear lines. The soft belly of field hospitals and comm stations behind the fighting front were the first to go. It was heard over the vox that the Ironclad were running their heavy tanks over surgical tents along with the occupant wounded.

It had been traumatising to listen to the voices of infantry officers he recognised, broadcasting last good-byes over the vox-net as their positions were overrun, one by one. First it had been the frantic voice of Sergeant Samir of 40th Battalion radioing enemy positions, then it had been Captain Ghilantra, commander of Zulu Company of the 55th screaming sit-reps before his link went dead. They were all men that Krusa had worked with at one point. One after another, and now the Arch-enemy were on them.

'Load the case-shots! Case-shots in the line!' yelled an artillery officer. The call was echoed along the batteries and Bombardier Krusa took the command to his loaders.

His loaders moved quickly despite the ceaseless days of toil. Their cotton shirts were stiff with salt and their braces sagged by their breeches. Sweat rolled in beads along their grimy necks.

'Case-shot loaded,' announced Private Surat. A shell of close-range ordnance was loaded into the breech of the sixty-pounder.

Ironclad troopers appeared over the crest of their plateau – thousands of them at once with no semblance of spacing or tactical manoeuvre.

'Hold! Hold!' shouted the artillery officers.

The Ironclad charged across the open field of broken rock towards them. There was less than fifty paces of open ground between them. Krusa took hold of the firing chain with both hands.

'Fire!'

There was a jagged crack of guns. Jets of smoke and muzzle flash rocked the massive field guns. They jerked back on recoil pistons. Eight guns fired in unison, vomiting a dense cloud of hyper-velocity ball bearings. It blackened the open space between them like a swarm of insects. The bandits on Mon Sumlayit had always baulked at a whiff of canister-shot. No matter how hungry or desperate the bandits got during the arid seasons, canister shot had always been enough to scatter, force them into trading shots with poorly maintained autorifles. Never in his service had Krusa seen the enemy run headlong into a wall of shrapnel. Like crumpled puppets the first rank of Ironclad shed away onto the ground. Unabated, the ranks behind them kicked and stomped their way over the wounded. One volley was all they had time for before the Ironclad were swarming over the sandbags.

Bombardier Krusa was amongst the first killed. A beaked warhammer punched through his thin orbital bone and spiked into his brain. His last thoughts, even as the warhammer was protruding from his eye, was that it would have been better to have died like his friends on Sumlayit. Bombardier Susilo had been shot by a machine pistol while on night sentry. Even Private Riau who was shot by a sniper while on border patrol had been killed cleanly by headshot. It took Bombardier Krusa some time to die. He was still very much struggling to live, spasming in shock and bleeding out from his face as the Archenemy stomped over him. This war was much worse than any he had seen.

CHAPTER THIRTY-ONE

KHORSABAD MAW WAS in his gunsights.

Khorsabad Maw, the King of Corsairs. Arch-heretic of the Rimward East. Sworn servant of the Apostles Martial.

Silverstein had the Chaos warlord wavering under the targeting reticule of his autorifle. With each steadily drawn breath, the reticule rose and fell.

Down from his minaret balcony, three hundred metres down on the streets below, Khorsabad was marching with his garish procession, singing, chanting, the column macabre in its harlequin manner. Spilling out to either side of the Chaos lord were his Iron Ghasts, surrounding him with no semblance of rank or order to their unruly mob. They brandished ornamental paper banners and papier-mâché scenes detailing four thousand years of misdeed. Amongst the forest of vibro-pikes, Ironclad were rattling hand drums, warbling discordant horns and dancing in a stiff-limbed frenzy. As their warlord's procession ebbed past, Ironclad troopers pushed towards their Arch-heretic in a show of adoration. The Iron Ghasts kept them at bay with their pikes, fighting on the verge of rioting. To the untrained eye it resembled more of a carnival than a military motorcade. Silverstein even spotted an Ironclad trooper, starkly naked but for his face-bindings, dancing about, swinging a smoking censer and cutting himself with a razor in the other hand.

Once a long time ago, Silverstein had visited Mura-haba during their festival of love lost. The people there had paraded, some dancing in a possessed frenzy that was eerie to behold. The crowd toted papier-mâché masks of monstrous proportions and chanted in tongues. Paper effigies were burned and discordant instruments were drummed ceaselessly. The Chaos lord's procession had a similar taint of the mystic macabre.

'Frightening, isn't it? Do you see him?' said Asingh-nu, peering down at the dizzying drop below.

'Yes. I see him.'

Silverstein made sure to see the warlord through the filtered lenses of augmetics. He dared not study the warlord in such clarity with his naked eyes. Silverstein was sure that only bad would come of it. Under the intensified spectrum of his bioptics, Silverstein could measure every detail of Khorsabad Maw.

He was still a man. Or rather, he still held the shape of one.

Khorsabad was not at all the brutal monstrosity Silverstein had expected. Maw was slim, and well articulated to the point of being doll-like. The litheness of his limbs could not be hidden by the overlapping warren of silk, splintmail and chain that wadded him. His face was of elaborately woven iron, slightly reminiscent of a porcelain doll. It was smooth and featureless except for a small, up-turned pinch of the nose. At one and a half metres tall, Khorsabad would have looked like a finely

costumed iron toy had it not been for the antler of quills
running along his shoulders and back.

He was borne aloft on a gaudy litter of painted paper
and textured fabric, by a solid phalanx of Iron Ghasts.
The Ghasts stood upright on a crab-shelled super-heavy
tractor, as if forming some unholy ziggurat. Escort FPVs
and mounted outriders rolled alongside the pedestrian
traffic. Parting the crowds like oceanic leviathans were
the hulls of broad, super-heavy flamer tanks, their trawl
turrets snorting wisps of fire.

'Asingh-nu,' Silverstein began, 'I only have one shot at
this. This is the only shot, of all my shots so far, which
matters. I need you to sit here and not say a word. Do
not move. Do not sigh. Do not tremor. You have been a
good friend up until now and I expect you will not let
me down.'

The guerrilla nodded warily and settled down into a
hunch, hugging his autogun. Silverstein adjusted his
scope bracket and snuggled down behind it.

He began by tracking for a weakness on Khorsabad.
His entire spine was exposed and pitted like raw ore and
sutured with his silks. The iron quills formed clusters of
scaly scuttles at his lower back and lengthened gradually
into the fifty-centimetre long pikes that branched out
like floral growth along the top of his back. Silverstein
decided that shooting the natural armour of any creature
would not be a killing shot. He tracked his scope to the
Chaos lord's head. It was dainty and perfectly formed
with a complex braid of iron lattices. There were no
vision slits or mouth pieces. It was more than likely the
Chaos lord's head, and that was where Silverstein hov-
ered his target reticule.

Silverstein closed his eyes, loosening the muscles of his
shoulder and neck. He took two breaths and then
adjusted his aim to be several centimetres in front of his
target's expected path. The ambush method was the

basic method for hitting moving targets, and Silverstein's favourite. He settled himself, slowed his breathing and his body's intake of oxygen.

The huntsman thought back to his days as a scout for the senior hunters of the lodge. Back to his youth in the conifer woods of Veskipine, when the northern lights would shine at dusk and air was crisp with cold. He had tracked exotic off-world game on the estates for days at a time. His favourite had been hunting the sentient primates. Those animals fought back, organised and used tools; sometimes the primates even hunted them. Those had been the best hunts and Silverstein had spent much of his formative years shouldering his brother's autorifle and mimicking the mating dirges of the meso-ape.

Silverstein opened his eyes. Khorsabad Maw was ghosting towards his centre of aim. Silverstein exhaled, allowing the scope to sink. His gradual inhalation buoyed the reticule back on target. Khorsabad Maw's polished cranium slid perfectly and precisely within the target's sights. The huntsman allowed the target a nanosecond shift to the left, allowing for wind direction and the natural curve of trajectory.

Silverstein fired.

The trigger pull was smooth despite the speed with which his nerves had wired the command to the muscles of his hand. The trajectory, the fall of mark, the wind current. Everything was as Silverstein knew it would be.

But the round never made its mark. Khorsabad Maw's force shields crackled with static film as the round impacted with it. The sudden discharge showed a perfect semi-sphere of iridescent force where it had been invisible before.

Silverstein jumped up from his post, his eyes wide. Suddenly, up on that minaret balcony he felt utterly vulnerable. The eyes of all those Archenemy soldiers below looked up at him, as one.

'Get down, Asingh!' shouted Silverstein. He threw himself backwards as the entire balcony erupted and literally shook apart. The assembled masses below opened up on the tower with all their combined arms. The stone balcony became a rapidly deteriorating sponge as chips of rock disintegrated under the storm of fire. Asingh-nu took a round in the stomach. Silverstein dragged the guerrilla into the tower proper. Heavy-calibre rounds punched holes through the walls and shattered the windows. Smoke and brick-dust was making him gag.

As the dust settled, the balcony was no longer there. There was just a scorched hole in the wall and empty space beyond.

'I'm hit,' Asingh-nu groaned. He shrimped up into the foetal position, clutching at his abdomen. Blood seeped out from between his folded arms.

The fire died down as quickly as it had started, but the huntsman still heard the frantic pounding of weapons. Only now, he was no longer the sole target of their ferocity. He expected to hear the sounds of forced entry at the tower below, but when none came, he decided to hazard a peek from the holes in the wall. The sounds of fighting below were too enticing.

Fifty storeys down, he saw Khorsabad's procession engaging with targets to their front and flanks. Further up the road and along a side junction, Silverstein saw an approaching column of armour. Imperial armour. They were charging at full power, turret weapons flashing.

Leman Russes rammed into the procession, pintle mounts throbbing and battle cannons seeking out Maw's motorcade escorts. The Ironclad replied when the flamer platforms began belching horizontal tornados of fire. They fired indiscriminately, at Ironclad and Imperial alike, spewing masses of flame that consumed oxygen with audible roars.

Amongst them, Silverstein picked up the distinct profile of a Siegfried siege-tank, with a pugnacious snout of
its dozer blades and its swivelling tower turrets. There,
leaning out of the cylindrical turret and firing the tank's
pintle-bolter, Silverstein saw Inquisitor Obodiah Roth.

KHORSABAD'S VICTORY PROCESSION was moving down the
central high road of Angkhora, a broad access-way that
was wide enough to accommodate the legions of Ironclad streaming out behind the advance of the Chaos
lord.

As the Imperial column hooked in at a mid-route
intersection, Khorsabad's procession lurched into view.
Immediately, hundreds of Ironclad troopers greeted
them with small-arms fire. Some took a knee, their shots
spanking off the metal tank hulls. Others threw themselves before the tank treads, laying prostrate in sacrifice
to their Khorsabad.

Lancer cavalry burst in ahead of the tank charge, their
sabres flashing. There was an audible crunch as the
Lancers rushed amongst the Archenemy in a wall of lashing hooves and slashing swords. Men flew off horses, or
were trampled in the press. Khorsabad Maw's Iron
Ghasts braced themselves around him, standing back to
back and shoulder to shoulder in a semi-sphere of
bristling vibro-pikes.

The firing became frantic. The statues that lined the
street began to explode, one by one. The walls along the
streets looked as if they were being sand-blasted.

Roth didn't even bother hunching down behind his
turret. There were too many rounds in the air and he'd
just as likely get hit standing up or squatting down. A frag
missile reared up and shot out at Roth's tank from the
jolting mass of Ironclad. The warhead punched through
the plating of the turret, the tip of the missile emerging
around a flower of ragged tank metal at waist-level. It was

suspended there, quivering but dormant. Looking at the unexploded missile, Roth began to laugh. The laughter was solace. It held him together and came easily.

In the pandemonium of shooting, Roth's Siegfried bulldozed into the line of Ironclad. Vibro-pikes snapped holes into dozerblades and reached up alongside the hull, jabbing at his turret. Someone was blasting a machine-pistol at him at point-blank range, the fat-calibre rounds ricocheting off the tank with angry sparks. The surprise of being shot at overrode the compulsion of fear. Rather than ducking, Roth gripped the pintle-mounted bolter and shot off a few loud, booming spurts.

'I'm taking fire to our flanks and front!' Roth shouted down the turret at his crew. It wasn't necessary. The crew knew it was all close quarters from here. The Siegfried's multi-laser swivelled and unleashed a short cyclical pulse, hosing the turret from left to right. Ironclad toppled and the rest scattered, trying to put some distance and other bodies between themselves and the spitting turret.

'Everyone is taking fire everywhere!' an anonymous crewman shouted back up at Roth from the interior.

By the time the fight had boiled into a close-quarter street fight, the column had already taken some heavy damage. Every vehicle was low on ammo; they had expended thousands of rounds just fighting their way through the city towards the objective.

The siege-tank to Roth's immediate left had its turret disabled and could only fire along its axis of advance. The Siegfried to his right had blown both tracks and was being pushed along by the Leman Russ behind it. All of the Imperial tanks Roth could see were punched through with holes, so badly in places that the hulls looked like perforated mesh. A Kurtis tank several metres in front was smoking, a gaping rocket wound in its front.

Ironclad were swarming over the vehicle, dragging the crew from the hatch.

Through the seething press, Roth could make out the throne of Khorsabad Maw. The Chaos lord looked child-like in his swaddling mantle of silks, plate and chain, his porcelain hands folded neatly atop each other. He did not seem at all fazed by the fight that raged around him. If it were not for the spinal quills that rose in majestic wreaths from his shoulders, Roth might not have recog-nised Khorsabad Maw at all. The guards who carried him took care not to jostle his throne, even as they lashed out with their pikes. The Chaos tank on which the warlord's sedan was mounted rolled along at a lumbering pace, gouting sheets of flame at everything before it.

The sight of the Chaos lord made Roth's breathing sharp and shaky. He had the architect of this entire hell-fight before him. Adrenaline coiled like a spring in his belly, pressurised and loaded. It compelled him to jump up and down, fury and anticipation thrumming from his fingertips. It was like a fist-fencing prizefight. Roth's focus became singular. His vision tunnelled in on Khorsabad Maw; everything else became distant, detached and utterly incomprehensible.

Roth sharpened his words into a psychic spear: +Min-ion of the Apostles Martial. I have come for you!+

The words did not seem to startle the warlord. Instead Khorsabad Maw looked at him. Even without vision slits, Roth felt the Chaos lord actually look at him. Roth couldn't shake the feeling he had incurred the attention of the Ruinous Powers at that very moment.

Roth lifted his Inquisitorial rosette in challenge.

Khorsabad Maw leapt from his litter with a tremen-dous jump. He went up high like an ordnance shell before coming down sharply, bouncing from tank hull to tank hull. He was moving at speed, clearing a distance of fifty metres before Roth could draw his pistol. As

Khorsabad leapt, the multiple capes of his regalia flew out behind him. The carapace armour beneath could not hide the lithe, powerful body, fine-jointed and perfectly proportioned like a dancer's.

He landed on an FPV, blowing out its windows and crumpling it flat like an anvil.

He must weigh at least half a tonne, thought Roth. He hit like a little wrecking ball.

The Siegfried opened up all its support weapons on the Chaos lord at a distance of less than ten metres: turret multilaser, hull-mounted heavy stubber and pintle-mounted storm bolter. The deluge of tracer had drummed Khorsabad's force field like a deluge of molten orange rain. It was so bright that Roth had to shield his eyes away from the point of contact. Despite the slight twitch of electrical static, the ammunition cycled dry before the force field would short. Immediately the Chaos lord was on them, jumping onto the front hull with enough force to rock the tank.

The Chaos lord moved with such liquid speed that Roth barely had time to throw out a timid jab with his power fist. Restricted in his turret, the punch had no weight or vinegar behind it. It agitated the force bubble and staggered Khorsabad Maw. Suddenly wary, the Chaos lord circled the turret, stomping fracture dents into the top of the tank as he moved.

'Are you done reloading this bloody thing?' Roth screamed at his crew as Khorsabad stalked him in circles like a hungry predator. Those dainty hands – Roth was sure – could dismantle him like boiled poultry.

He had never seen such raw power before. The Blood Gorgon who had claimed Pradal had been a behemoth of strength and towering rage. But Khorsabad Maw did not possess the visual size and power of an Astartes. Khorsabad Maw was a full head and shoulders shorter than Roth and he was not in power armour, yet there he was, about to shred the tank with his bare, delicate hands.

The multilaser suddenly popped into life, juddering a spray of incandescence at Khorsabad. The Chaos lord bounded backwards off the tank and out of sight.

Roth slapped the side of the turret with his hands. 'Reverse the engine!'

The Siegfried lurched backwards sharply before jolting forwards again.

The siege-tank ran into and over the Chaos lord. With a dull thump, the tank went over, heavy treads grinding. Roth could hear the squeal of mangled metal, yet when Roth turned to inspect the damage, the Chaos lord was standing. Roth fumbled to reload his plasma pistol.

Faster than Roth could react, Khorsabad Maw snatched the rear of the Siegfried in his hands, fingers denting buttery holes into the metal. The Siegfried's gas turbine engines were pushed to their limit, grunting like a wounded bull. Khorsabad fought the tank, digging his heels into the rubble. Then with an explosive cleaning motion, Khorsabad Maw launched the entire vehicle over his head and into the air.

The Siegfried came down, bottom side up, after flipping cleanly in the air. The weight of the tank virtually destroyed itself. Armour plating flew, the engine block compressed the crew compartment. Tracks flipped high into the air. If the initial shock of crash-landing had not killed the crew, the physical trauma of six tonnes of steel imploding and exploding surely would have. Roth lay prone some metres away, having been thrown out of the open turret during the tank's spiralling descent. He had landed badly.

When Roth came to, he was sure his leg was broken. It was the pain that roused him from unconsciousness. He felt the edges of his femur grate against muscle and test his sinew.

Khorsabad Maw stalked towards him. The Chaos lord's force field was flickering in and out, but he was otherwise unscathed. The tank had done little to hurt him.

Khorsabad Maw spoke to him. The words had a soft metallic hum to them, like a wind being blown through the tubes of an iron organ. 'You are a dead man. I am going to kill you, I am going to break you and I am going to pour molten silver in your ears.'

With a wild cry, two Cantican Lancers wielding their sabres overhead charged at the warlord. Khorsabad Maw dealt them one soft tap to the neck each. The movement was so casual that it was barely perceptible. Both Guardsmen fell sideways, their necks so utterly shattered that their chins rested in their chests. More Cantican Colonials rushed the Chaos lord. Horse cavalry ringed a rough box around them, pushing against the Iron Ghasts who formed a mauling scrum towards their lord. Sabres clattered against vibro-pikes. Guardsmen were fighting to form a desperate ring around the wreckage of Roth's tank. They knew full well the outcome of engaging the Chaos lord but they did it anyway. Five or six Lancers rushed at the Chaos lord. Roth didn't want to see. He closed his eyes, propped himself up on his elbows and reloaded his pistol.

As Khorsabad turned his attention back to Roth, the inquisitor shot him. The force shield blinked but held. The Chaos lord sprinted towards him, his acceleration inhumanly fast.

Roth braced himself. Khorsabad closed the distance. Roth shot with his plasma pistol. The spheres of atomic energy warped as they made contact with Khorsabad's force field, dissipating with bright flashes. Blue static convulsed across the shield's surface.

A fraction away from striking distance, the Chaos lord's head snapped up. At first Roth thought Khorsabad

Maw had tripped. Khorsabad Maw, Arch-heretic of the Rimward East, did not trip.

Someone shot him. Twice.

The two bullets had passed the flickering shield as Roth's plasma rounds tested the generators. A neat entry hole opened up on Khorsabad Maw's left temple and exited in a fist-sized crater out his opposite cheek. Another went through his neck. At first there was no blood. Then there was lots of blood. It burst in great arterial spurts, filming the inside of Khorsabad Maw's force bubble. Someone had shot the great Khorsabad Maw.

Roth was lying at the Chaos lord's feet. The inquisitor watched the four-thousand-year-old Arch-heretic fall to his knees, batting his hands weakly against his ruptured head. It was all that mattered. The rest was in the Emperor's hands now. CantiCol and Ironclad swarmed around them in a surging mess, but Roth lay down with his broken leg. He had already done all that he could for this war and no one could ask any more of him. He lay down and watched Khorsabad Maw die.

TAP-TAP.

It was an instinctive double shot. Silverstein had pre-empted his shots between the electrical convulsions of the Chaos lord's force generators.

The huntsman had just claimed his one perfect shot. Twice. But that did not matter to Silverstein. He was already tracking with his scope. An Ironclad rushed towards Roth. Silverstein put a round through his sternum. The scope moved again, floating over an Ironclad charging at Roth with a maul. The huntsman shot him down too. The shots sounded with clarity from the minaret, putting down the Ironclad around Roth's prone form.

'Damn!' hissed Silverstein.

The fight condensed into a roiling, heaving mass of bodies. CantiCol and Ironclad obscured Roth from

Silverstein. He tried to pan in with his bioptics, zooming his vision into grainy pixels, but he could not see Roth. The Canticans were pushing forwards, the Ironclad momentum disintegrating with the demise of their Corsair King. Further back from the fighting, the empty paper throne toppled, its fluttering pennants crushed beneath the retreating tracks of an Ironclad super-heavy. The Ironclad were flooding back down the way they came.

Silverstein tossed a crumb of rubble in frustration. There was no way he could get to Roth through the killing down there. Reluctantly, the huntsman backed away from the stumps of the balcony. There would be no following Roth. Not through the dense lines of Ironclad. And he could not leave Asingh-nu to die by himself. Silverstein had grown rather fond of him. The huntsman stole one last look at the area where Roth had been.

'Good luck,' he whispered. With that, Silverstein returned to Asingh-nu to wait out the end.

THE REMNANTS OF the 1st Mech-Cav and their Lancer escort withdrew hurriedly once the damage had been inflicted. The armoured columns, now substantially reduced in size and leaving a wake of burning wreckages, fought their way back to the last Imperial-held district in Angkhora – the excavation site.

A squad of infantry dragged Roth into the back of a Chimera. The ride back to the green zone was crowded and bumping. He could hear the enemy weapons bashing at the outside of the vehicle and wondered if a heavy weapon might score a lucky shot and smoke them all. Every bump in the road jostled his broken leg. He blacked out several times, and the journey back was lost.

Roth came to in a darkened tunnel, with a field medic shining a torch into his eyes and applying smelling salts beneath his nose.

'Get that away from me!' Roth said, a tad snappier than he had meant to.

He tried to rise and realised that his left thigh had been stripped and given a field splint. His leg throbbed, but he had stimmed enough painkillers to settle the pain into a dull glow. The acrid ammonia of the smelling salts were still fuming his sinuses, rousing his pain-addled mind.

'Why am I down here? Where are my men?' Roth started.

'The lady, Madame Madeline, requested you be brought down here, away from the fighting,' the medic said, stepping away. Roth realised he was startling the young Guardsman.

'My apologies–' Roth began.

'Stow it, Roth. I don't mean to be terse but I wanted you to be here when I open the seal.'

Roth craned his neck to look behind him, squinting at the sodium lamps that lit the subterranean darkness. Madeline de Medici was standing behind him. She was wearing a curious outfit that resembled a diving suit. Roth could see her face through the porthole window of her bulbous helmet. Hazard work-suits – he had seen Guard engineers working with them in chemically treated environments. The rubbery leather overalls were lined with lead, and the wrist and ankle cuffs were seamed to the gloves and boots.

'You look good,' Roth said.

'You look a mess as usual,' Madeline said. She crossed over to him and helped him up with thickly mittened hands. Roth wobbled slightly as he adjusted to his crutches.

'Tell me that it's opened,' Roth said.

'We're about to open it. Once Medic Subah here helps you into one of these hazard suits.'

Roth raised a questioning eyebrow as the medic began to scoop the thick overalls and boots over Roth's leg. 'What is this for?'

'It's an embryonic star we are dealing with, Roth. Elementary knowledge of the galaxy would mean that there will be radiation if the star breaks free.'

'Elementary knowledge would also suggest that a star is likely not going to be standing behind that rock-door waiting to greet us. It *should* be contained, remember?'

'We don't know that for sure. It pays to be careful, Roth,' she said in a serious tone that concluded all argument.

The city-fight was so close to the excavation site that they could hear the echo of guns coming down the tunnel shaft.

'You better hurry, we have enemies at the gate,' Roth said, screwing the porthole of his helmet tight.

The industrial tunnel-boring machine was Guard-issue and no larger than a tractor. The driver gave a thumbs-up with his hazard mitten and the nose-coned drill started. With a monotone shriek it ground into the ancient bone disc. The drill spat a spray of sparks when molten bone shavings fizzed into the air.

There was no explosion, or sudden release of cataclysmic energy as Madeline had feared. The drill punched a wide hole into the thick disc and reversed its cycle as the tractor backed away. It revealed a circular cavity in the bone, rough and smoking where the polished bone had been drilled away. There was darkness beyond, and a hole big enough for a man to fit through.

The Guard platoon in their bulky suits all aimed lasguns at the smoking darkness. Madeline, aiding Roth on his crutches, hurried over to the break in the seal.

'THERE IS A whole other chamber in here,' she said, shining a phosphor torch into the entrance.

'I'll go first,' Captain Silat volunteered. Madeline stepped aside to let the captain shimmy through on his belly, rifle-first. They aided Roth through, passing the crutches over and then easing him through legs-first. Madeline and several other Guardsmen followed.

Inside, the chamber was immense. A perfectly cut cube inside the crust of Aridun's rock mantle. There was a sense of perfect symmetry to it. Roth perceived it because he had never been surrounded by an artificial structure so precise in its execution. It gave him a strange sensation of humbling vertigo.

'The carvings, look at the carvings,' gasped Madeline in awe as she played her torch beam along the walls and ceiling.

There on the smooth stone were the constellations of Medina and its surrounding systems. Like a cartographer's chart, lunar trajectories, planar cycles and heliocentric orbits were mapped out in sweeping lines and curves. Roth could see carvings of the Shoal Clusters, the Kingfisher's Belt and even constellations in regions that the Imperium had not yet explored.

'Are these carvings accurate?' whispered Captain Silat.

'Do you doubt them?' Roth asked. The captain had no answer for him.

The smooth floors were marked with carvings, too. They were standing on a map of the Medina Corridor, its planets all in proper alignment, the ley-lines across every planet's surface forming a conduit – according to Madeline's notes – of polar energy.

At the centre of the map, where Aridun should have been, was a bell-shaped silo. It was planted squarely in the otherwise empty chamber. The silo was about the height of a man, not particularly large by any means. Formed from verdigrised copper, its bas-relief surface was coarse with rust and mineral deposit.

'Is that it?' Madeline asked.

Roth limped towards the bell for a closer inspection. Slowly, he edged his hand out to touch it. The surface of it was cold. In a patch of green copper, Roth could make out carvings of crude straight-lined men dancing beneath depictions of flying ships. There were also inscriptions, written in a flowing cursive script that Roth could not understand.

'Madeline, this is ancient.' Roth beckoned her closer. 'Can you read it?'

The archaeologist pondered over the bell, examining it closely. 'Some parts. It's written in a very poetic form of Oceanic Terran language. It describes the correlation of the dormancy of this star-ancient, to the orbit of the star system and the helio-markings of each planet.'

'Time, Madeline, time. Please hurry,' Roth said, reminding her of the battle that threatened to overrun them.

'These are not the exact words. But it seems to suggest that when the planets are not in alignment, the embryonic star is in a stasis state of condensation, shrinking towards itself. It becomes dense matter. They describe it as coiling slumber.'

'Please, for us laymen?' Captain Silat asked.

'Dense space matter becomes immeasurably heavy. You would not be able to budge this silo anywhere with all your industrial machines. It would also be in a stasis-state of reduction.'

'I see. So what does it say about when the Medina Corridor is in the correct alignment?' Roth asked.

Madeline shrugged her suit. 'I can only gather from what I read here. When the polar lines are in alignment, it changes the polar alignment of planets. The embryonic star contained within goes into a state of expansion, and its mass becomes less dense. Light enough to be transported in its state of stasis.'

'Transported and perhaps released from stasis?' Roth said. He flexed the lead-lined leather across his neck to smear the sweat away. It was cold in the chamber but he was sweating profusely. A by-product of too much adrenaline.

'Correct. Once the stasis state of this star is broken, it will continue to expand and expand and expand.'

'The Archenemy do not need this star to destroy the Medina Worlds. That would bring them nothing. But once the stasis is broken, they can transport this star anywhere, even to Terra, or the Cadian Gate. Better it here, than anywhere else.' Captain Silat was thinking strategically, as he had been taught to.

Madeline left that statement unchallenged. For a while nobody said anything. Within that silo, captured in stasis, was an embryonic star. This was just one of the Old Kings that pre-Imperial Medinians had worshipped. But this one they had plucked from the sky with the help of the Early Sentients. This was the angry god they would unleash if ever their civilisations were threatened.

The very same angry god who had been unleashed in the Reclamation Wars. The star hadn't been in expansion then, the polar conduits had not been carved to the precise schematics ordained by the Early Sentients. Instead the gamma flare as the star sparked and returned to stasis had eroded Aridun's ozone and caused the mass extinction. This thing was a destroyer of worlds.

'I'll break it.'

Everyone turned to look at Roth.

'I'll break it from stasis right now,' Roth declared again.

Madeline opened her mouth to speak but Roth silenced her with a wave of his hand.

'There's no time to think about it. The Archenemy will take this and they will use it on the Bastion Stars. I cannot allow that. Better I release it from its sleep here. How big can a star get?'

'Big enough, probably, to consume the entire Medina Corridor. It's impossible to tell,' Madeline suggested.

'Medina is gone. Chaos has subjugated the whole damn system.'

Roth turned to face the silo, patting it gently with his Tang-War gauntlet. With one swift motion he pushed the silo over. It yielded like a ripe fruit and toppled from its base with a clang that echoed around the perfect amplification of the cubic chamber.

'Go now. Or stay if you must. I'm going to open this here.'

Madeline moved towards Roth, but Captain Silat stopped her and tried to usher her away by the elbow.

'Professor de Medici. Your service has been invaluable to me,' Roth said.

The inquisitor stood over the bell silo. He tugged the mitten off his Tang-War gauntlet and allowed his weapon to charge. He took one last look at the artefact that had cost him so much. The Old King, the Star Ancient, the astronomical body worshipped as something it had no right to be. Roth lifted his power fist and fractured the silo in one clean strike.

The tomb bell was split, opening a chasm down its centreline. Inside was the star, now released. At first it was subatomic, an infinitesimal particle invisible to the naked eye. Yet its existence was undeniable as it bathed the entire chamber in an ambient green glow. It was like a microbial sun casting its light for an interior universe, colouring the sweeping map of the Medina Corridor, illuminating the mathematical lines.

Roth could feel its energy, thrumming harmonics in the air, prickling heat upon his skin. He waited in reverent silence as the star continued to grow. Soon it was as large as a fist, a boiling sphere of emerald gas. The interior casing of the broken tomb bell began to scorch and bubble into molten slag. The temperature and radiation accelerated so quickly that Roth could wait no longer. Without a word, the Task Group scrambled for cover as the star began to awaken.

EPILOGUE

During the sixty-eighth hour of the Last War, the embryonic star was roused from its dormant state.

At the centre of the four hundred-kilometre wall of Fortress Chain, a swirling disc of light could be seen, even from orbit by the 9th Route Fleet. It appeared as a whirling nexus, the energies of thermonuclear fusion spearing outwards with solar flares. The pulses even disrupted communications equipment on board the *Carthage* at high anchor.

The last Naval craft to leave Aridun tried to evacuate as many personnel as it could carry from the excavation site. Brigade commanders and staff generals were crammed alongside shell-shocked privates and NCOs. The Naval pilots simply tried to get as many bodies into their hangars before the Ironclad overran the perimeter.

Inquisitor Roth – all that remained of the Conclavial Task Group – along with a Professor Madeline Rebequin Louise de Medici boarded the last flight out of Aridun. A Marauder fighter-bomber was risking one last sortie to evacuate Roth. They carried him up on a stretcher, the Guardsmen parting the crowd for Inquisitor Roth as he was rushed up the landing ramp. Already some of the NCOs nearby were barking at the younger soldiers to make way for 'their general'.

The CantiCol still fought, up until the last hour of the planet's existence. The resistance, however, was largely pyrrhic. Pockets of CantiCol Guardsmen who had been scattered during the Archenemy siege continued to resist. Wallowing through the smoke, Guardsmen sniped at Ironclad formations. For the many who had run out of ammunition, they took themselves out into the middle of the streets, clutching unpinned grenades to their chest. They walked out into the night to find a suitable patch of rubble and lay down to die. It was in the hope that they would fall asleep and release the grenade, or the Archenemy would disturb them. Either way it was as quick and dignified a death as they could manage.

Before the fourth dawn of the Last War, the CantiCol no longer existed as a fighting regiment of the Imperial Guard. But by then, the entire Medina Corridor was well on its way to extinction. The embryonic star had convulsed into a rapidly expanding swirl of dust and dark matter. It glowed and flashed like the heart of a scarlet hurricane. Cones of contrasting green gamma flashed from its pressure gradient as expanding gas clouds boiled around it in smoky wreaths. The incalculable heat and pressure entirely consumed the planet of Aridun, and as it gradually gyrated into an expanding sphere, it consumed Cantica, Orphrates and Kholpesh. Within the end of the lunar cycle, the star had expanded into a fully-fledged white sun.

As of 999.M41, the Old King star is one of the largest celestial bodies in the Eastern Fringe and a navigational marking for the rimward shipping lanes. It resides where the Medina Corridor had once been, having consumed the majority of planets and rendering the frontier planets of Naga and Sinope inhabitable by proximity.

Not much further is mentioned in the annals of Imperial history regarding Inquisitor Obodiah Roth, at least not in the chronicles of the Medina Campaign. He was transported back onto the *Carthage* and monitored for signs of radioactive exposure in the presence of the embryonic star. It is said that he recovered quickly, and spent most of the proceeding days viewing the demise of the Medina Worlds from the starboard ports until the star grew too bright to be directly gazed upon. It would have blinded him, had he tried. Roth would later write in his memoirs, that the fate of the Medina Corridor rested heavily on his shoulders and followed him to his deathbed.

Of his final decision, he wrote: 'To no great surprise of my own, I was never the general in shining armour or apostle of the martial virtues. History has a place for those but I was just a young man incumbent with duty. Everything I had ever accomplished, up until that point, had led to this... [The Medina Extinction] The consumption of an entire star system was entirely my doing. I often wondered what Gurion, back on board the *Carthage*, truly thought of me. He had not been there. And if he had, would he have done the same? It is a point I regret never having discussed with him until his passing. To this day, I am not sure whether this had been my ultimate victory or most infamous failure. The Archenemy had been denied their objective. In military terms, that should rightly be considered a victory. Yet it is a difficult view to reconcile. In achieving it, I had lost the entire Medina Corridor, billions of lives, vanquished history and lost many, many friends.'

* * *

Bastiel Silverstein sprinted up the ramp of a docked troop carrier. Archenemy soldiers surged around him, fighting for position onto the frigate. There was no order to their retreat. The raiders pushed and elbowed, some were even stabbing or hacking their way onto the vessel. To his front, an Iron-clad Elteber raised a flak pistol and fired into the air in an attempt to restore order. Someone shanked him with a blade to the ribs and the underlord disappeared beneath the tidal crowd.

Silverstein kept his head down low, pushing a stinking metal mask over his face. The inside smelled of coppery blood. A chainmail tabard hung loosely from his wiry shoulders and greasy scraps of metal dangled like bead strings from his ill-fitting rags. He had never thought he would strip an Archenemy corpse for its attire. Perhaps several months ago, a different Silverstein would have scoffed at the idea. But now, anything was better than the alternative.

Behind him, rising like a hemisphere on the horizon, a star was expanding. The atmosphere was burning in searing flashes of red and black. It was melting like a photo-lith exposed to acid, black holes popping and yawning across its surface. The very ground shook as the planet began to lose atomic integrity. For the first time in as long as he could remember, Silverstein became really frightened. Ironclad vessels filled the darkening skies in a mass exodus. His would be one of the last flights off Aridun.

The docking ramp began to shut with a hydraulic squeal. The huntsman, along with the Archenemy troops jostling on the ramp, spilled into the belly of the carrier. They tumbled into the dim, cavernous belly. Dozens more Ironclad spilled off the sides as the ramp receded upwards. Some hung on by their fingers, until the ramp snapped shut. Silverstein could hear the muffled shrieks from outside. Outside, Ironclad hammered away at the hull in a maddening metallic cacophony.

It was pitch-black inside the carrier. Silverstein chose not to use his augmetics to see. He didn't want to. He could feel the sour, tainted warmth of Archenemy soldiers around him. The vessel shuddered as its thrusters propelled it away from the surface, the air pressure in the cabin becoming heavy and oppressive. Pressing the broken fragment of iron over his face, Silverstein began to pray to the Emperor, repeating the same prayer again and again.

ABOUT THE AUTHOR

Henry Zou lives in Sydney, Australia. He joined the Army to hone his skills in case of a zombie outbreak and has been there ever since. Despite this, he would much rather be working in a bookstore, or basking in the quiet comforts of some other book-related occupation. One day he hopes to retire and live in a remote lighthouse with his lady and her many cats, completely zombie-free.